THE ROWDY COYOTE RUMBLE

Dear Reader,

I have a confession to make—this book is not fiction. Well not entirely anyway. You see, I have two sisters, both older than me, and as I wrote many of the scenes in this story the line between fiction and non-fiction often blurred.

My oldest sister has always been our leader and caretaker. She taught me how to read and made sure I was prepared for kindergarten. I often credit my good grades in school to the early boost she gave me. These days she's still taking care of me, acting as my publicist, playing part-time bookkeeper, helping to find new readers, and buying fun clothes for me to wear at book signings.

My "middle" sister was born a jester, always making wisecracks and entertaining us. She taught me some very important life lessons, including how to lose with grace (she was the World's Best Cheater when we were kids), and how to be humble (which came with me losing every game I played with her). Her best lessons were about how to laugh at my screw-ups and to find humor in even the crappiest situations. I credit her for my having a sense of humor, which you will find on the pages of my books.

With four decades of sisterhood under my belt, elements from my real life sister experiences kept slipping into my story world. I didn't realize how much had leaked in until I read through the book during the editing process and giggled during many scenes. I could easily picture the three of us in Jackrabbit Junction getting into trouble along with the crazy Morgan sisters.

I hope you enjoy *The Rowdy Coyote Rumble* and the wacky messes Ronnie, Claire, and Kate get into down in the desert. When you finish, raise a glass at The Shaft to my two funny and loving sisters along with me. They deserve a lifetime of free drinks for putting up with my "spoiled" hiney all of these years!

Ann Charles

www.anncharles.com

THE ROWDY COYOTE RUMBLE

ANN CHARLES

ILLUSTRATED BY C.S. KUNKLE

To Laura and Shelly, my rabble-rousing sisters.

You both have given me so much love and laughter over the years. I'm glad you've been there to lean on.

When I write about the Morgan girls, you two are often on my mind, inspiring me to dig deeper and make their escapades even crazier.

Thank you for providing great inspiration for my stories. Here's to many more years of sharing life's adventures.

I love you more every year!

Also by Ann Charles

Jackrabbit Junction Mystery Series:
Dance of the Winnebagos (Book 1)
Jackrabbit Junction Jitters (Book 2)
The Great Jackalope Stampede (Book 3)

Dig Site Mystery Series:
Look What the Wind Blew In (Book 1)

Deadwood Mystery Series:
Nearly Departed in Deadwood (Book 1)
Optical Delusions in Deadwood (Book 2)
Dead Case in Deadwood (Book 3)
Better Off Dead in Deadwood (Book 4)
An Ex to Grind in Deadwood (Book 5)
Meanwhile, Back in Deadwood (Book 6)

Short Stories from the Deadwood Mystery Series:
Deadwood Shorts: Seeing Trouble
Deadwood Shorts: Boot Points
Deadwood Shorts: Cold Flame

A Short Story from the upcoming Goldwash Mystery Series
The Old Man's Back in Town

Coming Next from Ann Charles:

Title TBA
(Deadwood Mystery Series: Book 7)

Title TBA
(Dig Site Mystery Series: Book 2)

Acknowledgments

Thank you to my husband and kids for putting up with me writing, writing, writing everywhere we go.

I also want to thank the following amazing folks:

My fantastic first and second-draft readers, my incredibly clever editors (Mimi Munk and Marguerite Phipps), and my eagle-eyed beta readers. Without your help I'd be plastered with tomatoes after the book released.

My brother, Charles (C.S.) Kunkle (cover artist and illustrator) for creeping me out with the guy in the freezer, and his wife, Stephanie, for picking fun stuff for him to illustrate.

Sharon Benton (cover graphic artist) for trying 1000 different colors and shades for the teddy bear.

My publicists and promoters—my sister, mom, and brother. You guys are the best monkey handlers around!

Wendy Gildersleeve for sharing Chubby Chipmunk chocolate truffles with me and for putting up with me texting, emailing, and calling at all hours of the day and night.

Diane Garland for her backup brain and spreadsheets.

Barney Fife (from *The Andy Griffith Show*) for carrying that one bullet in his shirt pocket "in case of emergency."

Jacquie Rogers, Amber Scott, Gerri Russell, and Joleen James for always being there for me when shit is hitting the fan.

Arlene "Sparkles Magoo" DaVee for inspiring some fun scenes.

My family, ex-coworkers, and Facebook, Instagram, and Twitter friends. You all inspire me to keep writing—especially when you crack that dang whip!

Finally, my brother, Clint Taylor, for your publicly declared ardor for women in yoga pants.

THE ROWDY COYOTE RUMBLE

Cast

Claire Alice Morgan (1,2,3,4)—Main heroine of the series, Mac's girlfriend, Harley's granddaughter

MacDonald "Mac" Garner (1,2,3,4)—Main hero of the series, Claire's boyfriend

Harley "Gramps" Ford (1,2,3,4)—Claire's maternal grandfather, Ruby's husband

Henry Ford (1,2,3,4)—Harley's beagle/dog

Ruby Ford (previously Ruby Wayne-Martino) (1,2,3,4)—Mac's aunt, owner of the Dancing Winnebagos R.V. Park, Harley's new wife

Jessica Wayne (1,2,3,4)—Ruby's teenage daughter, Harley's stepdaughter

Chester Thomas (1,2,3,4)—Harley's old Army vet buddy

Manuel "Manny" Carrera (1,2,3,4)—Harley's old Army vet buddy

Joe Martino (1,2,3,4)—Deceased; Ruby's first husband, previous owner of the Dancing Winnebagos R.V. Park

Deborah Ford Morgan (2,3,4)—Claire's mother, Harley's daughter

Kathryn "Kate" Morgan (2,3,4)—Claire's younger sister, Deborah's youngest daughter, Butch's girlfriend

Veronica "Ronnie" Morgan (3,4)—Claire's oldest sister, Deborah's oldest daughter

Natalie Beals (3,4)—Claire's cousin from back in South Dakota, Harley's granddaughter

Grandma Ford (1,2,3,4)—Deceased; Claire's grandmother, Harley's first wife

Valentine "Butch" Carter (1,2,3,4)—Owner of The Shaft, the only bar in Jackrabbit Junction, Kate's boyfriend

Sheriff Grady Harrison (1,2,3,4)—Sheriff of Cholla County

Aunt Millie (3,4)—Sheriff Harrison's aunt, leader of the library gang

Ruth and Greta (3,4)—Members of Aunt Millie's library gang

Mindy Lou Harrison (3)—Sheriff Harrison's niece

Steve Horner (3,4)—Jessica's biological father, Ruby's ex-lover

Lyle Jefferson (3,4)—Ronnie's ex-husband

Arlene (3,4)—Waitress at The Shaft, friend of Kate's

Gary (2,3,4)—Bartender at The Shaft

Deputy Ernie "Dipshit" (1,2,3,4)—One of the Sheriff's deputies

DANCING
WINNEBAGOS
RV PARK
FULL HOOKUPS
RATES
MONTHLY
WEEKLY DAILY

Chapter One

Sunday, November 4th
Jackrabbit Junction, Arizona

Will Rogers once said, "If you find yourself in a hole, the first thing to do is stop digging."

Unfortunately for Claire Morgan, she wasn't the one holding the shovel. With her two sisters both digging away, one fueled by paranoia, the other by temporary insanity, Hell couldn't be more than a few shovelfuls away.

But until the flames of Hell started burning her toes, Claire had a campground to prep for the flocks of snowbirds heading south. A few white-haired birdies had already rolled into the Dancing Winnebagos R.V. Park and set up for the season, motivating her to get her ass in gear. But first, her grandfather wanted to talk to her about something …

Claire slid onto a barstool at The Shaft, the one and only watering hole in the dusty two-bit town of Jackrabbit Junction, Arizona.

"Sorry I'm late," she said over the sound of Glen Campbell singing about how great Southern nights were. She preferred the cool desert evenings topped with a blanket of stars herself.

From the next stool over, her grandfather grunted in reply. He pushed a foam-topped mug of beer toward her. "I saved you a drink."

"Thanks." Claire took a swig, grimacing at the bitterness. Too hoppy for her taste, but she was never one to turn down free beer. Wiping off a foam mustache on the collar of the jean jacket she wore over her Tijuana Toads T-shirt, she glanced around the bar. "Where's Kate?"

She searched for her younger sister's blonde head over the

sea of cowboy hats and baseball caps bobbing and wobbling under the dim lights. She found Kate in the corner, delivering a pitcher of beer to a table surrounded by dirt-crusted men in orange road-crew garb. Several of them flirted openly, trying to peek down her sister's black blouse while she refilled their glasses.

Kate had been a hit with the guys since she'd blossomed back in junior high. She was a graceful willow whereas Claire was more of a sturdy oak with knobs. To top it off, Kate had the kind of blonde hair about which men wrote silly poems that mentioned "straw" and "sunshine."

In Claire's opinion, straw smelled musty and too much sunshine caused melanoma. But she loved her younger sister enough to go to jail for her … more than once. Way more than once, actually, and that was what had Claire feeling anxious tonight.

"She's doing her job," Gramps answered. "Why? What's got your eye twitching like that?"

Claire leaned closer to Gramps. Even though her sister was too far away to hear what she was about to say, she didn't want to take any chances. "Kate's flywheel is off balance."

Gramps's skin scrunched all the way up his bald head. "Her flywheel?" He set his beer down. "I thought she got her Volvo back from the garage last month all spit-shined and dent-free again."

"That's not what I meant." Claire leaned in again, changing her tactic. "Her nail gun is misfiring." She spoke his language this time.

Gramps had retired a few years ago, selling off his contracting business up in the Black Hills of South Dakota before heading down to the land of sunshine, dust, and huge creepy insects. He knew cars, but he knew construction better.

"Nail gun? You mean one of those doohickeys you girls use to paint your toenails at the salon?"

Claire wrinkled her upper lip. "When was the last time I visited a salon?"

"How should I know? I'm not your beauty consultant."

"Gramps, I'm a handywoman, not a hand model." She

snorted into her beer. "Beauty consultant. You've been playing cards with your daughter too much."

"Speaking of your mother," he started.

Claire set her beer down on the bar with a clunk. "What I'm trying to say is that Kate's 'shooting the moon alone' with a handful of nines and tens." Since the old grump ate, slept, and breathed Bid Euchre along with his Army cronies, he should be able to figure out that euphemism.

Gramps stared at her, his light blue eyes shadowed under his crinkled brow. "What's wrong with you tonight, child? Did you hit yourself in the head with a hammer again fixing that back fence?"

"You're being a real buzzkill," she pointed at her half-full glass, "and I haven't even finished my first beer yet."

"Just speak plain old English."

"Fine. Kate's gone *loca.*"

"That's not plain English."

"You know what I mean."

"Is this about that mess you two got into on Halloween up in Deadwood?"

"How'd you hear about that?"

As far as Claire knew, only three people had any inside information about her field trip to the Deadwood cop shop: her, Kate, and Mac whom Claire had called to put money in her bank account in case she had needed to bail out Kate "the Bruiser." Thankfully, Mac hadn't asked too many questions that night on the phone. After seven months of sharing Claire's bed, he'd learned that sometimes it was better to give her the money and save the questions for when hard liquor was plentiful.

Gramps shrugged. "Jackrabbit Junction is a small town."

It dawned on Claire who had done the snitching. She should have figured Kate would panic and call the third musketeer. "Yeah, and Ronnie has a big-ass mouth." Her older sister always had been a first rate tattletale when it had come to keeping secrets from their grandfather.

"Ronnie was only concerned you might need some cash to get sprung from cellblock C."

"Cellblock C?"

"You know," Gramps smirked at her, "where they keep the other *clowns* who are dumb enough to tag team up on a bartender."

"Kate should've known better than to call Ronnie," Claire muttered. "She'd have been better off calling Butch."

"I thought they weren't snogging anymore."

Claire gaped at her grandfather. "Did you just use the word *snogging?*"

"What? I thought that's what you kids call sex these days."

"No, snogging is mostly just kissing." She chuckled. "You've been hanging around your stepdaughter too much."

Gramps's fifteen year younger new wife came with a "plus one," as in a sixteen-year-old daughter who was going on twenty. Poor Gramps hadn't had a moment's peace since he said "I do."

"That teenager won't leave my side lately," he told Claire. "She's more dogged than a shadow and won't shut up to save her damned life," he grumbled into his beer before tipping back another mouthful. "I'll tell you what else. That rotten, no-good father of hers has only managed to make things worse since he dragged his sorry ass down here and started trying to bribe her to come live with him. We all know that he only wants her for the money that comes with custody of her. If this was the Old West, I'd have him dance to my six gun all of the way to the state line, and then shoot 'em up for another ten miles for good measure."

"That scum needs a kick in the pants," Claire agreed.

"I've got the perfect steel-toed boots for the job." Gramps scowled. "So are Katie and Butch dating anymore or not?"

"Well, the official answer is 'not' if you ask Kate."

"But unofficially?"

"Unofficially, she's being a hard-headed nincompoop and insists she will not force him into a relationship that exists only because she's carrying his baby."

"That's a different tack than what your mother took when she got pregnant with Ronnie."

"And look where that got Mom and Dad." A lot of yelling and screaming throughout the years, along with plenty of bitterness and misery, finally ending in a nasty divorce.

"Speaking of your mother and her—" he started again.

"I see Kate's point, but she's not giving Butch a chance to change her mind about him." Claire lowered her voice as her sister headed in their direction. "On top of it all, she's totally crazy now thanks to those pregnancy hormones."

"Katie seems fine to me. She's a little tired, that's all."

Crazy Kate joined them at the bar, her blonde hair escaping her chignon and dancing around her face like she'd recently jammed a bobby pin in a light socket. She turned their way after giving the bartender a drink order, several ink smudges crisscrossing her face. "Do you two see that silver-haired biker over there in the red stocking cap and white handlebar mustache?"

Claire glanced in the direction of Kate's nod, zeroing in on the man in question. While he was built like a steel safe, block shouldered and square jawed, he seemed harmless enough, laughing with another biker who was probably traveling with him. "What about him?"

"Two words—polar bear."

"Polar bear, huh?" Claire repeated, giving Gramps a see-what-I-mean stare.

"Yep. Dark brown eyes, big paw-like hands, and a Coca-Cola tattoo. Definitely fits."

"That was only a marketing campaign for the beverage company. You realize that, right?" Claire asked the normally intelligent, rational Kate who was loading her tray with drinks.

"He may seem like your everyday friendly biker, but he's looking for trouble." She hoisted the drink tray, shooting Claire a determined look. "Before the night is over, I'm gonna teach him a lesson about messing with the Morgan sisters."

"Kate," Claire warned.

"You got my back again, right?" Kate didn't wait for Claire's answer. She waded back into the flotsam and jetsam floating around on The Shaft's dance floor, leaving Claire in a cloud of her sweet and fruity smelling perfume.

Ah, hell. Claire didn't want to go to jail again. That would be twice in a week. A new record.

"See that right there," Claire pointed her thumb behind her in the general direction Kate had gone. "That is batshit crazy. We need an intervention or a séance or some kind of exorcism before her head spins completely off."

"She's pregnant," Gramps said, as if that gave Kate a total right of way to the Insanity Express Lane.

"I know, but that's a baby inside of her, not some demon spawn. I can't believe I'm the only one worried about this."

"I need to hit the latrine." Gramps pushed back from the bar. "Don't go getting into any fights while I'm gone."

"If I do, it's Kate's fault."

Gramps hobbled off toward the bathroom, his mending leg no longer requiring a crutch but still slowing him down.

Claire stared up at the bull horns nailed to the wall above the liquor lining the shelves behind the bar. When Butch got home from his trip to that classic car auction in El Paso, he'd better throw a lasso on his woman and get her under control or Claire was going to …

"What're you doing?" Her older sister, Ronnie, interrupted her plans for locking crazy Kate away in the back of Gramps's Winnebago for the next seven to eight full moons.

"What am I doing?" Claire pointed at her glass. "I'm drinking a beer with Gramps."

She looked Ronnie up and down, noticing there were no beer or food stains on her sister's pink tunic and white capris, nor an order pad tucked away anywhere. Ronnie's shoulder-length brown locks curled around her face making her look cool and classy compared to Kate, who appeared to have been dragged behind a horse for a half mile at some point tonight.

"Why aren't you helping Kate wait tables?" Claire asked, irritation mounting. She was tired of always feeling like rumpled sheets around her sleek, perfectly creased older sister. "She's pregnant for crissake."

"Only eight weeks pregnant, not eight months."

Claire scoffed. "Some fine sister you are."

There was a distinct tightening of Ronnie's glossed lips. "I don't see you getting off your butt to help her."

"I'm here by appointment," Claire said. "Besides, I helped her open the place this morning."

"Well, not that it's any of your business, Miss Pissy, but I've been helping her, too, for most of the evening. Then I got a call from Butch and needed to take it in his office."

"Butch called *you?*"

"I believe that's what I said. Are your ears stuffed with tumbleweeds? Or did you clock yourself in the head with a hammer again?"

"Shut it." Sheesh, one miscalculated swing and everybody had a heyday with the wisecracks. "Why did Butch call you instead of Kate?"

"Because I'm helping him with his bookkeeping."

Claire about fell off her barstool. "Since when?"

"Since Kate and you went up to South Dakota. I went to his office the day after you two left to chew him out about his responsibility as a soon-to-be-father. While I was there he offered me a bookkeeping job. So I took it."

Tipping her head back, Claire let out a gut roll of laughter. "Well," she said still snickering, "it sounds like you really gave him a talking to in that meeting."

"Take your sarcasm and shove it up your ying-yang." Ronnie used one of their childhood insults.

"Remind me, where exactly is my ying-yang?"

"I needed a job, you ninny." Her sister nailed her with a squint. "With this gig I can keep an eye on the wallet of Katie's baby-daddy in case she changes her mind about raising the kid on her own and decides to take Butch to court for child support."

Actually, that was a pretty smart chess move. "I thought Butch had a bookkeeper."

"No, he has an accountant, but with all of his traveling lately, he's getting behind on paperwork and needs help. Katie told him about my organizational skills and he hired me on the spot."

"Organizational skills?" She grinned at her older sister. "You mean your ability to sort your costume jewelry according to stone color?"

Ronnie pulled Claire's hair in response.

"Ouch! Not so hard, you oaf." Claire smacked Ronnie's hand away as she tried to grab and pull again. "Seriously, does Butch know about your ex-husband's money laundering skills and current prison sentence?"

"That dickhead was never officially my husband."

"You're splitting hairs."

"Just because I was unofficially married to a lousy, no-good thief doesn't mean I'm going to cook Butch's books."

"I'm sure you won't. I was only curious what Kate has spilled about your current situation to Butch."

As in Ronnie's position way up shit creek thanks to her ex-husband skimming the money he'd laundered and sniffing it up his nose in the form of cocaine. According to the FBI, those goons he had stolen from were now coming for Ronnie, because they somehow had gotten the idea she knew where he'd hidden the dough. Unfortunately, there was no dough, and the only thing that had saved Ronnie from being in debt up to her zirconium earrings was nothing had been put in her name. Her lack of money didn't matter to the men who wanted their pound of flesh, though. Her skin would do just fine.

Ronnie slid onto Gramps's stool and spoke close to Claire's ear. "Did you find out anything about the diamonds yet?"

"No, not yet."

The diamonds Ronnie was talking about were goodies she had skimmed from a pair of rare artifact smuggling "mules." The two mules had been staying at the R.V. park a month ago, helping an archaeology crew excavate one of their new step-grandmother's mines. It seemed Ronnie had learned a thing or two from her ex-husband about *borrowing* from criminals.

Then again, maybe she hadn't learned from her ex's mistakes, because now Claire had more to worry about than the goons coming for Ronnie. Now she had to worry about someone coming for those missing diamonds, too.

Claire glanced around the bar, suspicious of anyone staring at her and Ronnie too long. "I told you not to mention those stones in public."

Ronnie's brown eyes widened. She scoped out the room. "You think someone in here is dirty?"

Downing her glass of beer, Claire scowled. "Yeah, I think most of the guys in here are dirty, especially those road crew workers. Stop looking so paranoid, you spaz."

"I'm not paranoid."

"Please. You think any man who looks at you is going to kidnap you and torture you for information on your ex's hiding places when all they're really doing is checking out your hooters."

"Hooters? Nice language. Kiss your new grandmother with that mouth?"

"Only on the cheek." Claire patted Ronnie on the forearm. "You know the first step to recovery is admitting you suffer from the affliction. Gramps told me you put up a trip wire alarm around his Winnebago last week while Kate and I were gone."

"I was only being cautious."

"The alarm woke up the whole R.V. park."

"It wasn't my fault Gramps's dog slipped his collar and came to visit me."

That damned beagle would have given Houdini a run for his money. "What about the eight canisters of pepper spray you have all over the Winnebago?"

"You never know when a grizzly bear might cross your path on the way to the bathroom in the middle of the night."

"There are no bears in Jackrabbit Junction." Well, except for Kate's polar bear.

Ronnie shrugged. "You don't know that for certain."

"I'm 99.9 percent positive. Besides, Gramps's R.V. has a bathroom."

"It could be occupied."

"At two in the morning?" Claire shook her head, dumbfounded. Was something in the water around here making everyone wacky?

"You're in my seat, Ronnie," Gramps interrupted them, patting her shoulder. "How about you scoot over one?"

Ronnie stood. "That's okay," she said as Gramps slid back onto his barstool, "I need to grab my order pad and help Katie." She peeked at Claire over Gramps's head, pretended to be looking through binoculars, and mouthed *diamonds*.

Claire rolled her eyes and returned to her grandfather. "So what did you want to talk to me about tonight?"

"I want to take Ruby up to South Dakota for a couple of weeks." He stared down at his beer before taking a drink.

"You want me to watch the R.V. park for you two?"

He nodded. "And Jessica. Teenager that she is, she doesn't want to come with her mother and me. She'd rather stay here with you and your sisters."

Claire thought about the responsibility Gramps was asking her to shoulder. "Did anyone talk to Mac about this?"

She had a feeling her boyfriend wasn't going to be thrilled about Claire running the park on her own with all of the near-death shit that had happened over the past few months. Nor the fact that it would mean she'd be staying in Jackrabbit Junction a while longer. Earlier today, Mac had been working on convincing her to come back to Tucson with him for a solid month now that Gramps's leg was doing better.

"Not yet." Gramps cut through her worries about Mac. "Ruby wanted to see if you were game first."

"I'll do it."

"Great, then you can let Mac know."

"What! Come on, he's Ruby's nephew." Their family tree was beginning to look more like a family vine with the relationship branches growing all twisted together since Claire's grandfather had married Mac's aunt.

"Yeah, but you're the one sleeping with him."

Not often enough thanks to the miles keeping them apart.

"Fine, I'll break the news to him," she said, "but you need to let me drive Mabel around for a week in exchange."

Gramps had named his 1949 souped-up Mercury "Mabel" after his first wife, Claire's grandmother. With twenty-five coats of hand-rubbed paint and a pristine white leather interior, he got persnickety any time anyone even got skin oil on his baby.

"I'll tell you what. If you do this, I'll let you have Mabel for the whole time we're gone."

"Really?" Wow, he was desperate. She should have bargained for more. Wait a second … "You're not leaving that damned dog of yours behind with me, too, are you?" Gramps's beagle turned his little black nose up at her every chance he got.

"He's coming with Ruby and me. If I leave him behind with you, he'd probably 'disappear' again."

"You know that wasn't my fault. Not entirely anyway."

"Let's just hope you don't manage to lose Jessica."

"You're a real hoot. So when do you plan on leaving?"

"This week. We want to beat the snowstorm that's supposed to hit the Black Hills next weekend."

Claire pushed her empty beer glass around. "I'll call Mac tomorrow and let him know we're bunking in your room for the next couple of weeks."

She couldn't wait to get a break from the R.V. where she'd been holed up with Ronnie and Kate for the last few weeks. There'd been so much sisterly bonding lately that she didn't think even a jackhammer could split them apart.

Gramps ordered her another beer without asking her.

Claire frowned. "I was gonna head home and crash. Working on that back ditch area all day wiped me out."

"Not yet." When the beer arrived, he shoved it in her direction. "Drink up."

Her gaze narrowed. "Why are you pushing alcohol on me?"

"Because there's something else I need to talk to you about."

"What?"

"Your mother."

Claire took a drink. Bitter, just like her mother. "What about her?" Ruby had mentioned that Claire's mom was in Tucson for a long weekend. They'd both warned Mac to keep his head low.

Gramps grimaced at the suds on his glass. "While you and Katie were in South Dakota something happened."

"Did Mom buy another pair of fake alligator skin boots?"

"No. She took a little trip."

"She's tripping all right." Her mom had been bitchier than ever since signing those divorce papers. Claire envied her father and his newfound freedom.

"I mean an actual trip."

"Really? She hates to drive long distances. Where to?"

"Vegas."

That was even weirder. Gambling wasn't really her mother's thing, but whatever. Claire wasn't sure why Gramps was making such a big deal of it. "Okay."

"She didn't go alone."

Claire shrugged. "The more the merrier I always say."

"She eloped."

Time screeched to a halt. A clanging racket filled her ears.

"Come again?"

"Your mom got married in Vegas."

The room tipped, slipping off its axis. Claire clutched the bar. "What did you say?"

"Congratulations, Claire." Gramps lifted his glass of beer in mock cheer. "You have a new daddy."

Chapter Two

Monday, November 5th

Kate Morgan was going to kick somebody's butt, as soon as she finished puking her guts out.

Sitting back on her heels, she grabbed a wad of toilet paper and wiped off her lips. "This pregnancy business isn't for wussies," she told the gleaming white porcelain toilet, aka her breakfast partner these days. Especially one wussy in particular who had no full-time job or health insurance and lived in her grandfather's Winnebago with her two bossy older sisters.

Actually, Claire wasn't normally bossy. At least she hadn't been before Kate's baby had come along. Lately though, Claire's normal attitude of swing-first-and-ask-questions-later seemed to have traded places with Kate's tendency to retreat in a cloud of dust.

Take last night at the bar with that polar bear biker dude. In the past, Claire would've been all squinty-eyed and hovering over him, demanding he fess up to his reason for being in Jackrabbit Junction. Instead she'd dragged Kate from his table and had sent her home with Gramps to be locked away for safekeeping, insisting she finish Kate's shift and stay to help Ronnie close the bar.

Kate used the toilet paper holder to stand up. Another bout of nausea threatened, but she kept it down, blinking through the accompanying tears. "That's enough for today," she told her stomach and took a few deep breaths.

Thankfully the restroom in this section of the R.V. park was brand new, so the place smelled like fresh concrete and vanilla thanks to the air fresheners attached to the wall above the stalls. The only thing lurking in the corners and behind the toilets were dust bunnies.

Her hand trembled as she wiped the sweat off her brow and tucked back the loose tendrils of hair that had escaped her ponytail. Pregnancy had shaken the shit out of Kate's universe, sending her tumbling ass over teakettle. But she was done starring in the real life version of Linda Ronstadt's *Poor Poor Pitiful Me.*

Something inside of her had snapped while she had been up in South Dakota with Claire last week. If it weren't for the threat of a restraining order, she'd send a Thank You card to that dickhead bartender whose snide comments had lit a wildfire that now raged inside of her. For the first time since she'd found out she was carrying Butch's child, she felt ready to face the world.

And maybe a little crazy.

But crazy was better than night after night filled with self-pity parties. Crazy was energizing, fueling Kate to start moving forward again instead of standing there catching flies.

The substitute teaching job in Yuccaville was the first step. Next came moving from the couch in Gramps's Winnebago to an actual bed.

But not Butch's bed. No way. No matter how much the panicky voice in her head tried to convince her that running back to him would solve all of her problems, she would not give in to it. After his comment about not having time in his life for kids with starting a new business and traveling, she refused even to daydream about what life could be with him.

But he said that before he knew ...

No! Kate squelched that thought, stomping it out before it could catch flame. There would be no future with Butch. Period. Especially if his heart wasn't in it.

Her mother could yap at her until her pink-painted lips fell off, but Kate had her mind set. She refused to end up in a loveless relationship, dragging her child down with her. She'd witnessed firsthand how that ended for all parties involved. She and her sisters were still screwed up after decades of their parents screaming and fighting into the wee hours.

With another round of morning sickness on the back-burner, Kate stepped out of the bathroom stall and crossed to the bank of lockers next to the showers. She double-checked under the stalls before pulling open the locker door.

Her hidden treasures were crammed together in a small basket. She fingered the note Butch had written to her after they'd first gotten together listing the steps to close up the bar. It was signed with a little heart and arrow in place of his name. She pushed aside the keychains he'd given her. One set held the keys to his house, the other had keys to his garage and the El Camino parked inside. She took out the stun gun she'd bought at a pawnshop in Yuccaville and tested it. She doubted it would drop a horse like the greasy salesman had said, but what about a man who called himself the Polar Bear? Maybe she could bribe Claire to let Kate test it on her. Better yet, she and Claire could test it on Jessica's loser of a father.

She put the stun gun aside and took out an old picture of her early teenage self with her sisters and her cousin, up on Pilot Knob overlooking the Black Hills. She'd never forget that day—the warm sun on her head, the cool fall winds freshened with pine whipping her hair here and there, and the giggles and laughs with her three best friends. Leaning the picture against the back of the wicker basket, she pushed aside the empty Baby Memories book she'd found at a drugstore on the way home from South Dakota and pulled out her journal.

Flipping it open, she fanned through the pages of notes she'd made on potential criminals lurking around Jackrabbit Junction until she reached her entry from last night about the Polar Bear. She pulled the pen from the spine. Under her other notations about the brute and the motel he was staying at in Yuccaville, she scribbled: *Driver's license had somewhere in Illinois as address. South Barren-something, probably a suburb in Chicago.*

Claire was wrong. That guy was up to no good, and Kate would bet it had something to do with the thugs who were coming for Ronnie and her ex-husband's mythical hidden stash. Before the week was out, Kate was going to have proof that her suspicions were spot on this time. Then maybe Claire would quit being such a chicken shit and help Kate send the Polar Bear whimpering home to the cave in Illinois he'd crawled out of.

Kate's cellphone vibrated in the pocket of her pajama pants.

She closed the journal and shoved it into her locker behind the wicker basket, then fished out her cellphone.

The name on the phone's screen made her breath catch.

Butch!

No.

Not now.

Her stomach roiled again.

Not so soon after worshiping the porcelain goddess, which had left her wanting to yell at someone while shredding the purple teddy bear her mother had given her as an early baby shower gift.

She let it go to voicemail, her hands trembling again for a whole different reason. Then she leaned back against the lockers, waiting to see if he left a message this time. The last few had been short, his voice terse.

A fly buzzed around the fluorescent light over the bank of sinks. Someone in the adjoining men's restroom flushed the toilet. Another bout of nausea stampeded through her stomach, glazing Kate's forehead with sweat before passing.

Her phone dinged.

Butch had left a message.

She hit the Play button, holding her breath as his honey-smooth voice filled her ear.

"Stop ignoring my calls, Kate. We need to talk. I'll be home Wednesday night."

Yep, still curt.

She puffed her cheeks and blew out a sigh. What was there to talk about besides her going part-time now that she had a substitute teacher gig in Yuccaville? She doubted he'd had a change of mind about playing Daddy. She'd learned early on that her life wasn't a Disney movie. There'd be no hunky prince and ballroom dancing at the end for her.

Stuffing her phone back into her pocket, she grabbed her toothbrush and toothpaste from the locker before closing it.

She had two days until Butch would be back in Jackrabbit Junction. That gave her a little over forty-eight hours to figure out how to face him without falling to pieces at his feet.

* * *

"Jeez-louise, Claire. Why are you driving so damned slow?" Ronnie leaned over to check the speedometer for the umpteenth time in the last few minutes. She sighed in frustration. "Hit the gas already, would ya? I could walk back to Jackrabbit Junction faster."

Downtown Yuccaville was a busy little beehive this Monday mid-morning. With people buzzing here and there, Ronnie wanted to get the hell out of town. It was too hard to spot any potential gun-toting strangers when this many probable gun-toting locals were filling the sidewalks and alleyways. Had Wyatt Earp felt this bug-eyed when he'd walked the streets of Tombstone with his brothers? Maybe she needed to hire a modern day Doc Holliday to be her sidekick.

Claire adjusted the seatbelt, loosening it across her purple *Deadwood Rocks!* T-shirt. "I'm not getting a speeding ticket just because you're having one of your fits of paranoia."

Ronnie stared down a couple of long-legged cowboys leaning against the side of a dusty white pickup. One of them tipped his hat at her as they rolled past. He looked familiar, but then again while helping out at The Shaft over the last month, she'd seen more cowboys than she could count.

She turned back to her sister. "Call me paranoid again and I'm going to have Henry lick your face while you're sleeping."

Claire shuddered. "Don't you dare! That dog licks his balls on a daily basis." She frowned across Mabel's leather bench seat at Ronnie. "What's up with you this morning? You've been acting all skittish and freaky-eyed since you came out of the library."

"Something feels weird here today."

"Have you considered that maybe you're the one feeling weird today?"

Ronnie saw a black Hummer parked a block ahead with tinted windows and shiny rims. She slid lower in her seat. "Listen, dear sister of mine, you're supposed to be helping me keep an eye out for thugs and instead you're spending all of your time pointing out my faults."

"As your loving sister," Claire started.

"Loving?" Ronnie let out a bark of laughter.

Claire continued, speaking over Ronnie's sarcastic laughs. "It's my job to be honest with you. So here's a hard truth you need to swallow: You have not only moved into paranoia-ville, you're running for mayor now."

"It takes a paranoid nut to know one."

"Oh, so I'm paranoid, too?"

"Yeah. Look at how obsessed you were about someone coming for that antique gold watch before we got rid of it." Ronnie tried to see through the tinted window of the Hummer as they cruised by but had no luck.

"Obsession and paranoia are two different monsters."

"Whatever, Miss Denial, but I'm not paranoid." Ronnie had thought about her actions a lot last week when her sisters were up in South Dakota. She'd lain in bed alone in that dark Winnebago night after night, listening for the sound of footsteps outside of the bedroom window. Many times throughout the long early morning hours, she'd wondered if she'd see the morning sunlight again, hating the way her heart rattled at the smallest sound. "I'm merely suffering from an overly heightened state of awareness."

"You're like those munchkins in Oz, always freaked out about the potential for blue monkeys in their little Shriners caps to come flying in and drag you off."

"You can point fingers and call names all you want, but I bet you'd be singing a different tune if you had goons coming to torture you for money you don't have."

"Maybe." Claire started picking up speed as they reached Yuccaville's city limits. "But after being *obsessed*, as you called it, about that gold watch and all of the other shit probably stashed around the R.V. park thanks to Joe and his criminal past—may he *not* be resting in peace—I've come to a decision."

Ruby's previous husband, Joe, had been a real piece of work, no better than Ronnie's ex. Both men had brought a potential shit storm down on their wives' heads after they were safely tucked away—Joe in the ground and Lyle behind bars.

When Claire didn't continue, Ronnie glanced her way. "Well, don't keep me on pins and needles over here. What's your big decision?"

"Has anyone ever told you that you really suck at sarcasm? Don't quit your night job."

Ronnie sighed. "Sorry. I'll behave."

"I don't think that's possible for you these days." Claire softened her jab with a smile.

"Probably not. So what's your decision?"

"That it's better to play offense than defense day in and day out."

Ronnie slid back up her seat again now that the traffic had cleared and greasewood bushes were the only things lying in wait alongside the road. "Does that mean you're going to seek out potential criminals by placing 'Lost and Found Treasure' announcements on light poles?"

"I'm still working out the details, big mouth. But I recommend you follow my lead and switch to offense soon before you start wearing a tinfoil hat and camouflage overalls."

Maybe Claire was on to something with this line of thinking. Ronnie stared out the car window, the desert blurring as her focus shifted inward.

Damn her ex and his cocaine lifestyle. It was bad enough that he'd been laundering money for ruthless kingpins from Chicago to New York and Miami to Dallas, but why did he have to cross the addict line and snort up all his common sense along with the nose candy? If she made it out of this raw deal alive, she was going to pay Lyle a visit in prison and jam something else up his nose. Maybe that creepy four-inch centipede she'd seen in the campground laundry room last week.

It was his last phone call full of warnings and worries for her safety that had spurred Ronnie to get out of South Dakota; she'd come down to southeastern Arizona where she could live close to the Mexican border in case fleeing into anonymity became a necessity. Too bad her ex hadn't been as concerned for her welfare *during* their so-called "marriage" when he had been screwing every other blonde he came across and living high on gutter glitter.

Claire and Katie had talked her into staying in spite of Lyle warning her of impending doom at the hands of those he'd robbed. While she enjoyed being here with her family, she worried night and day about their safety and the risk of taking her in right now. If something happened to one of them because of this mess, she wouldn't be able to live with herself.

It was this fear for her family that had upped her level of paranoia lately and had her courting options she hadn't considered in the past, options having to do with men and women who carried badges for a living. The same men and women who'd done their damnedest to destroy her pride while smashing apart her previous life in pursuit of the criminals Lyle had called "associates." The same badge-carrying bastards who were hanging around Jackrabbit Junction and using her for bait these days, dangling her out on the line while waiting for the sharks to start biting.

Ronnie was getting damned tired of dangling down here in Arizona. Claire was right. It was time to start …

"Shit." Claire interrupted Ronnie's ruminations. "Looks like Sheriff Harrison is up and at 'em early today. You think he's running radar?"

Ronnie looked out the windshield. Up ahead parked next to a dilapidated gas station sat a Cholla County Sheriff's Bronco.

Speaking of badge carrying law dogs, Ronnie had a bone to pick with Sheriff *Hardass*.

Claire lifted her foot off the gas pedal though she was barely doing the speed limit.

"Why are you slowing down?" Ronnie asked.

"To be safe. I don't feel like getting pulled over this morning."

Ronnie peered at the Sheriff through his open driver's side window as they rolled closer. He had his cowboy hat on, his tanned forearm resting on the windowsill. Her heart sped up at the mere sight of his profile, damn it.

Why hadn't he stopped by last night after closing like he'd said he would? Had he been out on a call, or did this have to do with her theory about the Sheriff of Cholla County being too good to be seen in public with a member of the Morgan sister clan?

There was no time like the present to ask.

"Slow down some more, Claire."

"Why?" Claire took her foot off the gas.

"Let's see if he's paying attention." Ronnie rolled down her window as they drew near the Sheriff's Bronco. She grabbed Claire's empty soda cup from the floor. "Hit the horn."

"I will not!"

Ronnie reached across and honked the horn long and loud before Claire shoved her hand away. When they rolled in front of the Bronco, she leaned halfway out her window and dropped the cup onto the road.

"What the hell are you doing?" Claire clamped onto the waistband of Ronnie's jeans and yanked her back inside. "You can't litter right in front of him, you doofus. He's gonna pull us over. It's his duty."

"I know." Ronnie sat back with a grin and waited for the sound of his siren.

Seconds later, the sound of his siren came through the open window, followed by Claire's cursing as she pulled to the side of the road.

"You better fix this, Ronnie, or I'm going to catch that nasty centipede in the laundry room that you keep whining about and put him in your sheets."

"Oh, I'm gonna fix him all right." Ronnie heard a door slam behind them and straightened the wrinkles out of her jersey T-shirt, tugging the neckline down enough to show a hint of cleavage. She brushed nonexistent crumbs off her worn blue jeans. "Trust me, you won't get a ticket."

Sheriff Harrison approached Ronnie's open window instead of Claire's and leaned down. He pulled off his aviator sunglasses. His whiskey colored eyes raked down over her before returning to her face. The unconcealed attraction staring back at her got her engine revving.

Ever since the first time he'd pulled her over, he'd had a way of seeing past her subterfuge of bravery and cockiness and locking in on the angry yet scared woman inside. That always-vigilant gaze of his also made her want to tear his clothes off and have her wicked way with him—with or without his handcuffs.

"Step out of the car, Ms. Morgan," he said in that deep, deep voice of his that almost always gave her goosebumps, especially when it was gravelly with lust for her.

"Why, Sheriff Harrison, whatever for?"

"Out," he growled more than spoke, opening her door.

"I'll be back in a few," Ronnie told Claire and then climbed out of the car, strategically brushing past the Sheriff so that her knuckles glanced over his belt area.

He caught her arm in a solid but painless grip and hauled her back toward his Bronco. He opened both doors on the passenger side of the vehicle and moved her between them so most of her from the knees up was shielded from view.

She crossed her arms over her chest, meeting his glare head on. "You didn't show up last night."

A muscle in his jaw twitched. "Did you miss me?"

"No," she lied.

One black eyebrow rose in disbelief. "I saw Claire through The Shaft's windows when I cruised the lot after closing."

"We sent Kate home early. Claire stayed to help me clean up."

He stepped closer to her, the smell of his bay rum cologne making her libido run rampant. "You should have sent her home, too."

"Why's that, Sheriff Hardass?"

He grabbed onto both doors, pulling a Red-Rover-like move to fence her in. "I believe it's time for another handcuffing, Ms. Morgan."

She scratched a fingernail up his shirt alongside the buttons, from his belt buckle to his open collar. "Maybe it's time for me to handcuff *you*, Grady." She covered his shiny Sheriff's star with her hand, the metal cool on her palm while his skin under his tan shirt heated her fingers. "Although with my being a notorious Morgan sister and all, maybe you're afraid of my riding roughshod all over you."

His Adam's apple bobbed. "Fear is the last thing I'm feeling when it comes to you riding roughshod all over me."

"You talk tough, Sheriff, but I've seen you without your shiny badge and big ol' hat. Frankly, I'm not so sure of your ability to follow through."

His hand covered hers where it still hid that damned star. "God, you have a sassy tongue on you, woman."

"Oh, yeah? What are you going to do about it?"

He lifted her hand to his mouth, running his lips over her knuckles, lighting her up even more. "Trust me, I have all sorts of ideas."

So did she, and most of them had to do with Grady and a future she couldn't have because of who she was now.

"Well, see, Sheriff, it's that trusting part that gives me pause." She pulled free of his electric touch before it zapped her brain again. "And you, too, based on your actions lately."

"What in the hell is that supposed to mean?"

"You figure it out, law dog." She held her hands out, wrists together. "Now, are you going to handcuff me for littering or what?"

He grabbed her and whipped her around so she faced the Bronco. Holding her hands up so her palms were flattened against the edge of the roof, he came up behind her, his breath warm on her neck below her ponytail. "Don't tempt me."

She peeked over her shoulder at him. "But, Sheriff, that's what I do best."

His body pressed against hers as he pretended to frisk her, his fingers finding far more than weapons. "Tonight, Veronica." His lips brushed down the side of her neck. Chills spread up her spine. "In the dark behind The Shaft. Alone."

She trembled with aches only he could appease. In the short time she'd known Grady, he'd aroused a carnal side she hadn't known existed when she'd been married to her ex-husband. Now she couldn't get enough. There was no satiation when it came to Grady, just a continual hunger for more of him that ate at her night after night.

"I'll have to take a look at my schedule." She kept her voice smooth in spite of his heated touch. "I'll see if I can fit you in."

He stepped back, turning her around. "Make time."

She loved it when he got all caveman on her, but she was getting tired of being hidden away from his public life. She understood that his position was an elected one and how important public opinion could be, but her pride was beginning to sit up and take offense at being his secret lust.

"Maybe I will." She led the way back to Gramps's car, which sat idling as Claire fiddled with the radio. "Maybe I won't." She slipped back inside.

He shut the door and leaned down into the open window. "Claire, you need to turn around and make your sister pick up that litter."

"Will do, Sheriff." Claire shot Ronnie a narrowed glance. "Won't we, Ronnie?"

"Of course. That was purely an accident, Sheriff."

He stared at Ronnie for an extra few seconds before pushing upright. "You girls take it easy now," his deep voice came through the window along with a sun-warmed breeze. "Don't be speeding."

Claire leaned down to peer out at him. "I wouldn't take the risk in this car, Sheriff."

"Quit being such a kiss ass," Ronnie said to her sister as the Sheriff strode back to his Bronco.

"I was wrong. You're not paranoid, you're just plain psycho." Claire shifted into gear and did a U-turn, easing to a stop opposite the soda cup. "Go get it, litterbug."

Ronnie took her time retrieving the cup. The road was empty except for a passing eighteen wheeler. The rig driver honked when she waved.

Grady followed the semi-truck, both heading toward Yuccaville. He stared out the window as he passed by, his aviator sunglasses back in place.

She flipped off his taillights. Stupid badge. She liked him a lot better when he shed his pointy star and righteous ideals along with his pants and inhibitions.

When she climbed back in, Claire shook her head at her.

"What?" Ronnie set the cup down by her feet. "Let's roll."

"Why can't you two just have a normal relationship like the rest of us?"

"It's not my fault. He's the one who's ashamed to be seen with me in public."

"Ashamed? Why would you think that?"

"He only touches me when he thinks nobody else is

looking."

"Maybe that's part of the fun for him."

Could be. "Is it too much to ask me out to dinner like a regular guy would?"

"Your ex used to take you out to dinner and look how that ended up."

"Yeah, but he was a lying piece of shit." Grady was as honest as they came, sometimes too honest for her own good.

"I'm sure the Sheriff has a respectable reason for taking this relationship with you nice and slow."

Ronnie thought of what Grady's aunt had told her about his ex-wife and how the bitch had put him through hell. How she'd lied about the baby from another man until it was born and Grady's insurance had paid the bills. Then she'd up and skipped town with her lover and their child, leaving Grady alone to face the music. He probably didn't relish another public humiliation fest on his behalf.

"Maybe he does, but I'm not accustomed to back alley screw jobs."

"True, you're used to being fucked over with watered-down champagne and fake jewelry."

"Kiss my ass," Ronnie snapped back.

"Sorry, I'm just being honest again."

"I'm not sure I'm hip to this newfound honesty policy of yours. A straight up lie is fine with me."

"Bullshit."

Ronnie stared out the windshield at the black ribbon of open road melting into the wavy horizon. "You're right." Lies would only steer her down the wrong path again, back to a valley of make-believe happiness.

"About not lying?"

"About Grady and Lyle, and my past."

Claire was also spot on about playing offense instead of defense. It was time to stop living in fear and take the bull by the horns.

"I like the sound of it when you tell me I'm right," Claire grinned over at her.

"Don't get used to it."

"And while we're being so honest, I have to tell you something else."

"If this is about Mac and you having problems, you don't have to tell me. I already know."

Claire's mouth fell open. "What? Mac and I aren't having problems."

"Oh, sorry, I didn't realize you were still in denial about that one."

"What are you … we're not … never mind about Mac and me. We're just fine."

Fine? Is that what she called Claire obviously not wanting to live at Mac's place back in Tucson while Mac pleaded with her to return home with him every weekend? "If you say so."

"This isn't about me. It's about Mom."

Ronnie recoiled at the thought of their mother. Her constant badgering for Ronnie to get a real job and stop spending her nights at "that bar slurping down gin and tonics" had worn some thin spots on her few remaining nerves.

Besides, she didn't slurp, damn it. "What about Mom?"

"She's no longer single."

"I know. She sometimes sleeps in Manny's Airstream now." Gramps's old-time Army buddy had been taking one for the team for weeks, using good old sex to dull the edge of Deborah's usually razor-sharp tongue.

"I'm not talking about sleepovers." Claire slowed as they neared Jackrabbit Junction and the road leading to the R.V. park.

"What then? Just spit it out."

"Okay. Mom's married."

"Not anymore." Thank God for that, too. Deborah may still be a miserable bitch to her family, but she was tolerable now—at least when some gin and tonic were part of the scene.

"Ronnie," Claire spared her a glance as she turned off the highway, "She's married again."

Crickets sounded in Ronnie's ears. "What?"

"We have a new stepfather."

"No." Ronnie's jaw hit her lap before bouncing back up again. "Please don't tell me Manny actually married her!" Not the poor, wonderfully kind Don Juan wannabe. Deborah would tear his loving, over-sized heart into pieces and then grind them into the dirt with her pointy heels.

"He did, the poor sucker. Gramps told me last night. Mom had wanted to keep it a secret, but Manny insisted on telling Gramps."

Ronnie shook her head in disbelief. "We'll surely win the Most Dysfunctional Family award this year." Her laughter was bitter with a dose of acid. "Does Katie know?"

"Not yet. But she will after you fill her in."

"Why me?"

"Because she's crazy and that's right up your alley, litterbug." Claire reached across the seat and poked Ronnie's forearm. "Tag. You're it."

Chapter Three

Tuesday, November 6th

The General Store at the Dancing Winnebagos R.V. Park was on fire this morning.

Literally.

Claire sniffed. The back of her throat felt scratchy after inhaling the acrid smell of burning electrical wires and wood paneling still thick in the air. Thankfully the store only needed the smoke cleared, not damaged goods.

The fire had started in the wall in Ruby's rec room, which was on the other side of an ancient, musty smelling velvet curtain that divided the General Store from the rest of the house. The flames had crawled along a loose piece of paneling and licked at the velvet curtain until it had caught fire, too. By then the smoke detectors had screeched to life, scaring Claire and Ruby out of their breakfast time newspaper perusal.

Claire had stomped out flames while Ruby had hefted the fire extinguisher Gramps kept under the kitchen sink, covering everything with spray including the bottoms of Claire's blue jeans and her flip-flops.

Claire surveyed the black foamy mess, burned fabric, and charred paneling wondering how to begin fixing what was left of the wall where the fire had started.

It was a good thing those smoke detector batteries had been fresh. Ruby's store was too old to have sprinklers in the ceiling, so Gramps made a point of checking the detectors every week. His obsession with making sure the place was fire-alarm ready was ironic considering it was his fault the fire had started.

"There's nothing like the sight of a flaming curtain to light a fire under my ass," Claire told Ruby, who still held the extinguisher in case something sparked back to life.

Claire yanked down the tattered and burned fabric and hauled it out the front door, tossing it onto the gravel drive beyond the porch. Then she grabbed a hammer from the spare tool belt she kept tucked behind the store's counter and used the claw to tear off the blackened paneling. Together she and Ruby piled the charred scraps of splintered paneling and molding on top of the curtain.

"I think that's the last of it," Ruby said in her soft southern drawl. Her red hair stuck out every which way, reminding Claire of Lucille Ball after too many hits of Vitameatavegamin. Streaks of soot marked her freckle-spotted neck and forehead. Only a few years older than Claire's mother, Ruby seemed more like a stepmom to Claire than a step-grandmother.

Claire followed Ruby back inside. "It's a good thing Gramps already pulled up the shag carpet or it could've been much worse."

Last week while Claire had been up in South Dakota, Gramps had been bit by the remodeling bug and had decided it was time to tear apart the rec room. Never mind that he was still recovering from breaking his leg back in September.

She'd arrived back at the campground to find the 1970s orange shag carpet ripped up and most of the wood paneling torn off. He'd left the piece of paneling around the doorway into the General Store still attached because the molding needed to be popped off and he'd run out of steam. From what Claire could tell, he must have jarred the receptacle when he pulled the paneling partway free and loosened some wires, which had sparked into a nice little wall-burner this morning.

Too bad Gramps was in Yuccaville, filling the back of his new Ford pickup with supplies for tomorrow's journey north. He'd missed all of the excitement he'd caused.

"Maybe your grandfather and I should forget about headin' out tomorrow." Ruby handed Claire a cold bottle of Coca-Cola.

Ruby was anxious about leaving Claire behind to run the store and campground with a torn up house, but Claire was ready for Gramps to go away for a while. She loved her grandfather dearly, but after almost half a century of working with his hands, the seventy-plus-year-old couldn't stand to lounge around and enjoy retirement. He was always starting one construction project or another and then dragging Claire in to help finish.

Take the new restrooms at the back of the R.V. park. He'd gotten as far as nailing up the wall studs before falling off a ladder and breaking his leg. Never mind that the broken leg was a little bit of Claire's fault. If that damned dog of Gramps's hadn't been such a stubborn little … Anyway, Claire and her cousin Natalie had taken over building the restroom while Gramps had barked orders from his lawn chair in between chugging beers with his cronies, Chester and Manny. Claire had barely finished painting the restrooms before she and Kate had left for South Dakota.

Now she had a partially gutted rec room to put back together. Gramps had asked her last night to take over where he'd left off while he and Ruby were gone. Never mind that she'd be a teeny bit busy running an R.V. park at the same time. The damned man must think energy grew on creosote bushes down here. Or maybe he had her confused with Popeye after downing a can of spinach. As flattering as his confidence in her was, most days she felt more like Wimpy—hurting for cash and wanting nothing more than to dive into a stack of hamburgers. Better yet a box of MoonPies.

Claire washed the smoke out of her throat with several swallows of Coke. Then she set the bottle on the counter and went to work airing out the General Store.

It took two floor fans and about fifteen minutes to chase out the last of the smoke hovering up near the fluorescent bulbs. Ruby swept up the last of the ashes scattered across the varnished plank flooring and wiped down the burned wall with a wet rag.

"That's as good as it's gonna get," Ruby said, dropping her rag into the bucket. "Finish your drink before it gets warm, darlin', and I'll go rinse out these rags in back."

Not a minute after Ruby had disappeared, Gramps pulled up in front of the store in his pickup.

Claire watched him step down out of the cab, whistling as he swung a Roadrunner Auto Parts plastic bag with each step. Who was this happy old Smurf and what had he done with Grumpy the dwarf?

Gramps took one look at the pile of burned offerings on the gravel and seemed to choke on his whistle.

"Ruby?" he yelled as he hustled up the steps and shoved aside a fan on his way into the store.

"She's out back rinsing out some rags," Claire told him from where she leaned against the counter, taking a couple more swallows of Coke.

His pale blue eyes hopped from her to the doorway where the curtain used to hang. "What in the hell happened in here? I was only gone for an hour."

"Well, I'm no fire investigator, but my somewhat-educated guess is that you pulled a wire or two loose in the outlet when you were tearing off the paneling in the rec room."

"Ah, hell." He dropped his bag on the counter and crossed into the rec room, checking out the fire damage with a grimace that deepened as he followed the burn marks clear up to the ceiling. "I knew those wires were trouble. I'll have to cap them until I get back."

"They're already capped." Claire had taken that precaution, disassembling the guilty outlet as soon as the wires were cool enough to touch.

"Good thinking, girl."

She joined him in the rec room. "I was taught by the master."

"Yeah, well the master should have known better and checked the wires before taking a break from his project." He ran his hand over his bald head. "Jesus, I could've burned the whole damned place down with you guys in it."

Claire patted his shoulder. "Thanks to your weekly smoke alarm inspection, the place is still standing, so don't beat yourself up too bad."

He grunted. "Maybe we shouldn't leave tomorrow."

"No!" she said with more emphasis than she meant to. "This trip will be good for both of you. With Mom and us girls all living down here now, and Jessica's dad constantly adding to the stress level, Ruby needs a break. The Black Hills are a great place to relax, especially now that the summer tourists are gone and the winter skiers and snowmobilers aren't there yet."

"That's true. Ruby sure could use a vacation. The poor woman has been baking every damned day lately."

Baking heavenly but fattening goodies was Ruby's method of de-stressing. Unfortunately, eating those heavenly but fattening carbohydrates was Claire's way of dealing with her own stolen-treasure worries and mother-caused angst. Ruby needed to leave town so Claire could drop ten pounds and no longer have to shoehorn her butt into her jeans.

"I don't like leaving you with this mess, though."

"Ehh." Claire waved away his concern. "It'll keep me busy. Plus this will keep Chester entertained until you return. Manny, too, when he gets back."

Gramps's old Army buddies thoroughly enjoyed heckling Claire while she worked around the R.V. park. They reminded her of the two old guys in the balcony on the Muppet Show, always making smartass remarks and cackling at their own jokes.

"But you're not so good at wiring."

"I'll call Natalie and have her walk me through anything that I'm not certain about." Claire's cousin was a real chip off Gramps's block. Nat's skills at wiring rivaled his these days, whereas Claire's expertise was in plumbing, where soldering a joint very rarely involved possible electrocution.

"I don't know," Gramps headed back into the General Store. "Wiring can be tricky, especially in these old houses."

"Wait. Didn't you tell me back before I called Nat to come down and help with building the restrooms that Chester knows his way around wiring, too?"

Gramps shrugged. "He claims to have worked as an electrician once or twice in his younger years."

"See, no problem. Chester and I will take care of it, and we'll bug Natalie, if needed."

"Call *me* if you need help, not your cousin."

"No. You and Ruby are escaping. Take her up to Nemo and let her soak up the hills in all their snowy beauty."

"There's no snow there yet."

"I know that, Negative Nelly, but there will be after this weekend. You better get up there before this big storm they're calling for hits and snows you out instead of in."

The General Store's screen door slammed shut.

"Where's the fire?" Chester Thomas called out.

"In the rec room." Claire hollered back.

Chester's bowlegged scuffle drew closer. He paused in the doorway, his usual shit-eating grin in place around the unlit cigar hanging from the corner of his mouth. His silver hair looked extra bristly this morning, along with his unshaven jaw and the sprigs of hair sticking up out of his shirt collar.

"Dammit, Claire," he said with his eyes sparking. "You're supposed to answer, 'In my pants,' and then I reply with, 'I got just the right hose to put out hot babes like you.'"

"Your hose would definitely put me out, Chester. Right out the front door and ten miles down the road, screaming all the way."

"Keep your pants on around my granddaughter, Thomas."

"Relax, you old crab." Chester took out his cigar and stuffed it in his shirt pocket. "I'm just trying to educate Claire on some of the finer things in life."

Gramps snorted. "She's had enough education to get her Ph.D. She doesn't need any more."

Gramps wasn't exaggerating about that. Claire had taken enough college classes over the years to be a doctor; unfortunately she couldn't settle on one major so all her schooling amounted to a doctorate in absolutely nothing, which her mother liked to remind Claire of often.

"What's got your pecker in a knot today?" Chester asked Gramps. "We always joke in front of Claire. She's one of the boys."

Unfortunately, that was also true. Since Claire had joined Gramps and his Army vet buddies down here last spring, Chester hadn't once worried about what came out of his mouth in front of her—and out of his other end, too, which was unfortunate since most mornings he loved to eat *chili con carne* straight from the can.

"My granddaughter is a respectable girl."

"Thanks, Gramps."

"She just doesn't dress like it."

She resembled that remark this morning, damn it, with her torn jeans and stained T-shirt. "Hey! Clothing doesn't make a woman."

Chester snickered. "No, but a lack of clothing sure does separate the wheat from the chaff. Take that cute little snowbird who rolled into the park yesterday afternoon in her sleek new Airstream."

"What's your snowbird have to do with Claire?"

"Not a single damned thing. I just want to *take* that sexy bird, especially after I saw her out drinking coffee this morning wearing a short silky robe and fur-lined, high-heeled slippers." Chester winked at Claire. "I bet she has a pair of fur-lined handcuffs that came with that outfit."

Jeez-o-petes, it wasn't even *nooner*-time yet. "Did you confuse Viagra for your allergy pill again this morning?"

Gramps squeezed her shoulder. "Stay away from Chester while I'm gone."

"Take it easy, Ford. Claire and I ain't gonna elope while you're gone."

She pointed at Chester. "What he said."

"Claire's a real peach, but a bit too green for me. I like my peaches soft, round, and sweet-smelling with plenty of juice when I bite into 'em."

Claire wrinkled her nose. She'd never look at peaches the same way again.

"Besides," Chester continued, elbowing Claire in jest, "we both know good ol' Sweet Buns has Claire wrapped around his totem pole."

"Oh, dear Lord." Claire rolled her eyes and headed toward the General Store. "I'm gonna go get the mail."

By the time she got back from the mailbox, Ruby had joined Gramps and Chester, all three leaning against the long, saloon-era bar in the rec room like a trio of cowpokes. All that was missing was a player piano and a spittoon. Claire handed Ruby the mail and detoured into the kitchen to put away the breakfast dishes she'd left in her haste to put out the fire. But the table had already been cleared, so she returned to the rec room.

"Harley," Ruby said, frowning down at a letter. "What do ya

make of this?"

Gramps took the paper she held out. He scanned it, turned it over and then upright. "What's the return address on the envelope?"

"It's ours."

"No, the return address."

She held out the envelope for him to see. "Ours. The sender put our address in both places."

Claire joined them, her curiosity getting the better of her. "What is it?"

She took the paper Gramps offered and read the one sentence typed on it:

You are the proud owner of Humdigger mine.

"Humdigger?" Chester said from where he was reading over her shoulder. "Is that supposed to be Hum*dinger*?"

"Can you read the city on the postage meter stamp?" Claire asked Ruby.

"Not without my reading glasses." She handed the envelope to Claire.

"It says Yuccaville." Claire gave Ruby back the letter and envelope. "Have you ever heard of this Humdigger mine?"

"Nope, but I've had my nose buried in this R.V. park since I moved here."

Ruby's deceased husband, Joe, had bought her the Dancing Winnebagos R.V. Park as a wedding gift and then had left her alone to fix it up and keep it afloat while he went on his so-called weekly sales trips. Unfortunately, while Ruby might be decent at bookkeeping and running the store, she stumbled when it came to the park's upkeep and regular maintenance. By the time Joe had his stroke, she was hip deep in debt quicksand from maintenance bills and sinking fast.

"You should call Mac," Harley suggested.

Ruby and Claire both blinked at each other in surprise, and then nailed Gramps with a matching set of frowns. Gramps had pawed at the ground last month and snorted fire about Mac playing the white knight too often, especially when it came to helping his aunt.

"Is this some sort of trap?" Claire asked Gramps.

"What are you talking about, child?"

"Be careful, Ruby. Gramps's bite is worse than his bark."

"Maybe you can call Mac," Ruby passed the buck along with the letter and envelope to Claire.

"Good idea." Gramps touched his wife's shoulder. "We need to get packing if we're gonna get out of here at dawn."

Ruby nodded, her expression worried when it returned to Claire. "You sure you're okay with us leavin' you with a burned rec room wall and now this?" She pointed at the letter.

"Sure," Claire lied without a twitch. "But I'd be even more okay if you waited and took Mom with you."

Gramps scoffed, "Nice try." He patted Claire's head like he often did his damned dog and then headed toward their bedroom.

Ruby gave Claire a quick hug and a whispered, "Thanks," before following after him.

"Looks to me like they're leaving you with nothing but trouble." Chester jammed his cigar back into the corner of his mouth.

"True." She poked him in the shoulder. "After all, they are leaving me here with you."

He swatted away her hand and waddled toward the kitchen on his bowed legs. "What's for breakfast? I'm out of chili."

Thank the breakfast gods for that. "You must have me confused with your maid. Check the fridge." Claire grabbed the cordless phone off Ruby's bar and went out through the General Store's front door. Plopping down on the porch bench, she looked out across the desert.

She never tired of the view from Ruby's front porch. Over in the valley, a dust devil zigzagged across the desert floor, dancing to its own tune. To the east, the Tres Dedos Mountains backboned the length of the valley. At the north end of the ridge, a chunk of granite known as the Middle Finger jutted up, pointing at the sun.

Arizona's deep blue skies reminded her of summers up in the Black Hills; the occasional clouds were like huge ships drifting past on their way out to sea. More than anything, she loved the feeling of wide openness. No city pressing down on her, making her aware of all of her shortcomings on the career front.

She leaned back, taking it all in. Living among the tumbleweeds and coyotes made her feel an affinity with those brave souls of the Old West who dared to pass through this barren corner of the country, let alone set up residence.

A breeze rustled through the cottonwoods and desert willows down by Jackrabbit Creek and blew her way. The clean scent of baked earth was marred by the odor of freshly charred paneling, reminding her of all of the work she had to do while Gramps and Ruby were gone.

Her gut tightened.

Shit. There went her moment of Zen.

Moving further down the porch away from the pile of burned offerings to the electrical gods, she leaned against the railing and punched in Mac's cellphone number. Their phone conversation last night had been shorter than she liked; he had been tired and she had been henpecked by Chester to be his partner for a couple of games of Euchre.

"Morning, Slugger." Mac answered. "What kind of trouble are you getting into today?"

Claire smirked. He knew her way too well. "Let's see. So far, I've played firefighter and put out a one-smoke-alarm blaze in the rec room with the help of your aunt. She's a real pro with a fire extinguisher."

There was a long pause on the other end of the line. "Are you serious? There was a fire?"

"The outlet right by the doorway to the General Store sparked a fire. I think it was tired of being surrounded by that crappy 1970s wood paneling."

"Is everyone okay?"

"Yeah. We put it out before it did too much damage."

"Good. So when are you coming home?"

"Uh, well, there's a thing about that." She shifted against the railing, her legs antsy to walk somewhere far from her current situation.

"What kind of a thing?" Mac sounded wary.

She tried to think of the best way to deliver the bad news and ended up going for a bumbling blurt. "Gramps and Ruby are leaving, and I sort of need to stick around until they get back. They want a break from this place. Well, more like from the people here than the actual place. Anyway, they asked me to take care of the R.V. park. And Jess. She doesn't want to go. And now there's the burned rec room. Gramps wants me to finish remodeling it. Chester's going to help, although his version of helping is more like drinking beer and bossing me around while he sits on his bony ass. Mom and Manny are still in Tucson on their secret honeymoon that I told you about last night. We haven't told Kate yet about that crazy mess. It's Ronnie's job. Speaking of crazy messes, I think Kate's gone over the deep end. She's dead set that she's found the Polar Bear. And Ronnie isn't far behind Kate. She threw litter out the window right in front of Sheriff Harrison, so I got pulled over. Lucky for me, she's sleeping with him so I didn't get a ticket. And on top of it all, Butch comes home tomorrow, so Kate's a nervous wreck. She spilled three pitchers of beer last night, and I ended up staying to help Ronnie close again. Then this morning, I went out to the tool shed and found a javelina stuck inside. It must have squeezed in through that loose board in the back and couldn't figure out how to get free. The damned thing peed all over the floor, so it stinks something awful."

She paused to catch her breath and let her tongue rest.

Mac's silence made her twist her T-shirt hem this way and that. "Mac? Are you still there?"

"I think my brain just self-imploded."

"So, will you come back Friday and stay for the weekend?" She licked her dry lips, worried that he might be getting really tired of driving all of the way from Tucson to see her and start making demands about her returning home with him … or else. "I'll make it worth your while."

"How?"

"Lots of nakedness?"

"Are we talking about you or Chester? Because I've seen Chester nearly naked, and it made me nearly blind."

Chester had a sleepwalking condition that had earned him

the nickname *Flash Gordon* back in the Army. Unfortunately, that was an ailment that hadn't been cured with time.

"*Me* naked."

"Hmmm. Tell me more."

"Alone with you."

"Tempting. What else you got?"

"Both of those first two conditions behind a locked bedroom door."

"Locked, you say? Is there a no-interruption guarantee in the deal?"

"Sure, and I'll throw on the tool belt as a bonus."

Mac had a tool belt fetish that she didn't question. In her trade as a handywoman, trading in gauzy lingerie for a loaded tool belt meant she could save money by killing two birds with one stone. Trust her boyfriend, the geotechnician who could name the different layers of rock making up the surrounding mountains, to have a practical side even when it came to his sexual fantasies.

"Are you trying to tell me that if I wade into that maelstrom you like to call good ol' family bonding, you'll have sex with me?"

"Yep."

"Then you have a deal, Slugger."

"That wasn't so hard."

"I'll be sure to torture you plenty on Friday."

"You could take Friday off and come sooner." Mac had months of time off accrued thanks to his nose-to-the-grindstone mentality year after year until she'd come along.

"I'll see what I can do." She heard the sound of a garage door opening. "I still can't believe Manny married your mother. You would have thought he saw enough bloodshed in the Army to last a lifetime."

"Gramps keeps talking about more blood being shed when Manny gets back with Mom. He turns all red and starts huffing when he talks about how his friend cradle-robbed his daughter."

Mac chuckled. "He's one to talk. Aunt Ruby is only a few years older than your mom."

"Oh, speaking of your aunt. She got a weird letter today."

"Please tell me it's not another solicitor threatening her."

"Nope. All it said was, 'You're the proud owner of Humdigger mine.' Both the To and Return addresses were the R.V. park. The postage stamp shows it went through Yuccaville's post office."

"Did you say Humdigger mine?"

"Yeah, not *humdinger*. Ruby was stumped by it. Said she's never heard of that mine. Gramps suggested we talk to you."

"Your grandfather actually wanted you guys to come to me? Is it raining frogs out there in the desert?"

"Maybe he's been getting too much sun."

"Humdigger," Mac said, as if rolling it around on his tongue would spur answers from his brain. "I'll see if I can find anything out about it after work tonight."

"Maybe I can get Ronnie to visit the library over in Yuccaville, too." The hometown of the long-running, super huge Copper Snake Mining Company, Yuccaville's collection of mining records was one of the most extensive in the state.

"I have to go, Claire. The boss called a special meeting this morning, so I have to stop at the office before I head down to the project site." Mac's company was subcontracting on a new drainage system for a growing retirement community twenty miles southeast of Tucson.

"Okay. Call me if you find out anything."

"Will do."

"I'm good with phone sex, too, if you want to skip straight to that."

His laugh was low and husky. "I always appreciate your colorful descriptions, but I want to enjoy the real thing."

"If you change your mind, you know my number." He knew how to ring her bells and whistles, too. "Be careful out there."

"Always. Don't touch anything that hisses or rattles, Slugger, and that includes your mother. Love you."

He hung up before she could sputter that she loved him back. Those three little words were relatively new to her and her tongue got all shy whenever it was her turn to say them to Mac.

The screen door opened and Chester came out with what looked like a rolled pancake in his hand.

"What is that?" She pointed at his breakfast.

"A pancake wrapped around a stick of jalapeño cheese."

Really? "Can't you just eat a normal breakfast?"

"This is normal." He pointed his pancake roll at the phone. "Who was that?"

"Mac."

"What did Sweet Buns have to say about the Humdigger mine?"

"He's going to look into it."

"Did you tell him we're running the park for a while?"

"We? Are you going to help clean toilets?"

"I figure I'll play host and visit all of the campers. You know, make sure their needs are met."

Claire slapped him on the arm. "You better be good while Gramps and Ruby are gone."

"Damn it, girl, don't take the fun out of it."

"If you harass any of the female campers, I'll confiscate your snowbird-spying binoculars."

"Now you've taken the fun out of it."

Chapter Four

The Yuccaville Library was a regular snores-ville this afternoon with only a handful of patrons roaming among the shelves.

Ronnie spared the librarian a glance on her way over to the spot where the computers with internet access were located. Even she was sleeping with her head tipped back and her mouth wide open like a baby bird.

The telltale clicking of knitting needles drew Ronnie over to the gang of old ladies hanging out in their usual circle. From an outsider's viewpoint, the three appeared to be harmless retirees meeting for their weekly knitting bee. But Ronnie knew better. The Geritol gang could give the Dalton brothers a run for their money.

"Good afternoon, ladies," she said, dropping into the chair next to Millie, their leader, who also happened to be Sheriff Harrison's aunt. Oh, such wonderful irony. As a member of the notorious Morgan sisters, Ronnie felt a sort of camaraderie with Aunt Millie and her feisty friends. "You're missing a couple of ladies today." Usually there were five of them, but today only the three main players were present—Millie, Ruth, and Greta.

"I have a bone to pick with you, young lady," Aunt Millie told her, poking Ronnie in the thigh with her long needle.

"I brought goodies to trade if you want." Even though Aunt Millie and her friends no longer demanded bribes from Ronnie in exchange for time on the internet, Ronnie still brought glittery goods in case they had a change of heart.

"This isn't about the Fair Trade Act." That was Aunt Millie's codename for the extortion racket she and her compadres had going on at the library. Aunt Millie pointed her needle at the computers. "What sort of trouble are you up to these days?"

Grady's aunt knew too much about Ronnie for each other's own good. "Just the normal black market stuff." Ronnie tried to dodge her question. "Same as always."

Aunt Millie and her crew had helped Ronnie back in September. Without their help, Ronnie wouldn't have been able to figure out where the watch had come from. Nor would she have been able to ship it back before someone much more worrisome than the law came looking for the watch. Technically, Grady had shipped the watch back under a cloak of anonymity, saving Ronnie and her family from an even bigger heap of trouble than they were in already.

"Your eyes sparkle when you lie," Aunt Millie told Ronnie. "Has anyone ever told you that?"

"No, but thanks for the heads up. I'll be sure to wear sunglasses more often." Especially around Aunt Millie's badge-wearing nephew and his x-ray vision.

"Now quit being smart with me. Cough up the truth or I'll sic Ruth on you."

Ruth was Aunt Millie's second in command. She liked to joke about sharpening her knitting needles every night and delivered a wicked blow with her cane when push came to shove. This was the same Ruth who had left some bruises on Claire months ago thanks to said cane when the two had gotten into a scuffle over the length of time allowed on the library's internet computers. Claire had not only taken a few hits from Ruth, but she'd also been kicked out of the library for six months, which was one of the reasons Ronnie was there today. Claire wanted information on a mine, and Ronnie was the only Morgan sister that Aunt Millie and her bruisers let inside their clubhouse.

"We know you've been deleting the cache and clearing the temporary internet files after every use," Ruth told Ronnie without looking up from the cherry red sweater she was knitting. "We may be old, but we're not computer fuddy duddies."

Damn. She'd underestimated the old gals. "Maybe I'm just a clean freak."

"Good try." Aunt Millie pursed her lips. "Now you're going to tell us what you're really up to or else."

"Or else what?"

"We can do this the easy way or the hard way."

"What's the hard way?" A cane beating? Ronnie really didn't want to involve anyone in her diamond search besides Claire.

"I call my nephew and let it slip that Greta is helping you with your German again."

Greta could read and speak German. She'd helped Ronnie translate a German article about Claire's prized antique gold watch. One slip to Grady like that would have him sniffing around her for reasons other than sex on the sly. "Oh, you girls are good."

"You bet your ass we are, *Fräulein*," Greta said, sounding like Cloris Leachman in *Young Frankenstein*.

Ronnie knew when she'd met her match. "Fine. I'll share, but only if you three promise to keep your lips sealed. Nobody, and I mean absolutely not another soul, needs to know about this, especially not Sheriff Harrison."

Ruth's shrewd gaze narrowed even more. "Or what?"

"I'll have to jump the border and disappear for a long, long time."

"Can we go with you?" Greta asked. "I've always wanted to sleep with one of those mariachi players. They're so sexy playing their romantic music in those fancy outfits."

Aunt Millie's face lit with a smile that made her eyes glow. Grady's aunt had a penchant for danger. Maybe that's where he'd gotten his desire to face off with criminals day after day. Millie leaned closer. "You have our word. Now spill."

Ronnie glanced around to make sure nobody was eavesdropping. The librarian still snoozed away. A mom and her toddler were looking at books in the kids' section. Other than that, they were alone. Waving the three knitters in closer, she shared her tale about the diamonds hidden inside the fake glass eyeballs that she'd found stashed up under one of the camper trailers last month. She purposely left Claire's name out of her story in case of retribution.

When she finished, all three sat back and resumed knitting, as if Ronnie had shared today's weather, not some sordid tale about black market dealers and human "mules" carrying stolen treasure across international borders.

"Hmmm," Aunt Millie said after several stitches. "It sounds to me like you could use some training to improve your investigational skills."

"What do you mean? I've seen plenty of CSI shows."

"CSI is fiction. If you want to learn from television, you need to check out Rockford or Columbo."

"I always enjoyed Perry Mason," Ruth said. "He had those dark piercing eyes."

"I'm a Philip Marlowe fan hands down." Greta sighed and patted her heart. "Bogart still makes my old ticker race."

That could be dangerous at Greta's age. She could blow a gasket.

"Why do I need training?" Ronnie dragged them back to the present day.

"You've been using words like 'stolen diamonds' and 'diamond heists' in your searches," Aunt Millie said.

Ronnie's jaw dropped. "How could you see that from over here?"

Ruth giggled and pointed at Greta, who pulled a pair of binoculars from her knitting bag.

"They're Vortex Vipers."

Greta would fit right in with Manny and Chester and their babe-watching binoculars. Ronnie shook her head in disbelief. "You girls should really go pro."

"How do you know we aren't already?" Greta asked, placing her spy glasses back into her bag and returning to knitting what looked like a muffler.

"What do you suggest I search for?" Ronnie asked all three.

"For one thing," Aunt Millie said, "if these women you took the eyeballs from were mules, you need to dig through the border patrol records about drug mules and past busts."

Ruth pointed a needle at Ronnie. "And don't forget to look for any Spanish articles about the same topics. There are several newspapers in the border towns that may have write-ups about stolen treasure trafficking and what the *federales* have confiscated."

She had a good point. Ronnie hadn't thought about what might be available on the other side of the border. "Can any of you read Spanish?"

"Grady can," Aunt Millie said.

"He speaks English, German, *and* Spanish?" Sheesh! Ronnie struggled with English most days.

"His German is sketchy but passable," Greta critiqued.

"But his Spanish is spot on from what I hear," Ruth said.

"From whom?" Aunt Millie asked.

"Juanita Chavez. You know, that busty, pretty young thing with the dark red lipstick who works behind the counter at the post office." Ruth leaned forward, her smile conspiratorial. "I think she has a crush on Grady, because whenever I bring up his name, her cheeks get all rosy."

Ronnie was going to have to pay a visit to the post office and get a look at this Juanita Chavez and her big boobs and red lips. After all of the stress thanks to Lyle's misadventures with the law, Ronnie had dropped twenty pounds and a solid cup size, darn it.

"I can't go to Sheriff Harrison with this," she told the gang. Where could she find someone who spoke Spanish that could keep a secret …

Oh, duh!

Manny!

Her wonderful new stepfather.

Now that he was family, he'd be doubly sure to keep his lips locked about this. If not, Ronnie would sic his lovely wife on him.

"I'll figure out something for the Spanish stuff," Ronnie fibbed.

The suspicion in Aunt Millie's gaze spoke volumes, but she nodded and aimed her needle at the row of computers. "You'd better get busy before the senior center bus comes by and drops off a herd of old goats who want to check their email accounts for letters from their grandkids."

Ronnie hopped up, not needing to be told twice.

A half hour later, Katie pulled up in front of the library windows and honked once.

Ronnie gave her sister a one-minute finger and deleted the internet temporary files, cleared the cache, stuffed her printouts in her purse, waving goodbye to the Geritol gang on her way out. "See you all soon."

"Give Grady our love," Aunt Millie called after her.

Grady's aunt had once caught Ronnie and Grady kissing during a stakeout. There was no pretending she and Sheriff Hardass were just good ol' enemies in front of Aunt Millie, no matter how hard they tried.

The librarian was snoring when Ronnie placed change on the counter for her printouts.

Outside, the senior citizen center bus was unloading at a fast crawl. On her way to Katie's Volvo, Ronnie dodged a very round lady who smelled like she'd been rolling in a tub of baby powder.

The November sunshine warmed the top of her head. She could get used to these Arizona winters real quick-like. Jeans and a T-shirt were her standard uniform now that the blazing heat of summer had mellowed into fall. A comfortable breeze ruffled the shoulder length curls she no longer needed to keep pulled into a ponytail so her neck wouldn't roast. She slid her sunglasses on, striding over to where Katie waited for her with the car still idling.

"How'd it go?" Katie asked.

Ronnie had told her sister about searching for Claire's Humdigger mine but hadn't mentioned she was also looking into the diamonds. While Katie knew about the diamonds, the less Katie was involved in Ronnie's messes the better, especially since her youngest sister's gut instinct was almost always dead wrong.

"Not so good. I found some information on a *Humdinger* Mine in Oregon and another one in Arizona, but nothing on a Humdigger mine. Every time I typed those two words in the Search field, unrelated results with 'mine' in them filled page after page."

"That's not good."

"Why?"

"Claire's going to get obsessed again." Katie took off down the road, but instead of turning toward Jackrabbit Junction, she went in the opposite direction, cruising along a back street in one of Yuccaville's dingier neighborhoods.

"Maybe." Ronnie looked over at Katie. "You missed our turn back there."

"I know where the damned turn is. I've been down here

longer than you, remember? I want to show you something."

"Okay, sheesh, don't bite my head off." Ronnie settled into the plush leather seats; Katie's taste in vehicles always had been good. Too bad her taste in men leaned toward chain gangs. At least it had until Butch.

Several blocks later Katie frowned at the rearview mirror. "We have a tail."

Who? Sheriff Harrison? Ronnie's heart giddy-upped. Grady hadn't stopped by last night, undoubtedly because Claire had been there cleaning up again.

She was torn. After spending years as an untouched trophy wife, she didn't want to be polished and put out on a shelf to shine under the spotlight any longer. Matter of fact, she wanted to be good and tarnished. But she didn't like being tarnished and tucked away, hidden from the public eye. Was it so much to ask to be treated somewhere in between trophy wife and clandestine lover? A plain-Jane girlfriend, maybe?

She turned in her seat to see who it was and cursed at the blue pickup following them. "It's that damned FBI cowboy."

"I thought he drove a red pickup." Katie took a quick right.

The cowboy followed.

"He keeps changing vehicles," Ronnie said, still watching through the back window. "Apparently blue is the new red."

"How can you be sure it's him? Maybe it's someone even worse with a briefcase full of sharp surgical instruments or an electric dental drill in his glovebox."

"Jeez, Katie. A dental drill?"

"Sorry. I watched *Marathon Man* the other night when I couldn't sleep."

"You need to stick to happy movies for a while. As for how I can tell it's my FBI buddy, he always wears his cowboy hat tipped to the right." Ronnie saw a cloud of smoke seep out through his window. "He also smokes hand-rolled cigarettes like they're doling them out for free down at the Bureau."

"He sounds like the Marlboro Man. What's he look like?"

Ronnie had seen him close up only once, and she'd been about four gin and tonics to the wind at the time, but she remembered him being better looking than most of the rat bastard Feds she'd come across. "He's hot in a chain-smoking, cowboy-skirting-the-edge-of-the-law sort of way, but he carries a badge." In Ronnie's book that meant he might as well be carrying the plague.

"What a no-good, lousy jackass!" her sister snarled into the mirror.

Ronnie did a double-take. "I don't know that he's that bad of a guy."

"Your FBI douchebag just threw his still-lit cigarette butt out the window."

"He's not *my* douchebag." She faced forward in her seat.

"Doesn't he know how dangerous that is in the desert?" Without warning, Katie slammed on her brakes so hard Ronnie face-planted the dashboard.

"What the hell, Katie?!!" she said, rubbing her forehead.

Her sister grabbed something orange from the door pocket and was out of sight before the FBI guy's pickup tires stopped *skirrrrch*-ing.

"Katie!" Ronnie called out the driver's side door after her sister. "Where are you going?"

A horn honked from somewhere behind them, followed by a "Move your truck, asshole!" A diesel flatbed truck rumbled past Katie's car, the driver's middle finger held out for the world to see.

Ronnie shoved open her door and jogged back to where her sister was tapping on the FBI guy's closed driver's side window with one of those orange emergency glass breaking hammers.

Katie's lips were wrinkled in a scowl, her cheeks red and blotchy. "If you don't get out of that truck right now and go pick up that cigarette butt you threw out back there, I'm gonna break your freaking window, drag you out by your Federal Bunch of Idiots badge, and kick your smoking ass all of the way back there!"

"Lady, are you off your meds?" Mr. FBI hollered through the glass. "If you don't get back in your Volvo, I'm calling the sheriff."

Shit! Ronnie didn't want Grady to be dragged into this. It would give him another reason to frown about the infamous

Morgan sisters.

Katie didn't even blink about getting the law involved. "And then I'm going to cram that butt so far up your nose that you won't be able to blow it out 'til next Easter."

He held up his phone and pointedly looked at Ronnie. "You need to get your Shih Tzu back on her leash."

"Littering is a misdemeanor fine, you Federal dickhead." Katie tapped on his window again. "Not to mention this desert is a damned tinderbox full of tumbleweeds and other dead stuff."

"Katie, come back to the car." Ronnie grabbed Katie's arm, but her sister tugged free.

"Just because you work for the government doesn't mean you're above the law, you stupid monkey butt."

Monkey butt? Okay, it was time to wrap up this freak show and move the circus to the next town.

Ronnie caught Katie again, this time with a firmer grip. "Kathryn Lynette Morgan," she used her best impression of their mother's voice and tone. "Get back in your—"

The whoop-whoop of a police siren cut her off.

Ronnie froze, her eyes widening. "No," she whispered.

Kate whirled, her little orange hammer still raised.

"Is there trouble here, ladies?" said a voice nowhere near as deep as Grady's.

Her knees weak with relief, Ronnie turned slowly, wearing a smile so wide her teeth were probably visible from space.

Deputy Dipshit. Thank God it was only Claire's nemesis rather than the sheriff himself. The deputy had come from the other direction. His cruiser idled in the middle of the street while he eagle-eyed them from above his double chin through his driver's side window.

"No trouble at all, Deputy," Ronnie said.

"Then why is your vehicle stopped in the middle of the roadway?" His gaze swung to Katie. "And what is she holding?"

Katie pointed her orange glass breaker toward Mr. FBI. "This son of a—" she started.

Ronnie shoulder bumped Katie.

"Hey! Knock it off." She turned back to the deputy. "I was making a citizen's arrest. This asshole threw out a lit cigarette butt and that's illegal."

The deputy's face split into a grin. "A citizen's arrest by a Morgan sister for littering?" He chuckled. "Awesome. This doozy is sure to win me the pot in this week's pool."

The door to the blue pickup swung open. A pair of long jean-clad legs appeared, topped by a black T-shirt and a crooked cowboy hat. Ronnie stared at Mr. FBI, fighting down the heartburn that bubbled up her throat every time she got too close to a badge-carrying member of the cocksuckers who'd taken her easy snow globe life and shaken the holy hell out of it before smashing it on the ground.

"Sorry about this, Deputy." The sound of his voice was smoother than she'd remembered from that night when they'd danced and he had warned her about the Husky and the Polar Bear. He flashed his badge at Grady's deputy and then approached the window with both hands clearly visible. "My cigarette accidentally slipped out of my fingers," Ronnie heard him explain. "The ladies here were helping me find it."

Katie sputtered, but Ronnie covered her sister's mouth. "Not now." Not with a Spanish article about Mexican drug mules from a Nogales newspaper stuffed in her purse.

Shoving Ronnie's hand away, Katie wiped her mouth with her summer knit sweater. "I hope you washed your hands before touching my mouth."

"I'll walk back," the FBI guy continued, "and go find that cigarette butt if it's okay with you."

"I'm not sure that's necessary, Special Agent." Deputy Dipshit said, kowtowing to the FBI.

"It can't hurt to look." Mr. FBI thumbed in the direction of his idling pickup. "I apologize for any inconvenience this little incident caused. It won't happen again."

"Not a problem." Deputy Dipshit smirked toward Ronnie and Katie. "We have special instructions to keep an eye on these Morgan sisters. They tend to land ass-deep in trouble without even trying."

Special instructions from whom? Ronnie's jaw tightened. She had a good idea who had given that order.

The deputy's hillbilly-like cackle of laughter echoed out

through the open window as he rolled away. Claire was right. The deputy needed to be taken down a notch, and Ronnie was just the woman to do it … if Claire didn't beat her to it. Maybe they could tag team his ass.

Mr. FBI hit Ronnie with a glare. "You need to take your sister home. I wouldn't be surprised to see her start foaming at the mouth any minute now."

Ronnie bristled. Katie might be rabid today, but no FBI sonofabitch was going to insult her little sister. "You better mind your own mouth, cowboy, or I'll bust your lip."

He chuckled. "I've seen you hit."

"Then you know I'm not bluffing."

"What the hell is her problem?"

Katie waved her hand between them. "Hello! I'm standing right here."

"She's pregnant and not feeling like herself lately."

"Oh, Christ." He shook his head as if Ronnie had said Katie had thirty days left to live. "That's even worse."

He took off down the street, his strides long, his boot heels clunking with each step.

Katie huffed. "I'm going to go kick his skinny ass."

"No, you're not. You're getting back in the car. I don't need to have Grady breathing down my neck right now."

"I thought you liked it when he breathed all over you."

"Shush up." Ronnie took Katie's keys.

"Give those back."

"Not until you're behind the wheel."

"Fine." Katie stalked back to her Volvo. The slam of her car door echoed down the block.

"Here." Ronnie handed her the keys through the window. Out of the clear blue Arizona sky an idea hit her. "I'll be right back."

"Where're you going?"

"Just wait for me." Ronnie met Mr. FBI guy halfway back to his pickup, the now-squished cigarette butt in his hand. "We need to talk," she told him.

"Only talk? You mean you're not going to slam my face into the asphalt, yank my arms back, and ride me like I'm a rodeo bull?"

Crap. Ronnie winced. He must have heard about that incident last month at The Shaft. "I leave the ass-kicking to the pregnant bruiser these days." Ronnie held up her finger at Katie, who was leaning out her window, muttering something while gesturing with her hands.

"What do you want to talk about?" he asked.

"Not here." Ronnie glanced around at the houses lining the street, the windows shadow-filled. "Somewhere more private."

He stopped next to his pickup door. "Private, huh? Did you learn something we need to know?"

We? As in the holier than thou, leave no secret hidden FBI? Yes, she'd learned she didn't want to be used as bait anymore. "Maybe. Meet me tomorrow night at The Shaft."

"What time?"

"Closing time. Outside the back door."

Katie honked the horn.

"That's kind of late."

"Oh, I'm sorry. I didn't realize the FBI had an early curfew. How about I offer to read you a bedtime story in exchange for a moment of your time."

He grinned. "I like your fire, Veronica Morgan. I'll be there in my favorite pajamas."

Ronnie would bet they had lassos and horses all over them.

Her sister honked the horn again, long enough to be heard clear down at the Sheriff's office.

"Keep your pants on, Katie! I'm coming," Ronnie hollered. "Don't be late," she told Mr. FBI and returned to the car before Katie really did start foaming at the mouth.

"What were you talking to that jerk about?" Katie flipped off Mr. FBI as he rolled past them.

"I'm tired of playing defense." She buckled her seatbelt.

"What does that mean?"

"It means I'm going to take the bull by the horns."

"Quit using metaphors and just say what you mean."

"Fine." Ronnie watched the blue pickup make a left and disappear around the corner. "I'm going to have a meeting with Mr. Long Tall Glass of FBI and explain to him that it's time to start working with me instead of using me." And if that didn't work, she was going to threaten to bust him in the kneecaps with the baseball bat Butch kept tucked away behind his office door.

"You think getting into bed with the FBI will help you bring down the Polar Bear?"

Katie slowed in front of a slightly run down, 1960s era motor lodge called The Rowdy Coyote Motel. The No Vacancy light was half burned out, the stucco walls cracked and peeling. There had been a pool, but now it appeared the hole in the ground was being used as a boat graveyard with a rusted hull and cabin sitting next to the bones of what had been a small vessel. Buoys and old nets decorated the half torn down chain link fence.

The Rowdy Coyote ... why did that sound familiar?

"I'm not going to sleep with him," Ronnie explained, trying to place where she'd heard the name of this motel before. "Just join forces."

Katie pulled into an empty parking spot across the street from the motel and rolled down her window. "You know what I mean."

"Now who's using metaphors?" When Katie cut the engine, Ronnie frowned across at her. "What're you doing now?"

Katie pointed at the two-story line of concrete block stucco rooms with chewed and rust speckled brown doors. "Check out Room 9."

"It's hard to see inside the room through that closed metal door without my X-ray vision goggles." She sniffed and made a face. "What's that horrible smell?"

"I think something is dead in that culvert over there."

Ronnie waved her hand in front of her nose. "Close the window."

"Not until you take a closer look at Room 9."

"Quit messing around and tell me why we're here gagging from the stink of some rotting carcass."

Katie pointed at the motel. "Room 9 is the Polar Bear's den."

"The Polar Bear. You mean that poor guy you were harassing at The Shaft the other night?"

Katie slapped her steering wheel. "First Claire, now you. Why doesn't anyone believe me? I'm telling you, this guy is here for one reason and one reason only." She poked Ronnie in the shoulder. "You."

"What makes you so sure he's not a tourist? Maybe he's on one of those motorcycle long distance tours. You know, a rich early retiree who's trying to find himself while cruising across America on a Harley."

"If he has money, why is he staying in this old, undoubtedly roach-infested motel?"

"It's not as if fancy hotel rooms are a dime a dozen in Yuccaville, Katie."

"Yeah, but there are a couple of semi-decent ones. Much better than this place. But enough about the motel. I saw something here earlier while you were at the library looking up stuff for Claire, and I wanted to show it to you."

"Wait a second." Ronnie turned in her seat, taking in her sister's flushed cheeks and messy hair. Katie looked like she was short-circuiting both inside and out. "I thought you were dropping me at the library and then going to the grocery store."

Katie shrugged. "That took ten minutes."

"Please tell me you didn't do something stupid like sneak into the big guy's room while he was showering?"

"Who do you think I am, Claire?" Katie pulled out a spyglass and held it up. "I used this."

Ronnie laughed. "Avast ye! Here thar be pirates!" Actually, plundering pirates would explain the rusted boat shell in the pool.

"Poke fun, but when you see this, you'll be choking on your laughs."

Taking the spyglass, Ronnie hefted it in her hands. "Where did you get this?" It was heavy and looked expensive. "It's brass, isn't it?"

"It was in Ruby's office. I think it's one of Joe's antiques, but that doesn't matter right now." Katie lifted the opposite end of the spyglass, pointing it in the direction of the motel. "Look!"

Ronnie focused on the door to Room 9. It was beaten up by the sun and desert weather more than she'd realized. One solid kick and the sucker would probably crash in. "What am I looking for?"

"Check out the opening in the curtains."

Ronnie scanned to the right. "Something's sitting on the table." She leaned across her sister, looking out through the open window instead of the front windshield.

"Ouch!" Katie pushed her away. "Get off me. You're squishing my boobs."

"I can't help it. I'm not used to them being this big. They're like freaking cantaloupes now."

"They are not that big yet." Katie sighed. "Would you just look on that table and tell me what you see."

Ronnie focused again with her left eye, closing her right one. "It looks like a fish tank."

"Bzzzzt. Wrong answer."

Ronnie lowered the spyglass and glared at Katie. "Do that again in my ear and I'm going to jam this thing where the sun doesn't shine."

"You'd do that to a pregnant woman?"

"If that pregnant broad is my little sister, then yes. Besides, if I put the big end of it in first, it would make it easier for your

OB-GYN to check on the baby." Ronnie looked through the spyglass again. "If it's not a fish tank, what is it?"

"A snake tank. You just can't see the snake from here."

Ronnie sat back and shuddered. "How do you know there's a snake in it?"

"I drove through the parking lot earlier and got a closer glimpse."

"Right. On your way to the grocery store that's a couple of miles from here?"

Katie shrugged. "I took a detour."

"Damn it, Katie. You need to be more careful. You're pregnant, remember?"

"Just a second ago you were talking about jamming a spyglass up my hoo-ha. Now you're going to act protective?"

"I was joking." Ronnie pointed the brass peeper at the motel. "This spying business is serious. You need to leave this Polar Bear guy to me and Claire. We'll look into him more."

"Look into him more? What more do you need on this creep to get Grady involved? Or that FBI jerk?"

"Just because someone has a snake tank in his room doesn't make him a killer."

"True, but that's not just any snake."

Ronnie narrowed her eyes at her sister. "How would you know what kind of snake it is? Even if he held it up to snuggle with in front of that window while you were in the parking lot, you couldn't tell what it was unless you really know your snakes, and you don't because you run away screaming every time you even think you see a snake."

"I do not. It's Mom who does that. I don't like snakes, but I'm not that creeped out by them."

"Fine. You're a regular snake goddess. So what kind of snake is it?"

"A rattlesnake."

Chapter Five

Wednesday, November 7th

I don't think you should be doing that, Claire," Chester said from where he rested his keister on one of Ruby's barstools. Claire raised her safety glasses, setting them on the top of her head, and then pulled off her dust mask. She used the hem of her blue South Dakota State Jackrabbits T-shirt to wipe the sweat and speckles of plaster from her face.

"I told you when we came back from lunch break," she said, grabbing the glass of water on the bar next to his can of beer, "if you're going to sit there and watch, keep your heckling to yourself." She washed down the dust that had made it through her mask.

"Your grandpa said to repair the fire damage area and then put the room back together." Chester ignored her attempts to mute him with a glare. "He didn't say to tear out all of the lath and plaster in the room."

Claire looked at the piles of broken plaster and wood laths that she'd ripped off the wall where the fire had sparked. She was almost two-thirds of the way done stripping this wall down to its studs, which thankfully were still in great shape.

"You saw the wiring in this wall." She pointed her hammer at it. "It's knob and tube with cloth-coated wires. That old school stuff is a huge fire hazard. There's no way I can patch up the wall knowing I left that mess behind the plaster. It has to be updated with modern wiring, especially with the electrical load on these few outlets. Shit, you know this as well as I do. You're the electrician here."

"Plaster may not be the current trend, but it has its benefits, not to mention the historic value. It makes better soundproofing, too. With the store next door, Ruby may like it quieter in here."

"Yeah, but repairing plaster is a bitch. Not to mention the weight it's putting on the floor joists and supporting structure. The only reason there hasn't been any sag yet is Joe beefed up the support on the basement beams in his office." Although knowing Joe and his worthlessness when it came to anything other than stealing, it was probably the previous owner who had shored up the basement beams.

Chester grabbed his can of beer. "Plaster is a pain in the ass, but this house is built like a tank. The lath and plaster keeps the place rigid." Chester finished his beer and let out a window-rattling belch as if to prove how strong the walls were. "Besides, Ford is a penny pincher. It's gonna cost a few hundred to rewire this room, and once we finish here, you'll want to tear apart the kitchen and do the same."

"No, I won't."

He crushed the can and tossed it into the trash. "Bullshit."

"It's not my house."

"It's not your R.V. park either, but you sure seem to be the one fixing everything around here most of the time. Have you thought about why you care for this place so much?"

What was he getting at? "It's my job. I'm the handywoman, remember?"

"You think that's it, huh?" Chester scratched his stubble-covered jaw. "I'll bet you a crisp hundred that before we're finished here, this remodeling job will spread to the kitchen and the downstairs bathroom."

"The bathroom? What's wrong in there?"

"There're still galvanized pipes behind the walls."

"How can you tell?"

"Ford told me. The whole house needs updating, but he's not sure he wants to sink the money into it."

Claire didn't want to think about what that meant in the long run if Gramps didn't want to fix up Ruby's place, but a sort of melancholy plucked at her heartstrings anyway. "Yeah, well, my job is to fix this room and that's it."

"For now." Chester said, as if he were some kind of oracle. "I look forward to collecting my winnings from you."

The back door opened. "We're home!"

The sound of her mother's voice made Claire cringe.

Chester let out a barrel roll of curses.

"Claire Alice Morgan!" Deborah gasped with an extra helping of drama. "What have you done to your grandfather's house?"

"First of all, it's Ruby's place, not Gramps's." She hooked her hammer on her tool belt in case her mother pissed her off enough to throw it at something. Or someone. "Secondly, what's it look like I'm doing? I'm fixing it."

"That's still up for debate." Chester laughed outright when Claire flipped him off.

"*Ay yi yi*, what a mess!" Manny Carrera lowered her mother's red faux leather luggage onto the floor. With his salt and pepper hair recently trimmed and his pleated trousers and Hawaiian button up shirt, he looked fresh in from lunch at the Country Club. A smile warmed his face when his brown eyes landed on Claire and her tool belt. "Ah, *chica*. It's good to see you in action again."

Deborah stood at the far end of the room in fancy Manolo heels and a sleeveless peach jumpsuit. An older, more pinched-faced version of Kate, their mother's perfectly lined lips crinkled as she surveyed the mess and then Claire, who couldn't move without making dust billow. "There's no way I can sleep in this house with all of this dust and Lord knows what mold spores in the air." She planted her hands on her hips. "Manuel, we'll need to move my things into your Airstream until Claire finishes with this remodeling phase she's going through."

Sweet potato fries! Claire hadn't even considered how remodeling the house would affect where her mother spent most of her time. She shot a double-wide smile at her remodeling pal. "You win, Chester. Next up, the bathroom."

"Don't forget the kitchen."

"You can't tear the whole house apart." Deborah sniffed and then sneezed, pinching her nostrils together when another sneeze tried to come out. "Where's your grandfather?"

Gramps must have kept his plans a secret from Deborah when she had called the other night to see how things were going. "They're on their way to South Dakota."

"What? Since when?"

"They left this morning. I'm running the R.V. park while they're gone."

Deborah turned to Manny, who'd joined Chester at the bar. "Maybe we should head north and meet them up there."

"No, Mother. They needed a vacation from *everyone*." Especially Deborah's pointy horns and flaming pitchfork. "Besides, I need Manny's help."

"You do?" Manny asked, glancing around the room in surprise.

"Since when?" Chester scowled at his retired partner-in-babe-hunting as he grabbed another beer from the mini-fridge behind the bar. "That old fart doesn't know a ground wire from his Johnson."

"Chester Thomas," Deborah chided. "Bite your tongue in front of the ladies!"

"Show me a lady and I'll get to biting." He handed Manny a beer and added, "starting with her inner thigh."

Claire groaned when he wiggled his bushy eyebrows at his buddy and they both wheezed.

"*Es verdad.*" Manny took the beer and pulled on the tab. "I stay far away from things that can zap me to death with one touch."

"Yet you have sex with *her*." Chester pointed at Claire's mom.

Deborah tiptoed her way through the piles of plaster and wood, joining the other two at the bar. She slapped Chester on the arm. "Behave yourself. Manuel is an amazing and considerate lover."

Claire gagged openly. "Please stop. My mental stability cannot handle another jolt this soon."

A month ago, she'd burst in on her mother and Manny doing the wild thing. Refried beans, tequila, and whipped cream had been on the bedside table next to them. No amount of electroshock therapy would ever cure Claire of the ongoing nightmares, nor could she look at a can of refried beans without considering lobotomy options.

"Oh, I see." Deborah stroked Manny's hair. "It's okay for you and Mac to talk about having relations but nobody else."

"Mac and I don't talk about 'relations' in front of anyone."

Cracking open his beer, Chester scoffed. "You just get caught riding bareback in your grandfather's hot rod."

"Oh, for crissake. We have not had sex in Mabel."

"Not for want of trying." Bristle-head elbowed Manny, laughing at his own wiseass comeback, ignoring Claire's snarls.

He was right on that one, though. Claire had tried to get Mac to have sex in Gramps's car only to get caught by her grandfather with her pants almost down. It wasn't her fault there was nowhere else to go to be alone with Mac most weekends.

Claire heard the General Store's screen door creak and then slam shut. An interruption, thank God.

"Claire?" Jess called from the other room. Ruby's daughter pushed aside the blanket that was strung up in the doorway, keeping plaster dust from seeping into the store. In her oversized gray sweatshirt and jean shorts, Jess looked twelve instead of sixteen.

Was school out already? Claire had lost track of time in the midst of playing demolition derby with her hammer.

"Whoa, dude! What happened in here?" Jess tossed her backpack on the bar and headed for the kitchen.

"Claire is making a godawful mess of your mother's house." Deborah let out a fake little cough and waved away plaster dust like it was attacking her.

"It's called remodeling," Claire told her audience of critics.

"Claire!" Ronnie pushed the old blanket aside. "I saw Manny's pickup outside." Her gaze moved to the bar. "Oh, there you are. Manny, I need your help with something."

Deborah cleared her throat, holding her wedding ring up, making a point of admiring it in front of everyone. "It seems congratulations are in order."

Claire and Ronnie rolled their eyes in unison.

"More like consolations if you ask me," Chester muttered and belched. "I need to see a man about a mule." He waddled off toward the bathroom.

"Claire and I are both very ..." Ronnie started saying to

Deborah and then seemed to choke on her words. Looking to Claire, she nudged her head toward their mother. "What was the word we used, Claire?"

"Traumatized."

"No."

"Appalled."

"Nope."

"Disturbed?"

Ronnie's eyes narrowed warningly. "Not that one either."

"Stunned."

"That was it—but in a good way." The smile Ronnie flashed Deborah didn't come close to the corners of her mouth. She focused back on their new stepfather. "Manny, can I drag you away from your marital bliss for a few moments?"

"You can have him later, Veronica." Deborah grabbed her new husband by the wrist and tugged him off the stool. "He's going to help me pack up my things and move them to his camper. We're not staying in here with this mess."

Ronnie turned back to Claire. "I call Mom's room."

"What about Kate?"

"She can have the Winnebago to herself."

"You'd leave a mentally unstable pregnant woman alone in a camper to fend for herself?"

"Katie isn't crazy." Ronnie paused, grimacing. "Not usually, anyway. Besides, I don't see you giving up Gramps and Ruby's big comfy new bed for *your* pregnant sister."

That was because Claire had plans for that bed. Since Katie wasn't going to be getting lucky anytime soon, it made sense for Claire to take advantage of the situation so that she could take advantage of Mac.

"Kathryn won't be alone," Deborah cut in. "Manuel and I will be right next door to her. If she needs anything, her mother will be there to take care of her."

Oh, boy. Crazy Kate was going to break something—make that several somethings—when she learned about her new neighbors.

Frowning at Ronnie, Claire asked, "You'd leave Katie alone in the camper next to Mom?"

"It's a great opportunity for some mother-daughter bonding."

"I agree," Deborah said.

Claire had a feeling that the only bonding that would be going on would be Kate tying up Deborah, duct-taping her mouth shut, and dumping her into Jackrabbit Creek.

Manny followed his new wife through the rec room's battlefield toward the spare bedroom she'd been occupying for the past couple of months. "You do realize, *mi amor*, that this will be the first time we sleep in my Airstream as man and wife."

Deborah flirted with him over her shoulder, her eyelashes batting. "Who wants to sleep?"

"*Gato montés*," Manny growled and smacked her on the bottom, making her titter and run away with him chasing after her tail.

"I'll find you when your mother finishes having her wicked way with me," Manny called back down the hall to Ronnie from the bedroom threshold.

Ronnie shuddered, easing back into the General Store.

Claire pulled out her hammer and eyed it. Maybe another hit to her head would block out the horrible refried bean and whipped cream memory that kept resurfacing.

"What'd I miss?" Chester asked, settling down on the barstool again.

"Something that a year of therapy won't even touch."

"Hey, Claire?" Jess strolled out from the kitchen with a sandwich in her hand. She hopped up on the barstool Manny had just vacated and bit into her snack, speaking through a mouthful of bread. "Did Mom leave me any money?"

Of course Ruby had left money in case Jess needed anything, but Claire hadn't been born yesterday. "Why?"

"I need some cash. Dad wants to take me to Tucson this weekend."

"What happened to your dad's wallet?" Chester asked, speaking around the cigar he was lighting. "Did he accidentally drop it in the mud pit at Dirty Gerties again?"

Jess's legs swung as she chewed. "He said he's a little short."

Ah ha! Once again, the asshole was trying to get Jess to give him whatever she had in her piggy bank.

Ever since Ruby had married Gramps and come into some money thanks to unearthing a couple of her dead husband's stashes, Jess's previously nonexistent father had shown up with both hands held out for Ruby's charity. Never mind that he owed years of back-pay on child support. Had it not been for Jess, Ruby would have sent the son of a bitch packing straight off. But Jess was at a vulnerable age and had been having troubles at home and school. Ruby was walking a tightrope, trying to keep her child from running off with a piece of crap father who only recognized his child now because he had dollar signs in his eyes.

"What happened to that primo job he landed with the Copper Snake Mining Company?" Claire asked while stuffing plaster pieces in a big garbage bin.

"Oh, he's still working there. He said he's on probation, whatever that means, and isn't getting his full pay until he puts in ninety days."

Chester snorted his feelings on the matter, but a head shake from Claire kept him from saying more. Until Ruby returned, it wasn't Claire's or Chester's place to tell Jessica what a huge cow patty her father was.

"Your mom left a little cash, but she said it was supposed to be for school lunches and a night or two at the movies with your friends, nothing more."

"Ah, man. Come on, Claire, you know where she keeps my college savings stashed. Can't you get more out so I can get some new jeans in Tucson? Dad said he'll take me to the mall."

Of course he would … on Ruby's dime. "Nope. I have to do as your mom says, Jess. I don't want to get in trouble with Gramps."

"Her grandfather is gonna be pissed enough when he sees what she's done to the rec room."

"Seal your loose flaps, Chester." Claire pointed at Jess's backpack. "Why don't you take your pack into the store and get your homework done while you're watching the register. I need to haul some of this garbage to the pile back behind the toolshed."

"Give me five bucks and it's a deal."

It never failed; Jess was always wheeling and dealing. "How about you do it for free and I don't tell your mom you were at the movies last Friday with your college boyfriend."

Jessica was sweet on one of the young college kids who had been doing some fieldwork for the University of Arizona's archaeology department over the last couple of months. The whole team was using the R.V. park as a base camp while excavating some ancient cave dwellings Mac had found in Ruby's Lucky Monk mine. Being that Jess was only sixteen and the boy was closer to twenty, everyone had been keeping an eye on the two to make sure nothing more than hand holding and stolen kisses were making headlines in Jess's daily news.

Jess's face turned as red as her shoulder length curls. "Were you spying on me?"

"I don't have to spy, kid. You're horrible at hiding the truth. Ask Chester."

The old boy tsked. "Your face is one big freckled tell. You're gonna need to work on it in the mirror if you want to partner with me in Euchre in the future."

Grumbling about how unfair life was, Jess grabbed her backpack and hopped off the barstool.

"Don't eat anything else after that sandwich." Claire called after the kid as she shoved through the old blanket. "Chester said he's going to barbecue some burgers later for supper."

The blanket hadn't stopped moving before Ronnie pushed through into the rec room. "Hey, Claire, there's a lady out here who needs change for the laundry room, but the cash drawer is locked."

Claire pulled the keys from her pocket and tossed them to her sister. "Give those to Jess. She's going to run the store for me for a while."

"Got it."

"You working at The Shaft tonight?" she asked Ronnie.

"I wasn't scheduled to, but I'm going there anyway to help. Katie could use the support. I have a feeling she may want to get out of there early tonight."

"That's right. Butch comes home today."

"I saw his pickup in the parking lot," Jess yelled,

eavesdropping from the other side of the blanket. "But Kate's car wasn't there."

Claire frowned at Ronnie. "Where's Kate?"

She hadn't seen her younger sister all day, and that had Claire a little worried. Kate had really locked her jaws on the idea that the biker guy at the bar the other night was the Polar Bear. Something told her that Kate wasn't going to let this rash notion go until Claire could prove the biker's innocence.

"She got a phone call this morning from the school in Yuccaville. They needed her to substitute."

Claire had forgotten about Kate getting state approval to be a substitute teacher. "Oh, good." At least she wasn't stalking the biker. Then she remembered how nutty Kate had been of late and wondered if a classroom full of kids would knock her more off her axis. "Or maybe not."

Maybe Claire should help out at The Shaft, too, after she wrapped up demolition. A full day of teaching and a night of waiting tables wasn't easy for anyone, let alone a pregnant woman.

The phone rang.

Ronnie disappeared back through the blanket as Claire picked up the phone extension Ruby kept on the bar. "Dancing Winnebagos R.V. Park."

"Hey, Slugger." Mac's voice in her ear made her smile. "How's life in Jackrabbit Junction?"

"Dusty." She drew a heart in the layer of plaster dust coating the bar. "So can you get Friday off and make it a long weekend?"

"Yes, but we need to talk this weekend. Alone."

"About the Humdigger mine?"

"And something else." His tension registered on Claire's uh-oh radar. She drew a sun with a wavy worried smile. "Did Ruby and your grandfather take off this morning as planned?"

"Yes." But that didn't matter right now. First off, she'd been burning with curiosity for long enough. "What did you find out about the mine?" She didn't want to wait until this weekend to hear. "Is it real? Does Ruby own it?"

"According to the Arizona Department of Mines and Mineral Resources, it's legit and it's owned by one Joe Martino, or rather his widow since he's no longer alive to claim it."

"Where is it?"

"In the area."

"Weren't there coordinates listed in the records?"

"Yes, there were, but I'm not going to give them to you."

"Mac," she started.

"No way, sweetheart. I know you too well. You'll hang up the phone and go out looking for it."

"I won't either."

"Claire." He echoed her earlier tone.

"Okay, maybe I'd go take a peek, but I'd wait for you to go inside."

"I'm not taking that risk. Besides, there's no easement to get to the property. You'd have to trespass to even go near it."

"No easement? Who owns the neighboring property?"

"I'm not telling you that either."

She growled through the line at him, drawing an unhappy face in the dust. "What if I promise I'll be good?"

He laughed. "I wasn't born yesterday, Slugger. You'd be crossing your fingers behind your back when you promised. I'm not going to tell you anything more than I have already. You can wait for me to get there, and we'll check it out together."

"Spoilsport."

Chester leaned over and wrote in the dust next to her doodles: *Mine?* She shook her head in reply.

"Hey, I want you to deliver on all of your promises about nakedness, which you can't do if you're behind bars in Sheriff Harrison's jail for trespassing."

Mac had a point there, and she really didn't want to end up in jail again so soon after the Deadwood mess. "Okay, okay. I'll be patient. What's the other thing you want to talk to me about?"

"Some good news."

"I could use good news right now."

"Why's that?"

"I sort of have a tiny mess to clean up here."

Chester guffawed. "Tiny? This place looks like someone threw a grenade in here."

"You want to muzzle that yap trap, Thomas?"

"How's life with Chester?"

"He's helping me with the rec room remodel." Claire pinched Chester, making him grunt and curse.

"You mean drinking beers, smoking cigars, and critiquing your work?"

"Bingo. So, give me some good news."

"Maybe I should wait on delivering that, too."

Claire's heart thudded a little faster at his somber tone. "No way, teaser." She tried to keep things light, now worried about more than the messes she was dealing with in Jackrabbit Junction. "Spill it, Sweet Buns. I could use a little sugar here."

Her use of the old boys' nickname for Mac drew a chuckle from him. "You've been hanging around Chester too long. How are your sisters?"

"Ronnie is pissed at the law and Kate is cuckoo."

"So nothing has changed since the last time I asked?"

"Not a thing."

Actually that wasn't true. Ronnie seemed to have turned some corner. Or maybe she'd just reached a new level of anger in the stages of grief brought on by her divorce from her ex-piece-of-shit.

"Mom and Manny are home now, though."

"Damn. I was counting on a few more days of reprieve from your mother's scorn."

Claire's mother continually made it clear to Mac how unfit she felt he was for her daughter, even though Deborah never hesitated to tell her daughter how unfit she was for life in general.

"You and me both." Pleasing her mother was impossible. Manny would soon find out the prize fish he thought he'd caught was really a Great White Shark with a never ending supply of sharp teeth. "On a high note, Mom is moving into Manny's Airstream."

"How did you accomplish that miracle?"

Claire glanced around the demolition zone. "I let the house get too messy for her fancy clothes and sensitive allergies."

"Whatever you do, don't clean it."

"No worries on that front." She wiped the top of the bar clean. "So quit stalling and tell me your news."

Silence filled the line.

A whirlwind spun to life in Claire's gut. She gripped the bar, bracing for whatever had him hesitating. Oh, crud. He hadn't gone and bought an engagement ring or something foolish like that, had he? She'd been working hard on overcoming her commitment phobia, and while saying 'I love you' was getting easier, she was nowhere close to stomaching the 'I do' freefall.

"I've been offered a promotion at work," he finally said.

She sagged against the bar in relief. "That's great." When he didn't agree with her, she added, "Isn't it?"

"Yes and maybe."

"What do you mean maybe?"

"Well, it's a position I've been wanting and working toward for years and would mean a lot more pay."

"More money is always good."

"It would also mean a lot more traveling."

"You mean to job sites each day?" Mac often worked long hours driving to and from job sites, so that wasn't a big stretch.

"And even further a few times a month via airplane."

"Oh."

"But the raise would easily cover the cost of you traveling with me. You wouldn't need to work at all anymore."

Claire looked around the rec room, taking in the disorder that resembled her life. "Oh," she said again, her brain unable to process what this meant to her future while surrounded by so much clutter and chaos.

"I haven't accepted the position yet."

"Why not?" If it was what he'd been working for over the last few years, it was his dream. He should jump on it.

"Because of you."

"Me?"

"Yeah, Claire. You. I want to know what you think of my taking the promotion."

"Mac, it's your dream job, not mine." She didn't want to hold him back or stand in his way.

"That's true," he said. "But I love you."

"I lo …" she coughed on some plaster dust and swallowed a gulp of Chester's cheap beer. "I love y …" she coughed again, her throat tickling so much her eyes watered.

"Let's drop it for now." He sounded tired. Or maybe frustrated. "I had a feeling you wouldn't be jumping for joy over this news."

"No, it's just," she coughed, "I have dust in my throat."

"Dust. Right. Listen, I need to get back to work."

"I love you." It came out sounding gargled, but at least she'd gotten it out.

"I'll see you tomorrow night, Slugger."

The line went dead.

"Shit sticks!" She fell back onto the barstool next to Chester, feeling like a wrecking ball had torn through her world. Even more so with the piles of construction debris surrounding her.

What a mess she'd made.

Of everything.

She took another swig of Chester's beer.

And now Mac was going to want an answer this weekend about taking that promotion.

She pulled the hammer from her tool belt and turned it over in her hands. *You wouldn't need to work at all anymore.*

"I'm no mind reader," Chester said, stealing his beer back, "but you look like a girl who's up to her hips in alligators."

"Not my hips." She sighed, leaning back against the bar. "More like my neck."

Chapter Six

Kate leaned against the wall of the bathroom stall, closing her eyes for a moment while she caught her breath. The throbbing bass din of The Shaft reverberated through the ladies room door. Butch's face floated across her thoughts, spurring another geyser of panic up from her stomach. She bent over the toilet again.

Panting in between gulps of air, she tried not to think about the fly carcass on the floor next to the tampon wastebasket or the myriad of smells that came with toilet bowl close-ups. She'd taken to carrying travel packs of antiseptic wipes in her purse to save herself from catching some icky disease from all of the toilets she'd face-planted over the last month.

After a few swallows of stomach acid, the nausea ebbed. She leaned back against the stall door, wiping her mouth with a piece of toilet paper and flushed away her woes. "Stupid morning sickness."

She had a feeling this churning gutful of anxiety had more to do with the return of one Valentine "Butch" Carter to Jackrabbit Junction than the hormonal effects of his child growing inside of her.

What am I gonna do?

There was no avoiding him anymore. Butch was back, those broad shoulders and long legs right here under the same roof as she. Even worse, his heartbreaking smile and mesmerizing blue eyes were waiting for her in his office at this very moment.

Fifteen minutes ago she had been delivering a pitcher of beer to a table full of spandex-clothed cyclists who were cruising down U.S. Route 191, aiming for the finish line in Douglas, Arizona, when Butch walked up behind her and shattered her thin veneer of calm.

"Kate, I need to talk to you."

She'd nearly dumped the beer in a cyclist's lap at the sound of Butch's voice. Her heart took off like it was being chased by a man in a hockey mask wielding a chainsaw.

"I'm a little busy right now." She'd avoided meeting Butch's gaze, making a stage production out of smiling at the cyclists, trying to keep her ruffled feathers hidden.

"Meet me in my office in five minutes." His tone left no room for argument. Then he was gone.

Thank God the cyclists had been too busy chowing down on their sandwiches to notice how badly Kate had been shaking as she topped off their mugs of beer. After making sure they were good for the time being, she'd made a mad dash for the bathroom.

Now as she stood there debating whether to crawl across the bar's floor to escape without being seen, she wondered what Butch would do if she didn't show up in his office. Maybe she could send him a text saying how tired she was after babysitting a classroom full of sixth graders all day and needed to take off early. Ronnie was there to cover for her, so it wasn't like she'd be leaving Butch shorthanded.

The bathroom door creaked open.

Kate froze, breath held.

"Katie-doll?" Arlene asked. "Are you in here?"

Kate's knees about buckled in relief at the sound of the other waitress's voice. "Yes," she called over the top of the stall door. "I needed to use the bathroom quick."

Arlene was well aware of Kate's rabid state of pregnancy—as in sick as a dog and foaming at the mouth most days when she wasn't having to pee for the umpteenth time during her shift. She'd been a good friend since starting at The Shaft back in September. In spite of Claire's numerous suspicions about the fifty-plus-year-old who seemed to have appeared out of nowhere, Kate believed Arlene's tale about why she'd chosen this dusty corner of the world to enjoy her pre-golden years. Yuccaville wasn't Sedona, but there were plenty of men thanks to the Copper Snake Mining Company, in case a woman got lonely and wanted some company to make her forget about life's kicks and punches for a while.

"Butch is looking for you," Arlene told her.

Damn that man was persistent. "I'll be out in a minute."

Footfalls drew close, pausing on the other side of the stall door. "Are you okay, sweetie? Do you need me to get you some ice water? A wet rag? Crackers?"

Arlene was always so good to her. Kate thought about telling her the truth. How Butch had once had a girlfriend try to hornswoggle him into marriage through a fake baby claim. How he'd told Kate when they'd first started sleeping together that he didn't see kids in his future, not with the business he was trying to build and all of the traveling to various classic car auctions.

Maybe Arlene would empathize with Kate, understand why she was so nervous about being near him. Maybe she'd agree that Kate couldn't give in to her heart, which had no qualms about trapping Butch in a life he didn't want if it meant staying by his side. Maybe she'd help Kate find a way out of this corner of hell and set up house where she wouldn't have to see Butch day after day. Maybe she'd let Kate climb up on her back and escape out the little square bathroom window right then without Butch seeing her.

No, it wasn't fair to put Arlene in the middle of the mess Kate had made of her life. "I'm fine. Thanks."

"Alrighty then, sweetie. Oh, I keep meanin' to ask you if you were in Yuccaville yesterday trying to find me."

Kate's scrambled brain tried to remember where she'd been yesterday. Oh, The Rowdy Coyote Motel and the Polar Bear. "I was in Yuccaville, but it didn't have anything to do with you. Why do you ask?"

"I thought I saw your car leaving the parking lot of the motel where I'm livin'."

"You're staying at The Rowdy Coyote?" Surely Arlene must have seen the Polar Bear in passing? Would she be willing to let Kate hide out in her room to spy on him?

"Sure am. The monthly rent is dirt cheap."

"Oh, yeah?" Kate could imagine, what with the way it looked so run down, not to mention the dead boat carcass. But why was a henchman with ties to a rich mobster hiding out there? Then it hit her—he was undercover, trying to fit in with the locals. The Polar Bear might look like a big meathead, but he was as clever as an Arctic fox.

Arlene's footfalls moved away, over toward the sink. "I'm fixin' to stay on there until I've saved enough to rent a house." She was probably checking her beehive hairdo in the mirror, something she did often in the mirror behind the bar, too.

"That's smart." Kate stared down at the dead fly, wondering if she should look into renting a room there for a month or two until she got back on her feet. Then she thought about that swimming pool turned boat junkyard and cringed. On second thought, her grandfather's Winnebago worked just fine for now.

"Anyhoo, Katie-doll, let me know if there is anything I can help you with tonight. You've been looking more worn out than usual lately, and I mean that as a concerned friend."

"Thank you, Arlene. You're always good to me."

"It's the least I can do to help. Ronnie and I will cover your tables while you and Butch catch up."

Kate heard the bathroom door creak open and shut, a wave of bar-related racket rising and falling.

Tucking back several tendrils of hair that had come loose while she worshiped the porcelain goddess, she blew out a breath. She could do this. Hell, she was about to become a mom. She needed to bone up, get ready to take on the world while single-handedly raising a child.

Besides, she reminded herself, Butch wasn't a monster. He was a nice guy who didn't want kids. It wasn't his fault she'd screwed up and gotten pregnant.

She buttoned the black shirt she was wearing over her white tank top, trying to flatten out some of the wrinkles. She could face Butch without letting him see how much she wanted to cling to him and never let go. Besides, she needed to let him know about her substitute job at the school, and now was as good a time as any.

The door creaked again, the bar ruckus louder for a second or two, then muffled again.

She waited while water ran in the sink, picturing one of the pretty young brunettes playing pool in back checking her lipstick.

Kate stood there without making a sound. She didn't feel like looking all disheveled in front of the un-pregnant, flirty thing in skinny jeans.

She counted to ten after the door opened and closed again to unlock the stall door and walk out.

"Butch!" she gasped, stepping back in surprise.

The source of her panic stood in front of her, bigger than life, in the women's restroom. His arms crossed and cowboy boots planted, he barred the door in his white T-shirt, faded blue jeans, and squinty glare.

Kate took another step backward, bumping into the outer corner of the stall. "You can't be in here."

"I own the place. I can go wherever I damned well please."

"What if someone needs to use the bathroom?"

"They can wait. We need to talk."

"I was on my way to your office."

"Were you?" His face was rigid with disbelief. "Hell, I was surprised to see your car still sitting in the parking lot after the way you've avoided me and my calls for the last couple of weeks."

"I wasn't avoiding you," she lied. "I had a lot of things going on."

"Right and your phone only takes incoming calls, making it impossible for you to call me back?"

She opened her mouth to lie some more, but then decided it was time to stop playing cat and mouse. "No, I could have called you back."

His jaw tightened another notch. "But you didn't."

"No."

"Why not?"

Because it hurt to hear the sound of his voice, and she'd rather avoid pain whenever possible. "I didn't want to hear what you had to say."

He took that in with a slow nod. "At least you're finally being honest with me."

She walked to the sink, turning on the cold water. "I've been honest about most everything lately."

Well, except when Chester had shown up at The Shaft the

other night in a long, pimp-style zebra suit jacket and satin black pants, asking her if she thought he had a chance with one of the new snow birds at the R.V. park who was twenty years his junior. Damn Manny and Gramps for putting younger-wife ideas in his head.

Butch watched her in the mirror as she washed her hands and then splashed her face.

"Good. Then tell me the truth about something."

She tore off some paper towel. "What?"

"Is there another man?"

His question stopped her mid-face dab. "Another man?"

"As in someone else you're seeing?"

Did he mean someone else who had fathered this kid? Did he think she was trying to trap him for his money?

Her forehead heated in a flash of anger. "There's no other man and hasn't been one since long before you." She threw the paper towel in the trash, fighting to keep the bubbles of rage from surfacing as they often did so quickly these days. "The baby is yours, Butch. But don't worry, like I told you before, I don't want anything from you. I'm choosing to have the kid because I want it. I can provide for the two of us just fine without your damned money."

That wasn't necessarily true yet, but Kate was more determined than ever to make it so now. Since the moment she'd seen those two little pink lines on the pregnancy test, she'd been worried about making him feel stuck playing daddy, and what did she get for her troubles and tears? Accusations about another man? Oh, this was rich.

Butch frowned. "You misunderstood my question."

"Oh, I think I understand what you're looking for here crystal clear—an escape clause." She closed the distance between them, her chin jutting in ire. "You don't want to be saddled with a kid. Well, don't worry, you won't be, because I don't want to put up with a piece of shit father who breaks my kid's heart without thinking twice about it."

She'd witnessed how that worked first hand with Jessica and her dad, the poor girl.

He cursed under his breath. "Kate, shut up and listen."

"No, you listen." She crossed her arms, matching his stance. "I have a new job."

His eyebrows wrinkled. "You're quitting?"

"Not yet, it's still part-time. But once I land a full-time teaching position, I'll be out of your life. Until then, Ronnie said she will help out, covering for me when needed."

"But you hate teaching."

"Yeah, well my priorities have changed. Teaching isn't as exciting as traveling from one classic car auction to the next, but it pays the bills, offers insurance, and provides stability."

"Don't forget the respectability level and retirement options."

"That too."

"I always thought teaching would be nice because you get holidays and summers off."

"It is a nice benefit, but believe me, by the time you've had a good portion of a year with twenty-five or more kids day in and day out, that time off goes way too quick."

"I bet."

Kate stared up at Butch, her anger fizzling. What the hell? This wasn't how she'd envisioned this conversation going at all. In her daydreams, Butch had begged her not to leave The Shaft, shoving a wedding ring on her finger and delivering a happily-ever-after ending. In her more rational fantasies, he'd offered her a raise to stay at the bar, provided paid time off for maternity leave, and thrown in a bonus for when the baby was born. In reality, he kept frowning at her like she'd grown a hairy wart between her eyes since he'd seen her last.

Apparently their big talk was over. She'd gotten all worked up for nothing.

"If you'll step aside now and let me out of here, I have some tables to wait."

"No."

"What do you mean *no*?"

He leaned back against the door. "We're not done."

They were done the moment she got pregnant, but since he was bigger than her and blocking the only feasible exit, she threw up her hands. "What else do you need to talk to me about? My overtime hours? The twenty bucks we were short in the till last night? Changing the exemptions on my W-2?"

"I've had some time to think about things."

A hot blast of frustration made her start to sweat. She snorted, her hackles up. "Oh, yeah? You mean while you were traveling in luxury all over God's green earth buying expensive old cars, and I was here in your hot stinky bar sweating and puking in between serving drinks to lonely cowboys and weary miners?"

His lips twitched. "Yes, Kate, while I was traveling."

Oh, she double-dog dared him to laugh at her. "Please, do share these grand thoughts that are so important you had to burst into the ladies room to tell me."

"I've changed my mind."

"About what?" Her temper was racing out of control yet again, the reins ripped clear out of her hands. "Whether Pluto should be classified as a planet or what beers we're keeping on tap this holiday season?"

Dear Lord of the Rings, what was wrong with her? Who was this mad woman in her head running around screaming obscenities? Was this what stumbling down the rabbit hole into insanity felt like?

Butch's hands snaked out, catching her off guard. He hauled her against him, his mouth coming down fast before she could think about pulling away. By the time her brain caught up, she was kissing him back, damn it.

As she melted against him, his touch softened. His lips became gentle and coaxing, his hands caressing a moan out of her. Hells bells, she'd missed him. She lifted her arms and draped them around his neck.

The door opened, slamming into his back, making him stumble forward with her in his arms.

"Oops!" The pretty pool-playing brunette peeked around Butch's shoulder. "Sorry, you two. I'll come back."

Kate stepped back from him as the door closed, her whole body burning with a confusing mixture of want and humiliation. Criminy, she was supposed to be strong, showing Butch she didn't need him in her life. Instead she'd suctioned onto his mouth and shoved her tongue down his throat like one of those alien face-huggers.

She straightened her shirt and tried to forget the scent of his skin, the heat of his touch, both of which she'd pined for in the middle of long and lonely nights for way too long. "So, what did you change your mind about?"

Butch's gaze searched her face, and then traveled down past her heaving chest and settled on her stomach. "That's my kid in there."

No shit, daddy-o. "If you want me to take a paternity test, my answer is *hell no* and *go fuck yourself*."

His focus returned northward, his eyes suddenly hard. "I believe you. Contrary to what you thought I was asking earlier, I never once questioned that fact."

"Well," she scoffed, "there's something."

"Here's something else—you're not shutting me out."

The steeliness in his voice gave her pause. She purposely played dumb. "You're the one blocking us in here."

"Whether you like it or not, Kate, my kid is going to have a father." He pointed his thumb at his chest. "Me."

Without another word or kiss or by-your-leave, he opened the door and walked out, leaving Kate alone with her pounding heart and pale-faced reflection.

* * *

The Shaft was a ghost bar. The evening's hooting and hollering a memory, the jukebox dark and resting for another night.

Ronnie swallowed the last of her soda water and cleaned the glass in the sink behind the bar, setting it on a towel to air dry. She checked the main door, making sure it was locked, and hit the lights before pushing through the swinging doors leading into the kitchen area and beyond, which included the supply room, Butch's office, and the back door.

She hesitated in the doorway of the office, watching Butch's chest rise and fall as he slept kicked back in his chair, boots resting on his desk. He should go home and get some sleep, but

Ronnie didn't rouse him. Something had gone down earlier between him and Katie, but she'd been too busy tonight to corner her sister and find out the details. Whatever it was, the poor girl had come out of the bathroom at one point looking like someone had used her to mop the kitchen floor, all blotchy-faced and frazzle-haired.

Right about then Claire had shown up with a bandage wrapped around her finger. She'd downed a Corona with her burger and sautéed mushrooms, mentioning something about needing a break from Chester's bristly personality, Jessica's nonstop mouth, and their mother and Manny's love-fiesta. When Ronnie inquired about the bandage, Claire had shaken her head. Ronnie had played bossy older sister then and ordered Claire to take Katie home with her. Katie had gone without much fight, which worried Ronnie even more.

Tiptoeing inside Butch's office, she grabbed her jacket and purse, dimmed the overhead can lights, and quietly shut his office door behind her.

Arlene had taken off a half hour ago at Ronnie's urging. While she appreciated the other waitress's concern about leaving her alone to walk out to Katie's Volvo, she wasn't going to be alone. A certain cowboy had stopped by the bar at the end of the evening, sipped on a beer until a few minutes before closing, then had given Ronnie a quick nod and left. The FBI was waiting for her out there under the stars. She'd rather it were Grady and his badge, but there'd been no word from the Sheriff of Cholla County tonight. Maybe he'd given up on getting a moment alone with her in the dark.

She hoped not.

She headed out the back door. Her eyes adjusted to the light of the half-moon as she crossed the gravel to Katie's car, which was parked outside the reach of the orange parking lot glow. Sitting in the shadows next to the Volvo was Mr. FBI's pickup. Inside of the cab, his lit cigarette burned red then faded to a pale orange.

She paused next to his open window, slipping on the jean jacket she'd borrowed from Claire. Hank Williams Sr.'s *Your Cheatin' Heart* came from his speakers. "It's chilly tonight."

He blew a lungful of smoke through the window. "Desert nights can sneak up on you that way." He tapped his cigarette on his side mirror. "So, tell me about this big idea of yours."

Ronnie waved away the smoke while glancing around. She was fairly certain they were alone, but she was still antsy. "You and I need to start working together."

"You have information to share with the FBI?"

"No, but if I'm going to be used as chum, I need to know what sharks are in the water."

"I already gave you that detail."

"Right, the Polar Bear and the Husky."

"And maybe a few others."

Didn't that extra threat just make her feel like tap dancing? "See, that's what I mean. If trouble comes to town I can't do much to help you catch your bad guys if I'm a sitting duck waiting for that lucky shooter to aim and pull the trigger."

"A duck?" He took a draw from his cigarette, blowing it out at her. "I thought you were chum."

"Blow that second-hand smoke at me again, you badge-toting tool, and I'm gonna shove that stupid cigarette up your anal cavity and laugh when the smoke puffs out your ears."

His laugh was husky, what she would expect from the Marlboro Man. He put out his cigarette and set the butt on the dash. "Work together how, spitfire?"

"Nobody ever expects the FBI to be friendly with anyone, right? Especially a potential witness. I propose we establish a fictional relationship."

His teeth glowed in the feeble moonlight. "You want me to pretend to be your boyfriend?"

"No." She had her hands full with one badge carrying pain in the ass. "I'm thinking more of a pal. You know, someone to shoot pool and drink with on nights I'm not working. That allows you to keep an eye on me without causing suspicion, and it gives me the peace of mind knowing you *might* have my back if someone pulls a gun on me."

"Might?"

"Well, you are the FBI. The company retreats I've attended with your people skipped the trust building exercises entirely and went straight to the humiliation-based breakdown training."

"That's too bad." He sounded like he meant it, too.

"I'm not looking for a shoulder to cry on here, just a partner in catching the bottom-feeders my ex-husband screwed over."

He watched an eighteen-wheeler roll by on U.S. Route 191, his eyes glittering from the dash lights as old Hank wrapped up his cheating heart blues.

The desert breathed a sigh of relief after the rig passed, blowing Ronnie's loose curls around. Sage infused the fresh breeze along with something Claire always complained about— oh yeah, greasewood.

"Okay." He was still looking straight ahead. "But we need to be careful. This isn't normal protocol."

"Well, you're not a normal FBI ass-clown either."

That drew his shadowed gaze. "What makes you say that?"

"Your cowboy hat and boots are for real, not freshly store-bought."

"I was called in because they needed a genuine cowboy to fit in down here. They didn't want your sister blowing another agent's cover."

Ronnie snickered, remembering the way Claire had gone head-to-head with the previous FBI schmucks, exposing them as the fake cowboys that they were.

"What's your name?" Ronnie asked, wrapping her arms around herself, trying to hug away the shivers. She wasn't sure if it was the desert night or being this close to the FBI again that had her shaking.

"Just call me Brown."

She scoffed. "Come on. That's one of the most obvious FBI fake names. Mr. Black, Mr. White, and Mr. Brown. It's like you guys can't be original and think you have to steal from the game CLUE."

"Not Mister," he clarified, "just Brown."

"No. This fake friendship plan isn't going to work if we're formal with each other. You can call me Ronnie and I'll call you what?"

He tapped his thumb on the outside of the door for several beats in rhythm with Jerry Reed, who sang about his ex-wife getting the goldmine while he got the shaft.

"Call me M," he finally conceded.

"Agent M? For real? Are we starring in a *Men in Black* spinoff here? Sheez, just give me your first name."

Jerry Reed complained about working two shifts and eating bologna. Ronnie smirked. She could one-up good ol' Jerry. Not only had she gotten the shaft, now she was working there, too.

"Mississippi." Mr. FBI had spoken so quietly she wasn't sure she'd heard him right.

"Did you say Mississippi? Like the state?"

He nodded once.

"Damn it, I'm serious."

"So am I."

Ronnie chewed on her lower lip as she stared at him through his pickup window. "You mean to tell me your name is Mississippi Brown?"

"That's correct."

"You're pulling my leg."

"Both of my hands are right here." He held them out for her to see.

"Why Mississippi? Were you born there?"

"Nope, but my great-grandfather was."

"Do you have any other state-named siblings?"

"I have a cousin named Montana."

"Like I said before, you're not a normal FBI ass-clown."

"I'll take that as a compliment. So, what now, friend? Do we get matching tattoos or just exchange phone numbers?"

"I don't have a phone and you don't look like the kind of guy who'd want a girlie tattoo on your ass."

"You have a girlie tattoo on your ass?"

"Don't you remember it from the FBI-confiscated files taken from the hidden video camera in my bedroom?"

"We have videos of you in your bedroom?" Either he really hadn't seen them or he was an A-list actor.

Ronnie fumbled with the keys to Katie's car in her coat pocket. "I was kidding about the tattoo. How about you stop at the bar tomorrow evening?"

"You working until close again?"

"No. I have the night off, but we could shoot some pool, have a couple of drinks, start the process of old pals in the making."

"Your sister isn't going to like that."

"You leave my sister to me."

"Which one?"

"Both."

He nodded. "If you say so, but the pregnant one makes me wonder if it's time to get a tetanus shot again just to be safe."

"She's having a rough time with morning sickness."

The sound of tires crunching in the gravel made them both freeze. A pair of headlights rounded the corner of the building, spotlighting Ronnie before going dark.

The engine cut out.

It took a few seconds for the temporary light blindness to fade. She recognized the white Bronco and its logo on the door at the same time a familiar deep voice spoke through the open window.

"Funny," Sheriff Harrison said, "the weatherman didn't mention anything about Hell freezing over tonight. Yet here stands Veronica Morgan getting all friendly with an FBI agent. It just boggles the mind."

Ronnie stuffed her hands in her pockets as another breeze blew past. She could swear each one was five degrees colder than the last. Or maybe it was the frigid tone in Grady's voice.

"What brings you around tonight, Sheriff Harrison?" She kept up their public appearance of outlaw and sheriff, since Mississippi didn't know she'd shared more than just heated words with Grady.

"I need to talk to you, Ms. Morgan."

Mississippi lit another cigarette. "Do you hold all of your clandestine meetings with lawmen in the middle of the night?" His lighter clinked shut.

"Of course. It's common knowledge that you guys turn into regular old vermin after midnight. Puts me and my lack of glass slippers on an even level with you boys."

Grady chuckled. "She's all sugar this time of night, isn't she?"

"And plenty of spice." Mississippi started his pickup. "I'll see you tomorrow night," he told her and rolled out, leaving her alone with the Sheriff of Cholla County.

At the sound of the pickup tires moving from gravel to asphalt, she turned to Grady, standing her ground. "I didn't think you were coming by tonight, *Sheriff.*"

"I needed to see you."

"It's hard to see me in the dark." Especially from the inside of his Bronco. "You should've come earlier."

"I would have, but there was a fender bender a few miles out of Yuccaville on 191 that slowed me up." He leaned back in his seat. "Why don't you climb on in here and get warm."

No way. She overheated almost every time she was in close quarters with him and his bay rum aftershave. Tonight she wanted to keep her head on her shoulders, not floating up near the stars. "I can hear you fine and dandy from here."

"Christ, woman. You're as prickly as everything else around this desert." Sounding more tired than angry, he took off his hat and shoved it onto the dash. "What was that little get together about?"

"I'm joining forces."

"With the FBI?"

"No, with one Agent M. Brown. The FBI can go blow a goat."

"Joining forces how?"

She shivered through another cold gust. "I figure since we're both keeping an eye out for the same killers, we might as well hold hands and sing *Kumbaya* while we wait."

"It makes sense he agreed so easily."

"Why's that?"

"You're a good looking woman."

That was the last thing she cared about with her life on the line. "I'm not interested in sex with yet another law dog."

"And he probably got word that a dust devil might be blowing your way," he added.

A dust devil? "What does that mean?"

"We may have a problem." He opened the Bronco door and stepped down. The slam that followed echoed across the vast openness of the dark desert.

"How big of a problem are we talking here?" she asked as he closed the distance between them.

He stopped just out of reach. "Sex with *yet another* law dog? How many have there been, Veronica?"

She waved away his question. What did he mean by dust devil? "Mississippi didn't say anything to me about trouble coming."

"Mississippi? No, they found the body over in New Mexico, just south of Albuquerque in the high desert."

"Agent Brown's first name is Mississippi." Another gust peppered her with specks of dirt. "Who found what body and what's that have to do with me?"

"You might be in trouble." He grabbed her by the lapels of her jacket and drew her closer.

She should have retreated, but it was too late now. "I have an alibi," she whispered up at him.

"Not that kind of trouble." He hauled her against him, wrapping her in his warm leather coat, surrounding her with his heady scent. "How many other law dogs are we talking about, Veronica?"

"There's only you so far, Sheriff Hardass."

He bent down, his mouth angling toward hers. "Good."

She started to lean into him, but then pushed back enough to look him in the eyes. "Tell me about my trouble first."

He tucked her under his chin as he explained. "A friend of mine in the Bernalillo County Sheriff's Department called today. They found one of their snitches in a culvert. He suspects the killer may be the man you know as the Polar Bear and warned me to keep an eye out for him."

Had Grady put out feelers without telling her? "How does he know the killer might be the Polar Bear?"

"The snitch appears to have been squeezed to death. He had a broken back and ribs, as well as internal hemorrhaging. The bruising on the corpse is similar to what's been found on other bodies left behind by the Polar Bear."

Ronnie sucked in a breath through her teeth. "Jesus."

"If it is the Polar Bear, and the FBI is right about him being one of your potential enemies, he may be heading this way, taking care of other business *en route*."

Or was he already here? As in Katie's big biker dude?

Should she tell Grady about the biker? She thought about several what-ifs and weighed them against corresponding but-if-nots. No, she'd wait until she knew something more definite. She didn't want to sic the law on a guy who might be totally innocent. She knew what it felt like to be wrongfully accused and have her life destroyed thanks to the Feds' fuckups.

"You need to be careful, Veronica." Grady's lips brushed over her forehead. "No more walking out of The Shaft alone in the dark."

She wrapped her arms around his waist, soaking up his body heat. Her chills ebbed. "I'm tired of constantly looking over my shoulder."

"I'll do whatever I can to protect you."

She snorted against his shirt buttons. "Serve and protect, isn't that right, Sheriff Hardass? Even for a tarnished Morgan sister."

He cupped her chin, tipping her head up. "Kiss me with that sassy mouth."

"You didn't say the magic words."

"Kiss me or I'll arrest you, Veronica Morgan."

"Arrest me for what?"

He slid his hands down her back, his palms rounding over her hips. "Lewd and lascivious behavior." His lips trailed down from her temple.

She moved her hips against his, her laughter at his carnal response sounding breathy, wanton even to her own ears.

"Using your body to bribe an officer of the law," he added.

She sank her hands into his wavy black hair, pulling his mouth to hers. "Don't forget attempting to corrupt the Cholla County Sheriff," she whispered and ran her tongue over his bottom lip.

"Too late. I'm already corrupted." He bent her backward with his kiss.

She held on for dear life. God she'd missed him. She'd missed the scent of his skin, the feel of his hands rubbing all over her body, the teasing of his tongue in her mouth. Craving much more than hot kisses on this cold night, she tugged at his shirt, yanking it from his trousers, seeking flesh on flesh.

"Sweet Jesus, Veronica," Grady spoke between huffs several kisses later. "If you don't get your hand out of my pants, I'm going to tear your clothes off and slam you up against the side of my Bronco."

"You say that as if it's a bad thing, Sheriff Hardass."

His lips came down again, more brutal now, his touch rougher. His restraint was slipping; she could feel it in the tightness of his muscles. His kisses grew more frenzied, firing her up along with him. There was nothing like the rush she felt when the big tough sheriff lost his iron grip of control.

The sound of a door shutting dimly reached through the raging hunger for more of Grady rumbling inside of her.

"Christ, you two!" Butch's voice doused her lust like a firehose blast. "You guys really need to get a room. You're giving The Shaft a bad rep."

"Sorry about that." Grady pulled his hands out from under her shirt and buttoned up her jacket. "Good thing he didn't come out five minutes from now, Ms. Morgan," he said for her ears only.

"I don't need the damned Sheriff coming around and writing me up for allowing lewd conduct in public here in my lot." Butch leaned back against Grady's Bronco. "Oh wait, you are the Sheriff. Can you write yourself up? How does that work?"

"I'm off duty, smartass." Grady put his arm around Ronnie's shoulders and faced Butch. "When did you get home?"

"Earlier today."

"Any good finds over in Texas?"

"A couple. They'll be here later this week. You should come to the house after they get here, toss back some beers, and tell me how much I overspent on them."

The sound of the police radio pierced the quiet night. A series of numbers crackled out the Bronco's window followed by some scratchy mumbling.

"Shit," Grady pulled away from Ronnie, striding over to his door.

"I thought you were off duty," Butch said as Grady reached

inside the Bronco for the radio.

"I am, but we're between shifts and have one guy out sick. There's only one deputy on duty right now and he might need backup." Grady lifted the radio to his mouth, speaking back a series of numbers and police mumbo-jumbo. He ended with, "Any identification on the prowler?"

"You're gonna love this, Sheriff," Ronnie heard come through the radio. "It's a Morgan sister."

Grady and Butch both looked at her.

She held up her hands. "It wasn't me."

"You got a first name on that Morgan?" Grady asked.

"Sure do. One Kathryn L. Morgan. Five foot six, one hundred and twenty-five pounds according to her driver's license. But if you ask me, she looks about twenty pounds north of tha—"

"Shove that twenty pounds up your ass, Deputy Dipshit!" Katie's voice blasted through the radio.

"Just hold steady," Grady told his deputy. "I'll be right there."

"Meet me at the station, Sheriff. She assaulted me."

"Assaulted you how?"

"With her middle finger."

"Oh, damn," Butch said, scrubbing his hand down his face. "I should've seen this coming."

Ronnie frowned at him. "What? Why?"

"Carter babies make women go *loca*. It's a known fact in my family."

"It is? They do?"

"Yeah. My sister-in-law landed in jail three times during her pregnancy."

"Jail?"

"Yep. The chief of police was her uncle. He did it for her own safety as much as the rest of the town."

"You've got to be kidding me." Ronnie shook her head at the stars. Claire was right. Katie was going off the deep end.

Grady lifted the radio to his mouth. "Keep Ms. Morgan in the holding cell until I get there," he told Deputy Dipshit. "Don't bother with the paperwork yet."

"10-4, Sheriff. What do you want me to do with the sister?"

"The sister?" Grady locked gazes with Ronnie.

"Yeah. The middle one, I think. You know, the one we had in the lock up before that swears with every other word."

Grady cursed off radio. Then he returned to his deputy. "What did Claire Morgan do?"

"When I tried to put handcuffs on Kathryn, the sister stole them from me and threw them in the bushes. Then she refused to go look for them, so I'm taking her in, too."

Grady's shoulders shook. Ronnie couldn't tell if he was laughing or shaking with frustration. When he spoke, his voice was level again, control back in place. "Put them both in the holding cell until I get there and can sort this out." He tossed the radio back into his Bronco and turned to Ronnie.

"It's Butch's fault," she said, pointing at the father of the child causing her sister's temporary insanity. "He made Katie go *loca*."

"Come on," Grady said to Ronnie. "Let's go get both of your crazy sisters out of my jail."

Chapter Seven

Thursday, November 8th

Jail.
Again.
Twice in one month's time.

Claire wasn't talking to Kate anymore. Not today. Not tomorrow. Not for the rest of the year, damn it. Sitting in that piss-stinking holding cell was the final straw. That's what she got for letting her little sister play the poor-pregnant-me ploy, landing Claire in yet another altercation with the law.

"I'm telling you it's not Katie's fault," Ronnie said. She stood in the kitchen archway dipping a banana in a container of yogurt while watching Claire thread electrical cable through the holes in the rec room wall studs.

"Oh, really?" Claire pulled yellow cable through another hole with more force than necessary. "So whose fault was it that she tried to run from Deputy Dipshit when he pulled up next to Mabel and then proceeded to poke him repeatedly in his doughnut belly when he threatened to take her into the station for questioning?"

Claire should've known better than to let her nutty sister talk her into driving to Yuccaville for some mint chocolate chip ice cream to appease her late-night cravings. Then she was foolish enough to take the shortcut Kate suggested on the way to the grocery store.

That was no shortcut. The Rowdy Coyote Motel was several blocks out of their way. That's what Claire got for trying to make Kate feel better after facing off with Butch. She yanked on the cable, cursing under her breath.

"Ease up there, Incredible Hulk," Chester said from the

other end of the rec room where he was feeding her the cable. "You about dragged me through the hole on that last pull."

"Sorry, Chester." Claire let go of the cable for a moment and shook the stress out of her hands, rolling her shoulders a couple of times. "I'm just sick and tired of having my personal effects analyzed by Deputy Dipshit while I sit on a pee-stained cot behind cell bars."

Ronnie swallowed a spoonful of yogurt. "What were you doing with a condom in your jacket pocket anyway?"

Chester snickered. "I'm bettin' it had nothing to do with protecting your firearm in the water."

"If you remember," Claire grabbed the cable and poked it through another stud hole, "*you* had my jacket, so I had to borrow one."

"From whom?"

"Mom."

"Ewwww!" Ronnie made a gagging face. "Why would she have a condom?"

"You're lucky it wasn't used." Chester took the disgusting factor to the next level.

"Chester!" Claire shot him a glare. "We're talking about my mother here."

"Yeah, well you don't have to listen to Carrera go on and on about her bazookas like I do. That's Ford's daughter, for shit's sake. I've known her since she was in diapers."

Claire pulled the cable through the last hole and lined it up with where Chester had the junction box nailed to the stud. "There, that's the last one." She pulled off her gloves and stuck them in her back pocket.

Chester joined her at the junction box. "Ford is gonna be pissed when he sees this wire."

"Why? We're just replacing the old stuff, plus an extra outlet or two per wall."

"You paid too much for the wire."

Here they went again, round and round about money, and it wasn't even his she was spending. Chester seemed to have been channeling Gramps since this construction project started. "What was I supposed to do? Run into Tucson? I had to pay what

Creekside Supply Company wanted." Jackrabbit Junction's hardware store was pricey, but a hell of a lot closer than the big box stores in the city.

"You could've driven to Yuccaville."

"It's not much cheaper there."

"And you should've bought the 14/2 cable. I told you we didn't need the 12/2 for in here."

"And I told you that if Ruby's going to run an air conditioner, flat-screen television, and multiple fans and other electronic gadgets in the rec room, it's better to be safe and get the wire rated for 20 amp circuits. I'll cover the extra cost."

"With what money? You haven't held down a full-time job in months. Did the tooth fairy stop by and leave you a mint under your pillow?"

Correction—Chester was channeling her mother. "I have some money, damn it." Not much, but enough if Gramps squawked.

"You could always try bartering with condoms if you run short of cash," the peanut gallery said from the kitchen doorway. "Butch has a bunch stocked up in the supply room at The Shaft."

Claire hit her sister with a smirk. "You would know."

With her cheeks pink, Ronnie backed into the kitchen and out of sight.

"Why would she know?" Chester asked. "Because she works there?"

No, because Ronnie and Grady had been caught screwing around in the supply room by Butch. "Something like that." She tapped on the junction box. "Now quit giving me shit about the wire and get to work on this, or I'll tell Mom you want to hear all about how Manny proposed to her again."

"Damn. That's blackmail. You've been hanging around your grandfather too much." He got out his wire strippers and got to work.

Claire joined Ronnie in the kitchen, taking in how clean and tidy the place was. "You cleaned again," she said, filling a glass with water from the tap and gulping it down.

"A little here and there, that's all."

Ronnie had a fetish for tidiness and organization that reared its ugly head whenever she was stressed about something. She must be worrying about the men her ex had sicced on her through his stupidity and selfishness.

"So, what were you two doing last night in front of The Rowdy Coyote Motel?" Ronnie spoke quietly next to Claire. "Did it have anything to do with Room 9?"

Claire set the empty glass on the counter and frowned at her sister. "What do you know about Room 9?"

"Katie told me that the Polar Bear is staying there. We took a gander through a spyglass at his big snake."

Claire tried to process that last line. "His what?"

"Big snake."

"Jesus, Ronnie. Were you spying on him while he was in the shower?"

Her sister made a horrified face that was almost comical. "Not that snake." She smacked Claire's shoulder. "You need to stop spending so much time with Chester. He's rubbing off on you."

Claire covered her eyes. "I know. I can't look at a woman now without hearing his voice spouting some dirty comment in my head about her hooters or her sweet ass. I think I need someone to strip my brain down to the studs and rewire it with 20 amp wire."

"The snake I'm talking about is a rattlesnake."

"Who keeps a rattlesnake as a pet?"

"That's what Katie and I were wondering."

"I don't want to even think about *your* sister right now."

"Katie feels horrible about you getting dragged to jail."

"Blah blah blah jail. That's what I just heard."

"Stop being such a baby, Claire." Ronnie moved closer again, her voice a whisper. "Grady told me last night that he got word from a friend in the sheriff's department in Albuquerque that they found a body that had the Polar Bear's calling card on it."

"The Polar Bear carries business cards?"

"You've been sniffing too much plaster dust. Not business card, nitwit. The person was squeezed to death." Ronnie glanced at the doorway then back. "Grady's friend thinks the Polar Bear might be on his way here, taking care of business along the way."

Claire grimaced. "So, you think Kate's loony-toon theory about that guy is right?"

"I don't know."

"Did you tell Grady about the guy in the bar?"

"No."

"Why not?"

"Because what if Katie's guy is innocent? Just some biker dude who looks like he could have that nickname? I can't condemn someone without some sort of proof. I know how it feels to get the rubber glove treatment. I won't put another innocent bystander through that."

Good point. They needed more proof.

"So what really happened last night? And don't try to sell me that bullshit story you told Grady about trying to rescue a stray kitten from behind The Rowdy Coyote."

"Ask your sister."

"Katie was gone this morning when I woke up. She left a note on the fridge saying she got a call to substitute again today."

Wouldn't the school principal just love to hear that their new substitute teacher was in the sheriff's holding tank last night? "Kate was creeping around behind the motel, peeking in windows."

"You let our pregnant baby sister sneak behind a seedy motel in the middle of the night?"

"No. I had to go pee. She went with me to an empty lot a short way down from the seedy motel to keep an eye out for creeps and meth-heads while I watered the weeds. The brat sneaked off when my pants were down, leaving me bare-assed in the dark."

Ronnie chuckled until Claire pulled on her ear. "Ow!"

"By the time I got my pants up, Kate had already made her way behind the motel and was looking in windows."

"So, that's why someone called in about a prowler."

"Yep. I managed to drag her back to Mabel and found Deputy Dipshit waiting for us. Kate took off running and everything went south from there until you showed up at the station with the Sheriff and Butch."

The sheriff had let Claire and Kate out as soon as he'd

walked into the building, and Butch had kicked back in the waiting room while the Sheriff sorted out the whole mess with Deputy Dipshit and Kate. After Claire got her condom and other personal effects back, Butch had loaded the three of them into his crew-cab pickup and hauled them over to where Mabel was still parked in front of The Rowdy Coyote.

Kate had ridden up front with Butch on the short trip, but neither had spoken a word. Ronnie had nudged Claire's leg and raised her brows about the silence, but Claire was too pissed about having to wait in that damned cell while Deputy Dipshit gave her crap about her mother's condom to care about Kate's love life or lack thereof.

"So, when do you want to go check out the Polar Bear's den?" Ronnie asked.

Claire snorted. "How about the day after never?" She headed back into the rec room. "As in if I *never* see The Rowdy Coyote Motel again, I'll be a happy girl."

"What do you have against The Rowdy Coyote?" Chester asked, securing the receptacle he'd wired into the junction box. "I knew a bikini mud wrestler who lived there for a few months. Talk about dirty sheets."

"Yuck." Claire grimaced.

"The rest of the room was clean as a whistle though. The owner has a no-pets and no-smoking policy."

No pets. Claire glanced at Ronnie. Did that include rattlesnakes sunning in the window?

The phone rang.

Claire squatted down to pick up the pieces of wire Chester had snipped off. "You want to grab that, Ronnie?"

"Dancing Winnebagos R.V. Park," Ronnie said into the receiver.

Claire stood and dumped the pieces into the waste bin. She looked over at Ronnie and did a doubletake at the sight of her sister standing there with her cheeks all pale, the receiver almost slipping from her grip. "Who is it?"

Ronnie whispered, "He's coming."

"Who?" Claire looked at her watch. Mac wouldn't be here for hours.

"The Polar Bear."

"What in the hell is she babbling about?" Chester said, stuffing the wire snippers in his shirt pocket.

Claire walked over and took the receiver from Ronnie's limp hand. "Hello?"

Nobody answered. The line was dead.

Setting the receiver back on its base, she frowned at her sister. "Who was it? The Sheriff?"

Ronnie shook her head.

"The FBI cowboy?"

"He didn't say," she breathed more than spoke.

"Well, what exactly did this mystery man say?"

"He's coming for you."

"Someone's coming for me?" Claire asked. "Or did they mean you?"

"I think they meant me."

"Nothing else was said?"

Ronnie shook her head.

"Did you hear anything in the background?" Chester asked. "Honking horns, barking dogs, strip club music?"

When Claire shot him a glare, he added, "What? Am I the only one who makes phone calls from strip clubs?"

"Do that trick that calls the phone back," Claire told her, picking up the receiver and holding it out. When Ronnie shook her head, backing away, Claire punched in the numbers herself. The phone rang and rang and rang.

And then someone picked it up.

"Hello?" a woman answered. Ronnie had said it was a man who'd called.

"Uh, hi. Who is this?"

"You called here, honey. Who are you?"

"Where is *here*?"

"Dirty Gerties."

Claire covered the mouthpiece. "It's Dirty Gerties," she told them.

Chester let out a bark of laughter. "I told you so."

"I'm Claire from the Dancing Winnebagos R.V. Park over in Jackrabbit Junction," she said in the receiver. "Did you happen to see someone just make a call from this phone?"

"Nope, but I was cleaning the john. This here is the payphone right outside the men's room."

"Can you tell me if there are any guys sitting at the bar who might have just made a phone call?" Claire had been in Dirty Gerties only once, and that was to drag Manny and Chester out of there when they called claiming they were too many sheets to the wind to drive home.

"There's nobody at the bar. The club doesn't open for business until three during the week. I'm part of the cleaning crew."

Claire thanked the woman and hung up, turning to her sister who had plopped down on a barstool as if her legs had given out. "There's nobody there besides the cleaning crew."

"I always wondered who spit-shined that place. There's mud everywhere after a night of bikini bouts."

"He's coming for you," Ronnie repeated the message. "Grady's friend was wrong."

"About the Polar Bear being on his way here?"

"Yeah, he's not on his way. He's already in Yuccaville." Her brown eyes were wide when she looked up at Claire. "I need to get out of here and go far away."

"What in the hell is she yapping about?" Chester joined Claire at Ronnie's side.

"Calm down," she told her sister. "We should talk to the Sheriff about this first."

"You're right." She jumped up. "I've got to get a hold of Mississippi."

"The state or the river?" Chester asked.

"The cowboy."

"Did you hit her on the head with your hammer when I wasn't looking?" Chester asked Claire.

"Leave my hammer and me out of this."

Ronnie scooped up Ruby's pickup keys from the bar. "I'll be back."

Claire snatched the keys out of her sister's hands. "Hold up. I need the pickup. I have to go to Yuccaville for some more supplies."

"Where are the keys to Mabel?"

"No way! Gramps said only I could drive her."

Ronnie grabbed a set of keys sitting on the corner of the bar. "Fine. Chester, I'm borrowing your truck."

"Okay, but don't wash the footprints off the inside of the windshield."

Without another word, Ronnie raced out of the room and slammed out through the General Store's screen door.

Claire turned to Chester. "My sisters are losing it."

"I've got bad news, girl. Your whole family is nuttier than squirrel shit."

Chester's words to Ronnie about footprints made Claire wonder about his level of nuttiness. "Why do you have footprints on the inside of your windshield?"

His bristly cheeks widened with a grin. "I had a stargazing date inside my truck with a snowbird the other night."

The Milky Way was amazing in the cold, clear desert night. "Did you show her the North Star?"

"Nope. Before I could find it, she grabbed hold of my big dipper and knocked my boots right off my feet."

Chapter Eight

I could use a stiff drink, Mac thought. He'd been working twelve hour shifts out in the desert southeast of Tucson so long now that he knew all of the lizards by their first names.

The Shaft beckoned like Apache Spring on a hot, dry summer day along the Butterfield Stage Route. He pulled his rig into the parking lot, killing his engine under one of the orange lights. If he were lucky, Claire would be back at the R.V. park holding down the fort, because he had some business with Butch that she didn't need to hear. Mac checked the half-full lot for Mabel or his Aunt Ruby's pickup, breathing a sigh of relief when he didn't find either.

He did see Chester's truck, though. Maybe he was on yet another date. Chester's ability to hook up with women made Mac wonder if there were a witch doctor somewhere doling out Love Potion #9. How else could someone as bristly and crude as Chester score with woman after woman?

The slam of his pickup door echoed across the lot, fading into the dark shadows beyond the glow of lights. On the eastern horizon, the waning moon crested the Tres Dedos Mountains, spotlighting the jagged ridge from behind. The breeze rolling in off the prickly pear and greasewood dotting the valley's alluvial floor had a chill tonight, biting through his thin flannel shirt and the T-shirt beneath it. He jammed his hands into his pockets and hauled ass across the gravel lot.

The Shaft smelled like booze and bodies crammed together in too small a space. He rolled up his shirt sleeves and headed for the bar, taking one of the open stools between a pair of grizzly old guys whose attention was riveted to the flat screen television. Mac couldn't see what had them so entranced, especially since he couldn't hear anything over the sound of Eddie Rabbitt on the jukebox singing about driving his life away.

Nobody was tending the bar at the moment, so he looked around for an available bowl of Butch's complimentary peanuts. The sound of Ronnie's laughter drew his gaze to the back of the bar by the pool tables. He did a doubletake when he saw her playing pool with a tall dark-haired cowboy who wore the whole Western garb—hat, Wranglers, and boots. All he was missing were spurs that jingle-jangle-jingled and Champion the Wonder Horse.

Who was this new guy and hadn't Claire said Ronnie and Sheriff Harrison were still an item?

It's none of my business. He turned his back and focused on popping peanuts.

"Hi, Mac," another familiar voice said from behind him. He swiveled again, taking in Kate's flushed forehead, red eyes, and messy hair. Her left cheek had a dark pink crease and her shirt collar was stuck half in and half out. Damn. Pregnancy was taking a toll on Claire's usually perfectly groomed blonde sister.

"How are you doing, Kate?" he asked, tossing a shelled peanut in his mouth. "I hear you got another job."

Kate opened her mouth like she was going to reply, but then tears filled her eyes and overflowed down her cheeks. A sob croaked from her throat.

Frozen, Mac sat palming the other half of the peanut shell wondering what he'd said. Before he could do more than gawk at Kate, she wrapped her arms around his neck and buried her face in his shoulder, almost knocking him off the barstool.

What the hell? He had déjà vu. On a visit to The Shaft back in September he'd made the mistake of asking Kate how life had been treating her. Dropping the other half of the peanut on the bar, he brushed his hand off on his jeans and then patted her on the back. When she pulled back, his shirt was damp from her tears.

She dabbed her eyes with a bar napkin. "Thanks for asking. I'm doing okay even though nobody believes the sky is falling."

What did she mean the sky was falling? Was that code for something about Butch? Did it have to do with the baby? Something about Butch and the baby? Hadn't Claire mentioned on the phone that …

It's none of my business.

Concerned as he was, he needed to stay out of Claire's sister's troubles and focus on the Humdigger mine and any other problems his aunt had at the moment.

Kate smiled at him, but it looked too big, extra toothy. The sort of freakish sight he'd be wary of when visiting an insane asylum. "I'm sure glad you're here now." Her left eye twitched several times. "Claire isn't speaking to me, and I really need you to talk sense into her about going with me to sneak into the Polar Bear's den." She shot a suspicious glance to the left and right at his grizzled companions, then moved in closer and spoke next to his ear. "I think we can flush him out before he comes for Ronnie."

Stepping back, she pulled an order pad from her apron and left without another word.

Mac stared after her. Was Kate taking drugs?

Reeling from his Kate-encounter, Mac watched her across the room where she was taking orders at a table of gray-haired ladies. Open books covered their table, several others stacked two and three high in the center. Birders, he'd bet. He wondered if that flock was staying at the R.V. park. Ruby had mentioned that the place was beginning to fill up with some long-term winter visitors.

Someone tapped him on the shoulder.

He spun around and stared into a pair of brown eyes that he knew well from his fantasies and frustrations.

Claire.

A flame flickered to life inside him. God, he'd missed her cute nose, full lips, beautiful smile. His gaze traveled down over her faded green Dancing Winnebagos R.V. Park T-shirt. He'd missed her other parts, too.

Then he jolted with the realization that Claire was there, standing right in front of him. Shit! He didn't want her at The Shaft tonight, at least not until after he'd talked to Butch.

"Hey there, McStudly. What'll you have first? A drink or a kiss?"

The old guy to Mac's right leaned forward. "I'll take a kiss, babe. Throw in some tongue action and I'll even give ya a tip."

Claire recoiled for a split second before covering it with a fake smile. "How about another drink instead?" She grabbed the guy's nearly empty glass and topped it off, sliding it in front of him.

"Now where were we?" she asked Mac, leaning over the bar. She grabbed him by the shirt and pulled him close. "Oh yeah, right here."

Her lips were soft. She tasted sweet and salty, spiking his hunger for more. Now. Outside. In the dark. His hands all over her. He sank into her kiss, forgetting all about Butch and the Humdigger mine for several pulse pounding moments.

"You two need to get a room," Ronnie's voice interrupted his fantasy about dragging Claire to his pickup for some even heavier breathing.

"We have a room," Claire said, winking at Mac after pulling away. "I just need Gary or Arlene to come back from their break and we'll get to it."

"What about Butch?" Ronnie asked.

"He's not here."

"Yes, he is. He came through the front door about ten minutes ago and headed toward his office while you were in the bathroom."

"You have some kind of Butch radar now?" Claire asked.

"No, Katie does. Her forehead glows red like Rudolph's nose whenever Butch is in the same room with her. On top of that, she gets all skittish and klutzy. The poor girl ran into that post back by the pool table because she was so busy watching Butch grab something behind the bar."

That explained the mark Mac had noticed on Kate's face.

Ronnie held up two empty glasses. "We need two more, bartender, only make mine a soda water."

"Who's your new friend?" Mac asked while Claire got her sister's drinks. Then he remembered he was going to mind his own business.

"Mississippi."

The guy's dad must have been a fan of James Caan in *El Dorado.*

He decided to mess with her a little. Hell, he owed Ronnie for all of those mornings when she'd added fruity-tasting sweeteners to his normally black coffee, insisting he expand his "refreshment palette." Grapefruit-flavored coffee was for the birds.

"Mississippi," he said. "Is that with four S's and two P's?"

Ronnie thought on that for a breath. "How else would you spell it?"

"Like M-R-S period and Sippi."

"Why would a man be named Mrs. Sippi?"

"Because Ms. Sippi doesn't roll off the tongue as well." He took a swallow of his beer, trying to keep from laughing at the perplexed expression wrinkling her forehead.

Then she reached out and knuckle-punched his shoulder. "Stop messing with me, Mac, or I'll sic the FBI on you."

Damn she had hard knuckles. Grinning, he rubbed his shoulder. "For what?"

"I'll come up with something." She pointed her thumb over her shoulder at her pool table buddy. "Mississippi works for the FBI. I have them in *my* pocket now."

Mac stared at the tall, lean cowboy as he racked the balls for a fresh game of 8-ball. "He doesn't look like he fits in pockets."

"You're right. Maybe I'm hiding in his."

"You're playing pool with the FBI? That must mean I somehow slipped into a parallel dimension on the way out of Tucson. What's next? You staffing the jail for the Sheriff?"

She took the drinks Claire handed her. "Well, if I did take that job, I could help keep my two sisters from landing in the holding cell every week." The glare that passed between Claire and Ronnie had guilt and threats threaded throughout it.

As Ronnie walked away, Mac focused on Claire, who was suddenly extra busy wiping down the bar.

"Claire?"

"I don't know why she'd say something so wacky. She's been under a lot of stress lately, acting paranoid. Just ask Kate."

He wasn't going to risk making Kate cry again. "Claire."

"Fine! So I spent an hour in jail last night. It wasn't my fault. Kate had ice cream cravings at midnight and ended up getting the cops called on her for prowling outside The Rowdy Coyote Motel."

Mac scratched his jaw, trying to figure out how ice cream cravings landed them in front of The Rowdy Coyote. That motel was a mile or two from the only all-night grocery store in town. "And how did your pregnant sister prowling around a shady motel in Yuccaville end with you in jail, too?"

"Kate's nuts."

"So you said, repeatedly I might add, when you called me Halloween night from Deadwood's police station."

"Yeah, well it's getting worse. Last night, when Deputy Dipshit checked her license and made the meathead mistake of commenting on the weight she has listed, she went off on him and his many, many shortfalls, which got him all jacked out of shape. When he said he was going to arrest her for assaulting an officer, I stole his handcuffs and threw them in the bushes."

"Christ, Claire." Mac had to laugh. It was that or hit his head on the post back by the pool tables, too. "Who sprung you this time?"

"The Sheriff. He brought Ronnie along to calm us down and Butch to haul us over to get Mabel. Kate's just lucky nobody touched Gramps's car while we were in the slammer. The Rowdy Coyote Motel isn't in the best part of town, just around the corner from Meth Lane and Heroin Drive."

"Did you manage to keep this incident from landing on your record, or do you and Kate have an upcoming date at the courthouse?"

"Grady let us off, but I don't think he bought that we'd only stopped there to pay Arlene a visit. Especially with the stupid zip-it hand signals Ronnie was giving off to the side during his questioning."

"Arlene lives at The Rowdy Coyote?"

"That's what Kate told Deputy Dipshit last night." Claire tossed the bar towel into the sink behind her. "So does the Polar Bear."

He was about to ask who this Polar Bear was when Butch walked out through the door to the kitchen. He paused at the edge of the bar, his gaze searching the room until it landed on something that made his lips squeeze tight.

Mac followed Butch's line of sight and saw Kate taking drink orders from a crowd of young ranchers who looked not quite old enough to grow mustaches, let alone drink. One of them was getting handsy with Kate. First he touched her arm, then placed his palm on her back, and then trailed his fingers up the side of her leg. Before he could get far, she smacked him on the top of the head with her order pad and grabbed his wrist, placing his hand firmly on the table.

Mac looked over at Butch in time to catch a flash of irritation slide across his face.

As Kate came toward them with her order pad in hand, Butch joined Claire behind the bar.

"Hey, Mac," he said with his gaze still locked on Kate, tension in his voice. "You in town for a while?"

"Not long enough." Mac turned to Claire with a wrinkled brow, wondering what was going on between Butch and Kate these days. Last he'd heard, Butch was wanting in on the baby's future.

Claire shook her head and backed away.

Butch spoke over Mac's shoulder. "Kate, did you check their IDs?"

"Of course." She handed him a piece of paper, her forehead seeming redder than usual. "This isn't my first rodeo, you know."

After a glance down at the drink order, Butch hit her with a scowl. "Well, it sure looks like you have a table full of rodeo clowns over there. If you need me to take over, let me know."

"And lose a good tip? I don't think so."

His eyes narrowed further. "Remind your young pals that I have a hands-off policy when it comes to my wait staff."

"I can take care of myself."

"That's what worries me."

"What is that supposed to mean?"

Mac frowned at both of them in turn. They had a whole big bar in which to fight. Couldn't they move this somewhere other than over Mac's shoulder?

"Damn it, Kate. I know you're a Morgan sister, hell bent on tearing up this town and everything in it, but as long as you're carrying my child, you need to let me help you."

"At what price, Butch?" Kate huffed next to Mac's ear. "First you spring on me that you've changed your mind about playing daddy, and now all of a sudden you want to act like my bodyguard and hide me away in your office."

Wincing, Mac looked over at Claire.

She mouthed *Run!*

He grabbed his drink, hesitating. He hated to interrupt their tussle, but he didn't want Butch to storm off without talking to him first. "Butch, I need to speak with you when you have a moment."

At Butch's nod, Mac waved Claire over to an open table. She grabbed a Corona and joined him, taking the seat next to him. Her hand found his thigh under the table, her lips grazed his neck. "I missed you."

"Good. My diabolical plan is working."

Her palm crept higher, fingernails scratching over his inseam. "What do you need to talk to Butch about?"

He shook his head. "You don't miss a thing, do you?"

She laughed, her whole face lighting up. "Not when it comes to you."

Damn, there was no way she'd let this go now that she'd sunk her teeth in. "I need Butch's help getting up to Humdigger mine."

She raised her brows. "Why Butch?"

"He's neighbors with the owner of the property we need to cross in order to get up to the mine."

Butch joined them at the table, yanking out a chair across from Mac. "Sorry about that deal with Kate," he told both of them. He shoved his fingers through his blonde hair, blowing out a sigh. "She's driving me nuts, bucking everything I say."

"Morgan women can really mess with your head."

"Hey!" Claire elbowed him.

He winked at her. "I meant it in a good way."

She wrinkled her nose at him and then pointed at Butch. "Ronnie told me it's your gene pool that opened the cage of mad monkeys in Kate's head."

"Yeah." He sniffed. "Now you know why I'd decided not to

have kids. After the stories I'd heard about my mom's pregnancies and then witnessing my sister-in-law's temporary insanity for nine months, I didn't want to be responsible for sending another female over the edge." He frowned over at where Kate was delivering a tray of drinks. "Especially one I like as much as your sister."

Claire held up two fingers. "Jailed twice within a week."

Butch laughed and then apologized. "You shouldn't have taken the deputy's handcuffs away. Grady told me the guy has a thing about polishing his weapons. He's aiming for a promotion this year, trying to impress his moneybags father." Butch's eyes crinkled. "I wonder if he found his handcuffs after we left."

"I threw them way farther into that patch of weeds than where he was looking." Claire took a drink of Corona. "Maybe I'll go look for them tomorrow."

Mac shot her a warning look.

"So," Butch leaned his elbows on the table, focusing on Mac. "What can I do for you?"

"I need to get to a piece of property that's surrounded by your neighbor's land." Mac fiddled with his glass. "If memory serves me right, Dick Webber isn't fond of trespassers."

"Old man Webber has two loves—his collection of coprolites and his Remington 12-gauge pump-action shotgun. He won't hesitate to use the latter to protect the former from anyone stepping foot on his land."

"What about you?" Claire asked.

"What about me?"

"He lets you on his land, right? Didn't you take Kate for a hike up to some ruins on his property?"

Butch's gaze swung across the room to Kate again, his smile creasing his face. "She showed up in sandals and a sexy little skirt that day. I decided right then and there we'd be climbing the ladder up to the ruins."

Claire laughed. "I always knew you were a scoundrel."

He shrugged. "What can I say? One glance at your sister's legs, and I was plotting ways to get a closer look at them."

Mac stared at the curve of Claire's neck, one of his many favorite spots. He could relate to Butch's demise. The damned

Morgan sisters were trouble that way.

"Can you sneak us past Mr. Webber and his 12-gauge?" Claire asked.

Whoa! Mac hit her with a narrowed glare. "You're not going up to the mine with me, Claire. It's too dangerous."

"You think I can't handle a few varmints in an old mine?"

"It's not the varmints that concern me. There may be someone watching that mine."

"Besides Mr. Webber?"

"Exactly." Mac swirled his beer around in his glass. "Whoever sent Ruby that letter may be trying to lead her into a trap. I don't want you up there. It's too dangerous." He looked at her, his eyes lowering. "And you're too distracting."

Butch chuckled.

"What if I promise to blend into the scenery?"

"Impossible, Slugger." Mac looked across at Butch. "Do you think you can take a couple of hours off tomorrow and go with me to talk to Webber? Maybe get me clearance to go see my aunt's mine if I promise to hand over any petrified gems I come across?"

"No can do. I need to run to Tucson in the morning and pick up a new fry station. Mine is on the fritz."

Mac didn't want to wait another day, but he didn't want to end up full of shotgun holes either. "What about Saturday?"

Butch shook his head. "I have a shipment coming in from the auction last week. I need to be here."

"Damn. I'd really like to get up there and take a look inside the mine."

Butch sat back. "Do you know the coordinates?"

"I have the latitude and longitude from the claim paperwork. I plotted it out on a USGS quad map I have out in my truck."

"How about we go tonight?" Butch offered.

Mac sat back. "Right now?"

"Why not? Dick should be in bed, but I'll drive to be safe. He knows the sound of my truck."

"In the dark?" Claire frowned from Mac to Butch.

"With the moonlight, all we need is that fancy GPS of Mac's and a couple of flashlights," Butch continued.

"Once we're in the mine, it doesn't matter if it's day or night," Mac told Claire, adding for Butch, "I have some high-powered flashlights."

Claire finished off her Corona and set it down with a clunk. "I'm going with you."

"I'd rather you wait here next to a phone, ready to call the Sheriff if Butch and I don't come back." After ending up trapped in a mine not so long ago, Mac liked to make sure someone back home was at the ready to call for help.

"We can tell Kate and Ronnie where we're going. Let them take phone duty."

"No, Claire."

"Damn it, Mac. Quit treating me like a girl."

"You are a girl."

"I'll let you two hash this out on your own," Butch said, pushing back his chair. "I'll grab my stuff and let Gary know we're heading out for a bit."

"I'll meet you outside," Mac told him.

"*We'll* meet you outside," Claire said, standing as Butch headed toward his office.

Mac rose, locking onto her arm. "You're not going."

"Wasn't it you who told me we're a team?"

"That was different. I was talking about financially."

"Oh," she huffed, "so we're only a team when *you* decide. Silly me, I thought we were partners on all playing fields."

He grimaced. "Listen, Slugger, I don't know what's going to happen up there. You could get hurt."

"So could you."

"I don't want anything to happen to you."

"I don't want anything to happen to you either, Mac, and I nearly lost you twice in those damned mines." She stepped closer, catching his hands, squeezing. "I want to go with you. Waiting back here, worrying if you're alive or dead, is a worse fate than being hurt on the way up to that mine. Don't make me stay behind again."

He wanted to stand firm, but the pleading look in her eyes was his undoing. "Fine, you can come, but you need to do as I say in that mine. Got it?"

She nodded, going up on her toes to kiss his jaw. "I'll be good, I promise."

"I've heard that before," he muttered to her back as she went over to let her sisters know the plan.

Mac waited out under the stars while Claire collected her jacket from behind the bar before joining him. He shivered on his way to his truck, where he grabbed his coat along with his GPS, backpack, and flashlights. He pocketed his favorite compass, too, along with a can of spray paint in case they decided to hike into the mine and needed to leave a trail of breadcrumbs.

Butch met them behind The Shaft. "You got your gear?"

"Yep."

"Claire won the argument, huh?"

Mac held the back door of Butch's Chevy Silverado SS open for her. "Like I said, the Morgan sisters can really mess with your head."

Smiling, she patted his cheek as she climbed up into the truck. "It's all part of *our* grand diabolical plan." She threw his earlier words back at him in jest.

He pinched her butt before she sat on the backseat, making her squeak and laugh. In the front seat, he showed Butch the location of the mine on the quad map.

"Really?" Butch started his truck. "I've hiked close to that range. There are animal trails here and there, but no sign of a mine."

"Maybe the entrance is overgrown with bushes," Claire suggested from the back seat.

"Could be." Butch headed south out of the parking lot. "But I'd expect to have noticed tailings. Although I suppose they could have been dumped out a different entrance higher up or around the other side."

Or maybe, Mac thought, someone went to a lot of trouble to cover up the entrance and any other indications of a mine to keep it hidden. And maybe that someone was out there waiting for them in the darkness tonight.

Mac frowned out the window at the waning moon. Damn it. He wished to hell Claire had wanted to stay at the bar.

Chapter Nine

The moon had painted the desert using smears of silver and gray. Under its feeble light, Claire crunched across the gritty alluvial slope, a mixture of gravel and sand and undoubtedly other types of rocks that Mac could name in his sleep.

Playing monkey in the middle between Butch and Mac, she marched through the shadow-draped landscape dotted with grabby cacti—barrel, cholla, and prickly pear the worst offenders. To the right, a series of fin-like mountains loomed high and intimidating in the semidarkness.

Butch paused, sniffing the air. "You smell that?"

"Smells kind of skunky." Claire took a step closer to Mac. After being sprayed by one last summer, she steered clear of the damned striped stinkers.

Mac glanced around the darkened desert. "No, it's javelina. I saw a small herd of them grazing about a quarter mile back."

The sound of paper rustling came from Butch's direction. "From what I can tell on the map, the mine should be right up there somewhere." He pointed his flashlight up the steep hillside dotted with creosote bushes, diamond cholla cacti, and boulders here and there.

Mac added a second spotlight to the hillside, lingering on an area with a grouping of boulders high up on the left. "That looks like a trail coming from those rocks."

Butch redirected his light. "You sure that's a trail?"

Mac's beam followed it along. "Look at the depth of the shadows there and there before it goes around that bend and disappears. It's a trail. Not much of it's probably visible in the full sunlight unless the sun's angle is just right and sets off the shadows, like what we have tonight with these flashlights." He aimed his light at a small group of desert willows further down the slope. "I'm betting it comes out over there by those willows. When it rains, water probably pools there, drawing in the wildlife."

Claire squinted, noticing another trail leading away from the willows in a different direction. "So do we follow it up?"

"We could go straight up the slope," Butch focused his beam on the landscape in front of them.

"Maybe," Mac said. "The talus at the base is mostly small rock, not too steep. The footing appears solid enough judging by all of the plants that have taken hold. But there's one snag."

"What's that?"

"You haven't seen Slugger here climb."

"What's that supposed to mean?" Claire turned to him, hands on her hips.

"You're no mountain goat."

"I can climb just fine."

"Sure," he grinned down at her in the shadows, "with a winch."

Butch chuckled.

"Smartass." Claire poked Mac in the stomach. "I can climb that slope without a problem. It's not *that* steep."

"Your depth perception is off because of the dark."

"Maybe we should backtrack and try the trail," Butch suggested, playing referee.

"You can try that route, Butch, but I'm going straight up." With all of the work she'd been doing around the R.V. park lately, she wasn't as soft and doughy as she used to be. "I'm going to make Mac eat his words when I reach the top first." Without waiting for either of them, she pulled her own flashlight from her jacket pocket, flicked it on, and started up the hillside.

"Claire," Mac said, following her, "this is a bad idea. Let's take the trail."

"If I let every bad idea stop me from what I wanted to do in life," she dodged a large grouping of prickly pear, "I'd never have kissed you under Ruby's willow tree that first time."

"You were drunk, remember?"

Oh, yeah. "But not the second time."

"The second time I kissed you."

"True, but it was still a bad idea."

"And it still is."

She paused to frown down at him and noticed they were alone. "Where's Butch?"

"He's trying the trail. We might need a safer way back down."

"Why is kissing me still a bad idea?"

He caught up with her, tightening the straps of his backpack. "Because it usually leads to me removing your clothes."

"I like it when you remove my clothes."

"So do I. Too much. In fact, on the drive to Jackrabbit Junction earlier tonight, I was thinking about doing that very thing to you."

"Really?" She led the way further up the slope. "And how did that go for you?"

"Not as far as I'd have liked."

"Why's that?"

"You weren't there."

"I'm here now."

"Yes, you are and slowing down to boot." He stood next to her as she huffed and puffed a little, gearing up to blow down his house.

He on the other hand merely sniffed. "The javelinas are moving away."

"Thank God … for that." She sucked in a breath and pushed onward and upward.

At the halfway point, Mac offered to throw her over his shoulder and haul her up the rest of the way in firefighter tradition.

"Bite me." She massaged the pain in her side and took several more steps before needing another short break, holding up her index finger for Mac to give her a minute to catch her breath.

He caught her hand on the way past, tugging her along behind him. "Are you even trying, Slugger?"

"Damn you … and your …"

"How's it going?" Butch called down to them from what must have been the trail another twenty or so feet up.

"We should be ready to join you as soon as Claire finishes damning me." Lifting her hand to his lips, he kissed her knuckles. "Any last words, milady?"

She had plenty but had no breath to utter them. Instead she pulled her hand free and smacked him on the butt before trudging onward and upward.

Mac played bulldozer the rest of the way, pushing her rump northward until they reached the trail, his hands doing as much squeezing as pushing along the way.

"See," she said to Mac between breaths. "I told you … the climb … wasn't so tough."

He kissed her temple. "Well, you're certainly in better shape than you used to be."

"It's all the work … around the R.V. park." Not to mention the lack of smoking. She jokingly flexed her bicep in front of Butch. "I'm getting buff. See?"

Butch's hand practically wrapped around her little egg of a muscle. He whistled between his teeth. "You better be careful, Mac. She'll be wearing the pants in the family soon."

"I like her better without pants," Mac said, stepping around Claire. "Let's see if there's a mine up here or not." He led the way further along the trail.

The climb was much less steep now, but Claire's thighs continued their slow burn. Mac offered his hand at one point, but she refused, determined to keep up on her own. After insisting on coming along, she didn't want to be a burden.

Finally they came to the collection of boulders and dense cluster of creosote bushes and mesquite.

"I can smell the mine's breath," Mac said, pushing through the foliage. "It's up ahead."

Claire followed, catching a wiry branch in the face.

And then another.

"Dang it, Mac." She spit out a waxy leaf and hooked onto his belt below his backpack, trying not to weigh anchor too much. "Wait up."

On the other side of Mother Nature's camouflage was a hole in the side of the hillside. A couple of boards crisscrossed the entrance barring the way. Spray painted on the boards someone had written: *Stay out! Bad air!*

"Bad air." Claire stepped to the side, making room in front of the mine entrance for Butch, who was shoving his way through the last of the brush. "Does that mean what I think it means?"

"Usually it means there's a pocket of carbon dioxide somewhere in the mine," Mac answered. "A silent killer of canaries and miners alike." He fished in his backpack and pulled out something that looked like a fancy walkie-talkie with an LED screen. He hit a button and the sucker lit up the surrounding hillside.

"What is that?" Claire asked, leaning forward for a closer look. "An alien beacon?"

He grinned down at his toy. "A portable gas detector."

"Wow, you don't mess around, do you?" Butch asked, looking down at it over Claire's shoulder. "Does that thing do your taxes, too?"

Mac snorted. "No, that's one step up from this puppy."

"How many gases can that thing monitor?"

"Up to six at a time." Mac held it out for Butch and Claire to see it better. "It can operate as a single gas PID unit or multifunctional tool." He turned it this way and that. "It's dust and water resistant, plus comes with man-down and panic alarms."

"The LED display is incredible," Butch took the detector, pushing the button Mac indicated. "Is that one of those detectors that comes with a library of VOC?"

Claire was trying to keep up with the conversation, but she kept getting hung up on the acronyms they were tossing around. She waited for Mac to finish his show-and-tell presentation, noticing that several of the boards crisscrossing the entrance looked loose. She pointed at his fancy gadget. "Is that thing picking up any gases right now?"

"Nothing dangerous."

"What about when you hold it on the other side of the boards?"

Mac reached through the gaps in the boards, pushed a few buttons and waited. When he pulled the gas detector back out, he stared down at the bright LED screen. "It's all clear."

"Good." She grabbed onto a board. It wiggled slightly, weathered loose by years of sun, wind, and rain. Bracing her foot against one of the other boards, she yanked on it. With a solid tug, it pulled free.

"What are you doing?" Mac asked, taking the board she handed him.

She tugged a second board free, handing it to Butch. "*We're going inside, remember?*"

"No, we're not." Mac caught her arm in a no-nonsense grip. "Just because the air is clear here doesn't mean you won't get ten feet in and keel over. Let's wait until daylight."

"You're the one who said that once we're inside it doesn't matter if it's day or night out here."

"That was before I knew about the possibility of poisonous gas."

She pointed at the warning sign. "This mine belonged to Joe. If you'll remember, he has a colorful history of swindling, stealing, and lying."

"What's your point?" Mac was still holding onto her arm.

"I bet this Bad Air sign is another lie. It's a lot more effective than a No Trespassing sign."

Mac stared down at her in the glow of the LED display, his forehead creased. "What if you're wrong?"

"Then your fancy air-checking gadget will tell us." When he continued to hesitate, she added, "Weren't you the one telling me last month that most hard rock mines don't have problems with gas leaching out of the surrounding rock? Only the soft rock ones, like coal mines."

"I said 'most,' not all." He pointed his gas detector at the mine entrance. "This could be an exception to the norm."

"Mac, my gut tells me this," she tapped the Bad Air sign, "is another one of Joe's shams." Hell, the asshole probably had stashed those damned gold boxes stolen from England's Waddesdon Manor in here. Lord knows she'd looked everywhere else around the R.V. park and come up empty. "But to be safe we have your detector to lead the way and see if I'm wrong or right."

Mac still hesitated. "I don't suppose you'd be game to Butch and me going in while you wait out here until I make sure it's clear."

"Butch has a baby on the way. I don't. Let me go in with you. I won't touch a thing this time."

"You promise?"

She laid her hand over her heart. "Swear on my mother's grave."

That made him smile. "Okay, Slugger, just stick close to my side." Mac looked at Butch. "You cool with staying out here?"

He shrugged. "I'm easy."

"Is your phone working?"

Butch checked it. "Yep."

"If we're not back out in twenty minutes, call the Sheriff. Whatever you do, don't come in." He checked his watch and then held it up for Butch to compare time.

She wondered why only twenty minutes, but since Mac was running tonight's show, she didn't ask.

"We'd better get cracking," he said and slid between the boards.

"Any readings on the gas detector?" she asked before joining him. She was feeling brave tonight but not stupid.

Peeking between the boards, she watched Mac fiddle with the detector. The LED screens—all three of them—lit up the rock around him and on down to where the throat of the mine narrowed to only a shoulder width or so.

"All clear. Get in here."

He helped her through the boards, brushing off her backside.

"I don't remember getting the seat of my pants dirty."

"I'm just taking precautions." He pointed his detector toward the mine's throat. "Let's go."

She followed as they inched along the narrow tunnel, Mac pressing buttons on his detector as they walked. Several yards in he paused, sliding off his pack. "Hold on, I want to get something."

Claire nodded, glancing around. The mine looked pretty much like the others she'd been in: rock walls etched with fissure cracks, old timber support beams, dirt floors. No rails in this mine, at least not at the entrance, but there was what looked like an ore chute coming out of the wall about ten feet further ahead. Right below it, angled against the wall at the base of the chute, was a two-by-four that was several feet long. It had been left leaning against the rock wall partially blocking the way into the throat of the mine, as if someone would be coming back to grab it on the way out later.

Her gaze returned to the chute. Why would there be an ore chute if there were no rails? Then she remembered several old-time photos she'd seen of the miners in the area with their pickaxes and jackasses. Maybe one of the previous miners used pack animals to haul out chunks of ore, leaving one of those iron-wheeled ore wagons she'd seen in the museum up in Deadwood waiting on the desert floor below the trail.

"Mac," she whispered.

He looked up from where he was rifling through his bag.

"I want to go look at that chute."

He glanced down at his gas detector and then nodded.

She tiptoed back to the ore chute, shining her flashlight up into the square conduit cut into the rock wall. A sheet of rusted metal blocked the top. That must be the hatch, she thought. If the chute dumped out here, how many levels of drifts were above her? The hillside did rise for thirty or so feet above the mine entrance before slanting toward the peak.

At the base of the hatch door was a nest of some sort, along with a length of newer looking rope. Her gaze followed the rope from the hatch door rigging down along the bottom of the chute and then the wall. It ended at the leaning board, appearing to be looped around the base. Maybe the board had something to do with securing the hatch. That would explain why it had been left wedged against the wall.

Her focus returned to the chute and a nest of dead branches, cactus spines, and pieces of chewed plastic bags. It looked like something was living up near the hatch. She searched the nest for a shiny reflection, seeing if this one had any treasures like those she had found hidden in the stopes in the Rattlesnake Ridge mine. When her visual inspection turned up nothing, she used her flashlight to carefully push around the matted mess.

Drat. Just a nest.

"Find anything?" Mac came up behind her, his hand warming her lower back.

"Nope."

He checked his watch. "We have fourteen more minutes."

"You lead the way." She moved closer to the wall in front of the ore chute so he could step around her. "Oh, watch out for that boa—"

His boot bumped the two-by-four leaning against the wall. It clattered to the ground, the sound echoing around them and down into the mine.

Something slithered along the rock wall, and then Claire heard a clink from the chute above her. A screech made her wince, followed immediately by a loud rumbling noise that drowned out the last half of Mac's shout to *RUN!*

Before her feet had a chance to follow his order, he barreled into her, his shoulder knocking her sideways. She stumbled toward the mine entrance, her shoulder bouncing off the wall.

When she looked back at him, her breath log-jammed in her lungs as a flood of rocks crashed down the ore chute right into Mac. Several slammed into his left shoulder, their momentum and weight making him stumble backward into the wall behind him. She watched in horror as a melon-sized chunk careened into his upper shin, knocking his leg out from under him. Claire scrambled to his side through the dust as the last of the rocks trickled down the chute and rained around Mac, narrowly missing his head.

"Oh, Jesus, Mac." She dropped to her knees next to where he sat holding his left arm close to his ribs. "Are you okay?" She cleared the floor around him, her heart pounding loud enough to echo clear down to the valley floor.

"Yes and no." He shifted, grimacing from the effort.

"What does that mean?"

"I'm alive, but I'm pretty sure my left shoulder is dislocated. It's happened a few times before."

She reached out to touch his shoulder but hesitated, not sure how she could help him. "Can we pop it back in?"

His face was lined with pain. "I already tried while you were clearing away the rocks, but it's being stubborn." He coughed and groaned.

"So what do we do?"

"We get out of here and I go to the ER."

"You mean *we* go to the ER."

A light shined on Mac from behind Claire. "That sounded bad! What happened?" Butch asked, squatting next to Claire.

"The hatch release on an old ore chute gave way," Mac told him.

"It didn't give way," Claire told him. "The hatch held fine until you bumped that board loose."

"You think it was rigged?" Mac asked.

A sickening feeling spread through her. "I think Joe has this place booby-trapped."

"Booby-trapped?" Butch sounded skeptical.

She nodded. She had no doubt now that Joe was hiding something in there, or maybe several somethings.

Mac didn't comment. He was too busy trying to stand. He held out his right hand to Butch. "Help me up, would you?"

Butch carefully hauled Mac to his feet.

His face blanched when he put weight on his left leg. The tunnel was too narrow for Butch and Mac's shoulders to pass through side by side, so Claire came up beside him on his right. "Lean on me."

They started back to the entrance.

"Where all do you hurt?" Butch asked, leading the way.

"His left shoulder is dislocated." Claire told him.

"My left side hurts like a son of a bitch every time I breathe."

"Broken ribs?" Butch asked.

"No, I've had a broken rib. There's no mistaking that pain. This feels more like I went a few rounds in the ring with a heavyweight."

Jeez, what in the hell had Mac gotten into in the past? Dislocated shoulders and broken ribs? What else didn't she know about him?

Claire gripped him by the waist of his jeans, careful of his ribs. It was her fault he was hurt. She should have waited for him to go check out that ore chute, or at least warned him ahead of time about that board before he tried to slip around her. He'd probably saved her life by shoving her out of the way and now he was paying for her stupid curiosity.

"How's your shin?"

"Throbbing."

He probably had a big egg of a bruise on it. The rock that had hit it was no pebble.

They paused while Butch knocked the last of the boards off the entrance, clearing a path out under the stars.

"Damned ore chute," Mac said sighing. "I should've known not to trust it." He hauled her close and kissed her forehead. "Thank God you're okay."

"I'm sorry I dragged you in there."

He pushed her back, frowning down at her. "I wanted to go in, Claire. This isn't your fault, it's mine. I'm the one who kicked the board loose."

"I should have warned you sooner about it."

"Stop it, Slugger. I did this, not you." He shuffled toward the opening where Butch was waiting for them. "You really think that mine was booby-trapped, don't you?"

Knowing what she did about Joe, she had little doubt. "Yep."

"I like that son of a bitch less and less every time I go in one of his damned mines."

It took them an hour, but they made it down the trail to the stand of desert willows before taking a short break. Holding his arm close and keeping his breaths shallow, Mac walked the rest of the way to Butch's truck without help.

As they headed back to civilization, Claire turned to stare out the back window toward the shadowed hillside where Humdigger mine was hidden.

Someone had rigged that chute at least to slow down, if not kill, a trespasser. Someone who hadn't wanted visitors finding out what was tucked away inside of the mine. And most likely that same "someone" was a man who'd made a living as a dirty rotten no-good thief and went by the name of Joe Martino.

Claire turned away, fiddling with her flashlight. The question was why would he go to such lengths to keep everyone out?

Chapter Ten

Friday, November 9th

As seedy underbellies went, Yuccaville's was more dusty than sleazy, Ronnie thought with a smirk. At least that was the case with Dirty Gerties, the one and only strip club in town. The white cinderblock building was lined with a brown bathtub ring above a skirt of scraggly weeds bent sideways in the stiff morning breeze. The few windows gracing the place had bars covering them, making her wonder if it was to keep the voyeurs out or the customers in.

Tapping the brakes of his pickup, Chester bounced into the pothole-filled parking lot. Two other dust-coated trucks were parked up near the building, sandwiching a rusted, ancient boat-sized Thunderbird. Their bumpy entrance inspired a dust devil to spin to life, collecting loose trash and whirling it into the empty lot next to them.

Ronnie frowned across the pickup cab at the grizzled old coot. "Chester Thomas, when you asked me to come to town with you to pick up some mud, I assumed you meant drywall compound for the rec room walls Claire had noted on her honey-do list, not the goop you dip a babe in a bikini into."

"I did." He shut off the engine.

"Then why are we sitting in the parking lot of a strip joint known for its rowdy mud wrestling bouts?"

"We need to make a *pit* stop." He shoved open his door and slid out, chortling. "Get it? Pit? As in mud pit?"

She joined him in front of his bug-coated grill and followed him over to the solid steel entry doors. "If that's your way of proposing we hop into the mud pit for a quick wrestling match, you can forget it. I left my bikini back in my early twenties."

He held open the door. "That's too bad. I was planning to put money down on you and win me a fortune. Carrera told me about your hogtying party for that poor cowboy over at The Shaft."

"Don't remind me of that asshole."

"Come on, girl. That's no way to talk about your stepdaddy."

Ronnie poked him in the ribs on her way inside, then let him lead the way into the dimly lit club. She took the seat he indicated next to him at the bar which surrounded a square ring. Currently the ring was dark with boards covering the mud pit. Stripper poles graced each corner, all four shined up and ready for a whirl. The smell of lemons and pine filled the place, surprising Ronnie. She'd expected something spicier and sex-inspiring—something musky perhaps with sultry notes of tawdry lap dances and one night lust affairs.

"You're early, Thomas," the platinum-blonde bartender said, leaning onto the bar across from them. Her low-cut T-shirt emphasized an impressive rack of what Ronnie would bet were man-made boobs judging by the wrinkled and freckled skin of her upper chest. Lines fanned from the corners of her long-fringed eyes, and she had deep parentheses around her mouth. "Where's your usual partner in crime?"

"He went and bought the damned cow when he could've gotten the milk for free, so I brought along a new playmate."

"Oh, yeah?" The bartender smiled, warm and friendly. "She's a little young for you, don't ya think?"

"Only in years. Cherry Haywood, say hello to Ronnie Morgan. She's Harley's granddaughter."

"Well stick a feather in my cap and call it macaroni." Cherry held out her hand to shake, which Ronnie did. "Who knew Ford had it in him?"

The bartender at Dirty Gerties knew Gramps? Ronnie shot Chester and then Cherry a raised brow. "My grandfather comes here?"

"Not lately, but he used to have one of our punch cards." Cherry grinned at Chester. "Although he was never brave enough to climb into the pit, unlike this horny toad."

Ronnie grimaced. There were some things she didn't need to

know about her grandfather's life, like anything involving the opposite sex. Anything at all.

"What can I get you two?" Cherry wiped the bar down with a wet rag. "The kitchen isn't open yet, but I can throw something together to wet your whistle in the meantime."

"I'll just take a Dr. Pepper." When Cherry looked at him with raised brows, he explained. "I'm driving. I don't need that sharp-eyed sheriff pulling me over on the way out of here."

Actually Ronnie wouldn't mind getting stopped by Grady. Last night, not long after Claire had left, he'd swung by The Shaft, still in uniform. He'd locked gazes with Ronnie, his stare narrowing when it landed on her pool playing FBI pal. But before she had a chance to sink the 9-ball and explain, he'd spoken into the walkie-talkie on his shoulder and exited without even a "See you later, alligator."

Ronnie ordered a gin and tonic. "What?" she replied to Chester's scrutiny after Cherry walked away to pour the drink. "When in Rome."

"Burn it down?"

"Something like that." She lowered her voice. "Why are we really here? And don't tell me you wanted me to meet your pretty bartender girlfriend."

"Cherry owns this place."

"She does?"

He nodded. "She bought it about seven or eight years ago and spruced it up. The place was a real dive before then—stunk like sex most days, and the girls looked dried-up and ragged from too many twirls around the ol' pole."

Ronnie glanced around, noticing the polished brass rails fencing the pit and black leather booth seats. Now that she thought about it, the floor hadn't been sticky or peanut shell-covered, unlike The Shaft most nights. The place smelled like a basket of lemons. The plain concrete block exterior hid a lush den ready-made for all sorts of vices of the wicked sort.

"These days, Cherry provides health insurance to her employees and helps pay for child care."

"Talking about me, Thomas?" Cherry set the drinks down in front of them, draping the towel over her shoulder. "I hope it's juicy. I could use something exciting in my life."

Says the owner of a strip club, Ronnie thought, stirring her drink with a small smile.

"Actually," Chester said, "we have some questions for you, Cherry."

"Shoot."

"Yesterday morning before you opened for business, someone called The Dancing Winnebagos R.V. Park from your payphone." He took a sip of his Dr. Pepper. "You wouldn't happen to have any idea who might have been in here before hours, would you?"

"Besides the cleaning crew?"

He nodded. "The voice was male, if that helps."

"My janitorial crew is all female. In my experience, when it comes to keeping everything clean and sanitary, female janitors are less likely to be distracted in a club where girls run around topless more often than not. Plus it makes my employees more at ease." She snickered. "There's nothing more painful to watch on stage than an uptight pole dancer. Imagine a giraffe trying to slide down a fire pole."

"Did anyone stop by to use the latrine?"

Cherry rubbed her lips together in thought. "Let's see, I came in around nine and holed up in my office going through last month's expenses one more time before shipping it all off to my bookkeeper. I can't remember seeing anyone other than … wait." She held up a finger. "Dory stopped by."

"Who's Dory?" Ronnie asked.

"Dory Hamilton. He works for Tucson Electric & Power. He's about two inches taller than me, has a big belly, and wears lots of thick gold chains and a look-at-me big gaudy watch. Nice enough but a little too greasy around the edges for my taste. He said there'd been some calls about power outages in the area and asked if we'd had any issues."

"Did you see him make a phone call?" Chester asked.

"No, but I do remember hearing his voice. I assumed he was talking on his work phone."

Chester and Ronnie exchanged speculative glances.

"How close is the payphone to your office?" Ronnie asked.

Chester answered for Cherry. "It's just down the hall."

"So you could easily hear someone talking on it when the place is quiet."

"Definitely." Cherry pointed at the gin and tonic Ronnie had sucked down without realizing it. "Want another?"

"She's good." Chester slurped the last of his Dr. Pepper and threw some cash on the bar. "Thanks for the drinks, Cherry. Always a pleasure to hear your sultry voice."

Cherry swatted the bow-legged flirt with her towel.

"Thanks for the answers, too," Ronnie added.

"Not a problem." Cherry scooped up Chester's bills and tucked them into her bra. "Don't be such a stranger, Thomas. The twins have been missing you lately."

Grinning through his unshaven whiskers, Chester led the way out into the sunlight.

"The twins?" Ronnie asked as they headed back to his pickup. "Is that code for something?" Like Cherry's chest?

"Yeah, it's code for the twin sisters who like to tag-team me and give me a lashing in the ring." With a wink and a snicker, he climbed in the pickup and started it up.

Ronnie joined him in the cab. "You're hopeless."

"Only when it comes to women." He looked out at the road. "Keep your eyes open for a white Chevy S-10."

She buckled her seatbelt. "Why? Is that what the twins drive?"

"No, it's Dory Hamilton's company vehicle. He checks the meters for Tucson Electric and Power both here in town and out in Jackrabbit Junction." Chester shifted into drive and bounced out of the lot onto the road.

"How do you know who Dory is?" Was Dory a frequent customer at The Shaft? Had she seen him in there before and hadn't noticed him?

"He was a steady lunch customer at Sophy Wheeler's diner across the street from The Shaft, back before Sophy got hauled off to prison for trying to blow your sister to smithereens and they had to shut the place down. I saw him in there watching Sophy's legs more often than not when we'd stop in for a burger or her famous chili. That babe might have been a grade-A wacko, but she made a bowl of chili that would bring you to your knees."

Ah, yes, Sophy, Joe's ex-wife. The psycho, shotgun toting and dog stealing bitch who'd done her best to remove not only Claire from the face of the earth, but Mac as well. Ronnie had heard all about Claire's nemesis while living in Tucson with the two of them.

"So why would this Dory guy have called with that message?" Was he working for the Polar Bear? One of the big-money crime bosses that her ex-husband had laundered money for? Was he also undercover for the FBI? Mississippi's partner? Or had he overheard Katie or Claire talking about Ronnie's sitting-duck situation while eating at The Shaft and just liked to scare the hell out of skittish women?

"I don't know." Chester rolled past the side street Kate had taken Ronnie down a few days back, the one with the motel where the S.S. Minnow's rusted twin was docked in the defunct pool.

Ronnie glanced down toward The Rowdy Coyote, doing a doubletake when she thought she saw a familiar Volvo parked parallel to the motel. Was that Katie's car? She turned in her seat to peer out the back window, but they were too far past the street now. Facing forward again, Ronnie shook her head. No, it couldn't be Katie. Claire had said she was substituting at the school today. It must have been a different black Volvo.

"But if it really was Dory," Chester aimed a grizzled grin her way, "I'm thinking you may want to use his rolls of gold chains to hog-tie him while Claire nails his greasy ass to the wall."

"I agree. That bastard had better have a good reason for making prank phone calls, or he's going to pay some painful consequences."

* * *

Kate was beginning to think she needed a different car.

Her black Volvo was a dead giveaway in a town full of dirty pickup trucks and Sheriff Department Broncos, like the one easing up behind her curbside parking spot across from The Rowdy Coyote Motel at that very moment.

Damn it, now what had she done? It wasn't illegal to park across from a public business and eat lunch in Yuccaville, was it? She'd made sure to park far enough away from the fire hydrant to be in the clear. If Ronnie had sicced Grady on her after the mess the other night with Deputy Dipshit, Kate was going to cut holes in all of her sister's underwear.

She glanced over at Room 9, worrying that her cover was now blown thanks to the sheriff. Not that much had been happening through the gap in the curtains today. The snake was gone, though, along with its tank. Maybe the manager had gotten wind of it. Or maybe the Polar Bear had used it on a victim and been forced to dispose of the slithering weapon in case the cops came sniffing around the joint.

The thump of the Bronco's door slamming behind her brought her back to her current predicament. Would Grady buy that she'd parked here in hopes of catching Arlene at home? That she hadn't remembered the other waitress was working the lunch crowd at The Shaft today? Probably not. Grady had been good at sniffing out her lies from their first meeting when she'd crashed into Butch's pickup. He hadn't bought it back then when she'd tried to place the blame for the accident partly on Butch in order to keep her insurance company from dropping her, and she doubted he'd believe her now.

As footfalls approached, she rolled down her window, wondering if she should call him Sheriff Harrison now that her sister was sort of seeing him or if Grady would be okay.

"What's your business here, Ms. Morgan?" a voice that was very much NOT Grady's came through her window.

Her neck bristled on cue, her gaze whipping upward. Deputy Dipshit! Jowls, sneered lip, handcuffs, and all.

"I'm eating my lunch, Deputy." She held up her half-eaten peanut butter sandwich as evidence.

His mirrored cop sunglasses reflected twin distorted versions of her upturned face. "You sure picked a funny spot to have a picnic."

"I like the view here."

He bent over, resting his forearms on her car door, filling the window with the smell of onions and French fries. His blatant attempt at intimidation made her want to smash her sandwich in his face. "Where did you find that fancy spyglass?"

She glanced at the brass spyglass lying on the passenger seat. Shit! She'd forgotten to stash that under the seat. "It's a family heirloom."

That was kind of true since Ruby was her step-grandmother and Joe's stolen treasures were now hers, whether she wanted them and the headaches that came with them or not.

"I sure hope you aren't using it to peek in any windows around here. I'd hate to have to haul you back to jail. The Sheriff has today off and won't be able to come to your rescue anytime soon."

Her chin lifted. "Is it illegal to carry a spyglass, Deputy?"

"Not currently."

"Is parking along a non-painted curb on a public street illegal for a substitute teacher who's enjoying a quick lunch off-campus?"

"They're letting you teach now, huh? They must not have checked your criminal record." His crooked smirk needed to be straightened out with a frying pan. Lucky for him, she hadn't packed one in her lunch bag today. "They must be really desperate for teachers these days."

Her forehead burned along with the ball of fury heading toward supernova in her gut. "For your information, *Deputy*, I happen to have multiple teaching credentials along with my master's degree."

"From where? Clown college?"

"Is that the best you can do, Deputy Droopy?"

The use of Claire's other nickname for the dipshit made his nostrils flare. He pulled out a pair of handcuffs and held them up between them. "Nope. I could slap these on you and we'll laugh all of the way to the station." His lips flat-lined. "Your sister's not here today to play interference and save you this time."

God, she wanted to hiss and bite him.

Instead she gripped the steering wheel, telling herself that no judge or jury was going to buy that she temporarily turned into a zombie and couldn't control her teeth. Especially when zombies usually hungered for brains and Deputy Dipshit obviously had only a walnut rattling around inside his thick, meaty skull.

She smiled, all teeth and sarcasm. "I don't need my sister to save me from your bumbling attempts at a false arrest."

His white knuckled grip on the handcuffs gave away how deeply her verbal jab had gotten under his skin. "Be careful, Ms. Morgan." He stood up straight, giving her breathing space again. "You may have the Sheriff fooled into thinking you're just a pretty blue-eyed blonde, but I'm onto your game."

"And what game is that?"

He looked over at The Rowdy Coyote Motel. "Stalking."

Oh, sheesh. Did he ever have this backward. She was here trying to stop someone from stalking Ronnie, not the other way around.

"One slip up," he continued, "and I'll be on you like flies on shit." He clasped his big shiny belt buckle with both hands. "Now, why don't you move along little teacher and run on back to school before you get into trouble here."

Kate bit into her sandwich, taking her time chewing and swallowing as she glared at him. The shithead wanted to dance, did he? "You ruined my lunch, Deputy."

"Shucks. That's too bad, Ms. Morgan. I'll be sure to make up for it next time you're behind bars." He patted the roof of her car. "Off you go now."

She keyed the engine to life, rolling up her window as he stood there with his legs wide, his cocky grin even wider.

He pointed two fingers at his eyes and then his index finger at her.

Shifting into gear, she rolled away, her chest tight.

"You better be watching, Deputy Dipshit," she told his reflection in her rearview mirror. "Because the dance has begun, and this little teacher is going to school you on what happens when you bully the wrong scrapper."

She stared back at herself in the mirror, a smile creeping onto her face. "Let the ass kicking begin."

* * *

Mac woke with a pounding head and aching body, feeling

like he'd had his ass kicked and been left out for the coyotes to fight over.

He opened his eyes and looked around, realizing that it wasn't his head pounding, it was the rec room. Or rather somebody in the rec room.

Gingerly he sat up in the shadowed room, groaning at the stab of pain in his ribs. Late afternoon sunlight poked through the blinds in his aunt's bedroom, making stripes across the nasty bruise on his shin.

The pillow next to him was empty and indent free. He wasn't surprised. Claire had told him on the drive home from the ER that she was going to sleep in the spare room with her sister so that she didn't bump him in the night. He'd insisted he was fine, but the painkiller they'd given him in the hospital had fogged up his brain, so he didn't remember much besides the sight of the sun cresting the Tres Dedos Mountains and Claire tugging off his jeans.

He adjusted the shoulder sling holding his arm mostly immobile and stood wincing. He was getting too old for this shit. His shoulder felt like he'd spent yesterday on the shooting range with a 12-gauge shotgun kicking back into it over and over. Putting on jeans one-handed was slow going, causing several more winces in the process. He grabbed one of Harley's button-up shirts from his aunt's closet and slid one arm into it, letting the other side drape over his sling. He'd need help maneuvering into the left sleeve.

Running a hand through his hair in lieu of a comb, he headed out into the hall to find out who was making all the racket in the rec room.

Chester glanced his way from the middle of a pile of plaster and lathe debris. The bow-legged bristle-top was the guilty party, his hammer in one hand, a blue electrical box in the other.

"Claire," Chester called around the nails in his mouth. "Sweet Buns is awake."

"Coming," she called from the General Store. The sound of other female voices carried through the curtain. Afraid Deborah might show before he'd had enough caffeine to stomach her ever present scorn, he detoured to the kitchen.

Mac was pouring himself a cup of cold coffee when Claire joined him. His gaze widened at the sight of her in a long beige crocheted skirt, white shirt, and blue jean jacket. Damn, she looked good enough to make him forget about his aches and pains for a few minutes.

"How are you feeling?" she asked, taking the cup from him and directing him to one of the kitchen chairs.

"Not so bad that I can't make my own coffee." She smelled like a fruit cocktail. His mouth watered at several sweet and juicy ideas that outfit put in his head.

"Here, let me help with this." She unhooked his sling, delicately maneuvered his arm into the shirt sleeve, and put the sling back on, nudging him over to the table. "Now let me play June Cleaver for a moment and get you something to eat and drink."

"Who are you and what have you done with Slugger and her tool belt?" He lowered into the chair, keeping his breath shallow until he'd settled onto the seat.

"I have my tool belt hidden under my skirt," she smiled over her shoulder at him as she fished in the refrigerator.

Jessica breezed in through the doorway, gasping at the sight of him. "What happened to you?"

He looked to Claire, wondering what she'd told everyone.

"He tripped," she lied smoothly, closing the fridge door.

"And did all of that damage? Jeezo-weezo." Jess sat down across from him. "You are *really* getting old, Mac."

He grabbed a cloth napkin from the Lazy Susan centerpiece, wadded it up, and threw it at his cousin, making her giggle.

"So is Mac coming with us tonight?" Jess asked Claire, who placed his now-warmed-up cup of coffee in front of him along with a thick ham and Swiss sandwich.

He tore into the sandwich, groaning through a swallow. It'd been over twenty-four hours and a shitload of pain since he'd had something to eat.

"That depends on how he feels." Claire took the seat next to him, sipping from a bottle of Coca-Cola.

Actually he'd hoped to have some time alone with Claire. They needed to talk about his promotion opportunity without interruption. "Is there a reason you two are talking about me as if I'm not sitting here?"

Jess giggled.

Apparently not. "Where are you two going?" he asked.

While Claire looked dressed for a night on the town, Jess was wearing blue jeans, a ponytail, and an old Cleveland Browns sweatshirt her father had sent years back for Christmas. It was one of Steve Horner's yearly token of affection gifts that had continued to make Jessica think her father actually cared about her. Ruby often had complained in private that she rather would have had some of the child support Horner didn't pay than more clothes to remind her of the asshole who'd gotten her pregnant.

"The Shaft."

"With Jess?" At a bar? Had he played Rip Van Winkle and slept through five of her birthdays?

Claire nodded. "Butch is having a private party out on the patio. Drinks and food on him."

"He's celebrating a big sale in his cactus nursery business." Jess explained. "Since I work for him I get to come, too."

Mac looked over at Claire. "You're going to The Shaft dressed like that?"

"What's wrong with this?" She looked down at her outfit. "I borrowed it from Ronnie."

"Are you supposed to be undercover or something?"

She crossed her arms over her chest. "MacDonald Garner, what are you insinuating?"

"Nothing. I'm just confused by the sight of you wearing your sister's stuff." She looked clothes-catalog-model good, but he sort of preferred her in a T-shirt, blue jean shorts, and a tool belt. "Are those actual hole-in-your-ear earrings?"

She fingered the golden circle dangling from her right ear. "Yep. The real deal."

"I didn't know your ears were pierced."

"I'm not the open Do-It-Yourself book you think I am."

Between her initial un-thrilled reaction over the phone when he'd told her about his promotion opportunity that would allow her to avoid having to find a day job and now this, Mac was beginning to wonder if he understood Claire at all. After so much time apart lately, they needed to play catch up—in and out of the bedroom, his body willing and able.

"How could you not know my ears are pierced?" Claire asked. "You've kissed my ears dozens of times."

"When I'm kissing your ears, my mind is usually thinking about other places on your body."

"Ewww, gross." Jess wrinkled her lip. "Young ears are at the table, you know."

"What? You don't want to listen in on a private conversation?" Claire asked Jess, her grin taking any sting out of her words. "Any other time you have no problem eavesdropping."

"That's because you two are old news now. Everyone knows you're a couple, so there's nothing juicy and exciting about your relationship anymore."

Mac frowned. That didn't sound like a good thing. He glanced over at Claire, wondering if she felt the same way. She was sticking her tongue out at Jess.

He returned his focus to his plate, his sandwich not nearly as appealing as before. Was that why Claire avoided going home to Tucson these days? The excitement in their bedroom had flat-lined? It certainly hadn't dulled for him. Hell, most nights he missed her enough to ache a little.

He eyed her outfit again, considering her grandfather's warning months ago about her history of running away from relationships. Was she dressed to the nines tonight in hopes of finding someone new while he stayed home in his sick bed? Someone more exciting who didn't work so much overtime each day and sleep in a bed two hours away from her every weeknight?

Jesus. What in the hell was wrong with his head? He rubbed his face, wondering what that damned ER doc had given him for pain that was making him have melodramatic thoughts and stupid doubts.

"You feeling okay?" Claire asked, her forehead creased with concern.

"I'm fine." Butch was right when he had joked last night about the rocks rattling his gray matter. "What time is Butch's deal tonight?"

"Seven," Jess answered. "Claire said she might let me have a glass of wine."

"I said no such thing."

"Come on. Mom lets me drink all the time."

Mac snorted. "You're so full of crap, Jess."

"Are you up to coming with us?" Claire asked him.

With her looking like that, hell yes. "Sure. But you may need to help me get dressed for the shindig."

"What you're wearing will do just fine."

"Claire!" Deborah called from the other room.

The sound of Medusa's voice made Mac cringe.

"In the kitchen," Claire returned.

Deborah sashayed in wearing something pink and absurd as usual. "What time shall Manuel and I plan on being at Butch's for this fancy dinner of his?"

"It's not a fancy dinner, Mom. It's just a barbecue, and it's on the patio at The Shaft, not in some elegant dining room with chandeliers and a wait staff. Don't overdo it."

"Fine, I'll keep my silk in the closet then." She pinched her red lips. "Although Manuel does like to touch me more when I wear it."

"Ewww!" Claire and Jess jinxed.

Deborah tittered and flounced out.

Mac turned on Claire. "You tricked me."

"What do you mean?"

"You didn't tell me your mother would be there."

"Yeah, well you're not alone." She leaned over and kissed him on the cheek, her eyes sparkling with mischief. "I didn't tell Butch either. You think he'll change his mind about wanting to be the baby daddy when he hears the grandmother of his unborn child cackling in the night?"

Chapter Eleven

As parties went, this one was making Claire's head spin.

She frowned into the ladies room mirror at The Shaft, wondering what else could happen out on Butch's patio before the night was through. The evening had started off promising. Mother Nature had kept the cool desert-fresh breezes to a minimum while filling the night sky with sparkling starlight. But Claire's mother quickly had sent things off kilter by having too many pre-dinner drinks on an empty stomach. After Deborah's second attempt at table dancing, Claire and Manny had made a pact to secretly take turns watering down Deborah's drinks for the rest of the night.

Then there was Jessica's blood curdling shriek when she thought she had seen *El Chupacabra* under the parking lot lights, the sound of which made Deborah spill her nearly full drink in Chester's lap.

The mythical goat-blood sucking creature Jess claimed to have seen turned out to be a harmless jackrabbit with a piece of sagebrush tangled around its torso, but thanks to all of the boogeymen in Claire's life these days, it took a bit of negotiating to coax her heart down from her throat and back into her chest.

Chester proceeded to stuff wads of paper napkins down the front of his wet pants, which inspired a long string of racy jokes and lewd comments from him and Manny, every other one inappropriate for the sixteen-year-old girl and her sponge-like brain who sat at the table with them. With Deborah too full of tipsy titters to chastise the old boys, Claire stepped in with glares, pinches, and several swats. Ruby was going to be appalled by her daughter's sailor-like vernacular when she returned from South Dakota.

In the midst of the chaos, Claire tried to keep things smooth and functional in front of Butch's other guests. But putting a diaper on a pissed off porcupine would've been easier than keeping her family's crazy antics from dominating tomorrow's talk of the town. Not that she was concerned about the gossip column, she just wanted to keep flying under the radar in case some of Joe's old enemies were sneaking around looking for weak spots in her defenses.

After returning from her trip to the bathroom, she stepped out onto The Shaft's patio and scanned the crowd for Mac, finding him over by the grill where Butch was teaching Jessica how to cook burgers. A contemplative expression lined his face as he stared out into the darkened desert. Did he see something? Something attracted by the aroma of charred beef and chicken? Or was he thinking about the Humdigger mine secluded out there in the night on that hillside, its secrets waiting to be unearthed? She sure as hell was obsessed with it since coming to the conclusion it was booby-trapped.

A cool breeze blew her skirt around, spurring her to move closer to one of the kerosene patio heaters Butch had set up among the tables. Randy Travis was crooning on the patio speakers about digging up some bones. Claire had already been there and done that. She'd moved on now to burying Joe's illegally acquired treasures to keep thieving buzzards from circling.

Ronnie joined her, looking warm and comfy in her jeans and black cable-knit sweater. "You look good in that outfit." She brushed something off Claire's shoulder.

"The skirt is too long. I had to roll it up at the waist."

Claire should have stuck with jeans and a sweatshirt instead of trying to dress to impress Mac. After he'd risked his life up in that mine for her, she was out to thank him via seduction—actions speaking louder than words and all that jazz. The outfit had seemed to catch his eye initially, but judging from the frowns he kept shooting her way when he thought she wasn't paying attention, she was stumbling now that she was out of the gate.

She grabbed a bottle of Corona from the beer-filled tub in the corner of The Shaft's patio.

"We need to talk," Ronnie said, moving closer.

"If this is about Mom's current semi-drunken state, my vote is to pour her another cognac and look the other way. She's less critical when she's soused."

"Are you crazy? Butch just pulled her down off the table again while you were in the bathroom. Her latest attempt at dancing the Charleston up there could've ended with her in the ER." Ronnie dragged her gaze from their mother, who was now sitting in Manny's lap while laughing at something Chester was describing with numerous bawdy hand gestures. "She's going to have one hell of a hangover in the morning."

"I don't ever remember her letting go and getting sloshed with Dad, do you?" Manny seemed to have brought out the rowdy side in their mother.

"No," Ronnie said. "But enough about Mom; I need to talk to you about Dory Hamilton."

"Dory who?"

"Hamilton. He works for Tucson Electric Power. He drives a white Chevy pickup around Yuccaville and Jackrabbit Junction checking meters. Does that ring a bell?"

Claire took another drink of Corona, swishing it around in her mouth as she tried to remember where she'd heard that name before. Was it someone who'd come to the campground? One of Ruby's friends? Someone Mac knew?

Her gaze found Mac again; he was chuckling at something Butch was telling him, the shadows emphasizing the angles on his face. Dory had something to do with Mac, she was pretty sure of it.

Then it hit her. Sophy Wheeler's house. Mac had been with her. They'd been snooping through Sophy's place while she had been working down at her diner, the one that was now closed since she was spending her days and nights in the slammer. A Tucson Electric Power pickup had pulled into the drive that day while Claire and Mac had been back in a bedroom filled with stolen antiques. The Tucson Electric Power guy had knocked on Sophy's door, almost making Claire wet her pants. Then he'd left and they'd gotten the hell out of there, but not before finding incriminating evidence against Joe's ex-wife that had made Claire certain she was up to more than just no good.

The guy in the white pickup must have been Dory.

"Sure, I think I know who he is," Claire told Ronnie, watching Jessica flip burgers under Butch's watchful eye. "Why do you ask?"

"He's the one who called the R.V. park the other day and left that cryptic message."

That snagged Claire's full attention. "Why would this Dory Hamilton call and say some guy is coming for us?"

"You tell me."

"How should I know?"

"No, I mean you tell me *after* you find him and ask him."

"Why me?"

"Because if this is related to the Polar Bear, Dory won't try to kidnap or kill *you*."

"And he might you?"

"Well, that's what I'm afraid of."

"How did you figure out it was Dory?"

"Chester and I paid a visit to Dirty Gerties this morning."

"Are you bikini wrestling part-time now for extra cash?"

Ronnie's gaze narrowed.

"I thought I noticed mud under your fingernails earlier."

Ronnie knuckle punched her.

"Ow! I told you to stop using your bony-ass knuckles on me,

or I'm gonna wallop you upside the noggin."

"Chester knows the owner of the place. She told us Dory had been there yesterday morning and she's pretty sure he was talking on the payphone. Cherry didn't hear exactly what Dory said, but the timing is right."

"Cherry?"

"She's the owner."

"A strip club with an owner named Cherry? No way is that her real name."

"Well, I didn't check her license, but she seemed really nice and was happy to help." Ronnie wrinkled her nose. "Especially after she found out who our grandfather is."

"She knows Gramps?"

"He used to have a loyalty punch card there."

Claire made a gurgling gag noise. "I didn't need to know that about our grandfather."

"Neither did I, but you and I are in this together. We have to share and share alike."

"So we figure out where Dory Hamilton lives and pay him a visit tomorrow?"

"I thought maybe you could take Katie with you to question him."

"What happened to share and share alike?"

"You two have always played good-cop bad-cop better without me there."

She was right. Ronnie's acting sucked. "You're just a chicken shit."

"Am not."

"Are too. You're afraid you'll wind up in jail with us."

"And why will the Morgan sisters be gracing my holding cell this time?" Sheriff Harrison's deep voice made both her and Ronnie whirl around.

Grady was out of uniform. Dressed in a cream-colored shirt unbuttoned at the neck, dark blue jeans, and black cowboy boots, he looked fresh off the rack and ready to break some hearts.

One look at Ronnie's flushed-faced, slack-jawed expression told Claire exactly whose heart was on the way to the chopping block.

"Will it be more of the usual shenanigans?" he pressed, his attention focused on Ronnie with only a sparing glance in Claire's direction. "Or are you three clowns going to try a new circus act with dare devils, flaming hoops, and freak shows?"

"I actually prefer the act where a bear rides on a teeny tiny tricycle," Claire told him. "How about you, Ronnie?"

"My favorite is when monkeys dress up like rootin' tootin' cowboys and ride horses around the circle."

Claire laughed. "Cowboy monkeys? I'd love to see that."

"The ones I saw even had toy pistols." Ronnie eyed Grady up and down. "They were quite adorable but not nearly as cute as Sheriff Hardass when he's all duded up in his cowboy hat, gun belt, and shiny star."

Grady's lips twitched. "You two are already on a roll tonight, I see." He held an envelope out to Ronnie. "This is for you."

She reached for it, but he pulled it back out of reach. "But first you need to explain why my Aunt Millie is having me play delivery boy."

"That's from your Aunt Millie?" Ronnie stared at the envelope as if weighing the chances of it biting her fingers if she reached for it again.

"She sealed it shut and made me cross my heart that I wouldn't open it before I gave it to you."

Ronnie laughed.

Grady didn't. "I'm serious. Make sure you tell her it was sealed when I handed it over so that she doesn't have Greta put some old German gypsy curse on me again."

"Again?" Claire asked.

He shook his head at her. "You don't want to know. Just trust me when I tell you not to cross that crazy *Hutzel.*" He turned back to Ronnie, holding up the envelope between them. "Why is Aunt Millie sending you letters now?"

Ronnie's gaze met Claire's for several beats, making Claire wonder if Ronnie had been blabbing her mouth about one of their so-called secrets to a particular sheriff's aunt, damn it.

"Well," Ronnie licked her lips. Claire could practically see the gears turning behind her sister's eyes. "Not that it's any of your business, Sheriff, but since I don't have an email address or cellphone, it's one of the ways we communicate. I'm old fashioned that way."

The lines fanning from the corners of his eyes said plenty regarding his feelings about the level of bullshit in Ronnie's reply, but he handed her the envelope anyway.

Ronnie quickly folded it and stuffed it in her back pocket.

"Aren't you going to open it?" he asked.

"I'll save it for later."

"Why?"

Her sister's gaze darted to Claire's, which unfortunately made Grady's frown include her in its scope. "Because I want to focus on the task at hand," Ronnie told him.

"Which is what?"

"Getting you to kiss me."

Claire glanced away, grinning. Smart girl, distracting the Sheriff with her body yet again.

"In front of your sister?"

"Claire doesn't care."

"She's right. I don't care." Out of the corner of her eye, Claire saw Ronnie catch his hand and pull him toward her.

"She knows what's going on," Ronnie added.

"She does?"

"I do," Claire confirmed, focusing on Mac to give them a little privacy. He was staring out at the desert again, a frown lining his brow. She knew very well what was going on with Ronnie and Grady, but she worried her thumb over the lip of her beer bottle and wondered what was going on with Mac and that promotion.

"But Mom doesn't know." Ronnie said. "So unless you want her to find out, you'd better hurry up and kiss me. She stumbled off to the ladies room when you walked up."

"But what about—" Grady started.

"Oh, for crissake!" Claire growled, glaring over at them. "Would you two hurry up and kiss so that I can ask him about Dory?"

They obliged a little too noisily. Claire made a face and went to get another beer while they had at it. A few lusty sighs from Ronnie later, Claire had stood all that she could of their public display of affection. She cleared her throat. When that didn't separate them from their lip-lock, she poked Ronnie in the ribs. Twice. "Jeez, break it up already. This isn't a breath freshener commercial."

"Ouch. Damn it, Claire." She backed out of Grady's arms and tried to knuckle punch her again, but Claire dodged and weaved away.

Grady shook his head as if to clear away the spider webs Ronnie apparently had woven during their reenactment of a nickel peep show.

Claire gave him a moment to collect himself before asking, "Do you know Dory Hamilton? He works for Tucson Electric Power."

The Sheriff dragged his gaze from Ronnie, who was busy dabbing her lips with some gloss she'd borrowed from Jess. "Sure. Why?"

"Any reason you can think of for why he'd want to prank call Ruby's place and try to scare your girlfriend?"

"I'm not his girlfriend," Ronnie clarified, capping the lip gloss. "At least not as far as the rest of the world knows."

"Oh, I'm sorry. I forgot that you two have this deranged, half-baked non-relationship going that includes criminal acts, jail threats, and sex with bondage."

Grady turned on Ronnie. "You told Claire about *that*?"

"No, Katie did."

"Christ! Don't you three know how to keep secrets?"

"Oh, we know all about keeping secrets, Sheriff Hardass," Ronnie snapped back.

Resisting the urge to knock her sister upside the head for admitting that to the freaking Sheriff, Claire tried to cover Ronnie's faux pas with, "Nothing you or your deputies would find interesting, though."

"I'm sure you'd spike the lie detector needle with that one." He crossed his arms over his chest, looking very cop like in spite of the missing badge and gun. "What did Dory say when he called?"

"*He's coming for you*," Ronnie told him.

"How do you know it was Dory? Did he tell you his name?"

"Of course not. It was a prank call." Ronnie grabbed two beers from the cooler. "Claire did one of those call back tricks and it rang on a payphone at Dirty Gerties." She held out a beer to Grady. "Chester and I talked to the owner this morning, and she told us Dory had been there yesterday morning at the same time we received the phone call."

"Cherry Hayworth was certain about the time of day when Dory was there?"

"How do you know Cherry?" Ronnie asked, her eyes shrinking to suspicious slits.

"We go way back."

"Way back to sex?"

"Ronnie!" Claire shot her sister a keep-it-together look before appealing to the Sheriff, "I move to strike that question from the record." Claire had little doubt that Grady knew everyone in the red light district by their first names since he was in charge of patrolling it.

After taking a deep breath, Ronnie continued. "Cherry was positive. She said she heard him talking but thought nothing of it at the time. Does Dory have any history of harassment or assault or stalking?"

He drank on that, watching Ronnie as he swallowed. "I'm pretty sure his record is clean—in Cholla County anyway."

Shit-sticks. Claire scratched at her neck, grimacing up at the stars. Dory's clean record didn't help their case, and now she'd gone and alerted Grady so that if anything happened to Dory "by accident" while she was questioning him—anything like a bent-backwards pinkie finger or lightly blackened eye—she'd be at the top of the Sheriff's list of suspects.

"I guess that means we're back to square one," Claire said.

"Which is where you two need to stay," he warned. "Let me talk to Dory next week and see what I can find out."

Claire nodded, agreeing to let Grady *think* she was going to do nothing about Dory. What the Sheriff didn't know wouldn't hurt him.

"I could ask Mississippi if the FBI has anything on Dory in their files," said Ronnie.

That earned her two glares—one from Claire, who was not

thrilled to have the FBI nosing around in her business, and another from Grady.

The Sheriff spoke his objection first. "Keep the FBI out of this. They'll only make things worse."

"I don't want the Feds coming around the R.V. park," Claire added. They'd see some of the illegal treasures down in Joe's office and start sniffing around Ruby, too.

"You're both paranoid. Mississippi isn't your usual FBI asshole."

"If you believe that, sister dear, you've been drinking the FBI Kool-Aid. Let's ask Kate what she thinks of your FBI pal." Claire would bet that the mention of those three letters would turn Kate into a rabies-infected version of Mr. Hyde.

"Where is your pool-playing buddy anyway?" Grady asked, scanning the patio like he was checking for roaches.

"I don't know," Ronnie told him. "I'm not his babysitter."

"Could've fooled me." His voice was cool, but his gaze was anything but when it returned to Ronnie.

"What's that supposed to mean, Sheriff Hardass?" she challenged.

Oh God, Claire shook her head in disgust. Here they went again.

"It's pretty clear. You've been spending a lot of time with the FBI these days."

Chin raised, eyes flashing, Ronnie got in his face. "Are you in charge of my calendar now?"

His only response was clenching his jaw.

Stepping back, Claire gave her sister plenty of room in case she started swinging.

Ronnie went up on her toes. Gripping the front of Grady's shirt, she pulled him down to her nose level. "Because if you are I'd like you to replace the scheduled flyovers by the Sheriff of Cholla County with actual touch downs, maybe even an overnight layover now and then."

"Oh, man." Claire groaned. "Come on! You two have an audience here." She turned her back on them. "I can't watch."

"Overnight layover, huh?" she heard Grady ask.

"Give me a few hours for once, Sheriff, and I'll make it

worth your time."

"That's it." Claire was not sticking around to hear any more. Across the patio, Mac now lounged in a chair between Jessica and Chester, both of whom were chowing down on burgers. She needed a solid dose of level-headed normalcy, something Mac offered in spades. "I'm outta here."

Her ears would bleed if she had to listen to Ronnie make those lovey-dovey sigh sounds again. They sounded too much like what she'd heard coming from their mother recently whenever Manny got handsy, which seemed to happen more often than not when the two lovebirds were screwing around in the kitchen while Claire was working on the rec room. She'd been tempted more than once to hit herself in the head with her hammer … on purpose this time.

She was halfway across the patio when Kate rushed out The Shaft's patio doors carrying two glasses of amber colored liquid. She made a beeline for Claire, intercepting her course to Mac's side.

In the glimmering light from the tiki torches and string of lights draped around the edge of the patio, Kate's face looked less worn, the shadows under her eyes not so heavy. But her hair bun sat crooked on her head, and two of her fingers had been bandaged together since Claire had seen her only thirty minutes ago.

"Claire," Kate shoved the two drinks at her. "Take these to Mom and Manny for me."

"Damn it," Claire held the glasses away from her, frowning down at the splashes of what smelled like cognac now on Ronnie's jean jacket. "Ronnie is going to cream you for that."

"She's got bigger problems than stained clothes."

Claire's frown lifted. "What's that supposed to mean?"

"Chester told me about the prank phone call." Kate leaned forward, her eyes wide and darting. "I bet the Polar Bear hired Dory to get Ronnie all flustered. He's trying to flush her out of her hiding spot."

"She hasn't really been hiding."

Kate chewed on her lower lip. "He probably likes his victims to run." She nodded, agreeing with herself. "The thrill of the hunt, you know."

"You're insane." Claire didn't mince words.

"Big predators are into hunting down their prey."

"Seriously, Kate." Claire set the drinks down on a nearby table. "You need to stop this erratic behavior before the Sheriff or Deputy Dipshit locks you up until that baby comes out."

"You leave Deputy Dipshit to me."

Claire recoiled a little at the zealous light in her sister's eyes. It matched the manic smile that flashed over her flushed features. "You're creeping me out. Are you feeling okay?" She reached out and rested the back of her hand on Kate's forehead. She felt warm but not overheated.

Kate whacked Claire's hand away, her arm swinging like she'd been taking lessons from the monkeys in Ronnie's circus show. "I'm coming with you to interrogate Dory."

"What? No. That's a bad idea." She'd rather go alone than take this pregnant orangutan with her.

"Ronnie already told me that I could."

Damn their sister's big mouth! Claire sent a laser beam glare over her shoulder at her sister, who had disappeared for the moment along with Grady.

"We should leave right after breakfast," Kate continued. "I've found three potential addresses for a D. Hamilton within a hundred mile radius."

"Kate," Claire grasped her sister by the shoulders, forcing her to meet her gaze. Kate's left eye twitched several times. "You need to stop this madness. You're pregnant. Now go home and get some rest. You're working too hard."

"She's right," Butch concurred from over Claire's shoulder. "And that shirt is way too tight to wear while serving drinks to the crowd here tonight."

The sound of his voice had Kate bristling in an instant. "And miss out on the biggest tips of the week? I don't think you two understand how much money a baby costs. I do. I've done the math. I need to work at snagging as many tips with this," she flashed Claire and Butch a big toothy smile, "and these" she pointed both thumbs at her breasts, "as long as they still bring in cash for me. As soon as my belly starts showing, the good tips will dry up, along with my appeal to the male sex. After that, it's stretch pants and drippy boobs until the baby is born."

Claire pinched her lips together to keep from laughing at her usually cool and sophisticated little sister. Pregnancy was turning Kate into Daisy Mae Scragg, Li'l Abner's voluptuous, barefooted hillbilly woman. Dress Kate in a polka dot peasant blouse and all they'd need was a shotgun for a proper weddin'. "You mean *droopy* boobs."

"No, drippy. I've heard they can start leaking colostrum before the baby is born."

"Then what?" Butch asked.

Kate's forehead wrinkled. "After drippy boobs?"

"No, sweetheart." He was working to hold in a smile, Claire could tell. "After the good tips dry up."

Kate shrugged. "I'll have to come up with a Plan B."

"Maybe Ronnie can get you in at Dirty Gerties now that she's made friends with the owner." Claire turned to Butch. "I'm sure there're men out there who'd pay to see a pregnant stripper, right?"

"I'm going to tell Mom what you just suggested."

"I take it back," Claire said, laughing as she dodged Kate's attempts to pinch her. "I was joking."

"We'll see how hard you're laughing when you're helping pay for diapers."

"Kate, you worked at the school today," Butch said. "You need to get off your feet and let your body take a break."

"Do you realize that women in some third world countries work in fields up to the moment of delivery, pause to push out their baby, and then get back to work?"

"There will be no delivering *our* child anywhere other than a hospital, where both of you will be safe if there are any complications."

"I'm not saying I want to have this baby in a field." She sniffed. "I just want everyone to stop treating me like I'm a Fabergé egg sitting on a shelf. I don't break easily, damn it. Between Mom checking on me night and day in Gramps's Winnebago and everyone else acting like I'm some delicate flower, I'm getting fed up with things." She tucked some loose tendrils of hair up into her crooked bun. "Look, I know I'm pregnant and I have to be more careful, but that doesn't mean I need to live in a bubble."

"Fine." Butch jammed his hands in his pockets. "How about you have a seat out here with your sister and take your shift break." It was a command more than a question. "Let me get you something to eat and drink while you're at it."

"I don't need your help."

"Yes, you do, starting with better health insurance."

Kate did a doubletake. "What are you talking about?"

"I signed you up for a low deductible health insurance plan. A nurse will be stopping by the bar this coming week to give you a quick physical."

"Butch, I can barely pay for the shitty insurance with an astronomical deductible that I have. There's no way I can afford this other insurance."

"I'm paying for it."

Kate opened her mouth and then closed it when nothing came out. Tears filled her eyes instead. She turned away, dabbing at her face with her waitress apron. "Damn you, Valentine Carter. I told you I don't want your handouts."

"This isn't a handout, Kate. I got a deal on a good plan because I'm a small business owner." After holding out a chair for Kate at a nearby table, he turned to Claire. "Matter of fact, I can have up to ten employees on the plan, so I was thinking your sisters could sign up, too."

"What?" Claire asked, taking the seat next to Kate. "Why include us?"

"It's the least I can do. Since Sophy's diner closed down, my lunch crowd has tripled. I couldn't have handled it without the three of you helping me out."

"I only did it for the free beer," Claire said with a smile.

Butch squeezed her shoulder. "Right and I'm sure Ronnie is in it for the amazing pay. Think about it for now. I have a little window of time before I have to have everyone signed up." At Claire's nod, he grabbed the two glasses of cognac and told Kate, "I'll be right back with something for you to drink."

After he'd left, Kate scooted her chair closer to Claire's.

"What should I do about Butch and this insurance stuff?"

Claire shrugged. "Take it. I don't know about you, but short of marrying Mac, this is the best chance of landing decent coverage I can find."

Kate's eyes widened, locking on something over Claire's shoulder.

Claire pinched her lips together. Crap. "Mac is standing right behind me, isn't he?"

Kate nodded.

"Lord knows you wouldn't want to have to resort to marrying me for health insurance coverage." Mac leaned down and dropped a kiss on the crown of her head.

Dang it! Men needed to quit sneaking up on her. She faced Mac, grimacing. "That's not what I meant."

One of his eyebrows inched up. "And here I was holding on to that health insurance trump card, hoping to blackmail you into a trip down the aisle with me."

Crud nuts. How was she going to fix this? She opened her mouth with the hope that something brilliant would roll off her tongue.

Mac beat her to the punch. "I'm kidding, Claire," he said, but the hint of coolness in his gaze gave her doubts. "I'll be back."

"Where are you going?"

"I need to make a phone call."

"For work?"

He shook his head. "I've been thinking about that mine."

Was that why he'd been frowning out at the desert off and on for the last hour? "You mean Humdigger mine?"

"Yeah. I'll be back in a shake, Slugger."

As soon as Mac was out of earshot, Kate leaned toward Claire. "What are you going to do about Mac?"

Huh? "Well, I was originally thinking about keeping him chained down in Joe's office to use as my personal sex slave, but now he's damaged goods with that messed up shoulder."

Kate reached out and flicked Claire on the ear. "I meant about his promotion deal, you dork."

"Brat!" Claire rubbed her ear. She'd told Kate about Mac's phone call the other night when Kate had found her sitting on the porch steps in the moonlight fretting about her future. "I'm afraid."

"Afraid of how being with him day after day will change your feelings?"

"That's one way of putting it." She rested her chin on the heel of her hand. "I'm afraid that if I don't have anything to do besides sit around hour after hour and wait for Mac to come home each night, I'll turn into one of those housewives who requires antidepressant pills along with bon-bons to find her happy place."

"So what? You'd rather continue to be a handywoman at Ruby's R.V. park than travel around the country with Mac?"

"Maybe." Claire looked down at her hands: the cuts, calluses, and broken nails. "Yes."

"But you love Mac."

"I know, but what if I go with him and start hating my life? Worse, hating him? How long until I sneak out some bathroom window during one of our so-called romantic anniversary dinners and run off to Bora Bora?"

Kate grimaced. "I've heard it's really expensive there."

"Okay, some other affordable tropical island."

"Maybe you should go up to Alaska. If the oceans rise due to climate change like they're predicting, you could lose your island home." Kate pursed her lips. "I should probably make a point of taking the baby to Bora Bora before the oceans rise and it's underwater."

"Oh my God. Do you hear yourself? I'm gonna ship you to Bora Bora until the kid is born, ya nut job."

"You're the nut job. Mac is offering you the opportunity not to have to work, but you're going to turn him down because you're afraid you might get a little bored?" Kate crossed her arms over her chest. "You know what I say? Quit being a bonehead about this. Tell him to take the damned promotion. He's been working his ass off for this opportunity for years. You can find a frickin' hobby to occupy yourself while you're on the road. Hell, you like college so much, you can take classes online and get your Ph.D."

Wow. Claire sat back feeling whiplashed. "Got a little

hostility tucked up under that apron there, dear?"

"Sorry." Kate blew out a sigh. "I'm willing to fly out to Bora Bora tomorrow if you still want to ship me there. I hope they have coconut milk there, because I think this baby is making me lactose intolerant."

Claire reached across and squeezed her sister's arm. "Come on, chin up. Butch will be back any minute."

Kate sucked it up, even conjuring a smile. "Mac's going to want an answer soon, you know," she told Claire. "He deserves your honest feelings about this. Don't do like Mom did and pretend you want the future he's offering. You'll make him hate you in your old age."

"I know, I know." Claire drained the last of her drink. "I wish I could figure out how to tell him the truth without making him hate me in our *young* age."

Chapter Twelve

The quiet, steady rumble of Mabel's engine calmed the chaos that had been whirring in Claire's head all night at The Shaft. The rhythmic thump-thump of the tar strips lining the road weathered away the tension in her shoulders.

"Where are you sleeping tonight?" Mac asked as he drove over the bridge that led into the R.V. park.

The General Store's porch light hailed, a beacon in a starlit desert ocean of greasewood and prickly pear. The crunch of gravel under Mabel's tires stilled. He killed the engine. Silence filled the car, interrupted only by their breathing and the soft whispers of clothes on leather.

She stared across the front bench seat at Mac. His face was streaked with shadows, cloaking his eyes. After the noise and disruptions she had suffered through on The Shaft's patio this evening, she'd sooner spend the night sharing a bed with her soused mother and her Don Juan loverboy than deal with the worrisome weight of this damned promotion of his.

But she'd missed Mac last night … and every night over the last week when he'd been in Tucson and she'd been here. Maybe she could come up with something that would take his mind off the promotion for one more night. "Are you up for some company?"

"Depends on the company."

"I was thinking of it being me." She leaned back into Mabel's warm leather embrace. "Maybe my tool belt too." She saw him smile in the feeble light. "Maybe a little nakedness thrown into the mix."

"I like your tool belt. I like it a lot. And nakedness is always good when we're talking about you and me alone." He shifted slowly, his breath catching in pain as he turned his body toward her and leaned back against the driver's side door. "Will this be a one-woman show? Or do I get to be part of the act?"

"What about that?" She pointed at his sling. "I don't want to hurt you." She'd already done enough with her curiosity up in that mine.

"I'm bruised, Slugger. Not broken."

"Yeah?" She rested her palm on his thigh. "So you're not going to make me resort to cheesy pickup lines to get you to surrender to my whims?"

"Oh, I don't know. Maybe I should make you work for it a little." He caught her hand.

Because of his bruised body, she planned on doing almost all of the work tonight, but verbal foreplay was always fun. "Okay, let's see what I can do after a couple of beers." She thought for a second and threw out one she'd heard several times over the years. "You know what would look good on you? Me."

"Lame. You're obviously a novice."

"Really, Mr. Expert? What do you have in your arsenal?"

"Hold onto your heart, Slugger, and get ready to be wooed." He flipped her hand over and tickled her palm with his thumb. "Hey, beautiful, how about you and I go in a dark room and see what develops?"

Claire giggled and threw back, "I'm no photographer, but I can picture us together."

"Nice one. Beat this." He pulled her toward him, his mouth hovering over hers. "Your lips look lonely. Would they like to meet mine?"

"Definitely." She kissed him, taking her time reacquainting herself with his mouth. When she pulled back, she inhaled the warm spicy desert scent of his cologne, everything inside her quivering with an eagerness for more. "Is your car battery dead, Mister, because I'd like to jump you?"

That made him chuckle and reach for the door handle. "I hope you know CPR, Slugger, because you've stopped my heart."

Claire joined him at the base of the General Store's porch steps. "If you were a burger at McDonalds, you'd be McGorgeous."

His laughter rippled out over the dark desert landscape.

"That was bad. This one is worse: Did you have Lucky Charms for breakfast? Because you look magically delicious."

"Oh, God. Where did you hear that one?" She unlocked the door and led him inside. The single fluorescent nightlight Jess had left on for them bathed them in a harsh flickering light.

"Your stepfather and Chester were throwing their favorite lines back and forth one night during Euchre."

She grimaced, locked up behind them, and then spun him around so he was pinned against the door. "My lips are like Skittles. Want to taste the rainbow?"

He bent down and did just that, taking his time turning her inside out. When he pulled back, he stared down at her, his gaze intense. "Do you have a sunburn or are you always this hot?"

"Stop, drop, and roll, baby." She rubbed against him, careful of his shoulder. "You're on fire."

So was she, both with corny pickup lines her brain had soaked up over the years and with a need for him that made her whole body feel fluid and pulsing. Catching his hand, she towed him across the store and through the makeshift curtain, weaving around small buckets of drywall mud, boxes of screws, and piles of tools and sanding blocks.

"Did you sit in a pile of sugar?" he asked from behind her. "Because you have a pretty sweet ass."

She grinned over her shoulder at him. "Someone actually used that one on Kate a couple of weeks ago." She kept her voice at a whisper level in case Jess was listening in at the top of the stairwell.

"What did she do?"

"*Accidentally* dumped his drink in his lap." Claire tugged him into the bedroom and closed the door. She leaned back against it, hitting him with her best attempt at flirty eye batting.

"Is there something wrong with your eyes?" he asked.

"I think so, because I can't take them off of you."

His chest rumbled, sounding a little like Mabel. "Damn, you are full of cheesy one-liners."

"Did I win the match?"

His eyes narrowed, challenging. "I don't know about that. I was feeling a little *off* today, but you definitely turn me on."

"That's sort of lame."

"How about this one?" He cleared his throat. "Is your name Daisy? Because I have a sudden urge to plant you right here."

"Who taught you that one? Chester?"

He nodded. "Here's another of his—I know where there's a good party. They've got liquor in the front and poker in the rear."

She snickered. "Chester's the worst. He taught me this one while we were tearing apart the rec room: If you were a floorboard, I'd take out all of the nails and screw you."

"You're pretty good at imitating his voice and everything." Mac pulled on her jean jacket. "Take this off."

She shrugged out of it and peeled off her shirt while she was at it.

His breath caught as he looked down at the fancy, black lace bra Kate had let her borrow since her chest had swollen right out of it. "I'm not staring," he said, whistling quietly. "I'm just stuck in a loop."

She'd heard that one before, too, only she'd had her shirt on when that guy had tried to use it on her and had kept it on after shooing him away. "Oh, dear, let me guess," she reached out and tipped his chin up so his hazel gaze met hers. "You'd like to herd your cattle in my fertile valley?"

"May I end this sentence with a proposition?" he came back without missing a beat.

Her laugh came out low and husky, her whole body feeling light and zingy with lust. "I'm no Wilma Flintstone, baby, but I can make your Bedrock."

She wasn't sure whether his groan was meant for her or her corny pickup line. Before she could ask he followed it with a kiss. Not just any kiss, the kind that reached down into her chest and squeezed her heart.

It was getting hard to think beyond wanting him naked and inside of her. Reaching for his zipper she undid his pants. "Were you in the Boy Scouts, Mac?" She reached inside his jeans, her hands exploring, teasing. "Because you've tied my heart in a knot."

"Shut up and have your way with me, woman."

She planned to do just that, helping him shed his pants and

then his shirt from around the sling, all while backing him toward the bed and then pushing him down onto it. The sight of the phone on the nightstand reminded her of something he'd said earlier. "Who did you call earlier tonight from The Shaft?"

He hesitated, frowning up at her for a couple of seconds. "That's a new one. I don't get the pickup part of it."

"It's not a line. It's a question." She wiggled out of her skirt, tossing it onto the chair in the corner of the room. "You left to make a call, remember? Who did you call and why?"

His focus seemed to be glued to her hips. "That's not important right now." He pointed at her underwear. "Do you need help removing those?"

She ran her finger along the waistline of her panties, snapping the elastic against her skin. "Tell me who you called and why, and I'll do a trick that will knock your socks off."

He gulped visibly.

Snagging both index fingers into the elastic waistline, she shimmied the flimsy satin down her hips an inch and then paused. "That's no cheesy pickup line either."

"I called Ruby," he said so fast she almost didn't catch it.

"Why?"

"The address listed on the Humdigger mining claim was different."

"You mean Ruby's address was different?"

"No, Joe's. It's somewhere in Yuccaville."

"I don't understand."

"I needed to find out if Ruby had been with Joe when he still lived at the Yuccaville address."

Joe had lived in Yuccaville? Of course he had, she answered her own question. He'd grown up in Yuccaville according to Ruby. But for some reason Claire hadn't considered that he'd lived somewhere else in the area besides the R.V. park. "Had she lived at the other address with him?"

"No. She said when they married he brought her here to the R.V. park straight away."

"Did she know anything about the other place listed on the claim?"

He shook his head, his gaze dropping to her hips again.

"Are we going to go check out this other address?"

"*You* are not."

"Come on, Mac. Take me with you. Please?"

"No, Slugger. I'm going alone." He reached out and snagged her wrist, pulling her closer so she stood between his knees. "Now, I held up my end of the deal, so let's see this trick of yours." He reached behind her and unclasped her bra with a quick flick of his fingers. "My socks are waiting to be knocked off."

She let the bra straps slide off her shoulders. The black lace-edged cups slipped little by little down over her breasts. Down, down, down, teasing Mac with a tiny glimpse of her …

Someone pounded on the door.

Horsefeathers! She reached back and hooked her bra back on, sliding the straps back onto her shoulders. This lack-of-privacy baloney was getting old. She should have jumped Mac in Mabel's front seat when she had the chance.

Claire held her finger to her lips, shushing Mac in hopes that their silence would make their late night visitor go away.

The pounding came again, harder. "Claire, I know you're in there." Ronnie's voice sounded muffled through the wood.

"Go away. I'm trying to sleep."

The door knob twisted. "Dammit, I need to talk to you."

"I'm busy. Can't it wait until tomorrow?"

"No! This is important," Ronnie said in a slurred stage whisper through the crack at the bottom of the door. How many gin and tonics had she emptied tonight? Hadn't Grady kept an eye on her?

"Not important enough." Claire wanted to finish what she'd started with Mac.

"It's about the diamonds," her sister whispered loud enough for Sheriff Harrison to hear her clear over in Yuccaville.

Claire squeezed her eyes shut. Mac had known nothing about the diamond-filled glass eyeballs Claire and Ronnie had found last month, and she'd really wanted to keep it that way.

"Unlock the door," the blabbermouth continued, oblivious to what she'd just leaked.

"Claire?" Mac's voice sounded constricted, like his vocal

chords were locked up in surprise.

She peeked at him with one eye, cringing at the sight of his rigid jaw and pinched brow.

"What diamonds?"

* * *

Saturday, November 10th

Mac woke in the semi-darkened room to the feel of a warm body pressed against him under the sheet. Sunlight was trying its damnedest to sneak in under the pulled window shades.

He frowned up at the ceiling. He could have sworn that he'd fallen asleep last night alone in his aunt's bed. Claire had gone off to deal with her somewhat drunken sister and the so-called little diamond fiasco she'd promised to fill him in on today.

Drunken sister … His eyes widened. It was Claire snuggled into his side, wasn't it? He pulled the sheet back and breathed a sigh of relief at the sight of her brown eyes opening.

"Morning, McGorgeous." She nuzzled into his good shoulder, her hair tickling his nose.

Stroking her smooth, bare back, he breathed in the fruity scent of her favorite shampoo and enjoyed her soft curves brushing his skin. Her fingers threaded through the hair on his chest, her nails scratching downward, circling around his abdomen, and then drifting over his briefs.

"What's this?" she asked, taking a firmer hold on him as she slid her warm body up along his.

His pulse leapt. God, this was pure ecstasy … and torture. He reached down and pinched her bare bottom.

"Hey! What was that for?"

"Just making sure I'm not dreaming."

"You're awake, trust me." She slid her leg across his thighs, climbing on top of him. "Very awake," she whispered while pressing her hips into his.

Sweet Jesus! He blinked up at her, unable to process fully what was going on. Things clicked into place one at a time. Claire. Naked. Rubbing all over him. Turning him inside out.

"Slugger, what are you doing? Is this an attempt to make me forget about those diamonds?"

"Sheesh, Mac. After all of those pickup lines you hit me with last night, I'd think you'd expect to wake up next to a naked, man-starved girl."

"I never *expect* that," he shifted her weight so she fit closer against him. "But I'm always open to having any naked woman in my bed."

"Any?" She leaned down and bit the skin above his nipple, then trailed her tongue down, circling, flicking, tantalizing. "Take that back or I'll tell my mother you are only using me for sex."

"I've told you before," he groaned when her teeth scraped over him, cranking him up even higher. "Never mention your mother while we're in bed together." He stroked his thumb along the side of her breast and then palmed it, forcing all thoughts of Deborah from his brain.

Claire pushed down his briefs, sliding all over him in the process, making him writhe under her in need.

He growled in his throat. "You're doing that on purpose."

"Maybe." She bit, nibbled, and licked her way down his stomach and further, toying with him until he teetered on the edge of bliss. He hauled her playful mouth up to his, plunging his tongue inside hers, unable to get enough.

"Mac," she whispered when he came up for air. Her body hovered just out of reach, tempting him with brushes of flesh on flesh.

"What?" he gasped at another brief touch. So close.

"Take me."

"Hell, yes!"

"No, I mean take me to Joe's old house."

His gaze nailed hers. "You play dirty, Slugger."

"I know." She slid down onto him in one smooth push, making his mind reel with a burst of pleasure that would've knocked his socks off if he'd been wearing any. "But you like it dirty, Mac."

"God, Claire!" He cupped her hip with his good hand, moving under her, urging her to finish what she'd started before he went blind from yearning. "I definitely do."

She stilled suddenly, staring down at him, her eyes dark with lust. She shook her head when he tried to get her to keep moving. "Take me with you to Joe's today, Mac."

He cursed at the ceiling. He'd give her anything she wanted right now, and the temptress knew it.

"Only," he tightened his grip on her, "if you finish," he pulled her hip forward and then pushed her back while arching under her, "what you started." His left side was beginning to ache, but he didn't care. Claire surrounded him with her scent and softness, spiking his adrenaline, masking the pain.

She leaned forward, running her lips along his jaw. "You just lie back, handsome," she whispered, a husky chuckle following. "Let me bring you over to the dark side."

"I need to touch."

"So touch." She moved over him, touching him plenty. "Wanna get some coffee, hot stuff?"

He couldn't make sense of her question in the midst of her rocking his world. "What?"

"Because I like you a latte."

He gave that pickup line a thumbs down and then slid his hand up her ribs, his body's RPM redlining. "All of these curves and me with no brakes," he threw back a stupid line he'd first heard in college. Then he sank back onto the bed and let her run rampant over him until he couldn't hold back any longer, slamming deep into her, every muscle locked tight.

Several gasps from her later, when her body stopped shuddering around him, he tipped her chin up. "You are a nefarious, seductive minx."

She winked at him. "But you still love me."

After this morning, he wanted to beg her to marry him and put him out of his misery for good, but he knew better than to bring up the M word with Claire. "More than zombies love brains," he said instead, tickling her ribs.

After she'd captured his hand and stopped squirming, she asked, "It was that latte line that really pushed you over the top, wasn't it?"

He rested his head back onto the pillow, laughing up at the ceiling. "Yeah, that was the tipping point."

She slid forward and kissed his chin. "Come on, I'll make you breakfast, and then we can go check out Joe's old place."

He squinted at her. "Two can play at that blackmail game, you know."

"I know. I learned it from you."

"Me?"

"Yeah, you. Remember that morning in your shower when you blackmailed me into saying 'Yes' to going to your company's summer picnic."

"Oh, right." He grinned at the memory of her all wet and panting. "I believe your exact words were 'Yes! Yes! Oh, God, yes, Mac!' There might have been one more 'yes' in there that I'm forgetting." He stroked his finger down her cheek. "You were pretty excited that morning to go to the picnic with me."

"That's it, wise guy." She rolled off of him. "Get your sweet ass out of that bed and let's get moving." She grabbed a pair of underwear from a stack of clean clothes on the dresser and stepped into them. "After we get back from checking out Joe's old house, I need to rewire that other wall before Chester heads over to Dirty Gerties for Saturday night mud fights." She hooked her bra behind her back and flipped the front of it up over her chest, ruining the view. "And I told Kate I'd close for her tonight at The Shaft so she can get some rest."

"Whoa, Speed Racer. You're like a Tasmanian Devil," Mac said, slowly sitting up and lowering his feet to the floor.

She zipped up her blue jeans, grinning at him. "You didn't mind me gyrating all over you a moment ago."

"For the record, you can gyrate all over me whenever you wish, devil woman. Hand me that, please." He pointed at his overnight bag. "Want to help me take a shower?"

"Ha! I've fallen for that one before." She handed him his bag and cracked the bedroom door, making sure the coast was clear. "I'll come check on you if you're not out by the time I have breakfast ready."

"Spoilsport." He paused to sweep a kiss over her lips on the way out the door.

Twenty minutes later, he stepped into the kitchen with another one of Harley's button-up shirts in his hand—this one dark blue with little Army tanks all over it. `

Jess wrinkled her nose at him from where she sat perched on the counter. "Your chest keeps getting hairier the older you get."

"Shut up, brat," he said, holding the shirt out to Claire. "I need your hands."

"I noticed that this morning," she teased and helped him slide into the shirt, buttoning it for him. Then she gave him a plate of scrambled eggs and slabs of fried ham and joined him at the table with coffee and cream.

"Eat up, big boy." She dug into her own eggs. "Jess is going to run the store while we go to Yuccaville for supplies."

He smiled like a lovesick idiot and dug in. He couldn't help it. Morning sex and fried ham. This was the fodder of fantasies.

A half an hour later, Claire pulled his pickup to a stop in front of a two-story haunted house down a dead-end street in Yuccaville.

"That place looks like it should be on the cover of *Halloween Illustrated*," she said, shifting into park.

Mac agreed. There was nothing ornate about the place with its tall, boxy bones and weathered clapboard siding. The A-shaped roof peaked above a small, broken circle window. The door and first-floor windows were boarded up, with NO TRESPASSING spray painted in black across the dry-rotted siding, along with plenty of other spray painted graffiti. A Property Condemned sign hung crookedly on the sagging front porch rail, broken glass littered the splintered floor boards. The front yard had been taken over by scraggly weeds which poked out of the dirt. The chain link fence surrounding it was bent outward in several spots like something had been trying to push its way out.

"Is that really it?" Claire asked, leaning over him to look out the passenger side window, her hand warming his thigh.

"According to my GPS it is."

"There must be at least ten families of packrats living in there."

"Unless the snakes have moved in and taken over."

She shuddered at that notion, her hand tightening on his leg. "I keep expecting to see some shadow move in front of that attic window."

"Maybe it's covered with flies on the inside."

She chuckled. "Another Amityville Horror wannabe."

"Exactly. I suppose you want to go inside."

Her face lit up. "Can we?"

"Not today, Slugger. I need both shoulders in shape before we go in there."

Her hand crept up his thigh. "You mean you'll really sneak in there with me?"

"Yes, but you have to wait." He focused back on the house. "I'm as curious as you to see if Joe left anything else behind."

"You got it." She squeezed his leg a final time and then sat up.

"Promise?"

"Cross my heart." Shifting into gear, she pulled away from the curb. "Creepy old houses give me the heebie jeebies."

He watched the dilapidated structure disappear in his side mirror. "Yet you skip through old mines like they're fields of daisies."

"Old mines are only spooky when there is a crazy, gun-toting bitch in them." She glanced at him while turning the corner at the end of the street. "Or they're booby-trapped."

He frowned, thinking about how that ore chute had been rigged to release. What was in that mine that was worth possibly killing a trespasser?

His phone buzzed in his shirt pocket. He looked down at the text message on his phone, frowning as he read the note from the general contractor on one of his projects. "Damn."

"What is it?"

"I have to go back to the jobsite tomorrow."

"What? Why?"

"A temporary wall gave out, which caused a landslide. They had to close the road. They need to clean it up and get a new structure in place ASAP."

She was silent for several blocks. "I wish you didn't have to go."

Him too. "I wish you could come with me."

"Yeah."

"I know you don't want to talk about the promotion, Claire."

"I'm that easy to read, huh?"

"On this, yes." He looked out the window at Yuccaville's dusty streets, staring without really seeing the cars and trucks they were passing. "I'm going to need to give them an answer soon."

She sighed. "How soon?"

"This week probably."

He didn't look her way, giving her the space he figured she needed on this.

"I love you, Mac," she said, surprising him.

He wanted to reach out to her and pull her to him, but his arm was in the damned sling, so he smiled across at her instead. "It's the sex, isn't it? I wore you down with the amazing carnal fulfillment in the bedroom, didn't I?"

She giggled. "You're a funny guy."

He turned back to focusing on Yuccaville's streets, his smile slipping. Funny. Right. If only that were enough to keep her from falling out of love with him if they ended up living hours apart for the next few decades until he could retire.

Not liking the way his thoughts were headed, he changed direction. "Tell me about the diamonds."

By the time she'd finished, they were parked in front of the hardware store.

He gaped at her. "Where did you get this article Manny translated?"

"Ronnie found it online. It's from a Mexican newspaper."

"This is bad, Claire."

She grimaced. "I know."

"Like more guns and bullets coming your way bad."

"Now you see why I didn't want to get you involved."

"If you're involved, I'm involved."

She leaned her forehead on the steering wheel. "So how mad are you at me right now for this? Like no sleeping with me tonight in the same room mad? Or more like you want to pinch me a few times in frustration?"

"Pinching won't cut it. I'm going to lock you and your sister away in Ruby's basement and only let *you* out for conjugal visits. The Sheriff can deal with Ronnie."

He watched an older couple stroll out of the hardware store pushing a cart filled with a big box showing a Christmas reindeer on the front. Would his life ever be as simple as shopping for holiday yard decorations? Probably not with the Morgan sisters in the picture.

Sighing, he unhooked his sling and carefully reached out, taking her hand in his. "Claire, I'm not mad so much as I am scared shitless of losing you. I don't think you understand how nuts I am about you."

She scooted over and kissed him. "I think I do, McGorgeous." She spoke low in his ear, making his blood rush.

And just like that he saw clearly what he needed to do.

Chapter Thirteen

Yuccaville was hopping for a Saturday afternoon, as in several long-eared jackrabbits jumping around, bounding through parking lots and crisscrossing the road. The scene reminded Ronnie of Alice in Wonderland only the setting was much dustier, and the rabbits were missing suit jackets, pocket watches, and an imaginative little blonde girl running after them.

She smirked over at Katie, who sat behind the Volvo's steering wheel. Her blonde sister might not be Alice, but Katie was quite creative of late with tales of a Polar Bear, a Husky, and a thick-headed Sheriff's deputy.

Katie glanced her way, looking more frazzled than usual with the sun backlighting her. "What was the name of the diner again?"

She'd just told her the name two blocks ago. Was it just her or was Katie's hair growing wilder, sticking up here and there and everywhere like Cruella De Vil's?

The sight of The Mule Train Diner up ahead on the left snapped Ronnie back to the sole reason she'd asked Katie to bring her to Yuccaville today.

"Park up there," she told Katie, pointing out the windshield. "In that spot across the street from the diner."

"No way." Katie slowed but cruised past the parking spot. "I suck at parallel parking. I'm going up here."

Ronnie tried to see in the plate glass window of the diner as they passed, searching for a glimpse of Aunt Millie. The meeting invite Grady had brought her had said don't be late. Thanks to Katie's lollygagging in the cookie aisle at the grocery store they were almost ten minutes late already.

Katie pulled up next to the curb. Ronnie was out the door before the Volvo's tires had stopped rolling. "Hurry up, Katie."

She waited for her sister to join her before crossing the street. "We're late and Millie explicitly said not to be. Trust me we don't want to piss her off, especially after the way your last encounter went."

"Wait!" Katie stopped halfway out the car door. "You didn't say we were meeting Millie. She's that crazy tyrant with the red dingle balls on her walker who threatened to drag me into the ladies room and kill me."

"She wouldn't have killed you. Maybe just smacked you around a little. None of that matters now."

"What!?"

"You need to let that negativity go and move on with your life. Focus on the positives, like this baby."

"Who do you think you are? Richard Simmons? You go on and enjoy your *Sweatin' to the Oldies* exercising without me." Katie sat back down behind the wheel. "I'm staying right here."

"Quit being a weenie."

"You're the weenie," Katie grumbled. "That woman scares the bejeezus out of me. I'm not going in there."

"What then? You're going to sit here for the next hour?"

"No. I'll have to pee before then. You need to get back in half that time, or I'm leaving without you and you can call someone else to come fetch you. I'm sure Grady would be happy to race over and find out why you're having a secret meeting with his bully-happy aunt."

"Jeez, you're such a pain in the ass." Ronnie sighed. "Fine, keep your head low if Grady or his deputies cruise by."

"We shouldn't have come in my car if you wanted to be incognito."

"Whatever. I'll be back as soon as I can." She pointed at Katie. "Don't you dare leave me here, Kathryn Lynette." Ronnie crossed the street and after glancing in both directions to make sure there were no Cholla County Sheriff vehicles in the vicinity, she slipped inside the diner's front door.

Not much had changed since she'd been in here last. Not the pictures and paintings of mules covering the walls, not the knickknacks of the stubborn animal placed on shelves, not the tablecloths dotted with cute versions of the beasts of burden. The only thing missing was the big mule with the Sheriff's star pinned on his shirt who had sat at the same table at which his Aunt Millie now waited, her fingers tapping. Her notorious walker with the red dingle balls sat at the end of the table within reach.

"You're late," Aunt Millie greeted her with a slight scowl on her painted lips. "I told you not to keep me waiting. Time is precious when you're as old as I am."

Ronnie sat down across the table from her. She reached into her purse and grabbed a small card she'd brought along in case some feather smoothing was required. She slid it across the table for Aunt Millie to take. "Here's a little thank you for your help. I really appreciate it," she told the older woman, then glanced around again, feeling antsy. "This is a bad place to meet." Grady's sister owned the joint, and he came here for lunch.

Aunt Millie picked up the fully stamped loyalty card for a free drink from the latte stand next to the grocery store and stuffed it into the handmade bag hanging off the front of her walker. "My niece never works on Sundays and Grady already left. So go teach your grandmother how to suck eggs. I was tooling around this town long before you were even born."

"I never have understood that 'suck eggs' thing. I can't get past how gross sucking raw eggs out of the shell would be, not to mention the risk of getting salmonella."

"You're missing the point."

A young girl brought a glass of water over and set it in front of Ronnie, leaving a menu behind and a promise to return in a bit.

As soon as the waitress was out of earshot, Ronnie asked, "Why didn't you just have us meet at the library like usual?"

"Because my nephew has a spy in there keeping an eye on us now."

"He does?"

"Well, I'm not certain, but the wife of one of his deputies suddenly got a job at the main desk, and she didn't even go to college to be a librarian. Two weeks ago she was giving mani-pedis over at the Silver Curl salon. Plus her hours always seem to coincide with when we have our group meetings. I'd bet my next Social Security check she's an undercover agent."

"But why meet here? This place is like one of his lairs."

"Because he'd never expect us to meet here, so it's a safe bet."

Nowhere was a safe bet for Ronnie. Grady seemed to have Morgan sister radar. Maybe he'd planted a bug in her purse.

Aunt Millie leaned across the table and waved Ronnie close enough to smell her citrusy perfume. "You've got a problem."

Ronnie had too many problems to count. "Which one?"

"I was poking around on the internet the other day following paper trails and came across this." Aunt Millie grabbed a folded piece of paper from the bag on her walker. She pushed it across the table to Ronnie.

"What is it?"

"Read for yourself."

Ronnie took the paper and unfolded it, scanning the article … make that the obituary column. Why was she reading obituaries? She looked up at the top of the printout. "Grand Canyon State Prison, Gila Flat Complex. How do I know that prison?" she asked more to herself than Aunt Millie.

"It's the prison where they sent that woman you told me about, the one involved in that stolen artifacts deal up in your step-grandma's mine." Aunt Millie lowered her voice. "You know, the one with the diamonds stashed under her camper who your sister *didn't* kill."

"My sister didn't kill the other one. She accidentally hit her in the head with a flashlight, knocking her temporarily senseless, which resulted in her taking a fatal fall down into the mine shaft."

Aunt Millie waved her off. "Semantics." She tapped her fingernail on the paper in front of Ronnie. "This obituary here is the other woman's. I remember her name from the write up in the paper last month."

"So the other woman is dead." Why did that require a clandestine meeting?

"Not just dead. She was murdered in prison."

"What?" Ronnie frowned down at the paper, scanning the obituary. Sure enough, there it was in black and white. Not a heart attack, not a stroke. She'd been stabbed to death with some sort of shiv. Twenty-three freaking times. "Holy fuckballs!"

"Well, that's one way of putting it."

Ronnie rubbed her forehead. "What a bad way to go."

"I can think of a few worse." Aunt Millie said, like they were talking about what types of flowers to plant in her garden this year.

"But why does this mean that I have a problem?"

"Because you took the box of eyeballs from her, and I'll bet my favorite pair of support stockings that her death is directly related to those missing diamonds."

"The article!" Ronnie felt her gaze widen. She covered her mouth, a sudden wave of nausea making her gulp.

"You mean the one we found the last time you were in the library? The one written in Spanish from that newspaper in Mexico?"

Ronnie nodded.

"What about it?"

"I had it translated." Aunt Millie didn't need to know that Manny had done the translation work for her. "It's along the lines of what we thought it was, only instead of one murder, there were five. All of them were shot down in one night. The wife of one of the victims tried to stop the killer only to get shot up herself, but she lived long enough to tell the cops the guy who did it had a tattoo of a bull on his neck, and he kept demanding to know where the eyeballs were before he opened fire on her husband. The police suspected she was incoherent at the time but mentioned that if anyone saw a man with a bull tattoo on his neck to contact them immediately. There was a reward of some sort."

The concern in Aunt Millie's eyes mirrored the sudden wallop of anxiety that had Ronnie's gut churning. "Someone is hunting down those diamonds, Veronica. You have to get rid of them before they follow the trail back to you."

A breath of fresh air blew across Ronnie's back. She didn't need to turn around to see the diner's door was open, and Aunt Millie's slight jerk of surprise told her exactly who the wind had blown in.

"Hello, Grady," Aunt Millie said, smiling up at her nephew who now stood over them, a six-foot-four wall of testosterone and suspicion.

"Good afternoon, ladies," he said in his deep, gravelly voice. "What are you two up to today?"

As much as Ronnie wanted to slide the copy of the prison obituary under the table, she knew Grady was too sharp to miss that move. So she did the only thing she could think of at the moment and reached for her water glass, knocking it over so that the water spilled toward Aunt Millie.

"Oh, damn it," she stood up quick, leaning over the table to try to stop the water from reaching his aunt, blocking his view of the paper. "Grady, grab some of those napkins up by the cash register, will you?"

By the time he came back with a handful of napkins, the paper was gone, tucked away safely inside Ronnie's boot.

She winked at Aunt Millie as she soaked up the water. "Sorry about that. Your nephew makes me nervous when he stands over me like that."

Aunt Millie patted her arm. "That's okay dear. You have a definite effect on him, too."

The Sheriff grunted.

Ronnie wasn't sure what to make of that—good or bad.

After the waitress carried away the wet napkins, Grady turned to her. "Your sister wanted me to tell you to hurry up. Her bladder has about ten minutes left on it."

Darn it. That explained why Grady was here. He must have seen Katie waiting in her car and put two and two together. She should have made her sister come inside with her, the big chicken.

"She was feeling tired and wanted to wait in the car," Ronnie explained even though he didn't ask.

"Right." He shot his aunt a smirk. "Or maybe she didn't want to have another altercation with a particular intimidator."

Aunt Millie sniffed. "I'm sure I don't know what you're talking about, young man. How's your mother's bursitis these days?"

"You know better than I do. You were there yesterday." He focused his sharp gaze on Ronnie. "Sorry I had to leave last night. Did you make it home okay after the party?"

"Yes."

Last night, in the midst of some serious window steaming in the semi-privacy of his front seat, he'd gotten a call from one of his deputies requesting backup. There had been a fight outside one of the seedier bars a few blocks down from Dirty Gerties, and the deputies on duty were tied up with a domestic violence situation on the other side of town.

"Alone?" he pressed.

Of course she'd gone home alone. What? Did he think she'd jumped into someone else's lap after he'd left her standing there in The Shaft's parking lot, still burning up for more from him and only him? "What exactly are you asking me, Sheriff?"

His eyes narrowed, but he didn't clarify. "Are you working at The Shaft tonight?"

"I offered to help cover breaks if needed."

"And after that?"

"I figured I'd hang around and see if Claire needed me. She's taking over the last half of Katie's shift so she can get some rest." Ronnie crossed her arms over her chest. "Is this interrogation going anywhere, or are you just trying a new method of keeping tabs on me?"

"I'd like to take you somewhere."

"With or without handcuffs?"

His eyelids lowered, his gaze dipping to the V of her peach-colored cashmere sweater. "Which would you prefer?"

Her cheeks warmed in a blink. Oh, God, she hadn't meant it that way. She glanced across at his aunt, whose smile nearly split her face in two. "I meant are you going to take me to jail or is this a date?"

His gaze returned northward, drilling for truth. "Is there a reason I should take you to jail, Veronica?"

Damn it, this was going downhill fast, and she had diamonds to worry about ditching before someone came shooting in her direction. Without making a further fool of herself and before she screwed up and gave away her secrets to the Sheriff of Cholla County, she stood and collected her purse.

"I need to go." She squeezed Aunt Millie's hand. "It was good to catch up with you. Give the other ladies my love."

Turning to Grady, she said, "If you feel like stopping by The Shaft tonight for a drink, Sheriff, I'll be there. If jail is on your agenda, go play bloodhound somewhere else. I'm sure the girls at Dirty Gerties could point out a crook or two to warm that nasty cot in your jail cell." Like Dory Hamilton, for example, and whatever game he was playing with that phone call.

"Oh, I'll be seeing *you* tonight, Ms. Morgan."

Why did he have to make it sound so ominous?

"Fine. Leave your hat and star at home for once." She patted his chest and left before she did something stupid like tell him that she couldn't wait to see him again.

* * *

Kate slipped out The Shaft's back door, hurrying through the cold blast rolling in from the open desert and the dark shadows layering the parking lot behind the bar. Nobody saw her leave, just as nobody saw her grab the black hoodie jacket tucked away in Butch's supply room or take the keys to Ruby's old Ford from Claire's coat pocket and replace them with her Volvo keychain.

The driver's door of the pickup creaked. She slipped inside and shut the door right as a volley of sneezes hit her. Her damned allergies were acting up tonight. Must be something the wind kicked up. Digging a wad of bar napkins from her pocket, she dabbed at her drippy nose. She needed to get some real tissues; those paper thin napkins of Butch's were scratching the hell out of her upper lip. She stuffed the wad of napkins back into her coat pocket and pulled out the pink lip gloss Jess had given her last week. Short of any other lip balm, this would have to do. As she coated her chapped upper lip, she focused on the task at hand, crossing her toes this didn't go south before the night was through.

Ruby's old Ford started up with a little gas pedal pumping. Kate rolled out of the parking lot and onto U.S. Route 191 heading toward Yuccaville. At the edge of town, about a half mile before she encountered the first street light, she saw a familiar white Bronco heading her way. Hitting her blinker, she pulled off onto a dirt road and slowly bounced along it, watching in her rearview mirror. A Cholla County Sheriff's Bronco blew past on the highway, no sign of stopping. Was that Grady or one of his deputies? She couldn't tell for certain. As soon as the taillights were out of sight, Kate turned the pickup around and returned to the main drag.

She rolled into town, searching for more of Grady's crew as she cruised the streets slowly. The regular stores were all dark and shut up for the night. Only the grocery store, a two-bit bar, and the Sheriff's office had lights blaring.

Deputy Dipshit was on duty tonight along with a handful of others from Grady's troupe of monkeys. Kate knew this because she'd seen it on the Sheriff's white board earlier this week when the deputy had dragged Claire and her to jail. She'd been paying attention to several details about the Sheriff's office that night, unlike Claire, who'd been too busy yelling and cursing about the injustice of her arrest and her rights being violated.

Kate found Deputy Dipshit coming out of the mini-mart several blocks from the Sheriff's office. She turned down an alley before he caught sight of Ruby's old Ford. While she doubted he'd look twice at the pickup, she didn't want to take any chances.

He was driving a Cholla County Sheriff's cruiser tonight. No four-wheel drive for him. She followed him back to the office, staying a couple of blocks behind to be safe. He parked on the street in front of the office. She left the pickup in a dark lot adjoining an alley a block away, out of sight but within a quick sprint if needed. By the time she peeked around the corner of the alley he was already inside.

Pulling her black hood up to hide her hair and shadow her face, she waited for a car to pass and then stepped out onto the sidewalk. Luckily she made it to the front window of the Sheriff's office without being seen and peeked inside. Deputy Dipshit sat at Grady's desk with his feet up, staring down at his cellphone with a big grin. His firearm was strapped on his hip, but his walkie-talkie thingie was on the desktop along with a set of car keys.

He stood up suddenly, and Kate stepped back out of sight. She counted to three and then looked inside again in time to see him grab a magazine from the drawer of one of the deputy desks and disappear through the men's room door.

Giving him to the count of thirty to get settled into his business, she moved quickly before she could chicken out. She tried the front door. It was unlocked. Slipping out of her tennis shoes, she tucked them out of sight around the side of the entryway and pushed inside the door. It buzzed, announcing her arrival.

The timeclock was now started.

Hood pulled down to shield her face, she made a beeline to Grady's desk and took a couple of the bar napkins from her pocket to hide her prints. First, she pulled the power plugs for the surveillance system, making sure all of the pretty lights on the black box sitting on the shelf behind Grady's desk went dark. It was times like this that she was thankful the Cholla County Sheriff's Department had put their tax dollars into the technology inside their vehicles instead of their office's security camera setup.

Next she opened Grady's top drawer making sure the jail cell keys were where he always kept them. Then she grabbed Deputy Dipshit's walkie-talkie and car keys and ran through the open steel door that led to the holding cells, her stocking feet silent on the concrete floor. Her blood was rushing in her ears as she zipped into the cell she and Claire had shared days ago—the one with a toilet—and lifted the corner of the musty smelling mattress. Cranking up the volume of his walkie-talkie, she tucked it under the mattress. His car keys made a little splashing sound when she tossed them into the rust-stained toilet on the other side of the cell. She slipped out and returned to the front office seconds before the bathroom door opened. She ducked behind Grady's desk, heart pounding, waiting to see if Deputy Dipshit would fall for her trap.

"Hello?" the deputy called out.

She heard something drop onto the desktop and tucked down tighter into a ball on the other side of Grady's desk. Andy Griffith would have sniffed her out in a heartbeat, but Deputy Dipshit seemed to lean toward the Barney Fife side of the law enforcement spectrum.

"Who's here? Riley is that you?"

As if on cue his walkie-talkie crackled and broadcast from the jail cell, spewing something about a possible hit and run over on Dragoon Drive.

His footfalls clapped on the concrete floor, heading back toward the cell. She did a quick look-see over the top of Grady's desk. The deputy was standing in front of the open jail cell door, scratching his head.

Katie rose onto her haunches and inched around the front of Grady's desk, still hidden from view but able to lean out and see the deputy.

His back was to her as he stepped inside the jail cell.

This was it.

She gulped, taking a shaky breath.

If she were going to make her move, she had to do it now.

Don't do it, a rational voice said in her head. *Go back to the bar and forget about this craziness.*

Kate looked over at the front door. She could make it out without Deputy Dipshit even knowing she'd been there. No harm done, no fouls made. Only keys in the bottom of a stained toilet bowl.

"Riley," the deputy called from the cell, "if this is another one of your practical jokes, after I kick your ass I'm going to tell your girlfriend what you did with that skanky slut last month out behind Dirty Gerties."

Skanky slut? Nice mouth. It was time for a lesson on humiliation for the dickhead.

Standing, she moved to the edge of the doorway leading to the cells, peering around the jamb.

The deputy was looking out the dirt smeared cell window. He pounded on the glass at whatever he saw in the alley behind the jail. All Kate had ever seen out there were ravens, rats, and feral looking cats.

"Get out of that garbage can, mutt!" the deputy hollered and pounded on the glass again. "Or I'll come out there and shoot your mangy ass." He pulled his gun from his holster, his focus still out the window.

Kate's feet were sprinting down the short hall toward the jail cell before she realized what she was doing. She watched her hand snake out and push the door. It swung silently, the hinges well-greased just as she remembered.

The deputy pounded on the window again, using the butt of his firearm this time. The sharp rapping sound along with his curses gave her the noise distraction she needed to close the cell door without his hearing it click shut.

She'd made it back out to the front office and hidden behind the doorjamb before his pounding and shouts stopped. As much as she wanted to wait there to hear his reaction to finding out he was locked in his own cell, she didn't dawdle. She'd left him his walkie-talkie so he could call for help. How long until his deputy buddies showed up to free him depended on his pride.

She rushed outside knowing the door's buzzer would start the realization process for the deputy. Grabbing her tennis shoes, she took off at a crouch, staying down until she was well past the Sheriff's office front windows. Then she hustled to the alley like the devil was on her tail. She paused long enough to slip on her shoes.

With mad cackles of laughter threatening to roll off her tongue and echo through the brick-walled alley, she made a mad dash to Ruby's old Ford. Her getaway truck rumbled to life with a couple more pumps of the gas pedal.

"Let's see how well you keep your eye on me from jail, Deputy Dipshit."

A giggle escaped as she pulled out into the alley and headed east toward The Rowdy Coyote Motel.

Chapter Fourteen

Ronnie sat back in Butch's chair, blinking in the low light from the desk lamp. His office cocooned her with its dark green walls, soft leather furniture, and fancy stereo piping classic rock via satellite radio. The spicy remnants of his cologne absorbed by the leather, along with the fresh air blowing in through the circulation system, kept the smell of fried food and sweaty bodies from trickling into his man cave.

She stretched her arms in the air, easing the kinks out of her back. Someone knocked lightly on the door. It inched open, her sister's head poking into the room.

"Have you seen Kate?" Claire asked.

"No. I thought you told her to go home a little early." Katie had been sneezing off and on all evening. She'd claimed allergies, but Ronnie was worried she was coming down with a cold, especially with how hard she'd been pushing herself lately.

"I did." Claire held up a keychain. Ronnie recognized the Volvo emblem on it. "I found her keys in my pocket. She took Ruby's pickup."

Ronnie frowned. "Why would she do that?"

"I don't know. That's why I asked if you'd seen her. I was hoping she'd explained herself to you." Claire glanced behind her at the sound of her name. "Who? For Ronnie?" she asked, speaking to someone over her shoulder. "I'll let her know."

When Claire looked back at her, Ronnie beat her to the punch. "Grady's here."

She nodded. "You want me to send him back here or have him park at the bar for a bit?"

Ronnie needed to tell Claire what Aunt Millie had told her earlier about the woman murdered in prison, but Mac seemed to be glued to Claire's side tonight. Since he was leaving in the morning, Ronnie decided that particular bad news could wait until tomorrow.

"Send Grady back." She gathered up the papers, statements, and other bookkeeping receipts she had spread out over Butch's desk. She carried the stack over to the built-in secretary, a floor-to-ceiling half bookshelf, half desk made of dark walnut. When she closed the desk and turned, Grady's shoulders filled the doorway, his star and hat nowhere to be seen.

"Hello, Sheriff." She smoothed her silver velvet tunic over her black leggings.

"It's *Grady* tonight." He leaned against the doorframe, his gaze following her hands down over her thighs, landing on her black knee high boots. "You look nice, Veronica." His voice was deeper than usual, gruffer. Her pulse giddy-upped at the intensity barreling off of him. "I like those boots."

She liked his cowboy boots, too, along with his dark jeans, tan flannel shirt, and black wavy hair. Did he smell as good as he looked? She couldn't wait to find out. "Thanks, Grady." Her voice sounded timid as if she hadn't already done more than k-i-s-s-i-n-g with him. She cleared her throat. "I'm done here for now. Did you really want to go somewhere, or do you want to hang around, grab a table and some drinks?"

"I want to get you out of here."

What did that mean? No, never mind. Tonight she wasn't going to overanalyze his every word. She was going to let him lead the way and pretend she was just a girl hanging out with the guy on whom she had a killer crush. And if they ended up naked and sweaty somewhere all the better.

She grabbed her jacket and purse, shutting the door behind them, and followed him out front.

Her sister was filling a pitcher behind the bar. "We're going to head out," she told Claire. "You and Arlene got this covered okay?"

Claire smiled. "Sure." She pointed across the bar at a familiar face. "Mac is going to help out until Butch gets back." Glancing over Ronnie's shoulder, Claire's gaze narrowed. "Keep her out of jail, Sheriff. I'm too busy serving drinks to come to Yuccaville and spring her tonight."

He saluted Claire and then caught Ronnie's wrist, leading her out to a Chevy pickup.

"Where's your work Sheriff's Bronco?"

"I'm off duty tonight."

"No radio even?"

"Nope." He held open the passenger side door for her, helping her up and in. A true gentleman clear down to the kiss he dropped on her knuckles before closing her door.

His manners made her feel awkward, stutter-filled, unsure of what to do with her hands. She clasped them together in her lap and waited to see what his next move would be.

He climbed behind the wheel, started up the pickup, and headed out onto 191 toward Yuccaville.

"Where are we going?"

"There's something I want to show you."

She stared out the window at the ghostly greasewood bushes they passed, a little smile playing on her mouth. "I've heard that one before."

"Not from me."

"True."

A few miles or so up the road, he made a right turn onto a gravel road. "It's not much further," he told her.

She sat in silence as the road dipped and swerved right and then left, letting the whir of the vent and the rumble of the engine soothe away her feelings of awkwardness. This was Grady. She needed to pull herself together, get her guard up, and prep mentally for his next interrogation.

In the middle of a valley painted silver by the moon with dark shadowy mountains all around, he stopped the pickup and shut off the engine. Out her window she could see a line of big cottonwoods meandering off around a hillside. Their big limbs stretched toward the moon, as if praising its luminescence.

Without a word, Grady crawled out and came around her side, helping her down. *Damn!* He did smell as good as he looked. Finger licking and back for seconds good!

"We're here," he said, leaning against the passenger door.

She looked around in the semidarkness, pulling her coat tightly around her neck. She should have worn a scarf. The spindly twigs on the greasewood bushes shivered in the breeze, clicking against each other. "Where's here?"

"My home."

She turned this way and that, searching the dark horizon but saw nothing other than the irregular lumps of flora and the mountains beyond. "Is it underground?"

"It's not built yet. We'll break ground this winter."

Ahhh. His future home. "You already own the land?"

"Yes. I've had it for years. I was saving up to be able to afford the house I want to build on it."

She soaked up the idea of Grady living out here while taking in the wide open feel, the moonlit landscape, the peacefulness of it all. "I can see why you like it here."

"Really?" He sounded surprised.

"Sure. It's easy to breathe out here."

"Some might not like the feeling of isolation."

"It's not isolation." She leaned against the pickup next to him, close enough to enjoy his cologne but without actually touching. "It's the freedom to walk out on your back porch in your underwear without worrying about the neighbors seeing you."

He chuckled. "You like to walk around in your underwear, Veronica?"

She shrugged. "Sure, when I'm alone." Then she remembered how she hadn't really been alone in her previous house thanks to the hidden cameras her ex had stashed in the most humiliating places. "Just ask the FBI. They've seen all of the damned tapes."

His hand caught hers and squeezed. "Let's leave the FBI off of tonight's agenda."

"Okay." She laced her fingers in his and squeezed back. "So, did you bring me out here to kill me and bury my body in the desert? Or did you plan to leave me out for the buzzards to peck at come morning?"

He tugged her closer, so their shoulders were touching. "Neither. Not this time at least. I wanted to show you all of this." He waved his free hand in front of him.

His dream? Why? She was too old and realistic to believe it

had anything to do with romantic notions of her joining him here with matching front porch rocking chairs.

"It's beautiful. I'd like to see what it looks like in the daytime."

"I also wanted to explain why I've been trying to keep my distance from you."

Ah ha! So it wasn't her imagination. She wanted to turn and look at him but resisted, giving him room to speak his piece. He'd obviously brought her out here under the protection of darkness to have this discussion.

She pulled her hand from his and shoved both her hands in her pockets, drawing her coat tighter around her.

"Are you cold?" he asked. "Do you want to sit inside the truck?"

"No." She glanced at him. If he were going to be honest, so would she. "I'm just bracing for what comes next." She had no inkling of how badly this talk might end. Had he brought her out here to dump her? Out here where her shouts and mad yells wouldn't be heard? Wait, were they even enough of a couple for her to be dumped?

"Fair enough," he said and frowned out at the valley. "What do you know about my past?"

Only that his ex-wife had royally fucked him over by pretending the baby she carried was his until it was born and paid for, and then the tramp had run off with the real father. That kind of betrayal was like being run down by a Mack truck, and then backed over before being slammed into again.

However, that inside information had come from his Aunt Millie with a promise from Ronnie to keep her mouth shut about it. So she would, but she didn't want to outright lie when he was in a sharing mood. "A lot less than you know about my past thanks to my piece of shit ex-husband."

"Right." She heard him take a deep breath. "How about we even the score."

He spilled his sordid tale of squashed dreams, heart-wrenching deceit, and broken pride. His story played out similar to Aunt Millie's, only with a throat thickening dose of anger and self-disgust that made Ronnie's chest ache.

When he finished, she turned and wrapped her arms around his waist, resting her forehead against his sternum. "I'm sorry," she whispered, wishing she had a magic potion that would fill the crack in his heart.

He pulled her closer. "I'm not."

That made her look up. His face was heavily shadowed, the moon lighting his cheekbones and forehead. "You aren't?"

"No. She opened my eyes about a few things."

"Such as?"

"I'm a public figure."

"You mean as the Sheriff of Cholla County?"

"Well, at that time I hadn't been elected Sheriff yet, but I'd been busting my ass while climbing the ladder." He stood up a little straighter against the pickup, repositioning her so her boots fit between his. "Until then, I didn't realize what being a public figure meant. After Elizabeth left me, everyone in town, and I mean *everyone*, knew all about what she had done. Hell, half of them knew far more than me. I'd been so caught up in my job, I hadn't been paying very close attention to my wife's whereabouts on nights I worked late."

In other words, public figure equated public humiliation for him, as in strangers witnessing his personal life imploding. Ronnie knew all about that thanks to the FBI's determination to break her pride with R-rated films in which she was the sole star. While the local yokels hadn't seen Grady in the shower or touching himself in the privacy of his own damned bedroom, the public shame was pretty much the same.

"After some time had passed," he continued, "the thrill of airing my dirty laundry faded for folks and the focus moved onto someone else's screw-ups. I kept my head down and worked like hell, eventually getting elected Sheriff. Since that day when I stepped into an empty house and found the letter Elizabeth left for me, I've been determined to keep my personal life uneventful. Boring even. I've avoided romantic entanglements and taken care of my," he cleared his throat, "uh … personal needs elsewhere, far away from this county and the busybodies and gossipmongers in it."

"Personal needs, huh?" Ronnie smiled up at him. "So you are

human after all. And here I'd figured you to have a rusted tin heart in here." She knocked on his chest.

"More human than you know." He leaned down and kissed her, pulling away long before she was ready. "For years I'd been existing. Going to work each day, doing my best to keep the law in this county, and heading home to an empty house every night. I bought this land a couple of years after Elizabeth left, deciding that if this was how I'd be living the rest of my life, then I'd at least make the coming home part less dismal."

She could see him with a big dog following him around out here, happy for pats on the head and scratches behind the ears now and then. Or was that her she was thinking of, not a dog? With kisses and caresses instead of pats and scratches?

No, she blinked that idea away. This was his dream. He wasn't handing out invitations to live with him, just giving her a view from the visitor's center window.

Grady touched her chin. "Then one day, I pulled a woman over for speeding and she tried to bribe her way out of a ticket with fake jewelry."

"But it was really good fake jewelry," she insisted. "Ask your aunt."

"And now that same woman has hooked up with my aunt, a fellow borderline criminal."

Ronnie chuckled. "Your Aunt Millie is an amazing lady."

"You would say that, being you're a Morgan sister."

"What is that supposed to mean?" She played dumb, pretty sure she knew exactly what that meant in his eyes and grinned with pride at being part of the family.

Leaning closer, he threaded his fingers through her hair, his mouth hovering over hers. "From the first time I met you, Veronica, you have been cruising just outside of the law."

He was taking too long to kiss her. "What's wrong with that?" she whispered against his lips and then went up on her toes, making the connection for him. Her hands crept up his shoulders, holding on for dear life as his tongue met hers and then took over, leaving her tingling when he was finished.

His uneven breath matched hers. "It's where you and your sisters seem to be most comfortable."

"That's not exactly true," she tugged his shirt from his jeans, seeking the warmth of his skin.

"Really?" He gasped at the touch of her cold fingers on his bare stomach but pulled her even closer, sheltering her from the chilly breezes. "Then why don't you tell me what you're hiding."

She hesitated.

"See, that's exactly what I'm talking about." He stole another kiss, lighting fires all over her. "You and my aunt are up to something. Your sisters are probably involved, too. But you won't fess up because of the badge I wear."

It had more to do with not wanting to end up back in a room with a spotlight shining in her eyes and a pack of FBI ass-clowns circling her. Or worse, having someone she loved winding up hurt or even dead due to her past bad decisions—marrying Lyle the crook, for example, or taking those diamond-filled eyeballs.

She leaned back so she could meet his gaze. "Have you considered that sometimes I keep secrets to protect rather than conceal?"

"You're withholding this business with my aunt from me in order to protect someone?"

"Yes."

His forehead wrinkled. "Who? Your family?"

"And you."

"Me? You're protecting me?" When she nodded, he pressed, "From whom?"

"If I told you that, I wouldn't be protecting you, would I?"

He stilled under her touch, his muscles tightening. "Veronica, if what you're withholding could endanger your family and me, it also puts my aunt at risk."

"I know."

"Tell me what it is."

She chewed on her lower lip, debating laying her troubles on his capable shoulders. But then she thought of Claire and what her sister would do to her if she found out Ronnie had spilled their troubles to the cops. What that might mean for the future of the R.V. park with the stolen goods stashed here and there. At the least Claire would stop talking to her. At the most Claire would give her a reverse Mohawk and figure out a way to make

Ronnie spend the rest of her life taking care of their mother.

"I can't."

He swore at the moon. "Why must I be hung up on a woman who hates my job and rides roughshod all over the law?"

Hung up, he said? How hung up were they talking? Hung up as in thinking about her day and night, wondering where she was, who she was with, and when he'd get to see her again? She knew plenty about being hung up.

"You don't understand," she told him.

"You're right, I don't. But what I do understand is that you're scared enough to get chummy with the FBI now for extra protection, and that makes me want to walk around carrying a big stick, practicing my swing."

"I appreciate that," she said honestly, thinking about how twenty-three stabs with a shiv would feel. Not to mention the bloodshed that had happened across the border. "More than you know."

He tucked her under his chin, her ear pressed to his heart. "I hate that you've made a new friend."

"You mean Mississippi?"

"Uh-huh. What kind of a name is that?"

"It's a family thing. Are you afraid I'll give him information and leave you out of the loop?"

"No. I'm afraid he'll talk you into spending the night in his bed for your protection."

"You're jealous?" She kissed the underside of his taut jaw. "That's nice. Nobody has been jealous at the thought of me with another man since long before I was married."

"It is not *nice*, Veronica. It's gut-twisting, and it makes me want to drag you by the hair back to my cave." He ran his hands down her sides, spanning her hips. "And then you wear something like this."

"What's wrong with my outfit?" It wasn't low cut or tight or showing too much skin or any of the other complaints he'd made about her choice of clothing in the past.

His hands moved up to her shoulders, holding her out at arm's length suddenly. "I want to see you."

She looked down over herself, then back up at him. "You are

seeing me." Well, it was a tad dark. Hold on, did he mean he wanted to see her, as in sans clothes?

"I mean officially." When she stared at him, unsure of what he was getting at, he added, "In public."

Oh, that kind of seeing. Her heart started breakdancing in her chest, but she cut the music before it had a chance to really get bouncing and flopping. Judging from the odd tone in his voice, something wasn't quite as it seemed. "Why do I detect a 'but' in there?"

"People will talk. They'll dig into your private life and gossip behind your back."

She let out a brittle laugh. "You're forgetting that once upon a time, before I became a notorious Morgan sister, I used to be a high-society wife. You have no idea how sharp the claws on those rich bitches can be."

"Some people might make a spectacle of our relationship," he added.

"That might be more of a problem for you than me. I'm a stranger here, and frankly, after the hell Lyle put me through, I could give a flying fuck what any Chatty Cathies have to say about me making whoopee with the Sheriff, especially when I supposedly have hired killers gunning for me."

His head cocked to the side. "Did you really just say 'making whoopee'? Have you been watching *Hee-Haw* on late-night T.V.?"

"More like *The Benny Hill Show*, it's one of Chester's favorites." Ronnie raised her eyebrows. "Tell me the truth, Sheriff? How do you feel about what your deputies and the residents of Cholla County might say when they find out you're dating me—the ex-wife of a known felon and a member of the notorious Morgan Sisters?"

Grady's cellphone rang from his pants pocket.

"Saved by the bell," she said.

"Hold that thought." He pulled the phone out and frowned down at the screen. "I need to answer this."

"Go ahead."

"Harrison here." He listened, his frown deepening. "Come again?" After another pause, he swore and scrubbed his hand across his brow. "Christ. Fine, I'll be there within a half hour."

He hung up. "We have to go to my office."

"Now?"

"Yeah." He held the door open for her.

"I didn't do it," she said and climbed up inside.

He squeezed her knee. "I may need to interrogate you up close and personal later to be sure of that."

Rounding the front of the pickup, he joined her in the cab and took off, flying faster than before over the gravel road.

"Is everything okay?" she asked, not wanting to nose into his business after their conversation back there under the moon but curious what had him moving so fast.

He shrugged. "My deputy is in jail."

"What?"

"He's managed to lock himself in the holding cell again."

Again? Ronnie chuckled. "You need to start calling him Barney Fife."

"I've already threatened to make him carry his bullets in his pocket." He shook his head. "He thinks one of my other deputies may have pulled a prank on him. Riley loves practical jokes."

"That sounds like something Chester and Manny would do to each other."

They rode along in silence until he hit asphalt. Then he glanced her way, his face softened by the glow of the dash lights. "I don't care."

"About what?"

"I'm tired of living like a monk."

Oh, he was referring back to her question. "I can't guarantee I won't cause more trouble than I'm worth."

His laughter filled the cab. "I've already figured that into the equation."

"But I will try not to blatantly break the law."

"Like throwing litter out the window in front of me?"

"Exactly."

"Or flipping me off and calling me a no-good bastard at the top of your lungs?"

She grimaced. "I'll work on curbing my tongue, too." She turned to him. "But you'll have to make some changes, too."

"Such as?"

"Take me to dinner somewhere nice."

"Yuccaville is currently experiencing a shortage of fancy eating joints."

"It doesn't have to be fancy, just somewhere in public. I won't play the part of your tucked away mistress."

"The role of 'mistress' is out, got it." His expression grew serious. "This thing between us has to be exclusive."

"Of course." The thought of him touching and kissing another woman made her want to stroll down Main Street with guns a blazin'.

"That means no more dates with your FBI buddy."

"First, there have been no dates. Second, I'm telling you, Mississippi and I are pretending to be friends. It's all for show."

He slowed as they made it to the Yuccaville city limits. "Show or not, I don't want to relive the past and put up with the snide looks and smartass jabs about my woman sleeping with another man."

Grady's woman. She tried that on for size. It fit like a glove.

She reached across the cab and pulled his hand from the wheel, resting his palm over her heart. "I'm not Elizabeth. I won't do that to you." She knew exactly how deep infidelity cut thanks to Lyle and his lust for young blondes. "Cross my heart and hope to die."

His gaze bored into hers for a heartbeat or three, and then he looked back out at the empty road in front of them, pulling his hand away. A smile tugged at the corners of his mouth. "Quit trying to get me to touch your breast, Ms. Morgan. That's lewd and inappropriate behavior in the presence of an officer of the law."

She laughed. "Wait until you see what other debauchery I have planned for you, Sheriff."

He pulled up in front of his office and cut the engine. When she opened the door and joined him on the sidewalk, he glanced down at her. "You're sure your reputation can handle walking into the Sheriff's office voluntarily?"

"It's all part of my criminal master plan."

"That's what scares me," he said with a wink.

She followed him inside, sitting on the edge of his desk as he fished the keys from his drawer. A noise down the short hallway leading to the holding cells made her turn.

Deputy Dipshit glowered at her through the bars. "What are *you* doing here?"

"She's with me," Grady said, heading down the hall with keys jangling.

"With you?" She heard the deputy ask.

Ronnie glanced down at the floor, not quite comfortable with her new girlfriend role yet. A wadded up paper napkin lay next to the leg of Grady's desk. From where she sat, she could make out the letters "HE SHAF" in one of the folds.

What the …

She knew that napkin. An image of Katie blowing her nose into The Shaft's branded napkins and then shoving them in her pocket replayed through her thoughts.

Oh no.

I found her keys in my pocket. She took Ruby's pickup. Ronnie remembered Claire's earlier words. Her pulse picked up speed as Claire's voice continued, *That's why I asked if you'd seen her. I was hoping she'd explained herself to you.*

Surely Katie hadn't been here tonight. She'd gone home to rest. Or had she?

Glancing down the hall to make sure Grady wasn't looking, she hopped down off his desk and scooped up the napkin, catching sight of a smudge of pink lip gloss on it.

Oh hell. It was Katie's color.

Ronnie wadded the napkin up again and shoved it in her pocket. Strolling over to the Wanted posters, she pretended to read the fine print as Grady and his deputy joined her in the front office.

"What do you mean she's with you?" Deputy Dipshit asked. "Did you bring her in for questioning?"

"No." Ronnie heard the sound of Grady stuffing the keys back in his drawer. "I was attempting to take Veronica out on a date when you managed to get yourself locked in the cell again and interrupted our evening together."

Ronnie watched the deputy, curious how he'd react.

After pulling his jaw off the floor, he shook his head in surprise. Or maybe that was just a tic he had. "Oh. Wow. Gotcha." He looked over at Ronnie, checking her out from head to toe as if suddenly realizing she was human. When his beady eyes reached hers, his squint deepened for a moment. His distrust shined through crystal clear. There would be no buddying up to Deputy Dipshit it appeared.

"When you're done eyeballing my date, Deputy, could you come over here for a moment?"

Deputy Dipshit's cheeks spotted with red. He rushed over to Grady's desk. "What can I do, Sheriff?"

"Before you managed to end up locked in the jail cell, did you notice that the surveillance cameras had been disabled?" He plugged in the cord leading to a black box on the shelf behind his desk. Lights lit up the front of the box, a whirring sound coming from the camera in the corner that was aimed at the front doors.

"No, sir. I heard a noise, but then my walkie-talkie squawked back in the jail cell and distracted me."

"And where were you when someone came in?"

"In the uh …" the deputy glanced at Ronnie and he lowered his voice, "the john, sir."

It was hard not to snicker aloud.

Grady leaned over his keyboard and typed something. The computer screen came to life, lighting his face.

Ronnie's pulse picked up speed to a full gallop. *Shit!* If Katie really had been here, Grady would know within seconds that it wasn't this Riley guy who had pranked Deputy Dipshit, but a Morgan sister.

"I need to step outside for a minute," she said, struggling to breathe suddenly in the middle of the Sheriff's lair.

"Okay." Grady didn't look up from the screen thankfully, or he might have noticed that her panic was turning her blue. "I'll just be a second."

She inched toward the door, her feet wanting to flee, her brain holding them in check. She needed to know for sure if it were Katie.

Behind her, he tapped at the keyboard. "Here we go."

Ronnie peeked over her shoulder, watching, waiting for him

to look up at her and glare accusingly. This would surely change his mind about getting romantically involved with a Morgan sister.

Deputy Dipshit leaned closer. "Who is that?"

"I can't see through his black hoodie."

"It's Riley. Look at those skinny shoulders."

"Maybe." Grady didn't sound convinced.

"It's Riley." The deputy sat down on the corner of the desk. "Who else knows about the cameras and our surveillance system?"

Ronnie gulped. Maybe someone who'd been in jail recently who was mad as a hatter thanks to baby hormones flying around inside of her and who might have Revenge on the top of her To-Do list.

She pushed out the front door before Grady saw the panic on her face. She needed to talk to Claire asap. God, if she only had a cellphone. Then she remembered that there was a payphone across the street in front of the library. She jaywalked to it, fishing quarters out of her purse. She called The Shaft, counting the rings. "Come on, answer damn it."

Arlene's voice came on the line.

"Arlene, can I talk to Claire quick? It's Ronnie."

"Sure, hon'."

There was a muted scuffle and then Claire picked up. "Hello?"

"We have a big problem," Ronnie told her.

Her sister's laugh was loaded with sarcasm. "What's new?"

Ronnie glanced over her shoulder, making sure Grady hadn't come up behind her. She saw him still leaning over his desk. "I think Katie was at the Sheriff's office tonight."

"What? Why would she go there?"

"I don't know, but someone locked Deputy Dipshit in the holding cell and left him stranded without the keys." Ronnie had to wait for Claire to stop laughing to continue. "It's not funny, Claire. If Katie did this, she might have been getting him out of her way so she could do something dangerous. Something that she didn't want to be caught in the act of doing."

"Or she was just paying the deputy back for being an asshole to her. How do you know it was Kate?"

"I found a wadded up napkin on the floor from The Shaft with her lipstick on it."

"No shit."

"What if she's in trouble and needs help?"

"I don't think that's the case."

"How can you be so certain?"

"Because she's sitting back in Butch's office waiting for me."

Relief washed over Ronnie. Katie was safe and sound. Then she remembered Grady's comment while watching the video replay. "Is she wearing a black hooded sweatshirt?"

"No."

"Did she say why she borrowed the pickup keys?"

"I haven't had a chance to ask yet. She showed up about ten minutes ago all big-eyed and skittish and told me she needed to talk to me alone. But we're slammed so I haven't had a chance to find out what's up."

That didn't sound good. What had Katie gotten herself into tonight? "Keep her there." Ronnie saw Grady putting on his coat through the front window of the Sheriff's office. "I'll be back there in about twenty minutes."

"Then what?"

"We're going to find out what the hell is going on."

Chapter Fifteen

Kate paced Butch's office, wringing her hands together as she tried to make sense of what she'd seen at The Rowdy Coyote Motel. It had to be a coincidence, didn't it? Surely she couldn't have been so naïve, so obtuse not to realize things weren't as they'd seemed. Not after all this time, all the laughs shared. How could she be so stupid?

She shivered, wishing she hadn't ditched the black sweat jacket in the dumpster behind the grocery store on her way back to the safety of The Shaft. She moved over to Butch's chair, dropping into it, needing to calm down and get a grip. His ultra-comfortable chair usually worked magic on her nerves between its butter soft texture and the whiffs of his cologne.

After sitting there trying to clear her mind and focus on her breathing, she started fidgeting. Apparently the chair wasn't going to cut it tonight. She leaned forward, her head below her knees, letting the blood rush to her head.

When she sat back up and the spinning sensation stopped, an idea popped into her head. Of course!

She hurried over to Butch's built-in secretary desk, grabbed the key from its hiding spot, and unlocked the bottom drawer. Hanging folders filled it front to back. She fingered through them, looking for one in particular.

There!

She found it and pulled it out, flipping open the file, fingering through the sheets of paper. After almost dropping the file twice, she moved over to Butch's desk, leaning over the open folder as she dug through the contents.

There! She found it. Lifting up the application for employment, she scanned it, looking for a clue to explain what she'd discovered tonight.

The sound of a voice made her look over her shoulder at the door. Someone was coming.

Before she could do more than stare in panic at the folder lying wide open on the desk, the door swung open.

Butch stared at her, his face showing his surprise.

"Kate." He hesitated on the threshold, the surprised expression quickly replaced by wary eyes. "To what do I owe the pleasure of your company tonight?"

"Uhhhh," she couldn't seem to get her tongue to kick into gear. Her forehead grew warm as she floundered for firm footing on what suddenly felt like black ice.

His gaze searched her face and then lowered to the file folder splayed out on his desk. Stepping inside the room, he closed the door and leaned back against it. "What are you doing in here, Kate?"

"You're here," she managed to croak out.

Of course he was "here" being that he was standing in the very room with her, but her brain was backfiring as it tried to get rolling in this new direction. She'd been expecting Claire, maybe Gary the bartender, possibly Arlene, but not Butch. He was supposed to be at home tonight taking care of the cars he'd bought at that last auction, she'd thought.

"And so are you," he walked toward her, keeping the desk between them. "Now that we've covered that neither of us is an apparition, why don't you explain why you're in here looking through the ..." he glanced down, flipping the folder around so he could see the name on the tab: Personnel.

"I was checking to see what phone number I'd listed on my application."

"You didn't fill out an application, sweetheart." He crossed his arms over his chest. "If you'll remember, after you crashed into my pickup the second time, we came in here and you showed me how skilled you are at one-on-one communication and multitasking right over there on that couch. Then you pretty much hired yourself while I lay there trying to catch my breath."

Oh, yeah. Her body warmed at the memory of that day on his couch and many others since. Thank God the walls of his office couldn't take paparazzi pictures.

"Let's try this again. Why were you looking in the personnel folder?"

Short of making a break for the door, and she had no doubt he'd catch her on the way, she was stuck. "I was looking for Arlene's application."

His brow wrinkled. "Why?"

"I saw something tonight."

"In the bar?"

"At The Rowdy Coyote Motel in Yuccaville."

His jaw tightened. "What were you doing at a seedy motel in Yuccaville on a Saturday night?"

She stared at him, swinging back and forth like a metronome. Lie or truth. Lie or truth. Lie or truth.

"I had some business to attend to there." There, that was a truth.

"With whom?"

"A guy who came in here last week."

"Jesus, Kate." His face blanched visibly. "What's his name?"

The Polar Bear? "I don't remember, but he's from Illinois."

"You don't even know his name!?" Butch wheezed, as if she'd sucker punched him. "Why?"

"Why what?"

"Why him?"

"Because he might be the one."

"He's not 'the one,' Kate." He rubbed his hand down over his face. "I am. You just need to give me a goddamned chance to show you."

What was he talking about? He wasn't the one coming for Ronnie. She opened her mouth to ask what he meant and something clicked into place. The flash of pain behind his eyes, the tension pulling his shoulders inward, the wheeze of breath— she had a feeling they were not on the same page.

"Butch, what exactly do you think I was doing at The Rowdy Coyote tonight?"

He grimaced but didn't answer.

He didn't need to. She gasped in outrage. Stalking around the desk, she punched him in shoulder. "Valentine Carter, what sort of a woman do you think I am?"

"What am I supposed to think?" He rubbed where she'd punched. "Last night you said you'd use your chest to draw bigger tips."

"That's not even in the same arena as using my naked body!" She punched him again, this time in the gut, making him *Oof*.

"That's for thinking I prostituted myself tonight, you big dope."

"Kate, I didn't actually—"

"For Christ's sake, I'm carrying *your* child!"

He caught her wrist, stopping her from delivering a third blow aimed at his chest. "Sweetheart, stop it before you hurt your hand."

"There are plenty of ways for me to make cash other than getting paid for letting some stranger use my body for pleasure."

"I didn't say that you had—"

"You insinuated it!"

"No, I—" he growled in his throat. "Listen, I'm sorry. The notion crossed my mind before I could think it through. Jealousy is blurring things."

"There are a lot of legitimate opportunities out there," she ranted, "that have nothing to do with selling sex." She glared up at him. "How could you think so lowly of me?"

"I don't think that low of you. I just know you have this drive to make as much money as possible before the baby is born and those hormones are making you do things you wouldn't normally do and … and …" he scowled down at her, his eyes scouring her face. "Damn it, Kate! You don't talk to me anymore. How am I supposed to know what's going on in that head of yours?"

"You could try asking before you go accusing me of having sex for money!" She bared her teeth at him. "Why can't you get it through your thick skull that just because I'm not sleeping in your bed at the moment doesn't mean I'm hopping into some killer's?"

His blue eyes narrowed. "What does that mean?"

"It means I'm not a slut."

He shook his head. "Not that. What do you mean you're not sleeping in my bed *at the moment?*"

Had she let that slip out? Crap. "Well, for example, I'm not in your bed right now because we're standing in your office." She tried to dodge his question.

"No, that's not what you meant, Kate." His nostrils flared. "Is this some game you're playing with me? Some kind of twisted revenge for me telling you that I didn't want kids back before I found out you were pregnant?"

"A game?" She lowered her voice to keep the indignation that was clogging her throat from getting in the way. "You think that I'm toying with you, Valentine? You think that I'm working my ass off every day at two different jobs for fun? That I'm scraping for every single penny to amuse myself? That I'm spending each night crying alone in my grandfather's R.V. for shits and giggles at your expense?"

"I don't think any of that." He grasped her by the shoulders. "But you need to understand something."

Her chin lifted. "What?"

"I. Want. This. Baby." With each word, he pulled her closer, his gaze nailing home what he was saying.

The fervor in his eyes along with the underlying force in his tone released a flood of affection for him that doused the flames fueling Kate's anger. Her eyelids lowered to half mast, her body leaning into his, wanting his support, needing the tenderness he'd always shown her. The tension in his hands eased. His grip on her shoulders turned into caresses.

Holy cheese balls, she'd missed him. Missed being cradled in his arms. Missed his quick smiles and easy laughter, his flirting glances and heart-zinging kisses. That Winnebago was so damned lonely as she lay there night after night, thinking about him, pretending he was there next to her.

"I believe you, Butch," she whispered and meant it. Her baby would have a loving father. The full realization that she wouldn't have to raise their child on her own made her head float.

His sigh of relief wafted over her face. "Kate, I want y—"

"Katie!" Ronnie burst into the office, freezing at the sight of her and Butch. "Oh! I'm sorry. I didn't realize that you were … that Butch was … Wait, are you two back together?"

Claire raced into the room after Ronnie, her focus on

shutting and locking the door behind her. "Okay, the coast is clear." She turned around and her eyes widened. "Butch! I didn't see you come in."

Butch looked down at Kate. "Do you three have family get-togethers in here often, or is this a special meeting called to discuss Kate's trip to The Rowdy Coyote tonight?"

Ronnie shot a worried frown from Kate to Claire. When she focused on Butch, she had her poker face in place. "What did Katie tell you?"

He stepped back from Kate and rounded his desk, lowering himself into his chair. It creaked as he leaned back, his gaze assessing the three of them one at a time before returning to Ronnie. "Why do I feel like I've stepped into an old episode of *Charlie's Angels?*" He aimed a smirk at Kate. "We just need you three to dress in polyester jumpsuits and then 'Charlie' will call to tell us who the bad guys are."

"I already know who the bad guys are, *Mr. Bosley.*" Well, only one of them for sure but possibly two after tonight.

"He went by just 'Bosley,' Kate," Claire, the television know-it-all, cut in. She pointed at Butch. "You need to corral Farrah Fawcett here. I'm tired of being the sole wrangler in this rodeo."

"I do not need to be corralled, damn it. I'm telling you, that guy is the Polar Bear."

"What makes you so sure?" Claire shot back.

"I paid a visit to the Polar Bear's motel room tonight."

Ronnie and Claire glared at her.

"Oh, stop looking at me like that, both of you."

"Who's this Polar Bear guy?" Butch asked. "And why is Kate stalking him and calling him a 'killer'?"

She'd called him a killer in front of Butch? Then she remembered her heated outburst. Damn, she needed to get better at controlling her tongue around him.

"I'm not stalking him," she told Butch. Okay, maybe just a little but with sort-of good intentions.

"Katie, are you out of your mind?" Ronnie jammed her hands on her hips. "Do you realize how dangerous that is?"

"Of course I do," she snapped back. "I may be blonde, but I have a higher IQ than both of you."

"Jeez, Kate," Claire said. "How many times do you have to go to jail this month to get it through your higher IQ brain to stay away from that motel? Deputy Dipshit's drooling at the chance to throw one of us in that cell again."

Ronnie snorted. "Oh, little Miss Brainy made sure her ass was covered on that front, didn't you?"

Crap. Ronnie knew about Deputy Dipshit and the jail cell.

"How do you ..." she started and then remembered Butch was sitting behind his desk, listening to every word. Since he was good friends with the Sheriff, she didn't want to spill the beans about locking up the deputy tonight. "Never mind."

"I can't believe the size of your *cojones* lately," Claire said to her. "Or maybe all of your screws have come loose at once."

Butch chuckled.

Claire's focus shifted to him. "What are you laughing at, Carter? This is partly your fault."

"He had nothing to do with what I did," Kate defended.

"That's not entirely true," he admitted.

She whirled around. "What do you mean?"

His grimace was back. "There's something about Carter babies that you should know."

"What?"

"They make women a little crazy."

"A little?" Claire scoffed, leaning against the door. "At this rate, she'll be locked up in a sanitarium by the end of her second trimester."

"What do you mean crazy?" Kate pressed.

"Our family has a history of perfectly normal women becoming a tad mentally unstable during pregnancy."

"You're kidding."

"Yeah, I am. It's more like they go completely nuts." He reached across the desk and took her hand, squeezing it gently. "But don't worry. It goes away after the baby is born."

"No way," she said. That sounded like something she'd see on one of those crazy Mexican soap operas Manny liked to watch.

He nodded, dead serious.

"That's over six months away!" Kate tugged her hand from

his and then paced the room.

"At least we know what we're dealing with now when it comes to you," Ronnie said, trying to cheer her up. "Maybe we can find ways to help you fight the urges to do something madcap when they hit."

"Like lock her in Ruby's basement," Claire suggested.

"I'll lock you in the men's bathroom with Chester after feeding him a #10 sized can of *chili con carne*."

"That might not work," Butch said, leaning forward, resting his elbows on the desk. When Kate and her sisters all looked at him, he added, "I mean the part about finding ways to deal with Kate's temporary insanity when it hits."

"Why not?" Ronnie asked.

"With my mom and sister-in-law, things got worse further along."

Kate's belly fluttered in apprehension. Or maybe it was early palpitations from the baby who was apparently engineering the crazy train flying off the rails inside her. "What do you mean 'worse'?"

He hesitated.

"Valentine," Kate circled his desk, standing over him with fists clenched. "What's going to happen to me?"

After a glance down at her hands, he looked up at her cringing. "Let's just say I'm glad your sister is sleeping with the Sheriff."

* * *

Sunday, November 11th

"There ain't no good in an evil hearted woman," Chester told Claire the next morning as he fished wire through the rec room's ceiling to her.

With a whole week left until Gramps and Ruby returned, Claire had decided to take the time to install retrofit can lights in place of the fluorescents throughout the room. The constant buzzing noise coming from the bulbs was making her eye twitch. Then again the twitch could be the result of inhaling too much of

Chester's icy-fresh Aqua Velva cologne over the last week of working with him day after day.

"I'm not evil." She frowned down at Chester from her perch high on the ladder while her hand poked through the hole she'd cut out of the ceiling. "I'm just headstrong, ask Gramps. And you stole that line from Johnny Cash and Waylon Jennings."

"I don't need to ask Ford. He's going to come home and see the mess you've made in here and call you all kinds of names, including 'headstrong.' Can you feel the wire?"

She felt for the cable. "No, not yet." She glanced around the messy room. It was drywalled, mudded, and sanded smooth, ready for the first coat of primer. "It'll be done by the time they get home."

She hoped so, anyway. Her plan was to present a finished room to Gramps and Ruby, dry paint, new flooring, and warm lighting. It would be her belated wedding gift to them. Although she wasn't sure it qualified technically as a gift since she'd paid for part of the supplies with the credit card Gramps had left behind.

Something bumped her wrist. "Got it," she told him and grabbed the wire, pulling it through. "That's one. Five to go."

She climbed down the ladder and positioned it under the next hole. Chester took the other ladder he was using and set it up where she'd just been. He cut a length of wire and started up his ladder with it.

"I learned something last night," he told her, shoving the wire through the hole and aiming it her way.

"Oh, yeah? Did one of the girls at Dirty Gerties teach you the half nelson in the mud pit?" She'd already heard all about the jiggling and bouncing fun he'd had over at the strip club during their breakfast of reheated coffee, toaster waffles, and the last of the brownies Ruby had made before heading north. A better breakfast for two people about to dabble with electricity she could not imagine.

"Nope. Tootsie wrangled me into a corner and used the double leg drop on me."

"Tootsie? That sounds more like the name of a floofy white Pomeranian."

"Nah, Tootsie likes to tan." He snickered. "I'll give you three guesses on how many licks it takes to get to her center and make her pop."

Claire wrinkled her nose at him. "You do remember that I'm a girl, right?"

"I'd sort of forgotten again." He wiggled his end of the wire around. "Anyway, by the time Tootsie finished, I was flat on my back and barely breathing."

Searching around in the ceiling for the wire, she asked, "Isn't the double leg drop a professional wrestling move?"

"It's professional all right," he climbed a step higher on his ladder, "but then I got my second wind. So I flipped her over and gave her the good ol' Thomas piledriver."

The piledriver was another professional move. Somebody was going to sprain a knee or crack a hip if those girls were performing those kinds of moves on golden oldies like Chester. "I thought the mud pits were for amateurs."

"Who said anything about mud? Tootsie and I were in one of Cherry's back rooms at the time. Her 'Jiffy Stiffy Special' is a fan favorite."

"Jiffy Stiffy?" Claire scowled at him. "You're making this shit up now."

"You got me." A grin split his whiskered cheeks. "I kept my piledriver in my pants last night. That was just a fishin' tale." He shook the wire in the ceiling. "Get it? Fishing?"

"You're going to get it as soon as I get down off this ladder."

"You talk tough for someone who was wearing a dress the other night."

"That was a skirt."

"I thought you were allergic to girlie clothes."

"I'm not allergic, just more comfortable in jeans and a T-shirt."

"Then what was with the fancy get-up?"

"None of your business. Just fish me this damned wire."

She didn't want to hear a rash of ribbing about dressing up for Mac, who'd left before dawn this morning with a promise to take it easy on his shoulder and to call her later when he got a chance. They hadn't cleared the air on his promotion opportunity yet. Claire had little doubt that she'd have to give him her feelings on it this week, and frankly she'd rather juggle scorpions than have that conversation.

Chester pulled the wire out, straightened it, and threaded it through the hole again. This time she felt it bump her hand first thing and pulled it through.

They waltzed with their ladders again, stepping to the next hole. Two done, four to go.

"You're lucky I went to Dirty Gerties last night," he told her as he climbed the rungs.

"Why's that?"

"Because while I was asking around about Dory Hamilton trying to get the dirt on how he's been blowing through cash like there's no tomorrow, the bozo himself showed up."

"Did I just hear you say you saw Dory Hamilton?" Ronnie shoved aside the curtain between the rec room and store. Judging from her yoga pants, torn gray sweatshirt, and bottle of water, along with her pink cheeks and windblown hair, she must have finished with her newest diabolical pastime: *running*. That was a hobby Claire was saving for when the zombie apocalypse hit.

"Aye, lassie," Chester confirmed, pushing another piece of wire through the ceiling.

Ronnie plopped down on the barstool, wiping sweat from her face with her sweatshirt. "Did you ask the jerk why he prank called us?"

"He was a little busy."

"Doing what?"

Claire rolled her eyes at Ronnie. "What do you think? Teaching the strippers how to knit their own string bikinis?"

Ronnie flipped her off. "What I meant," she said to Chester, "was did you notice anything suspicious about Dory?"

"Besides the fact that he tucks to the right?"

The wire poked Claire's palm. "He's been on this R-rated bender all morning," she told Ronnie, pulling the wire down into the room and then moving her ladder to the next hole.

"What's suspicious about tucking to that side?" Ronnie pursued.

Claire paused climbing up the ladder. "I'd advise you to take a different tack."

"I'm serious," Ronnie leaned back against the bar. "Is it a trait like liars who break eye contact during interrogations?"

"Nah," Chester said, moving his ladder. "It's more of a personal prejudice I have against right tuckers based off an asshole who stole my fiancé while I was away at boot camp."

"Did Dory do anything dubious while he was at Dirty Gerties last night?" Claire tried to steer the conversation back to the problem at hand—that phone call.

"Not so much while he was there, more like when he left."

"What do you mean?" Ronnie asked.

"He drove off in someone else's truck." Chester angled the wire through a hole.

"Whose?" Claire pushed her hand up through the cut out in the ceiling. "Tootsie's?"

"She's got too much good taste to dally with Dory." Chester pushed more wire through. "I'm ninety-nine percent sure it was Sophy's."

Claire did a doubletake. "Sophy Wheeler?"

"Yup. As in your nemesis."

"Why would Dory have Sophy's pickup?" Claire could hear the wire scratching its way closer.

"Could it be as simple as he bought it from her?" Ronnie threw out.

"Sure." Claire's fingers brushed the wire. It was through with a tug. She moved her ladder to the next to the last light.

"Or maybe not." Chester climbed down the ladder and moved it to the hole she'd just vacated. "Could be there's something else going on." He cut more wire, made a hook out of the end, and held it up. "Something fishy."

"Here we go again," Claire muttered. She caught the wire quickly this time and left it dangling for Chester.

"There seems to be a lot of fishy stuff going on these days," Ronnie said, crossing one leg over the other.

"Like what?" Chester asked from the top of his ladder.

"Last night Katie sneaked over to The Rowdy Coyote Motel and spied on the Polar Bear."

"The Polar Bear is the killer who is supposed to be coming

for you, right?" Chester asked, moving his ladder to go wire fishing once more. Claire had gotten the old goat caught up this morning on what they knew about the Polar Bear, just not the latest details from Kate's field trip last night.

Ronnie nodded at him. "She found something *fishy* in his room—Arlene's favorite hair scarf."

"Arlene the waitress?" Chester's forehead crinkled up. "In the Polar Bear's motel room?"

"Yep." Ronnie's leg bobbed. "Claire and I knew there was something suspicious about her from the start."

"What?!" Claire stopped mid-climb to gape at her sister. "I'm the one who kept warning you and Kate to be careful about what you said in front of her, and you guys thought I was being paranoid."

"That's not the way I remember it." Ronnie finished off the last of her water, capping her empty bottle.

"That's probably because you spent your first couple of weeks here half-schnockered on gin and tonic every night."

Ronnie stuck her tongue out at Claire.

"Is Kate sure she was in the right room?" Chester asked, sending the final length of wire through the ceiling toward Claire.

"She said she was in Room 9," Claire shoved her hand up through the ceiling cut out, "which matched his room key that she supposedly saw when he was at The Shaft."

"I still think Butch might have a point," Ronnie said.

"About what? You heard Kate, she was positive it was Arlene's scarf. She could even smell her perfume on it."

"Arlene's hair scarf could have flown out of her car one day when she got out and this guy found it and took it inside. It is made of silk."

She said "silk" as if it were one of the top five precious metals.

"Things aren't always as they seem," Ronnie said. "Take Katie's shenanigans at the Yuccaville Sheriff's office last night."

"Did she confess to locking up Deputy Dipshit?" Claire asked.

"Not yet."

Chester tsk-tsked. "That fool should have known better than

to mess with a Morgan girl."

Patting around in the ceiling, Claire looked over at Chester. "I'm not feeling anything yet. Are you wiggling it?"

"That's the same thing I overheard your mother saying to Carrera the other night through his bedroom window."

"Boo!" Ronnie said and threw her empty water bottle at Chester, who dodged it while guffawing.

Claire seconded Ronnie's bottle with a roll of electrician's tape, which bounced off Chester's shoulder.

"What's all the racket in here?" Kate asked, poking her head through the curtain.

"Well, well, well," Chester grinned. "If it isn't crazy big-nose Kate."

"My nose isn't big."

"It sure seems big to me with all the trouble I hear it's been getting you into these days."

Ronnie hopped up and grabbed Kate's arm, dragging her over to the bar. "I was about to tell Chester what happened at the Sheriff's office in Yuccaville last night."

Kate dug in her heels. "I need to go get ready for work."

"It's your day off." Ronnie pulled her sister down onto the barstool next to her. "Are you forgetting that Claire and I were standing there with Butch last night when he threatened to lock you in his office if you tried to go into the bar today?"

"Fine, I'll sit, but I don't want to talk about last night. Otherwise you could be accomplices." She looked over at Ronnie. "Especially you."

"Why me?"

"Because you found the napkin and you didn't tell Grady." Kate crossed her arms over her chest. "Where did you and Grady go last night after I left?"

Claire felt the wire scratch the back of her hand. She grabbed it and tugged it through the last light hole.

"Which time?" Ronnie asked.

"After our talk with Butch."

"Nowhere. Grady was wiped, I could tell, so I sent him home while I helped Claire close the bar."

"Where was Arlene?"

"Butch let her leave early." Claire answered while climbing down from the ladder. She pointed at the ceiling. "Okay, Mr. Electrician, it's all yours."

Chester dragged his ladder back over to the first can light hole. "Kate, where was this Polar Bear when you were searching his room?"

She shrugged. "The place was dark when I got there and his motorcycle was gone."

"I can't believe you broke into a strange man's room."

"Like I told Butch last night, there was no breaking in. The window was open a little. The screen popped off just like you showed me," she said to Claire. "I was in and out of there within a couple of minutes. No harm done, no touching anything, just a quick looksee."

That was the point where Butch had come unhinged and threatened to drag Kate up to a remote cabin in Alaska until the baby was born if she didn't stop putting herself at risk.

Claire glared at Kate. "You do understand that being pregnant means you have a baby inside of you, right? You shouldn't be doing this kind of shit."

"Not alone anyway," Ronnie said.

"Oh, get off my case both of you. I've already had several voice messages and texts from Butch this morning repeating his threat to haul me up to the frozen tundra. Excuse me for wanting to save you from a killer," she said to Ronnie. "And as for you," she pointed at Claire, "I tried to tell you this guy was trouble, but you were too busy insisting I was making something out of nothing."

"If you hens are done squawking, we should probably figure out what we're going to do next," Chester said.

"You mean about the Polar Bear or Dory?" Claire asked.

"I mean about your mother."

"What does Mom have to do with any of this?" Claire asked.

Chester pointed his wire cutters at the curtain. A shadow shifted behind it.

"Why don't you ask her," he said, "since she's been standing there listening to the three of you bicker for the last two minutes."

Chapter Sixteen

Claire's mom was on a rampage.

A weirdly happy rampage full of giggles and drunken titters. And flirting, lots of flirting with Manny as well as way too much touching.

"In fact," Claire told Mac over the phone while sitting out on the front porch steps in the dark, "I'd say Mom is downright grab-ass happy."

"Come on, Slugger. I'm eating here."

She grinned up at the starry sky. "At least I didn't tell you what she was grabbing. She made Manny blush."

"I didn't think that was possible after all of his years of chasing tail."

"Not with Chester, but apparently Manny still has some modesty left."

"He's a changed man since hooking up with your mother."

Claire had noticed that, too. "I think she's taken possession of his soul."

Mac laughed. "You and your sisters should perform an exorcism."

"No way. Then she'll come after one of us."

Deborah had already given them a royal butt-chewing earlier after eavesdropping through the curtain. Kate had taken the brunt of it, since she was with child and still considered the nearest-thing-to-perfect daughter because of her continued dabbling in the teaching profession. Although where Kate had been the golden apple in Deborah's eyes months ago, she was now a bit bruised thanks to the out of wedlock pregnancy dent on her World's Best Daughter trophy.

Lucky for Claire and Ronnie, Deborah had given up on either of them achieving great success in her lifetime. Their father on the other hand, had called recently and talked to Claire about coming to spend Christmas with his "wonderful" daughters—all three of them. Claire wasn't sure if he intended to bring his new girlfriend or not, but she was positive that as soon as her mother caught wind of this possibility, Deborah's head would explode.

"I learned something new about Humdigger mine," Mac's voice brought her back to the present.

"What?"

"The mine's previous owner was found frozen solid in a deep freezer here in Tucson a couple of weeks after the claim transfer paperwork went through."

Claire pressed the phone closer to her ear not wanting to miss a single detail. "You're kidding me."

"Nope and that's not all." She heard the sound of papers rustling from his end of the line. "According to the old news article I found on the internet, the guy who owned the freezer had a lengthy record of petty crimes starting when he was a juvie. But about six months prior to the body being found in his freezer, he turned state's witness against a smuggler who'd been busted sneaking high-end stolen goods over the Mexican border. The smuggler was convicted with a twenty-year, no-parole sentence."

"That's an odd career coincidence considering Joe's past."

"Yeah, here's another coincidence. They convicted the freezer owner and shipped him off to prison. About a year into his sentence, he was transferred. He landed in the same prison as the smuggler he helped convict."

"Let me guess," Claire said. "The freezer owner had a life-threatening injury a couple of months later."

"Not months, weeks. He somehow managed to have a barbell fall on his throat and suffocate him to death before the guards could get him to the prison infirmary."

A cool night breeze swirled over the R.V. park's drive and headed for the cottonwoods lining Jackrabbit Creek. Their leaves quivered and rattled in response.

"Shit." Claire rubbed her hand over her thigh, warming away the chills. "You think that Joe had a bigger part in this tale than just purchasing the Humdigger mine?"

"After what we've learned about Joe, I wouldn't be surprised to find out he masterminded it all out of revenge."

"You mean revenge against the freezer owner for testifying against the smuggler?"

"Maybe. The smuggler who went to prison could have been a partner of Joe's."

"Or," Claire said, an idea striking her, "maybe the smuggler paid Joe to frame the freezer owner and get him sent to prison where he could get his hands on him."

"That's another possibility," Mac said. "Here's one more—someone else paid Joe to set up the freezer owner, someone higher up the criminal chain than the smuggler."

"Like the smuggler's pimp?"

"For lack of a proper name, sure."

Claire pondered this. The depth of Joe's villainous potential reminded her of tossing a stone over the edge of the Grand Canyon. And the shit just kept getting deeper. "Criminy, Mac. Your aunt was married to this man."

"I know. We need to protect Aunt Ruby from this if possible. She already beats herself up repeatedly for not seeing his many shortcomings."

"If Joe had a hand in this," Claire had little doubt otherwise, "why did he kill the previous owner of the Humdigger mine? Did he need a body for some reason and the mine owner was in the wrong place at the right time, or was there another purpose for removing him from the equation?"

"Are you thinking that Joe may have used extortion to take possession of the mine before he offed the previous owner?"

"Sure. It would've been his version of a hostile takeover." Claire caught the faint musky scent of skunk in the air, glad Gramps's dog wasn't here to go after it and leave them both in a heap of stink again. Although with this creepy stuff going on, she wouldn't mind having Henry's bark alarm handy. "So now what?"

"We go inside the mine again," Mac said.

"How about we send in some kind of remote controlled camera instead?"

There was a pause on the other end of the line. "Why?"

"I don't want you to go back in there," she told him, her guilt weighing in with a whopping back-bending bulk. "You could get hurt again."

"Claire, I told you before, what happened up in that mine was not your fault. I should have been more careful."

"I distracted you just like you said I would."

"Stop playing the self-blame game and let's move on. After learning this story about the mine owner's death, I'm even more curious what might be in there."

"Me too," she admitted.

"Then we go back in the mine together, and I take plenty of

precautionary supplies with us to be safe."

"But not until your shoulder is healed."

"It's better already."

"Mac," she warned. "You're taking care of it, right? Doing the exercises they showed you in the hospital and not straining it harder than you should?"

"Slugger, I told you, this isn't the first time I've dislocated my shoulder. I know all about what exercises I need to be doing and when not to push it."

"I'll hold you to that." She stared out into the shadows, watching, wishing he hadn't had to go back to Tucson so soon.

"Did you get the can lights in today?" he asked.

"Yes." She massaged the crick in her neck that had developed from installing the lights. "I miss you, Mac. When are you coming back?"

"I just left this morning."

"I know. I'm pathetic and it's your fault."

His raspy laughter warmed her through the line. "It's my mastery in the bedroom, isn't it? I knew it. I've turned you into my sex slave."

She snorted in reply. "You're right, oh great sultan. I am your humble concubine."

"And here I tried to take it easy with my incredible prowess, but it's not easy to keep this tiger on a leash."

"Oh, Lord. I've created a monster."

"A *love* monster." He was chuckling before he even finished saying it. "Damn, I'm beginning to sound like Manny."

"How many beers have you had tonight, Mac?"

"None. I'm drunk on—"

"Don't say love."

He yawned. "I was going to say fatigue. It's been a long day and I'm ready to crash."

"Okay, I'll let you go, sleepyhead. I need to go inside soon anyway. With the rec room out of commission, the boys have set up the Sunday night Euchre game at the kitchen table."

"It's a little cramped in there, isn't it?"

"That's what I thought, but Chester came to the conclusion that they should've been playing in there all along. All he has to do is lean back to open the refrigerator and grab a beer. It saves him the hassle of standing up and walking."

"Well, there is that." Mac yawned again. "All right, Slugger, blow me a kiss goodnight."

She did. "Hurry up and get those sweet cheeks back here."

He hung up first, leaving her alone in the dark desert night with a sky full of stars and a smelly skunk on the loose. The moon should be rising soon, but her check on the eastern horizon found no signs of it yet.

Setting the phone on the step next to her, Claire stared up at the Milky Way painting a gauzy white swath through the black velvet sky. Stars dotted the mesmerizing view like sparkling sequins. God, she loved the nights out here in the boonies. It was one of several reasons she wasn't thrilled about Mac's promotion and the idea of traveling with him from city to city.

She'd come to realize this little R.V. park out in the middle of nowhere fit her personality like a pair of warm and fuzzy slippers, offering the breathing room she hadn't realized she wanted until now. On top of that she felt needed here, a necessary part of something important even, for the first time in her life. Though Ruby owned the place, she pretty much let Claire be her own boss, and that in itself was freeing in a way she hadn't experienced before.

Somehow in the jumble of Joe's crazy left behinds, Claire had found her happy place in life. Irony was such a practical joker. After all of the college classes she'd taken and all of the soul searching she'd done over the years, trying to figure out her purpose and station in this big fat world, she'd stumbled into it by accident in a dusty corner of Arizona. Now that she'd discovered where she needed to be for her own serenity, would she be able to give it up to follow the man she was head-over-heels for so he could live his dream?

The screen door creaked open behind her. "Claire?" Ronnie called out softly. "Are you out here?"

"I'm on the steps."

"You still on the phone?"

"No."

"Good."

The door clicked closed, followed by the light bang of the screen.

"Where's Jessica?" Ronnie asked.

"She's spending the night at her dad's place in town tonight." Claire wasn't thrilled with this plan, but earlier today Jess had called her mom and gotten permission. Then to be safe Claire had taken the phone and confirmed that Ruby was fully okay with Jess staying in her dad's motel room on a school night.

"You mean the lousy bastard doesn't have another new girlfriend sleeping over for once?"

Those had been Ruby's exact words when Claire first had gotten on the phone with her, but after a few more acidic remarks about Jess's dad, Ruby had talked about how much she was enjoying the Black Hills. She'd sounded happy, relaxed even, and was looking forward to a visit from Claire's cousin, Natalie, that evening. Go figure that a curmudgeon like Gramps could make a grown woman giggly.

"Apparently Jess's dad is between slumber party buddies," Claire told her sister.

"While I don't like the idea of Jess at that sleazy motel room for the night," Ronnie said in a hushed voice, which set off Claire's internal alarm, "I'm glad she's safely out of eavesdropping range. We need to talk about something I learned yesterday."

What had happened yesterday? Oh right, Kate had locked Deputy Dipshit in jail so she could spy over at The Rowdy Coyote Motel. "Is it something you learned from the Sheriff?"

"No, from his aunt." Ronnie lowered herself onto the step, her shoulder bumping Claire's.

"His aunt, huh? Is she teaching you some new bully tactics?"

"You need to get over that."

"Maybe I will after my suspension from the library is finished." She thought back to that humiliating moment that had started with the kickoff argument between her and one of Millie's gang members over sharing the computer. Things had escalated from verbal to physical in a pacemaker pulse or two, and before Claire knew it she was being escorted out of the library with a warning not to come back for six months. To top it off, Deborah had spent the whole drive home bitching at Claire for misbehaving in public. "You know, on second thought, maybe not. Someone needs to apologize for clocking me with her handbag. I swear she had compression socks filled with rocks in there."

"Oh jeez, you big baby! Are we on the playground in third grade again?" Ronnie pulled a piece of paper from her back pocket and handed it to Claire. "Anyway, Aunt Millie showed me this article."

Claire peered down at the paper in her hand, but the starlight wasn't cutting it. "I left my flashlight inside. What's it say?"

"The other mule-lady, the one we stole the diamonds from, is dead."

"What?"

"Someone in prison stabbed her 23 times with a shiv."

"Holy fuck," Claire whispered. "What a bad way to go."

"I know." Ronnie shivered and scooted closer to Claire, hip to hip. "To be totally honest, I'm scared."

"Why are you scared? She's dead. She can't hurt either of us anymore."

"No, but the person who had her killed can." Ronnie lowered her voice to a whisper. "Someone's going to come looking for those diamonds. I'll bet that's why she was murdered."

"What makes you think that's why she was murdered? Maybe she pissed off the leader of one of the prison gangs by refusing to give her a free pack of smokes, so they cornered her down in the laundry and taught her a lesson about respecting the boss in the hoosegow."

Ronnie stared at her for several silent seconds. "Dad let you watch way too much T.V. growing up."

"Most fiction is based on fact. It could've happened that way."

"Or not. Anyway, her murder times out right. She was killed about a week after those victims in Mexico who were brutally murdered according to that article Manny translated for us."

Claire grimaced. Ronnie had a point. There was a strong possibility that one of the victims over the border had clued the killer in on the two mules. And now a week later, the one remaining mule was dead. The question remained whether the dead lady had mentioned The Dancing Winnebagos R.V. Park before being stabbed to death. There was no way she could know it had been Ronnie and Claire who had taken the diamonds since nobody had been around at the time of the heist, but the killer might be zeroing in on the park nonetheless.

"Shit." Claire rubbed her eyes. "Where did the Sheriff take that camper those two mules were using where we found the diamonds?"

"I don't know, but I could ask Grady."

"That might make him suspicious."

"True. Grady is too sharp for his own good. What if we ask one of his deputies on the sly?"

"That's still risky. He has his crew on red alert when it comes to you, me, and Kate."

"I have an idea," Ronnie said. "Maybe his aunt could find out for us. She already knows about the diamonds, so she knows the stakes here. If she agrees, she'd only need to ask around, not really stick her neck out."

"I can't believe you blabbed to the Sheriff's aunt about the diamonds. She'll probably spill the beans to him somewhere between gobbling down their Thanksgiving turkey and licking pumpkin pie from her fork."

"I didn't blab. She spied on me while I was searching on the internet for information. You have to realize who we're dealing with here when it comes to Aunt Millie. Grady gets his eagle eyes and bloodhound nose from her." Ronnie linked her arm in Claire's. "But you should know that if Aunt Millie agrees to help, it may cost us some high quality jewelry."

"Where are we going to get jewelry? The only thing I have of any value is Grammy's ring, and I won't give that up. Do you have any pieces from Lyle that are actually real?"

"Not much, and I've already given Aunt Millie and her gang most of my high quality fake bling."

"Crap."

"When this is all over, remind me to have Lyle castrated."

"We can pick out the hedge trimmers together."

They sat in silence for a bit, staring out at the black desert, listening to the breeze rattle the cottonwood branches.

"Here's a thought," Ronnie said. "We could ask Mom for one of the necklaces or rings Dad gave her."

"You think she'd actually give up any of those pieces?"

"She might if Kate asked and claimed it would be a keepsake for the baby."

"Hmmmm." Claire considered that angle, but then something else that had been bugging her came to the surface and distracted her. "Mom is drinking too much."

"You noticed that, too, huh?"

"It's hard to miss that the Wicked Witch of the West has turned into Giggles Magoo. You should talk to her about it."

"Me? Why me?"

"Because you're the oldest. It's your job to handle this kind of family crisis crap."

"Bullshit." Ronnie chuckled. "You're being a typical middle child and pushing responsibility off onto someone else."

"Don't start psychoanalyzing me based on birth order. We all know I have my issues with authority and commitment, so let's not slap any other labels on my bumper."

"Please, I wish authority and commitment were my only hang-ups these days. I have so many labels now that you can't see my bumper anymore." Ronnie crossed her arms over her knees and rested her chin on them. "What should we do about Mom?"

"Let's start with talking to Manny. He must see it, too. He's always been a party guy but never a drunken mess night after night." Manny and Chester liked to drink, but they both knew their limit. "Maybe he has the inside scoop on what's fueling this drinking binge she's been on lately."

At any rate Claire sure hoped so. The idea of trying to peek into her mother's brain could result in her learning more deeply buried secrets. After the last mind-blowing revelation about her grandmother's cold heartedness when it came to showing her own children any affection, Claire would sooner try to slay a dragon with a Swiss army knife.

The door creaked behind them.

"Claire? Ronnie?" Kate called out. "Are you out here?"

"On the steps," Ronnie said.

"It's your turn to take on Chester and Manny," Kate said. "Mom and I lost the round."

"We'll be right there."

"Speak for yourself," Claire muttered, not looking forward to watching her drunken mother grope her new husband any more tonight ... or ever.

"What are you guys doing out here?" Kate asked, closing the door behind her. She stood behind them. "Avoiding Mom?"

"Something like that," Claire said, not wanting to get Kate involved in this diamond mess more than she already was.

"And before you ask," Ronnie looked up at their little sister, "we weren't talking about the damned Polar Bear."

"Whatever." Kate said, squeezing her butt onto the step next to Ronnie's. She leaned forward to look at both of them, her eyes glittering in the shadows. "Are you talking about Dory Hamilton? Because I think Claire and I should go looking for him tomorrow morning before my shift starts at The Shaft."

Claire let out a bark of laughter. "Butch will kill me if I take you with me."

"Butch is not the boss of me."

"And we're back to third grade." Ronnie snickered.

Kate poked her in the thigh, making Ronnie yip. "Besides, we're not doing anything dangerous, right, Claire? We're going to ask Dory a few questions and then leave. No harm, no foul."

Claire shook her head. "No way, Kate. Not with how nutso you've been lately. I'm going alone so I don't end up in jail again."

Kate huffed. "I'm going with you, or I'm going to tell Mom that you went out of your way to invite Dad and his girlfriend down here for Christmas."

"You wouldn't dare. That's not even true."

"Trust me, I'd dare."

"You better take her," Ronnie said. "If you don't, she'll probably go on her own and wind up in jail again instead of you. What's a good name for a baby born behind bars, Katie? Maybe Rocko if it's a boy? Lizzy or Bonnie for a girl?"

Claire heard Ronnie grunt.

"Would you stop poking me, you little brat," she told Kate and poked her back.

Claire leaned back on her elbows while her sisters wrestled around, bumping her now and again. What was the saying she'd heard years ago? *There's no better cellmate than a sister?* Or maybe it was "friend" instead of "cellmate." She shrugged. Both worked in her case.

When the two nincompoops beside her stilled, she asked, "Kate, have you thought about how you're going to act around Arlene now that you suspect her of sleeping with the Polar Bear?"

"Yes. I'm going to do what Butch suggested and act like nothing has changed."

Butch's suggestion had had more meat to it than that. His plan involved talking to Sheriff Harrison about doing a thorough background check on Arlene while they all kept on as if Kate hadn't found Arlene's scarf in the so-called Polar Bear's motel room. Butch had agreed with Ronnie and Claire that the request was going to require some finesse, including skipping over the part about Kate sneaking around The Rowdy Coyote Motel again.

While Claire, Ronnie, and Kate had come clean with Butch about the whole Polar Bear mess and Ronnie's impending doom, they'd kept their lips sealed about the mother of his child locking up Deputy Dipshit prior to her little fieldtrip. It wouldn't benefit Butch to know that detail, only put him in yet another awkward position between Kate and his good friend, the Sheriff.

"If Arlene is sleeping with the guy you think is the Polar Bear," Ronnie said, "and that's a big IF on every part of that sentence …"

"It's him and she is." Kate sounded overly sure of herself, which Claire figured was the "crazy" voice talking.

Ronnie continued, "That doesn't mean Arlene knows about his plan to take me out into the middle of the desert and torture me until I tell him where the money is that Lyle and his high-priced, skanky blonde whores snorted up their noses."

Claire did a doubletake. "Wow. That's still eating at you, huh?" At Ronnie's shrug, she added, "You might want to seek therapy for that."

"Why do you think I want to castrate the bastard? That has to be worth a handful of visits to a therapist."

"Good point."

"Anyway," Ronnie turned back to Kate, "Arlene could just have the hots for this guy. Didn't you say he was close to her age?"

"Yeah," Kate answered.

"And Arlene has a thing for big, burly bikers," Claire added. She'd once agreed to trade tables so that Arlene could wait on three leather-clad, tattooed up the ying-yang, Harley riders.

"There you go." Ronnie slapped her thigh as if the judge had spoken and the trial was over.

Claire sat forward. "You know, I'm still not sure this guy is the Polar Bear, Kate." When her sister sputtered, she interrupted with, "Don't go getting all pissed and throwing monkey poo at me for saying that. I just want to point out that this guy has not made a single threatening move toward Ronnie."

"He cheated me on a tip," Kate griped.

"Oh, well," Claire stood and stretched, "in that case, he's guilty as hell. Let's pull a Wyatt Earp and demand he meet the three of us at the O.K. Corral. We'll teach him a lesson about shortchanging a Morgan sister on a good tip."

"Kiss my ass, Claire."

"No thanks. I'll leave the dirty work to Butch." She stepped up onto the porch and held the door open. "Come on, you two hooligans. Let's go see if Mom is wearing a lampshade and dancing on the kitchen table."

"Not again." Ronnie stood and offered Kate a hand up. "Chester told me he was afraid to watch her shake her booty last time for fear he'd turn into a pillar of salt."

"If she's up there getting all bootylicious," Kate said as she passed over the threshold, "let's just hope Manny isn't up there with her."

Ronnie groaned, following Kate inside. "If I have to watch those two reenact *Dirty Dancing* one more time, I may need to fall in behind Claire in the lobotomy line."

Grimacing at what the evening might have in store for her,

Claire followed her sisters inside. "I believe I'm going to follow in Chester's footsteps tonight and find my Zen at the bottom of a bottle of beer."

She closed the door behind her and locked it, shutting out the rest of the world and its troubles.

Tonight she was going to focus on one thing and one thing only—kicking butt at Euchre. After that she'd see what she could do about saving the day.

Chapter Seventeen

Monday, November 12th

Have you thought about Thanksgiving?" Kate asked.

"Thanksgiving?" Claire shot a frown across the front seat of Ruby's pickup. Her sister nibbled on a granola bar she'd grabbed on the way out of the General Store. "We're on a stakeout here, not a grocery run."

Here being across the street from the Tucson Electric Power building in Yuccaville where two white trucks were parked in the lot. Claire assumed one of them was Dory Hamilton's work truck, since they'd watched him pull up in it and stroll into the building thirty minutes ago.

"That's what got me thinking about food," Kate said.

"What got you thinking about food?" Claire focused back on the main door to the building, willing Dory to get his butt back out here and in that truck. There was no way she was going to confront him on his home turf. The plan was to follow him until he was well away from here and then catch him off guard.

"*Stakeout,*" Kate answered. "That word always makes me think of a takeout joint that specializes in steak. Better yet, it's the perfect theme for a food truck. I could name it," she lifted her hands in front of her, as if displaying an invisible banner in the air, "The Stakeout Mobile. Like the Batmobile, you know. I could drive it around as if I'm on a stakeout. Get it?" She didn't wait for Claire to weigh in or to tell her to shove the rest of the granola bar into her pumpkin pie hole and shut it. "Maybe I should name the business *The Stakeout Lady.* Unless you want to be a partner in my venture. Together we could be *The Stakeout Babes.*"

Claire stared at her sister in baffled silence. Who in the hell was this woman sitting next to her and what had she done with Kate? And where had this desire to cook food for people come from? Kate had been born with a case of bad-chef-itis that hadn't gone away in her thirty-one plus years.

"What does any of that have to do with Thanksgiving?" Claire asked after easing her tongue out of its state of shock.

The look Kate gave her made it clear that she thought Claire was the one with the cotton candy brain. "The word stakeout makes me think of steak, which makes me think about a restaurant, which makes me think about eating, which makes me think of my favorite foods, which reminds me that we haven't made any plans for Thanksgiving dinner yet. So, what do you think?"

"I think the real Kate was abducted from Gramps's R.V. last night by aliens from the planet Goofball, and they sent you down here to muddle our brains while they are busy up in their spacecraft repeatedly probing her."

Kate wrinkled her nose at Claire. "I mean what do you think about Thanksgiving dinner?"

"Turkey, rolls, cranberries, and stuffing. The rest I don't give a hoot about, because I'll be so gorged after those four comfort foods, not to mention I'll be borderline catatonic from the carb overload, that nothing else on the table will matter."

"Well, we must have some pie and potatoes." Kate tapped her chin. "I wonder if Mom will be sober enough to make her infamous eggplant and pea casserole."

"I sure hope not." That dish should come with a skull and crossbones label. "Maybe we should keep topping off Mom's glass of cognac to ensure that concoction does not end up on the dinner table this year."

"I don't know. It's not so bad tasting."

"Butch wasn't lying. You're getting loonier every damned day." She was dodging Kate's fist when a movement in her peripheral vision made her turn back to the building. "Hey, there's Dory. Get down!"

Claire slid down the seat peeking out the side window, watching him climb into his pickup and back out of the lot. She waited until he was a block away and then started up Ruby's truck and rolled after him.

He stopped at the mini-mart in Yuccaville and came out carrying a two-liter of soda pop and a bag of doughnuts, one of which he held in his mouth while he unlocked his truck. He took off out of the parking lot and headed toward Jackrabbit Junction.

Kate ducked down in the seat again as they passed the Sheriff's office.

"Feeling guilty?" Claire asked.

"If Deputy Dipshit sees us he'll follow, I know it."

"You're getting paranoid."

"He's got a thing for me." When Claire hit her with a get-over-yourself glance, she clarified, "Not *that* kind of a thing—more of a grudge."

"It couldn't have anything to do with you insulting him to his face, could it?"

Kate pushed back upright. "He needs to grow thicker skin if he's aspiring to sheriff-dom someday. Look at what Sheriff Harrison deals with from Ronnie. I'm helping the butthead be a better cop."

"Right."

"Just shush up and drive."

Chuckling, Claire did as ordered, following Dory through Jackrabbit Junction and several miles past. When he turned down a dirt road, she hesitated on the shoulder of the highway. Should she follow or wait for another stop?

"What are you doing?" Kate asked. "Let's go."

"What if we follow and end up in the boonies and he pulls a gun on me?" Sophy Wheeler and her 12-gauge had made her gun-shy in all senses of the word.

"He's not going to pull a gun, especially if you take off your jacket and put some extra wag in your walk when you approach him."

"No jacket? The breeze today is freaking cold."

"Oh, poor baby. We wouldn't want you to get a little cold when you're trying to keep your family from ending up dead now would we?" She blocked Claire's playful attempt to whack her. "Listen, we are going to find out today why that asshole called and left that message if we have to string him up by his balls to get the answer."

Claire frowned at the gleam in Kate's eyes. "Are you running a fever?"

Pointing out the window at the dust trail Dory was leaving, Kate ordered, "Drive, Claire. Before we lose him."

"Fine." Shifting into gear, she turned down the road and sped after him. "Your bossiness is growing along with your baby. By the time this baby shows up, I'll be calling you Ronnie Jr."

Kate laughed. It was more of a cackle really, reminding Claire of their mother last night before Manny led her stumbling off into the night back to his Airstream.

"When's your next checkup?" Claire asked after the cackle quieted.

"In two weeks." Kate shifted uncomfortably. "Butch wants to go with me."

"Good."

"Right." She didn't sound too sure about that.

"Is there a problem with Butch going with you to the doctor's office?"

"It's kind of an intimate thing."

"So is making a baby."

"Funny girl." Kate wrinkled her nose at Claire. "Butch makes me nervous, if you want to know the truth. I'm worried about what he'll do when we're in the exam room together and I'm in that stupid hospital gown."

"You think he's going to want to don a pair of rubber gloves and play rock-paper-scissors with the doc to see who gets to go in first?"

"You joke, but how would you feel if Mac sat in with you during a pap exam? Do you have any idea how uncomfortable it will be for me with my ex-boyfriend sitting there while the doctor pokes around under my hood?"

Claire grimaced down at that general area on Kate. "That's more like your trunk."

"You know what? I don't want to talk about this right now."

"Calm down. I get your point." Claire squeezed her shoulder. "Hey, maybe I could come with you guys. We could make it a party in your exam room. You know Chester's going to be hurt if we don't include him, too."

Kate's glare didn't last when Claire made a face at her.

When they focused back out the front window, Kate grabbed the dash. "Look! Dory made a left turn."

Claire saw it too. She followed. They made another turn a short way down the road, crossed a cattle guard, and wound their way up a rutted drive.

"There's his truck," Kate said. "He's not in it. Pull up next to it."

"I know what to do." Claire parked and cut the engine. She shook her finger at Kate. "You stay in here."

"Fine."

"I mean it, Kate. Do not follow me, do not try anything crazy, and do not do anything that will land us back in jail again."

"I won't."

"Pinkie swear." Claire held out her pinkie.

Kate took it. "Okay, happy? Now hurry up before he gets back to his truck."

Shoving her door open and sliding out of the pickup, Claire jogged across the gravel drive. She passed in front of the older, half adobe/half wood ranch house and its large wraparound porch that sagged a little on one end. As she rounded the corner post, she nearly ran smack into Dory on his way back to his pickup.

He jerked back in surprise, almost knocking off his Tucson Electric Power cap. A weird squelching noise came from somewhere around his jowls.

Claire held up her hands. "Sorry if I scared you. I just needed to ask you a quick question."

His eyes narrowed, his lips following suit. "Who are you?"

"Claire Morgan."

He jerked again, this time not as much but a reaction nonetheless. Apparently he'd heard of her. Or maybe one of her sisters.

"I'm busy right now," he said, hitching up his blue work pants under his beer belly. "You need to contact our customer service number if you have questions."

"I have a question for you, Dory Hamilton. Not Tucson

Electric Power."

The red shade that crept up his cheeks and around his brown, scruffy, Elvis sideburns had nothing to do with the Arizona sunshine. His brown eyes darted around as if he were looking for an escape route.

Claire took a step back, bending her knees, ready to chase after him if he tried to run. "Why did you call the Dancing Winnebagos R.V. Park last week and leave a message?"

A movement in the corner of her eye drew Claire's gaze. When she looked over at the window on her left, the curtain was waving like a breeze had somehow blown through the closed window.

"I don't know what you're talking about, lady."

"Really? You didn't make a call from the payphone at Dirty Gerties and tell my sister, 'He's coming for you'?"

He lifted his chin. "Nope. You have the wrong guy."

"The owner of Dirty Gerties doesn't think so. She specifically remembers you being there at the time the phone call was made. She also heard your voice from her office."

"She was wrong. I was already gone by that time."

Ha! Got him. "By what time, Dory?"

The red crept higher. He puffed out his chest. "Listen, lady, I told you I'm busy."

She sidestepped as he tried to leave, blocking him. "Whatever game you are trying to play here, Dory, I will figure it out and come for you again."

"Is that a threat? Because I'm sure the Sheriff would like to hear all about it."

"I'm not afraid of the law, so don't try to throw it in my face. Why in the hell did you call the R.V. park? Who is coming for us?"

"Stay away from me, lady." He pushed past her, his shoulder nudging her hard enough to spin her around. "Or I'm calling the law and turning you in for badgering me."

She followed on his heels. "There's no law against merely badgering a person."

"They'll know what I mean."

"Maybe I should call them, too, and tell them about your

threatening phone call."

"I told you I never made a call." When he reached his truck, he rushed inside and locked the door like she'd turned into a zombie and was hungry for his brains.

"You're lying, Dory Hamilton," she yelled through the window, "and I'm going to find out what you're hiding."

He flipped her off while starting the truck.

"I'll teach you not to fuck with a Morgan sister!" she yelled after him as he backed partway down the drive. He yanked his truck around and spit gravel in her direction as he left.

"Well," Kate said, sidling up to her. "That was fruitful, Shaggy. You and Scooby Doo sure know how to make a bad guy come clean."

Huffing, Claire jammed her hands on her hips. "Did you see his reaction to me? He's guilty as hell."

"I have no doubt and I aim to prove it."

Claire frowned at her. "Oh yeah? What do you have in mind? Sprinkling him with your truth fairy dust?"

"No, smartass. I'm going to scope out his recent calls list." Kate held up a cellphone and smiled ear to ear. "That stupid asshole drove off and left his phone behind. Oops!"

Oh, shit! "You stole his phone?" Claire accused more than asked. Would that fall under burglary or robbery in Sheriff Harrison's book, since Kate undoubtedly had stolen it from Dory's truck while Claire had him distracted?

"Technically I'm only borrowing it."

* * *

Ronnie turned Chester's truck into the parking lot of Dirty Gerties. Apparently Monday afternoon was a good day to hang out at a strip club, because almost half of the lot was full of pickup trucks, older model cars, and a few Jeeps. With not a single minivan or soccer mom SUV in sight, she couldn't imagine a more testosterone laden place.

She cut the engine. After a quick check for any passing Sheriff vehicles, she headed inside. When Chester had brought her here, the venue had been mostly empty and quiet, echoing even. Today the place throbbed with deep bass. As Ronnie approached the bar, she breathed air heavy with the musty scent of humanity—sweat, cologne, and something else she didn't want to try too hard to identify.

She stopped at the bar on the way in and ordered a Roy Rogers mocktail since she was driving today. Cherry was nowhere to be seen at the moment. The bartender was a well-built, muscled woman with tattoos escaping the neckline of her T-shirt and crawling up her throat. Her body looked thirty without an ounce of fat in sight, whereas her extra-tanned skin was approaching Medicare eligibility.

Ronnie scoped out the room while she waited for her drink. Two of the four stripper poles were in use. She tried not to stare at the bottle blondes working the floor, their scantily clad bodies undulating in slow motion more than dancing, their limbs sliding up and down and all around the poles. Some of the men sat in small groups, others were solo, one was with a fully-dressed woman who was obviously not an employee. All were focused on the titillating scene on stage.

Movement in the back corner booth caught her eye. Someone was waving at her—someone whose notorious walker was parked next to the booth. Ronnie grabbed her drink, tossed some cash on the bar, and headed for the corner, weaving through the silent watchers.

Aunt Millie looked up from the scarf she was knitting as Ronnie neared. "You're late again, dear."

"Sorry about that. I had to shake one of the Sheriff's hound dogs." Even though she was in Chester's truck, a deputy had glanced her way when she had passed and then had followed her for a couple of blocks. She'd lost him after shooting down an alley and cutting through a parking lot.

Sliding into the booth opposite Aunt Millie, Ronnie set her drink on the table. "I can't believe you picked this place to meet."

Her life seemed to revolve around Dirty Gerties these days. She wasn't sure if she should take that as a good or bad sign. Maybe she needed to check her horoscope and see if a bright career in stripping was in her stars. She glanced down at her sad lack of an ogle-worthy chest, the result of being on the run-for-your-life diet for a couple of months too long.

"When you called," Aunt Millie said, "you specifically requested that we meet somewhere Grady would never think to look for us." She spread her hands wide. "Can you think of a better rendezvous location?"

"Nope." If Ronnie were going to continue living a life of *almost* crime, she needed to hire Aunt Millie as her mentor.

"Besides," Aunt Millie nudged her chin toward the dancers, "watching these girls spin and twirl reminds me of some burlesque shows I used to go to in Vegas with my first husband." She winked across at Ronnie. "He was a real hot rod in the bedroom if you get my meaning. That boy could go from zero to sixty before I even rolled up to the line."

Her smile was downright scandalous as she stared off over Ronnie's shoulder for a moment. Then she shook herself back to the present. "Anyhoo, how deep of a tar pit have you gotten yourself stuck in now? Judging from the fact that you needed to meet me in a top secret location, I'm guessing you're up to the top of your hip waders already."

More like up to her neck. Ronnie sipped on her drink, forming her request in her head. "I need your help again, but you can't say a word to anyone about this. Not even to the other girls. It's too dangerous."

One of Aunt Millie's eyebrows lifted. "I'm listening."

"The woman who was killed in prison, the one you told me about, along with her partner, was staying at my step-grandmother's R.V. park in a camper. They had hidden the box of diamonds underneath it, tucked up inside the frame. It was a freak happenstance that my sister saw it while she was under there trying to catch my grandpa's dog."

"This is the sister who attacked poor Greta in the library?"

"Uh, yeah." Ronnie ignored the guilt that rippled through her for agreeing that Claire was the instigator in that scuffle. But now was not the time for sister solidarity.

After a glance around to make sure nobody was looking in their direction, Ronnie leaned forward, lowering her voice. "I need to know where that camper is now." She'd scouted the impound yard but hadn't seen it there.

"Did Grady's boys take it away when the hubbub was all over and the mule carted off to jail?"

"Yes."

"Why don't you ask Grady then?"

Ronnie hesitated. She really wasn't sure how many details of her relationship with Aunt Millie's nephew she should share. While Grady was willing to go public now with their relationship, the waters between them were anything but clear.

"Ahh," Aunt Millie smiled, nodding. "You're sleeping with him on a regular basis now, and you're trying to keep your nose clean as far as he knows."

"Something like that." Truth be told they weren't sleeping together often enough for her satisfaction. Between the demands of his work and her crazy family's interruptions, more often than not Grady left her burning up and wanting more.

"I understand. I'm not so old that I've forgotten what that itch feels like and how much a good scratching can satisfy yet still leave you hankering for more."

The fact that they were talking about sex with Grady, the woman's nephew, had Ronnie squirming in her seat. "Grady is a good man," she said, taking the conversation out of the bedroom. "I don't want to worry him unnecessarily about this diamonds deal if I can help it."

"Good answer." She snickered. "Do you love him?"

Ronnie gave her best impression of a department store mannequin. "Uhhhh ..." Did she? No, it was too soon. Wasn't it? She thought about how much his presence made her light up like a jackpot-winning slot machine. "I don't know," she answered honestly.

"Another good answer." Aunt Millie lowered her needles. "I can find out what happened to that camper after it left your step-grandmother's campground, but what's in it for me?"

"More jewelry?" One way or another, Ronnie and Claire would figure out how to get their mom to donate to their cause.

Aunt Millie shook her head. "I have plenty now thanks to you."

"Okay," Ronnie leaned back in the booth, sipping the last of her drink, holding Aunt Millie's stare. "What do you want for this job?"

The needles clinked back to life, her focus returning to her scarf. "Thanksgiving," she answered.

"What?"

"You heard me."

"You want me to give you Thanksgiving? As in the holiday?"

Aunt Millie smiled across at her. "You're going to invite me to your family's dinner."

Ronnie set her drink down, frowning with a mixture of confusion and surprise. "You want to have Thanksgiving with me and my family?"

"Yes. I'm sick of the senior center's gravy. It tastes like gelled horse's hooves."

"Horse's hooves?"

"And their cranberry sauce is straight out of a can, no sugar added thanks to the damned diabetics."

Thanksgiving? With her mother? Why would Aunt Millie want to subject herself to such torture? What was the catch? "Is that it? Just an invitation for you to join my family for Thanksgiving?"

"No. There's one more thing."

"If you're going to insist we put raisins or broccoli or anything other than the basic ingredients in the dressing, I'll go find that damned camper on my own."

"You can have the dressing however you like. What I want is a second invitation."

"For whom? Greta?" That wouldn't sit well with Claire at all.

"I want you to invite Grady to Thanksgiving dinner, too."

"You want me to invite the Sheriff of Cholla County to the Morgans' dinner table?"

The logistics of Aunt Millie showing up were complicated enough after she'd threatened to drag Kate into the library bathroom months ago and teach her a lesson or two. But Grady too? In Ruby's house? Eating dinner with her family? Dear Lord, the potential for trouble was endless, especially since Manny and Chester would undoubtedly be there as well.

"Yep. And don't even think about taking 'no' for an answer from my nephew, or I won't deliver the information on that camper."

Ronnie crossed her arms over her chest, casting a shrewd look at Aunt Millie. "Besides salted gravy and real cranberries, what's in this for you? With Grady being there, too, I mean?"

Wouldn't Grady's family be unhappy about his not showing up for their own get together?

"My nephew has worked every Thanksgiving since his ex-wife left him, the selfish little tramp." Aunt Millie tucked her knitting into one of the bags draped off the front of her walker. "That boy needs to remember what living is about, and I imagine that your family's dinner table is the perfect place to get reacquainted with life."

Or not.

Claire and Kate would not be thrilled with either guest at their table, not with the troubled histories they shared with Grady and his aunt, and especially not with the secrets they were trying to keep tucked under the rug these days. But Ronnie wanted to know what had happened to that camper, especially if someone might be coming for her and Claire next.

She reached her hand across the table. "You've got a deal. Two invitations are yours."

Aunt Millie shook her hand. "You'll need to ask my nephew as soon as possible so he can schedule one of his deputies to work that day."

Grimacing slightly at the awkwardness sure to come when she delivered his personal invitation, which she fully expected him to decline, she nodded. "You have my word. He'll be there, even if I have to drag him there and tie him to the chair."

"Sounds like fun to me. Let me know if you need my help with the dragging part. The boy's sheriff britches get too big for his own good sometimes." Aunt Millie smiled at something over Ronnie's shoulder. "Heads up," she spoke through her teeth, "we have company."

"Hello, ladies," Cherry the owner said, hovering over their table. "I'm surprised to see you here again," she said to Ronnie and then winked at Aunt Millie. "But not you. What's with the walker? You fall and hurt your hip since I saw you last?"

"Something like that."

"Well, I hope it heals soon. You need to stay after closing again. I haven't had such a good time dancing up on stage since I was wearing ponytails, leotards, and tap shoes." Cherry squeezed Ronnie's shoulder. "Have you ever seen Millie here shake her booty?"

Her gaze bounced from Aunt Millie's pinched lips to her notorious walker and back again. Holy dingle balls! Was the walker a ruse? A con to fool everyone into thinking she was a tottering little old lady? Why? Ronnie chuckled. Damn, Grady's aunt was good.

"No," she told Cherry, "I haven't yet. But she's promised to teach me a few dance steps soon."

Aunt Millie's eyes narrowed a fraction, but then her lips rounded into an easy-going smile that she aimed at Cherry. "The place is looking good, sweetheart. I'm proud of all you've accomplished in here, and the girls you hired are the sweetest things. Maybe we should see about getting Ronnie up there on stage one day." Aunt Millie shot her a daring glance. "What do you think, dear? You feel like making some extra cash?"

Ronnie shook her head. "I'm more of a drinker than a dancer."

"If you ever change your mind," Cherry said, "I'm always looking for new talent, and I offer a solid health insurance package." Someone called the owner's name from over by the bar. She tapped the table twice. "You ladies take care."

After she left Ronnie nailed Aunt Millie with a gunslinger stare. "How long have you been conning everyone with that walker trick?"

"It's not a con. I slipped last February and hurt my leg, so the doctor gave me this walker."

"Does it still hurt?"

She shrugged. "Sometimes."

Ronnie wasn't sure whether to believe her or not, but a glance at her watch told her it was time to head back to The Shaft. Butch's bookkeeping called.

"Time for me to fly. I'll be in touch." Ronnie slid out of the booth and scooped up her purse. "As for Thanksgiving, you need to let me know what Grady's favorite dessert is."

Aunt Millie chortled. "Oh, sweetie. I'm sure he's already shown you exactly what he likes and how he likes it."

Oh, man. With Chester, Manny, Deborah, and Aunt Millie all sitting around the dinner table this year, it was sure to be a Thanksgiving Ronnie was going to want to forget.

Chapter Eighteen

The Shaft was cooking.

Ronnie's stomach growled at the aroma of seared meat in the air as she crossed the parking lot in the late afternoon desert sunshine. A cool breeze rolling in from the greasewood flats stirred the dust around her feet, promising another cold night under the stars after the warm rays disappeared behind the mountain range to the west.

A long row of Harley Davidson motorcycles lined the front of the building, chromed horses tied to an invisible hitching post, gleaming under their leather saddlebags. A few Kawasaki and Honda motorcycles were mixed in with the herd.

What was with all of the bikers? It was a nice day, but still, this was about three times more than usual. Then she remembered a conversation with Butch right after she'd started helping him with his bookkeeping. Word had gotten out about the specialty burgers he'd added to the menu after the only other eatery in Jackrabbit Junction had gone out of business. A well-known motorcycle enthusiast website had requested an interview and done a write-up on The Shaft. Judging by the number of bikes in the lot, the article had been posted recently. She wondered how much of a boon this would be for Butch's business.

When she stepped inside The Shaft and saw her little sister with her blonde hair hanging half out of her chignon, the tired sag of her shoulders, and the red splotches on her cheeks, she realized what was good for the gander wasn't necessarily good for the goose.

Ronnie made a beeline back to the storeroom and grabbed an apron. Butch's books would have to wait. She met her sister on the other side of the swinging doors.

"We're drowning out here," Katie hollered over the din of music, television, and conversation.

"I'm diving in." Ronnie tied her apron as she rounded the end of the bar.

Behind the beer tap handles, Butch's number one bartender, Gary, was working so hard pouring drinks his glasses were partially fogged up. He handed her a tray of foamy beers. "Take that to the group next to the pool tables."

The five chaps-wearing bikers shouted in appreciation when she arrived. She promised to check on the rest of their order and moved over to another table that hadn't been touched yet, starting there with drinks. She passed Arlene on the return trip to the bar.

"Hey, sugar, have you seen Butch?" she asked Ronnie, sounding like the same Arlene she'd been before Katie had found her scarf in a possible killer's motel room.

Ronnie couldn't see Arlene as a threat. She worked as hard as everyone else here, was never late, filled in whenever asked, and had kind eyes. Katie had to be barking up the wrong tree. It wouldn't be the first time. Unlike Claire, Katie's gut instinct had flunked Intuition 101.

"No, but I just got here."

"If you see him, tell him that I need to talk to him about taking a couple of days off soon. I have an old friend coming to town for a visit."

Old friend? Or an old lover? Ronnie shook her head, trying to get rid of Katie's suspicious voice playing through it. "Will do," she told the older waitress.

Ronnie left her orders at the bar with Gary and grabbed another tray of drinks he had ready to deliver. Through the narrow window behind the bar that opened into the kitchen she caught a glimpse of Butch standing by the grill with a spatula in hand. Arlene must not have looked into the kitchen in a while.

Ronnie took the drinks to a table with three gray-haired Harley couples, all six of them walking advertisements in their orange and black gear. On her way back to the bar after emptying the tray, Mississippi caught her eye. He was playing a game of pool against a skinny guy dressed in red and white leather motorcycle getup. This one had the Honda brand plastered all over it.

Mr. FBI waved her over.

"Hey, Mississippi," she said, pointing at his drink. "Can I get you a refill?"

Truth be told, with this much leather and testosterone in the place, she was happy to see the FBI agent.

"I'm good." He lined up a shot, called it, and sank the 4 ball in the corner pocket as he'd foretold. "Give me a minute," he told the Honda fan and looked at her. "Follow me."

He led Ronnie off to the side and leaned down to speak in her ear. "Your ex-husband is trying to work a deal with the FBI."

Terrific, what was that shit-bag up to now? "What sort of deal?"

"He's not happy living in a jail cell without a chance of parole for a decade."

"That's too fucking bad."

He smirked. "Yeah, that's what I say, but my superiors have other fish they'd like to fry."

"What's that mean?"

"Lyle and his lawyer have scheduled a meeting with the FBI for later this week. They want to cut a deal to shorten his stay in prison."

"Why do I have a feeling this is a bad thing?"

"Because you don't like the organization I work for?"

"You mean your boss and coworkers over at the local Fucking Bandwagon of Imbeciles office?"

An actual smile lit his face, a sighting as rare as the fabled jackalope. "That's a new one. I'll have to share that one with the other imbeciles."

A glance toward the bar found another tray of drinks ready for her to deliver. "I have to go, Mississippi. Thanks for the heads up."

Two customers flagged her down on her way to the bar and requested drinks.

For the next two hours, Ronnie's head spun as she helped Arlene and Katie keep up with drink orders. Was this the height of the rush from that website article? Or would things get worse?

If this kept up, Butch was going to need to add on to the bar and hire more staff or he'd be turning away customers.

As the light outside faded, so did the bikers. Her feet were killing her by the time she had a moment to plop down on a barstool and breathe. Usually when she waited tables she wore tennis shoes and jeans, not a knee-length knit dress and boots. Her tips today had been better than usual; but on second thought that actually might have had more to do with the non-local clientele than her outfit.

Katie dropped onto the seat next to her, her hair down, the chignon a thing of the past. Her nose shone, her eyes had dark circles under them, and her pink shirt had a big red ketchup smear down the center of it.

"I need to talk to you," Katie said to her.

"Shoot. I'm not going anywhere for a few minutes."

Katie glanced over one shoulder and then the other before leaning closer. "I borrowed Dory Hamilton's phone today."

It took Ronnie's brain a moment to remember who Dory was thanks to the exhaustion settling in for the evening. Then it came tumbling back, ending with Claire and Katie taking off early that morning to track him down and ask him what the hell that anonymous phone call had been about last week.

"You *borrowed* his phone?" Ronnie frowned. "How did you get him to ..." Ronnie let her question drop. The less she knew about Katie's law bending the easier it was to claim ignorance when Grady questioned her about her sister's next crime. She got to the point. "What did you find on his phone?"

"He's a shitty speller. Just about every one of his text messages has errors, and his grammar is atrocious. Makes me wonder about the meter readings he writes down for Tucson Electric Power. Ruby should probably start double checking her bills."

"Is that it, Miss Teacher? Because the last I checked being a bad speller doesn't automatically make you a conspirator in attempted murder, so I hope to hell you found something worthy of you breaking the law again."

"I swear you and Claire are such weenies these days. I told you I only borrowed it. I fully intend to give it back to him."

"Claire isn't a weenie. She's just tired of going to jail. As for me, I'm sleeping with the Sheriff, remember? It's a little tough to look him in the eyes when my sister keeps committing crimes."

"So face the other way during sex." Katie said and then giggled at her own smartass comeback.

Forcing a smile to her mouth, Ronnie said, "Funny. You've been hanging around Claire and Chester too much."

Katie sobered, searching Ronnie's face. "Oh shit, you're falling for Grady, aren't you?"

Ronnie didn't want to talk about the Sheriff and her growing feelings for the hardass at the moment. "Did you find anything else on Dory's phone?"

After another few seconds of studying Ronnie, Katie answered, "Only several calls to the Grand Canyon State Prison."

"What? Which one?" There were several of those throughout Arizona.

"According to the operator who wanted to direct my call, I'd reached the Gila Flats complex."

Gila Flats was the prison listed in the article Aunt Millie had given her, as in the place where the mule had been stabbed to death. Ronnie frowned at her hands, trying to line up the reels in her brain and land a jackpot with the diamonds, the mule, and Dory. "Dory called the prison?"

"Yep. He also received calls from the payphone there. It's a separate number from the other one."

"Did you tell Claire about this?"

"She was there when I made the calls confirming whose numbers Dory had in his phone." Katie grabbed Ronnie's chin and turned it toward her. "What's going on?"

"What do you mean?"

"You and Claire are hiding something from me. What?"

So Claire hadn't leaked the story about the murders in Mexico and at the prison. From the start, they'd agreed to shield Katie from this diamond mess as much as possible. There was even more reason to keep up that shield now. "Nothing."

"You're lying, Ronnie, just like Claire did when I questioned her." Her sister's face tightened, her eyes sparkling. "If you two won't come clean, I'll have to dig around myself and figure it out, the law be damned."

"Katie, you're making something out of nothing."

"Then what has you both so scared that your eyes are darting all around? Does this have to do with the Polar Bear somehow? You think Dory is connected to him?"

Ronnie tried to hold her eyes still. "No, I don't think either of those things."

But she did wonder if Dory were somehow responsible for the death of the mule. Was he the one who'd killed those people in Mexico? She'd never seen Dory but imagined him as a burly, menacing tyrant hiding behind a Tucson Electric Power uniform.

Arlene joined them at the bar, taking the stool next to Katie with a weary sigh. "My dogs are barking something fierce after that run," she said and squeezed Katie's shoulder.

To Katie's credit, she didn't pull away. She reached up and patted the other waitress's hand. "Maybe you should go home early tonight, Arlene. Get some rest."

"You're the one who should be resting, Katie-doll."

"Nah, I'm good. I got lots of rest last night." She shot Ronnie a sidelong glance and then asked Arlene, "How's life at The Rowdy Coyote Motel? Any troubles with your neighbors there?"

"Nope. Everyone has been behaving themselves." Arlene grimaced. "Although, I have heard talk lately about someone sneaking around the place in the dark, peeking in windows."

"It's probably a drunk stumbling through the neighborhood," Katie said. "There's a real seedy bar on that side of town. You should ask Butch for a raise, move somewhere safer."

"Maybe I should buy a camper and set up in the Dancing Winnebagos R.V. Park. Then I can keep an eye on you until this baby is born, make sure you're not pushing yourself too hard."

"I think Ruby has monthly rates, doesn't she?" Katie asked Ronnie, giving her a wild-eyed look that left Ronnie perplexed.

If Katie thought Arlene were up to no good, why in the hell was she inviting her to come live in their backyard? What was Katie's angle here? Or was this "crazy" talk again, dancing with danger for shits and giggles?

A glance at her watch told her she had a few hours until closing. Whatever Katie's reasoning was, Ronnie didn't have time to sit here and play psychologist-slash-detective at the moment. There was a pile of papers in Butch's office with her name on it. "Listen, I'm supposed to be working on Butch's bookkeeping. If you two can handle this for now, I'm going to go dabble in debits and credits in his office."

They both waved her away: Arlene pushing to her feet and limping back toward one of her still-full tables, Katie grabbing a rag from behind the bar and a bottle of cleaner.

Ronnie hobbled back to Butch's office and found him inside, lying on the couch with his arm over his eyes. His chest was moving up and down too fast to be sleeping. Electric Light Orchestra was on the stereo singing about an evil woman making a fool of them. Ronnie rolled her eyes. They needed to get over it.

"You okay?" she asked him, pausing on the threshold.

"When I close my eyes, I can still see burgers on the grill."

Chuckling, she skirted his desk and grabbed the pile of papers on the corner.

"I wish I'd never decided to start offering gourmet burgers. It takes twice as long to make every damned sandwich now."

"But business is booming."

"I'm still not sure if that's a good thing."

"Mind if I work on your books while you lie there dreaming about charred meat?"

"Not at all."

She sat in his chair, pulling out his general ledger and digging into the pile.

Ten minutes later, ELO had moved onto *Strange Magic*, but Ronnie was stuck in expenses.

"Ronnie?" Butch asked.

His arm still covered his eyes when she glanced over. "Yeah?"

"I don't know if I have what it takes."

"To run your bar?" He could always hire a manager.

"To make your sister happy."

Ronnie lowered her pen, realizing that he was dead serious.

She passed on several glib responses and asked, "You love her, don't you?"

"To the moon and back."

"Well, if that's not enough, you can always take her out for ice cream. She's been craving mint chocolate chip a lot lately, especially in the middle of the night."

* * *

Tuesday, November 13th

The wind was blowing through Yuccaville's streets this morning, dust billowing in the air like snow, making Kate hesitant to follow through with her plan.

"Maybe we should come back tomorrow," she told Claire, who'd agreed to come along and play lookout for her.

"No, we have to do it today." Claire parked Ruby's old Ford opposite the Tucson Electric Power building and shut off the engine. "His truck is the one on the left."

"How can you tell?"

"When we were following Dory yesterday, I noticed the 'How's my driving?' bumper sticker was crooked."

A blast of wind howled past, kicking a tumbleweed up the street like a soccer ball.

"It's too dusty out today," Kate said.

"It's perfect. Anyone driving by will be too distracted by the wind and shit in the air to be looking around. Plus, it'll drown out any sounds you might make."

"What sounds do you think I'm going to make?"

"I don't know. You have a way of getting caught lately."

"I managed to sneak into the Sheriff's office and lock up Deputy Dipshit without getting caught."

"That's true," Claire said. "I'm just saying this weather gives us a good diversion. Nobody is going to want to go out in it if they see you sneaking around Dory's truck."

"Nobody is going to see me." Kate zipped up the black windbreaker she'd borrowed from Ruby's closet, flipping the hood up over her head. "But for the record I think my idea was better."

She'd wanted to drop the phone in an envelope and mail it with an anonymous note saying she'd found it at Dirty Gerties.

"I disagree. We don't want Dory asking around about it at Dirty Gerties."

"Why not? Nobody will know anything about his phone disappearing. There's no way to trace it back to anyone there either, so he'll drop the subject and go on with his life."

"Kate, I don't want to put anyone else in danger."

"What danger? It's a cellphone, Claire, not those diamonds you and Ronnie took."

Claire started to say something else but then stopped, swallowing it. "Listen, this is better, trust me," she said with finality. "Dory will think he misplaced his phone and that's all. Now go."

"Easy for you to say," Kate grumbled, tucking her hair into her hood and tying the strings tight under her chin. "You're not the one about to inhale a shovelful of dust."

"Quit speaking in whine-ese and get out."

Kate slid on a pair of Ruby's cotton gardening gloves she'd borrowed along with the coat and shoved open her door. The wind promptly slammed it shut. "You see that?" she said to Claire. "It's a sign not to do this."

"It's a sign that you're being a wuss."

"You do remember that I'm your pregnant sister, right? Do you really think this is a good idea in my delicate condition?"

Claire pointed out the window toward the two work trucks. "Now, Kathryn Lynette!"

"You have no respect for a pregnant woman."

"I'm teaching your unborn child morals. Now go return that damned phone."

"You teaching morals? Oh, that's rich." She wrinkled her nose at Claire and then pushed her door open, keeping her back to the wind. Dust peppered the nylon windbreaker, sounding like thousands of tiny pellets bombarding her. She rounded the back of the Ford.

Looking up and down the street to make sure the coast was clear and nobody was watching, she jogged over to the back of

Dory's work truck.

Coughing on a gust full of dust that slammed into her, she frowned back at Claire, who gave her a thumbs up. With a thumbs down back at her sister, Kate slipped around the right corner of the tailgate, hiding between the two work trucks as she sneaked up to the passenger side door handle. The door opened with relative ease since the wind was partially blocked by the other vehicle.

Kate pulled Dory's cellphone out of her pocket, but it slid out of her gloved hand and crashed onto the gravel.

Shit!

She bent down to grab it and a gust blew the pickup door shut.

Damn it.

Growling under her breath, she flipped the phone right side up, grimacing at the scratch in the lower right screen. Had that been there before? She rubbed the screen on her yoga pants. The cotton and spandex mix smeared things around, but took care of most of the dirt. Yep, that was definitely a new scratch.

Crud!

She opened the pickup door again, blocking it with her body. The smell of stale French fries and musty dirt was the same as yesterday. So was the litter of papers and wadded up foil wrappers from the mini-mart. Apparently Dory liked to stop for snacks on his way out of town—a lot of snacks.

She shoved several of the wrappers and papers aside and laid the phone on the floor. The new scratch was plain as day in this light. She flipped the phone over, screen down, but then realized it was lying on a rubber floor mat. That wasn't going to work because she needed something to justify the scratch.

Bending down, she scooped up a handful of gravel from the parking lot.

The wind blew the door shut again.

"Son of a crikey!" She shook her fist at the sky.

When she yanked open the door again, a gust blew into the cab whipping the papers and wrappers around, filling the rig with a cloud of dust.

"Now you're just being an asshole, Mother Nature."

She blocked the wind as much as she could with her body and shoved wrappers back down onto the floor.

"It's perfect," she mimicked Claire's comment about the wind from earlier in Ruby's Ford. "The stupid freaking dust storm is anything but perfect." She scattered the dirt and gravel on the passenger mat and placed the phone screen down on top of some rocks.

Collecting the wind-blown litter from the dash and the driver's side of the pickup, she stretched across the seat to get a French fry wrapper plastered to the speedometer. The sight of the door to the building opening made her freeze for a split-second, her heart latching onto her ribcage like a startled cat.

A hand wrapped around the edge of the building's door, pushing it open against the wind.

Kate dropped down below the dashboard and melted backwards out of the pickup to the ground. She closed the pickup door quietly, the sound muffled by the wind whistling around the side of the building.

The boom of a metal door slamming shut made her peek under the pickup. A pair of black work boots were coming toward the trucks. On her hands and knees, she back peddled. The gravel poked through the knees of her pants, making her wince and curse under her breath.

She paused waiting for Dory's boots to turn toward the driver's side door, but the boots kept coming around the front of the rig. Why was he not … then she realized it must not be Dory's boots.

Shittle-de-doo! It was the other guy! She shot a look to the driver's side door of the other pickup. He was going to round the front of Dory's truck in a second and see her hiding down here.

What should she do? Fake dropping a contact? Roll over and play dead like a possum?

A horn honked loud and long behind her.

The boots stopped and turned in the direction of the sound.

Kate backed around the tail of Dory's truck, glancing over her shoulder at where Claire was hitting the horn and ending up with a face full of dust as another gust rolled passed.

"Excuse me, Mister," Claire yelled through her open window

at Dory's coworker. "Can you tell me if I'm close to Sunflower Street?"

"Sunflower is two blocks up to the left."

"Great. Thanks for your help." Claire waved at the guy as she rolled up her window.

Kate peeked under the back bumper, waiting for him to climb into his work truck and close the door before slipping around the other side of Dory's rig.

The sound of Ruby's Ford starting up made Kate look across at Claire, who was pretending to fish in Kate's purse for something. She made a show of it, appearing to haul everything out while the engine idled.

"That's enough theatrics, Claire," Kate whispered, spitting out the grit between her teeth thanks to that last blast.

As soon as the other work truck hit the pavement and rolled away, Kate stood. She shucked Ruby's gloves and stuffed them in her jacket pockets, heading toward the street.

Down the block, a testosterone-ized pickup lifted so high a Great Dane could have run underneath it without breaking stride turned in her direction, coming up behind Claire. Kate waited for it to pass, frowning across the street at her sister, who was making annoying hurry-up hand gestures at her through the windshield.

The blue monster truck wanna-be rolled in front of her and then locked up the brakes, adding the acrid smell of burned rubber to the dust in the air.

Kate frowned at the oversized beast of a vehicle as it reversed, coming to a stop in front of her.

The driver's side window rolled down and Deputy Dipshit's meaty head poked out. "Well, don't you look suspicious, Kate Morgan," he hollered, lifting his sunglasses.

A glance toward Ruby's truck showed it empty, or at least it appeared that way. Claire must have ducked down so the deputy wouldn't spot her. Wonderful. That meant Kate was on her own.

"What kind of trouble are you getting into now?" he asked, all smug from high up in his perch.

The way he was looking down his snub nose at her kick-started her temper. She jammed her hands on her hips, ready to hit the dickwad with a verbal firing squad. "I'm jogging, Deputy. You should try it sometime. Maybe you could actually catch and hold onto a criminal then."

His face scrunched like she'd reached out and pinched it. "You need to keep in mind that you're talking to an officer of the law."

"You're missing your Sheriff's truck, *Ernie*," she emphasized his first name, "along with that tin badge that you like to hide behind. Why don't you grab your ladder, climb down out of that ridiculous monstrosity, and face me here on the ground like the weasel that you are?"

He pointed his finger at her. "You watch that smart mouth, harpy."

"Are you on duty or not right now?" she asked, just to be clear.

"Not at the moment, but I will be later tonight."

"Well, in that case I have something for you." She pulled her hands from her coat pockets and gave him the old double bird. "Have a lousy day, Ernie," she said, and took off jogging down the sidewalk in the opposite direction, the wind pelting her back with more dust.

Two blocks later, Ruby's pickup pulled up next to her. Kate crawled inside, tugging her door shut in spite of the wind trying to rip it right off the hinges. She brushed the dust from her face.

"What did Deputy Dipshit want?" Claire asked as she pulled back out onto the street.

"To harass me. Same old, same old." Kate untied the hood and shook out her hair. Her scalp felt like it was coated with dirt. "Apparently, I'm going to have to teach him another lesson about messing with a Morgan."

Claire shook her head. "We're going to need to set up a collection box to cover the cost of your bail."

"I won't get caught."

"You will. Hell, you almost got caught back there at Dory's truck. What in the hell was taking you so long? Were you crocheting him a doily to put under his cellphone before you left it in his truck?"

"I dropped his phone on the gravel, smarty. Those gloves are all cotton. I told you that you should have stopped at the store so I could buy rubber ones."

"So you dropped the phone, oh well. You should have dumped it and left; then Deputy Dipshit wouldn't have seen you there and we'd have made our getaway without a hitch."

"It's your fault," Kate told Claire. "You're the one who insisted we return the phone. If you'd have let me mail it, none of this would have happened."

"Damn it, Kate, you don't understand what's at stake here."

"Then explain it to me."

"I can't."

"Why not?"

"Because you're pregnant."

"Here's a newsflash for you: pregnancy does not cause temporary deafness."

"No, but in your case it caused temporary insanity."

Kate leaned over and socked her sister in the shoulder.

"Hit me again, spud-knuckle, and I'll tell the Sheriff you locked Deputy Dipshit in his jail."

"You won't either." Kate sighed. "I wish you and Ronnie would stop treating me like I'm made of glass."

"We're trying to protect you."

"Well, knock it off and tell me the truth. What is it about this Dory guy that has you two freaked out?"

Claire stopped for the last light on the way out of Yuccaville and scowled across at her. "Someone killed the mule."

"You mean the woman in prison, right?"

"No, Kate, I mean the old mule Ruby keeps out behind the tool shed."

When Kate threatened to punch her again, Claire came clean. "Yes, I'm talking about the woman Ronnie took those diamonds from."

"That woman who tried to shoot Mac in the mine?"

"Yes. *That* woman. They stabbed her twenty-three times with a shiv while she was locked up in prison."

"What's that have to do with Dory Hamilton?"

"The prison where she was killed was the Gila Flats complex."

Kate's mouth opened. "The same one Dory has been calling."

Claire nodded, hitting the gas.

"So you think Dory is connected to that woman's death?"

"If not, it's one hell of a coincidence."

Kate sat back in her seat. "And Dory was the one who called Ruby's and said someone was coming for Ronnie."

"Bingo."

As the Yuccaville city limits shrank in Kate's side mirror, the weight of this mess pressed on her, making her stomach tighten. She reached over and squeezed Claire's shoulder. "I promise I won't let anyone hurt either you or Ronnie."

Claire gave her a troubled smile. "What does that mean?"

"Detective Kate is on the case." Dory Hamilton was going to wish he'd never heard of the Morgan sisters.

"Oh, God." Claire frowned out the windshield. "Now I'm really worried."

Chapter Nineteen

This is a big mistake," Chester told Claire that afternoon as she rolled out the final stretch of underlay material over the vapor barrier she'd spread out on the rec room's subfloor. Freshly back from a beer run to the kitchen, he sat down on one of Ruby's barstools with two unopened cans of beer in hand. "Your grandfather isn't going to like this cheap-ass flooring."

"First of all," Claire stood, brushing her hands off on her jeans, "it's not cheap. I made sure to get a high quality, very durable, drop-lock bamboo laminate."

"Laminate," Chester said with a sneer, cracking open one of the beers. "It's not even hardwood."

"Second," she walked over and grabbed the beer from him, "I'm not concerned if Gramps likes it or not, only his wife." She took a gulp and made a face. His taste buds must have been long dead from all of that *chili con carne* if he enjoyed that nasty, bitter shit. "Jeez, that tastes like crap, Chester. You need a new tongue."

After sticking said appendage out at her, he snickered. "No can do. This one has too many good memories attached to it."

A wheezy-sounding laugh came from Manny, who sat on the barstool next to Chester. "Remember that time we met those three spicy ladies from Ipanema and you wiggled your tongue around between their—"

"Beep!" Claire interrupted what undoubtedly would have been yet another X-rated tale of debauchery. Four in one afternoon was plenty. "No more old stories of loose women."

"How about some new stories of tight asses?" Chester's eyes danced with mirth as he cracked open the other beer.

"How about we get back to work so I can slap the first layer of paint on tomorrow?" She handed the open can of beer to

Manny and then grabbed the half-inch, square molding spacers that came with the flooring.

"Party pooper," Chester said, jamming his smoldering cigar into his mouth. "What makes you think Ruby will like this cheapo floor?"

Claire pulled the utility knife from her tool belt and cut open several of the boxes of bamboo slabs. "After all of the scrubbing and vacuuming she's done thanks to you boozehounds tracking in the whole damned Sonoran desert every time you come over, I think she's going to be happier than a dog with three balls."

"A dog with three balls," Manny repeated chuckling. "That reminds me of a dancer your grandfather and I met in Bangkok."

"You did more than meet her that night according to Ford," Chester said to Manny. He pointed his cigar at Claire. "You've misplaced your feelings."

Huh? *Misplaced?* "I don't think so. Let me check." She patted her back pockets. "Nope, I have them right here, Mr. Pain-in-the-Ass, exactly where I left them after putting up with your bitching and moaning about the lousy job I did installing those can lights and ceiling fans yesterday."

"Good one, *bonita*. I should be filming this," Manny said, toasting her with his beer. "You two could have a show on that home and landscaping channel."

Chester crossed his arms over his chest, giving her the stink eye. "You say that you have Ruby in mind when you're making these remodeling decisions, but if you really believe that you're lying to yourself."

"That's not true." Claire re-crossed her arms. "I'm trying to make choices that will make life easier for her."

"No, you're making choices that will make this place more comfortable for *you*. If you were truly concerned about Ruby's feelings, you would be calling her each day to ask what kind of lights and flooring she wants, or if she wants the walls white or tan or whatever color of green it was you picked out."

Claire hesitated. She'd told herself she was doing this as a belated wedding gift, but was Chester right? Did she really have only herself in mind? She did think that Ruby would like this type of floor better than … *OH! MY! GOD!* She covered her mouth in horror. "I'm being like my mother, aren't I?"

"*Un poco*," Manny said, making a pinching gesture with his fingers.

"More than that but with a lot less bitchiness." Chester swigged the last of his beer. "When your grandfather gets home next weekend, make sure you tell him that I had nothing to do with those lights and this floor." He let out a belch and then set the can on the bar. "Now what do you need me to help with next?"

Should she take the flooring back? She grimaced at the opened boxes, and then decided she might as well finish what she'd started and make it up to Ruby via free labor if she hated it. Onward ho, then.

"Who's better on your knees, you or Manny?" She'd grabbed two pairs of knee pads, one of them for her.

"Knee work is Carrera's specialty," Chester said, his smartass grin punctuated with his cigar. "He spent half of his time in the Army on his knees. How do you think he made it from private to sergeant so fast?"

Manny's laughter echoed off the freshly primed walls. "For that, *amigo*, I'm going to tell Cherry over at Dirty Gerties how you fantasize about her in a Cat Woman outfit and a little white apron making molasses cookies for you."

"Watch yourself now, Carrera, or I'll tell your fashionista wife that you secretly love the color pink and want her to rosy-up your wardrobe."

Lordy-be, it was going to be a long afternoon.

"Chester," Claire interrupted, "will you take the golf cart back to the tool shed and grab Ruby's miter saw? I left the key in the ignition."

As Chester hobbled out through the back door, she turned to Manny. "Here," she tossed him the other set of knee pads. "Let's get this floor done. I have a lot to do before Gramps and Ruby get home."

"The place is looking *muy bueno, chica*."

She thought so, but now she had her doubts. "Chester would disagree with you."

"Thomas wears plaid socks with pinstriped boxers. What

does he know about decorating?"

Manny had a point. Claire had seen Chester in clashing boxers and socks more times than she'd have liked. But at least she hadn't seen his bare butt, unlike her new stepfather's.

Speaking of asses: "Where's Mom?"

"She's still sleeping off last night's cognac-fest."

Still? Criminy. Claire laid out several slabs of bamboo on the floor, staggering them as she made a pattern. She contemplated how to phrase her next question and in the end went right to the point. "Manny, have you thought about why Mom is drinking so much lately?"

"*Sí.*" His knees popped as he slid down onto them and began to help her line up the bamboo planks. "I think about it each night as I watch her pour drink after drink, and then later as I undress her and put her to bed."

She frowned at him. "What's going on with her?" She worried her lower lip. "Are you two getting along okay?"

"*Tu madre* is having a midlife crisis."

Midlife? Wasn't she about ten years too old for that? "You sound as if you know that for certain."

"It's what she told me on our way back from Vegas."

"She said that to you?" At his nod, she asked, "Why did you two get married so fast?"

"She wanted to show up your father."

"What? And you agreed?"

"*Sí.* At my age, when a beautiful younger woman throws herself at you and begs you to marry her, you either run the other way as fast as your old legs will carry you, or you jump on the horse and ride off into the sunset with her."

"Please tell me you made her sign a pre-nup."

"Your mother will be well taken care of now, whether I'm in the picture or not."

"Why would you do that for her?"

"I didn't do it for her." He took her hand and patted it. "I did it for your grandfather and you girls. You all have been in my life so long that I think of you as *mi familia.* Marrying your mother simply made it official."

Claire's mouth fell open. "Manny, you shouldn't have done

that for us."

"Don't get me wrong, *chica*. I'm no martyr. I find your mother *muy bonita*." His eyes twinkled. "And when she's alone with me, she's very attentive."

Claire winced.

He chuckled. "I didn't mean in bed."

"Thank God."

"Although she is a wild cat between the sheets."

"Manny," she warned, "remember Gramps's number one rule for family members?"

Manny snorted. "Your grandfather needs to lighten up."

That was putting it mildly, but she wasn't finished fishing about her mother, so she switched back to Deborah's problem. "Do you think this drinking thing with Mom will pass?"

Manny nodded. "Divorce can cause ripple effects long after a relationship stops thrashing and finally drowns. Right now, *tu madre* is using alcohol to cope with big changes in her life that have her scared. Eventually she'll tire of the hangovers and learn how to get a grip on her fears. When that time comes, we'll see if this rebound marriage of ours works."

"What if it doesn't?"

"Then we go our separate ways." He handed her a slab of bamboo. "Only I'm not going anywhere, so she'll have to be the one doing the *adios*-ing."

As odd as their whirlwind courtship and marriage had seemed initially, she liked having Manny in the family. She leaned over and gave him a hug. "Manuel Carrera, I'm very proud to call you my stepfather. Thank you for marrying my mom and looking out for all of us."

"*De nada*," he said, but then he blushed and looked away.

The telephone rang.

She dropped a quick kiss on his cheek, and then headed over to answer the phone. "Hello?"

"Hey, Slugger, how's the rec room coming along?"

"In spite of all the beer drinking and dirty jokes, we're getting closer to being done."

"Chester is on a roll, huh?"

"Yeah," she looked over at where Manny was securing a

bamboo slab against the molding spacers. "And now he has a cheering section."

She took the phone through the General Store and out onto the front porch.

"You mean your mom actually let Manny leave her side for once?" Mac asked.

"She's in bed, still hungover." Claire lowered onto the top porch step. The wind wasn't so blustery on this side of the house with only a periodic breeze whipping her hair around. The full sun warmed her head and shoulders, keeping her from shivering.

"Again? That sounds like it's becoming a problem."

"You don't know the half of it. How's Tucson?"

"Lonely. I miss your smile along with the rest of your body. How are your sisters?"

"Freaking wacko." She filled him in on Kate's latest confrontation with Deputy Dipshit in his monster truck, which led to telling him about the phone number for the Gila Flats prison complex being on Dory's cellphone multiple times.

"That's the same prison where they took the other mule who got stabbed to death," he said.

"I know. Now we're trying to figure out if Dory is in cahoots with whoever killed her." She spent the next few minutes catching Mac up on the theories and worries she and her sisters had been tossing around lately, along with how Dory had acted so suspicious when she'd confronted him.

"Claire Morgan, you're going to be the death of me. Please, no more confronting anyone on your own who might be dangerous to your health."

"I wasn't on my own. Kate was with me."

He cursed under his breath. "Kate is temporarily out of order, and you know that. Taking her to an informal interrogation is asking for trouble."

"If I didn't take her, she threatened to go after him on her own."

"And do what? Jump on his back and pummel the hell out of him like a wild woman?"

She chuckled. She'd actually witnessed that very scene up in Deadwood last month, only Kate had used a rubber hand to wallop the crap out of the insulting dickhead. "She thinks she's Rambo now, I swear."

"Maybe you should let Sheriff Harrison know about Dory and get him involved."

"Maybe." But the thought of knocking on the Sheriff's door gave Claire the shudders. There was so much around this R.V. park she didn't want the law knowing about, things that might make them shut down the place and cart in the trouble-sniffing dogs and metal detectors. The more she learned about Joe's criminal past, the more she was afraid of what illegal treasures he'd buried. "I'll see what Ronnie thinks."

"Don't let Kate have a say. With the way she's heading, she'll land all three of you in jail, and that's a lot of bail money."

"I'd reward you for springing me."

"Oh, yeah? How?"

"Well …" There was a voice in the background, then a beeping sound followed by the growl of a diesel engine. "Are you still out on the job site?"

"Yeah, it's going to be a late night. We hit some snags today." The beeping stopped. "Listen, Slugger, the company wants me to give them an answer about the promotion by Friday."

She closed her eyes and leaned her head against the porch post. After much thought and angst and going back and forth over the last few days about his job and their future, she had an answer. "I think you should take it."

"What?" he asked over more beeping and racket in the background.

"I said," she raised her voice, "I think you should take the job promotion. It's what you've been working toward for years." The commotion on his end quieted. "It's what you want," she added at a normal level.

Silence came from the other end of the line. After several seconds, she checked the digital screen on the receiver to see if she'd lost connection, but the seconds were still adding up on the call.

"Mac? Are you still there?"

"What about you?" he asked.

"What about me?"

"What are you going to do?"

"Cheer you on."

"From Jackrabbit Junction?"

She closed her eyes, shutting out the vast valley in front of her. She didn't want to look at the landscape she'd come to hold dear or think about how in the cold light of dawn when the sun first hit the desert, the frost that was sprinkled over the ground sparkled like a field of diamonds.

"I'll go wherever you go, Mac."

More silence played through the line. This time she waited for him to break it.

"Let me get this straight," he said, his voice quiet, serious. "You want me to take this promotion *and* you're willing to go along with me, flying all over the place, not seeing your sisters and grandfather for stretches of time?"

"I sure am." She did her best to sound upbeat about it, too, while wondering how soon she'd have to leave Jackrabbit Junction and her family.

"Okay, Claire." But he didn't sound too convinced. "I'll go ahead as planned."

She'd have to play it up when she saw him next, convince him her heart was in this with him. "When are you coming back here? Thursday or Friday?"

"I'm not sure yet. Let me see how things go here tonight and tomorrow." Someone honked on his end of the line. "Damn, I gotta go."

"Call me tomorrow when you have a chance."

"I will." With a quick "love you" he was gone, the line truly dead this time.

She opened her eyes and stared out beyond the dust devils swirling across the valley between the Dancing Winnebagos R.V. Park and the Tres Dedos Mountains. Maybe she could take a picture from Ruby's porch or several shots at different times of the day. Then she could take her favorite place with her to pine over while she sat in hotel room after hotel room, waiting for Mac to finish with work each day.

She took a deep breath of the fresh desert air, wishing she

could somehow take that with her on the road, too.

"This is going to work," she told the three wrens perched on the bird feeder Gramps had hung off the side of the porch.

It had to, because as much as she loved spending her days in Jackrabbit Junction with her family nearby, there was one thing she had come to love even more—being with Mac.

* * *

Later that afternoon Ronnie's butt was temporarily planted on a barstool at The Shaft while she took a short break, waiting for Gary to finish filling a tray with the corner table's drink order. The sight of the Sheriff pushing open the swinging doors leading back to Butch's office and waving at her to join him made her blink in surprise.

She glanced over at the front door. Grady must have sneaked in when she wasn't looking. Then again, missing his arrival wouldn't have been tough since the joint was rocking and rolling with ZZ Top on the jukebox and another flood of hungry bikers.

That reminded her—she needed to thank Butch for listening to her request to mix in some classic rock with his collection of old-school country. If she had to listen to Jeannie C. Riley sing about taking down those fuddy-duddies at the Harper Valley P.T.A. one more time, she was going to beat the jukebox to death with her boot.

She pushed to her tired feet. "Arlene," she called down the bar to the other waitress who was handing off an order. "Will you please deliver the tray Gary's loading up to the corner table for me?" At the bouffant blonde's nod, Ronnie told the bartender she'd be right back and joined the Sheriff on the other side of the doors.

"I didn't see you come in," she told Grady, taking in his uniform minus the hat. He must have come straight from work. Or was he still on duty?

"I came in the back door." With his hand on her lower back, he propelled her down the hallway toward the open door at the end. "I needed to talk to Butch, and he wanted me to grab you before I got started."

"Why me?" Then a thought struck her. "Oh, hell, what's Katie done now?"

"You tell me," Grady said, following her into Butch's office and shutting the door behind them.

Butch sat on the corner of his desk, still wearing the cook's apron he'd slung on earlier when the orders had rolled in too fast for the cook to juggle. The paperwork Ronnie had been working on when the deluge of bikers had hit was spread out on his desk where she'd left it before heading out front to help.

"I know you're both busy, so I'll get right to the point," Grady said. "Per your request," he looked toward Butch, "I looked into Arlene. What I found doesn't really offer much help, but it does make her a person of interest."

"Person of interest? What does that mean?" Ronnie asked.

"In this case," Grady's somber gaze returned to her, "it means the only record of a woman named Arlene Hobbs in Florida is for a twenty-one-year-old college student going to the University of Florida in Gainesville. From what I can tell, if the woman out there taking drink orders is from St. Augustine, Florida, she was living off the grid without a driver's license, a mortgage or rent payment, or any other kind of paperwork that ties her to the Sunshine State."

Ronnie looked over at Butch. "You think Katie is onto something with Arlene?"

He rubbed his jaw. "I don't know." He turned to Grady. "Did you find anything on an Arlene Hobbs in one of the other states in that area? It seems like she mentioned living in Kentucky before taking care of her dying mother for the last few years. Maybe she never took up residence in Florida and everything identifying was under her mother's name."

"That's a possibility. That's partly why I say she's a person of interest. Usually when someone claims to be from a certain area but I can't find anything on them in the system, they are keeping their head low for a reason."

"So it could be something criminal related," Butch said.

"Or she could be running from an abusive spouse or someone with a criminal tie," Ronnie said. She'd been trying to disappear from the world in southeastern Arizona before Grady had figured her out.

"Or that," Grady said, his gaze somber.

A knock on the office door made Ronnie jump. When Grady opened the door, Katie was standing there.

She looked from Grady to Butch to Ronnie, her eyes narrowing. "What's going on in here?"

"I'll explain later," Ronnie told her.

"You better." She pointed at Butch. "Your presence is requested at the bar. There's a woman out there covered in tattoos, spandex, and a few well-placed swatches of leather who claims she writes articles for some motorcycle magazine and wants to ask you a few questions." She ended her monologue with a definite huff.

Butch eyed Katie for a couple of beats, and then a grin crept up his face and made his eyes twinkle. "Well, based on that tempting description, I'd better go see what she wants." He shucked his apron, hanging it on the coat rack next to the door. "I'll be right back," he told Grady and then slipped past Katie, leaving her glaring after him from the threshold.

When Katie didn't follow him, he came back and grabbed her hand. "You'd better come along to keep an eye on me, sweetheart. If this writer is dressed in as little clothing as you claim, I may need something to do with my hands so I don't touch anything I'm not supposed to."

"You have the right to touch whomever wherever, Valentine Carter." Katie shot Ronnie a scowl. "If you hear a bloodcurdling scream, you need to knock out the Sheriff, grab my keys, and meet me at my car. We'll make a run for the border."

"Come on, killer." Laughing, Butch tugged her after him.

After they were gone, Grady closed the door again, leaning against it this time, sealing Ronnie inside with him.

A nervous flutter filled her stomach at the intensity lining his face. "That's some wind we have out there today, huh?" she said to break the silence.

He crossed his arms, his utility belt making a creaking sound, his legs wide in the cop stance that always made her hackles rise. "I need to talk to you."

"About what?" she lifted her chin, preparing for a verbal

sparring match.

"You tell me. My Aunt Millie called me today and insisted that I come see you because we need to talk about something important."

Oh, right, Thanksgiving dinner. Ronnie had practiced asking him in the mirror this morning, but all of her attempts had sounded downright dorky.

Grady cocked his head to the side. "Maybe we can start with what you and my aunt were doing at Dirty Gerties on Monday afternoon."

Ronnie's cheeks heated. Busted, but how? "Sheesh! Did you plant a tracking device in my purse or something?"

"No. That would be illegal without a court warrant."

"Well," she threw her hands in the air, "there's a ray of sunshine in this shit storm."

"I know that you and my aunt were at the club because I recently talked to the owner."

"Cherry?"

He nodded once, his poker face firmly in place.

Why was he talking to Cherry? Did he like to hang out at Dirty Gerties on his nights off? Was he like Lyle and …

Grady growled in his throat. "Veronica, don't look at me like that. I'm not your ex-husband. I saw Cherry at the mini-mart yesterday morning when I stopped for coffee on the way into work. She asked about my aunt using a walker now and went on to tell me about seeing you two in her establishment."

Relief flooded through her, cooling her jets, leaving her feeling embarrassed and stupid. She ran her fingers through her hair, wishing she could shapeshift into a cockroach and scuttle away through the vent. "Sorry. Old habits die hard."

"Trust me, I understand." His face relaxed, his lips curving into a hint of a smile. "Let's start again."

She nodded, sweeping her insecurities under the rug. "Fine, ask away. But keep in mind that I suffer from a rare form of interrogation-intolerance similar to Tourette's syndrome and cannot be held responsible for the resulting verbal tics that may offend your delicate cop sensibilities."

"Delicate did you say?"

She matched his challenging look clear down to the wide-legged stance. "Extremely delicate, Sheriff Hardass."

"Well, Ms. Morgan," his gaze slid south, over hill and dale and the rest of her peaks and valleys before snapping back northward. Longing softened his hard features. "It sounds like I may need to use excessive force to compel compliance from an unwilling subject in order to get the answers I'm seeking."

"Bring the heat, Sheriff. You're going to need it if you think I'm going to roll over without a fight."

His mouth curved up on one side. "God, you're sassy, Veronica."

"What are you going to do about it, Grady?"

"I'm going to handcuff you to my bed and keep you there for a week."

"Sounds like police brutality to me."

"You don't know the half of it. Once I get started you'll be begging for release over and over."

The conviction in his voice gave her goosebumps. "Not if I corrupt you first."

His throaty chuckle enticed her even more. "Ah, but my beautiful *bandolera*, you had me corrupted as soon as I asked for your license and registration. The consequences since that day have been serious to say the least, violating my personal welfare more than you realize."

"Well, Sheriff, that makes two violations then—one for you and one for me. Now are you going to interrogate me or just keep standing there thinking about me naked?" Truth be told, she was the one with the naked thoughts, but he didn't need to see how weak-kneed he made her.

His eyes flashed, widening, but he kept his hands to himself, damn it. "Why did my aunt send me to see you?"

"I need to ask you something."

"I'm all ears."

She licked her lips, her cockiness waning, feeling like she was back in junior high trying to land a date for the Sadie Hawkins dance. "I would like to ... uh ... I was wondering if you would consider ..." she blew out a breath, scratching her neck. How could something so simple be so awkward and hard?

"Just spit it out, sassy."

She gave it a whirl. "I would like to request your presence at the Morgan family's dinner table on Thanksgiving Day." What the planets! That was her worst one yet.

Grady's forehead scrunched. "Are you asking me to Thanksgiving?"

"Yes."

Suspicion filled his gaze. "Why?"

"What do you mean why? To eat turkey and stuffing and pumpkin pie."

"What's the catch?"

"Why does there have to be a catch?"

"Because the Morgan girls are usually allergic to the law, especially you. Did my aunt put you up to this?"

Ronnie hesitated, wondering how much Aunt Millie would talk about their deal in front of Grady. She didn't want to lie, but the truth might not go over so well.

"I knew it!" Grady shook his head, cursing under his breath. "It drives her nuts that I choose to work the holidays."

"Why do you work the holidays?"

He shrugged. "It's just another day of the year, same as Christmas. Plus it lets my deputies spend the holidays with their families."

His irreverence when it came to holidays tugged at her heart. Now she understood why Aunt Millie had made his invite part of the deal.

"Grady." She stuffed her hands in her pants pockets to keep from reaching for him, figuring any evidence of caring right then would probably make him uncomfortable. "Please have Thanksgiving with me and my family."

He smirked. "Now you feel sorry for me." When she tried to deny it, he held up his palm like he was stopping traffic. "Trust me, Veronica, when I say there's no need for sympathy. I'm happy to work through the holidays."

This was going to be tougher than she'd thought, but she knew better than to show up at her next meeting with Aunt Millie empty handed. "Okay, fine. If you're too chicken shit to have dinner with us, I understand."

"That tactic isn't going to work."

She pretended to inspect her fingernails, trying another avenue. "Never mind that I was going to fill you in on a potentially illegal situation we're dealing with as of late."

"If you know of any illegal activity in the area," he gripped his belt, "you need to inform me before someone gets gun-happy."

Well, that didn't work either. What was next? Sex? It had been too damned long since they'd been alone long enough to do more than touch and tease. What the hell, it was worth a shot. "Not to mention that I was thinking we could steal a can of whipped cream and sneak out to the tool shed for some dessert."

"Dessert?" His voice sounded a little hoarse. Had she cracked his resolve?

She closed the distance between them, going in for the kill. "Dessert," she repeated, drawing a circle around his badge with her fingernail, and then scratching her way south until she bumped into his belt. "You see, Sheriff Hardass, I have this little idea."

"I'm listening."

"It involves you, lots of whipped cream, and my tongue."

His Adam's apple bobbed.

"What say you, law dog? Are you sure you don't want to come to Thanksgiving dinner with me?" She looped her hands around his neck, pressing her chest against him.

"You're playing dirty, Veronica."

No shit. She had to satisfy her part of a deal with whatever it took. She went up on her tiptoes, pulling him down to her, and whispered in his ear, "I promise not to wear panties to the tool shed." Then she flicked his earlobe with her tongue.

He caved with a deep groan. He wrapped his arms around her, crushing her lips under his with a kiss so overpowering that she didn't realize he'd lifted her off the ground for several seconds.

He pulled back, his dark eyes turning her into a smoldering mess of need. "I shouldn't kiss you, Veronica."

Fine. She kissed him instead and showed him what he'd been missing from her lately. When she came up for air, she asked,

"Why shouldn't you kiss me, Grady?"

"I'm on the clock." He let her slide back down to her toes, his body obviously taking her side.

"Screw the clock." Her fingers sank knuckle deep in his dark wavy hair, drawing him down to her this time. Her mouth taught him the error of his ways until he took over and knocked her seduction attempts out of the park. Damn, the man knew how to kiss. Her heart was dangerously close to leaping into his arms so he could carry it off into the sunset.

The office door opened, bumping into them.

"Hells bells, you two," Butch said, stepping inside and shutting the door behind him. "You're worse than the jackrabbits around here."

"Go away and come back later," Grady muttered against her lips, not letting her go.

Ronnie heard Butch's chair squeak. "Sheriff Harrison," he said, apparently not listening to Grady's order. "Aren't you still on duty?"

"I'm on break," he answered but then untangled from Ronnie and straightened his shirt. "Not that it's any of your business what I do with my time, Carter."

Butch laughed, leaning back in his chair. "Oh, how the mighty have fallen."

Ronnie blew on Grady's badge and then shined away a smudge with her sweater sleeve, saying over her shoulder to Butch, "I've heard that the bigger they are, the harder they go down." She gave the Sheriff a daring grin.

He smirked back. "Make a note of what the temptress said, Carter. She usually likes to taunt me with words like 'delicate' and 'tiny,' shooting her poisoned arrows at my ego."

"So what's your answer, Sheriff?" Ronnie pressed. "Are you up for a date with a turkey and some dessert or not?"

His brow wrinkled, his focus moving to Butch. "What are you doing for Thanksgiving?"

"Same as usual. Pouring drinks."

Grady turned back to Ronnie. "If you can get Butch to take the day off, I will, too."

"Take Thanksgiving Day off?" When Grady nodded, Butch

frowned. "Why would I do that?"

"Because you're going to have Thanksgiving with us," Ronnie told him.

"Who's us?"

"The mother of your child for one, along with the rest of her family."

He grimaced. "Is your mom going to be there?"

"Probably."

Butch steepled his fingers. "I'll make a deal with you."

"Let's hear it."

"I'll join you for Thanksgiving if we can have it here."

"At The Shaft?" Ronnie asked, confirming.

He nodded.

"Why here?"

"Because I like to leave the bar open for people who don't have family and don't want to spend the day alone. There's usually only a handful who come and go during the holiday."

"Okay." Ronnie looked from Butch to Grady. "We'll have Thanksgiving here and you both will be in attendance." Aunt Millie hadn't made stipulations on where dinner had to be, so it still fulfilled Ronnie's part of the deal.

Grady didn't look thrilled when he nodded in agreement. She wondered if it had anything to do with whipped cream and a certain tool shed. While it was his fault for insisting Butch be part of the deal, she'd have to find a way to make it up to him.

"Now where were we?" she asked.

"You were about to tell me what you and my Aunt Millie were doing at Dirty Gerties on Monday afternoon."

"Research," Ronnie shot back.

"What would you be researching at a strip club with my aunt?"

"Now, Sheriff," she patted his arm, "you know it's a woman's prerogative to kiss and not tell. And since I already kissed you ..."

His jaw tightened. "Technically, I kissed you first."

"Right, well, there's no *telling* what we were up to at Cherry's establishment, but I could be persuaded to show you."

"What's that supposed to mean?"

She smiled and reached for the door. "Mark your calendars, boys: Thanksgiving dinner with the Morgan family. Butch, you're supplying the location and furnishings. Grady, I'll expect you to provide dessert." She winked at him. "I like lots of whipped cream with my pumpkin pie. Try not to disappoint me."

Before he had a chance to continue his interrogation, she closed the door behind her. Whew! That had taken some fancy dancing, but she'd withstood his questions while managing to convince him to come to Thanksgiving. Aunt Millie had better deliver some answers on what happened to that damned camper.

Ronnie pushed out into the bar, searching for Katie among the crowd of patrons.

There was one tiny snag to fix—convincing her sisters that Thanksgiving at The Shaft with the Sheriff of Cholla County and his notorious aunt was a good idea.

Chapter Twenty

Wednesday, November 14th

Kate pulled her Volvo into the parking lot of Diggers Feed Store and took a spot near the back, far enough from most of the other vehicles so she'd have a clear view. Cars and pickups whizzed by on the side street, some turning into the lot, others leaving. None of them had any idea that a killer was milling among them on this sunny morning here in a dusty corner of Yuccaville—none of them but Kate.

She slid lower in her seat, hiding behind the steering wheel of her Volvo. Across the lot, the Polar Bear climbed off of his shiny Harley Davidson, shoving his leather gloves in his back pocket as he strode through the store's front doors.

As she waited for him to come back out so she could resume their game of cat and mouse, she opened the bag of dill pickle flavored popcorn she'd brought along for brunch and sipped on the strawberry milk she'd grabbed on her way out of the General Store. Today was the day; she could feel it in her bones. She tossed a handful of popcorn into her mouth, the dill seasoning twanging her taste buds. Something was going to give, and for once Claire wouldn't roll her eyes when Kate told her what she'd witnessed.

Ten minutes later, Kate was covered in popcorn crumbs and all out of milk. She also felt the strong, tickling sensation of a full bladder. Maybe the feed store had a bathroom she could sneak in and out of before the Polar Bear finished whatever he was doing in there. After a quick check to make sure the coast was clear, she grabbed her keys and stepped out of the car. As soon as she started walking, the pressure on her bladder increased twofold, making her move faster before she blew a gasket. She could imagine Claire's hysterical laughter if she found out Kate had peed her pants on a stakeout.

The restroom was right inside the main doors thankfully, but so was the Polar Bear. He was too busy unloading a small basket onto the checkout counter to notice her. As she passed by him, she scanned his purchases—a coil of rope, a roll of duct tape, a blow torch, and a bag of sour gummy worms.

Holy shit balls of fire! He was buying rope, duct tape, and a blow torch??!!! How much more obvious could he be? He might as well buy a "Murder for Idiots" kit while he was at it.

Kate's breath was short and quick the whole time she was in the bathroom. She hurried from the toilet to the sink and out the door. The Polar Bear was outside stuffing his purchases into his leather saddlebags. She fast-walked to her car, keeping her head down and maintaining a distance of several vehicles between them.

She was almost to her car when the chirp of a siren behind her stopped her in her tracks. "You've got to be fucking kidding," she said and turned to face her nemesis.

Deputy Dipshit pulled up next to her and rolled down his window, blocking her view of the Polar Bear. Today he was dressed up in his tan uniform and hiding behind the Sheriff's Department symbol painted on his white pickup door. His smirk rubbed her wrong, her claws automatically extending.

"Well, look what we have here," he taunted. "The one and only Kate Morgan, slinking around town. You looking to start some more trouble?"

"I wasn't slinking."

"What were you doing in the Feed Store? You don't have a bag to show for your time in there. Kind of makes me wonder if you have something hidden under your coat."

She spread her coat wide, showing her jeans and pink sweatshirt underneath. "Sorry, Deputy, but you're barking up the wrong tree today. I suggest you move along now, little dogie. They'll be out of doughnuts at the grocery store soon."

His upper lip curled as he snickered. "Hey, did you know your name is the same as a porn star?"

Of course he'd know that. She smiled back at the putz. "Hey, did you know your face looks the same as a baboon's butt?"

That wiped the smirk clean off his smug mug. He pointed at her. "You watch that mouth, or I'll haul you in again for assault."

"Criminy, you're like a broken record, Deputy. Did you study only two pages of the list of crimes in your How-to-be-a-Deputy picture book?"

The sound of a Harley rumbling to life made her curse under her breath. While this double chinned asshole made it his mission to try to one up her, a true-to-life criminal was getting away with saddlebags chock full of supplies for the death fiesta he was obviously planning to have soon. The only thing missing was the piñata, aka her oldest sister.

"If you think you can get away with breaking the law because your sister is bedding down with the Sheriff, you're wrong."

The Polar Bear rolled out of the parking lot and onto the street, the sound of his muffler heading toward downtown. Shit, there he went. Now she'd have to return to Go and start all over again.

Deputy Dipshit continued blustering. "I'm here to tell you that I'm making it my mission to keep a close eye on you Morgan broads and stop you from menacing around this town—*my* town."

She glared up at the meathead who'd screwed up her stalking opportunity for the morning. "First of all, Deputy, one does not *menace* around a town. I suggest you ask Santa for a dictionary this year instead of bigger tires."

She unlocked her Volvo with her remote. It was time to end this showdown at the Feed Store corral before someone ended up in jail for clobbering the witless dung beetle and missed her shift at work.

"Second, here's a concept for your squirrel brain—instead of harassing a pregnant substitute teacher every time she comes to town, how about you focus on finding criminals and protecting citizens like you're paid to do. Who knows, you might actually manage to handcuff someone before the year is out."

"You may talk smart, but I talk badge."

Talk badge? What did that even mean? Was that cop speak for something?

"Great," she said, opening her car door. "Well, how about you take that badge and move along. Your pickup is in my way, and since there is currently no legitimate crime you can think of to pin on me, I'm going to leave."

He rolled up his window, his beady eyes hating her to eternity and back.

By the time she'd gotten into her car and started it up, he'd reversed enough to let her leave. But the son of a bitch followed her out of the lot, down the street, and clear to the Yuccaville city limits. Kate glared into her rearview mirror when he pulled off to the side of the road and flipped a U-turn.

What in the hell did Sheriff Harrison see in that incompetent boob? They must be related by marriage somewhere down the line. Why else would the Sheriff not fire his ass and hire a real lawman?

Whatever the reason, Grady had better get a handle on his deputy, because if he didn't stop poking her with a sharp stick, Kate was going to go grizzly on his ass.

* * *

Ronnie glanced down at the scrap of paper in her hand and then back up at the single-story, dark red Craftsman style bungalow on Starlight Drive. The numbers posted on the cream-colored beam across the top of the porch matched those Aunt Millie had given her over the phone this morning. This must be it. Was this where she lived? If so, the older lady was taking good care of the place.

She parked on the street in front of the house so she didn't block the drive. The sun warmed her back through her blue flannel shirt as she walked up the sidewalk, admiring the tan columns and clapboard style siding. On the porch, she could smell a hint of fresh paint. She touched the siding. It was dry, but the joints were mostly dust free. Aunt Millie must have had it painted in the last month.

She rang the doorbell and glanced back out at Ruby's old Ford. On second thought, maybe she should have parked in the drive. If Grady passed over on the main drag, he might spot the pickup and come knocking for another round of interrogation fun and games.

The door creaked open.

Ronnie turned, looking down to Aunt Millie's level and instead found herself eye-to-eye with the neckline of a black shirt.

"Ah-hah," Grady said, "this explains why my aunt insisted I clean my house before she joined me for a late lunch."

It took Ronnie several stutters to realign her tongue so she could speak actual words. "This is *your* house?"

He nodded and stepped aside. "Come on in. Aunt Millie is in the kitchen."

Crossing the threshold, she stepped inside his lair and paused, taking in the setting. The place smelled like bay rum mixed with a lemon scent and a spritz of Windex. The inside was as well-kept as the outside, with plush textures and warm wood accents, dark green carpet and cream colored drapes.

There was something very intimate about standing inside Grady's home, seeing this side of him after being face-to-face with the rugged, hard-edged lawman more often than not. Something very dangerous, too, putting her heart at risk. Maybe it was seeing him in such a casual environment. Or maybe it was the dose of longing to share this life with him that left her trembling enough that she clasped her hands together.

He closed the door behind them and joined her, standing in his entryway, looking toward the living room and the adjoining dining area. "What do you think? I'm trying to get it ready to sell. Are the colors too masculine? My sister thinks I might want to include more neutral colors, like beige or gray."

"It's beautiful. I think it would be a mistake to go too neutral, especially with the wood accents." She reached out and ran her fingers over the polished wood chair rail running the length of the wall. "Won't you be sad to leave this place?"

"No. I lived here with Elizabeth. It has too many bitter memories attached to it. But I do like the lines and angles of this building style. The house I'm having built will be a Craftsman, too, only it will be about twice this size with an attached garage."

She liked this style, too, especially with the natural wood accents that he'd polished to a shine. But she kept her lips sealed, afraid he'd figure out that lately she was daydreaming about something more serious with him than good times and great sex. If he knew how much the picture he was painting of his future made her want to cling to him and share it all, he might change his mind about calling her his woman.

She glanced at him from under her lashes. In this cozy setting, he looked more attractive than usual, especially in worn blue jeans and that black Henley. The way it emphasized the width of his shoulders made her clasp her hands together even tighter. "I look forward to seeing the new place you're having built."

"I have the architectural plans and sketches if you're interested."

Trying not to appear too eager, she stared straight ahead, nodding slowly. "Sure."

A diesel truck growled by out on the street.

Something clinked in the kitchen, sounding like ice cubes in a glass.

"Veronica."

"Yes?" She looked up at him, knocked a little off balance by the warmth in his amber gaze.

He caught her by the elbow, turning her to face him. "You look amazing in that shade of blue."

"The store label called it sapphire." Now why on earth had that come out of her mouth?

"Okay."

"It's a cotton blend." Damn it! She needed to jam a wedge of cheese between her teeth to block the stupidity pouring out between her lips.

He chuckled, looking too irresistible for her own good. "Shut up and kiss me 'Hello'."

"Yes, sir." She stood on her toes, reminding herself that his aunt was sitting in the other room undoubtedly eavesdropping. It was really more of a peck on the lips than an actual kiss.

His grip on her elbow stayed firm as she tried to step away. "That was too short."

"We have company."

"Will you come back here again?"

"You mean to this house?"

He nodded.

"With you?"

"Just the two of us next time."

"For a visit?"

He shrugged. "I was thinking more like dinner and a movie."

She lifted one brow. "That sounds sort of tame for us." Truthfully she was thrilled with the idea of snuggling up to Grady on his leather couch in front of the television.

"I could throw in a ferocious tiger." He pointed toward the floor in the corner of the living room. As Ronnie looked over, the gray and tan mottled cat lying there yawned, looking very not ferocious.

"What's her name?"

"*His* name is Clyde."

Lyle hadn't let her have a pet because of his array of allergies. She would have loved a companion to curl up with during those lonely nights in that big fancy house he'd mortgaged out from under her.

Swallowing the sudden lump in her throat, she wondered if Grady had any idea that she wanted to be part of this idyllic scene with him so much it made her ache. If only … No, it wouldn't work. She was a wanted woman with a felon-linked past and a potentially deadly future. He needed to find a girl who'd wear red polka dot dresses, drink iced tea instead of gin and tonics, and organize the local community potluck dinners.

She lifted her chin. That girl wasn't here now, though. So, until he found that modern day June Cleaver, Ronnie would keep his lap warm. She wasn't going to dwell on how long it would be until she was pushed out of his life, left to live like a stray once again.

She took his hand, lacing her fingers through his. "Grady, I would love to come over for dinner and a movie with you."

"How about Saturday night?"

"It's a date." She started to lead him down the hall toward what appeared to be the kitchen at the other end, but he tugged her back to him.

"One other thing," he said, taking her face in his hands, his thumbs tracing her cheekbones. He leaned down and kissed her the way he normally did, smashing through her defenses and leaving her with swollen lips and a racing pulse. "Hello, Veronica," he whispered when he pulled back.

She stared at him like a robot on the fritz, unable to do much else at the moment with the overloaded circuits in her brain popping and sparking. He towed her toward the kitchen, leaving her at the round table where his aunt drank coffee with a clown-like grin pasted on her face.

"My what a rosy complexion you have today, Veronica," Aunt Millie said with a wink and pointed at the chair next to her. "Sit. The Arizona sunshine is treating you well. Wouldn't you agree, Grady?"

He chuckled. "You couldn't be more obvious, Aunt Millie." He held up a mug and a glass. "Coffee or water?" he asked Ronnie.

Sitting in the chair next to Millie, Ronnie said, "Water would be great." She could use something to douse the fires inside of her and cool her down enough to think clearly.

After he set the glass in front of her, he excused himself for a moment.

Ronnie swallowed a gulp, and then leaned closer to Aunt Millie. "Interesting location you chose for today's meeting," she whispered. "I thought we were keeping things on the down low when it came to your nephew."

Aunt Millie frowned back. "I made an executive decision."

"Oh, yeah? What gives you the right when it's my problem we're talking about?"

She shrugged. "Grady needs to know about this."

"I need to know about what?" Grady asked, returning at that moment and pulling out the chair next to Ronnie.

"Ronnie has a situation."

"I do not have a situation." She glanced his way. "At least not one that you need to know about."

"And she doesn't want you to know about it," Aunt Millie continued in spite of Ronnie's zip-it glare, "because she's afraid of how you'll react."

A second glance in Grady's direction made Ronnie wince. He had his Sheriff expression in place, along with his x-ray vision peepers.

"What's the situation?" he asked Ronnie.

She felt sweat bead on her upper lip. "Boy, it's warm in here." She unbuttoned her cuffs and started rolling up her sleeves. "Did you turn up the heat?"

"Not yet," he answered, his mouth tight. "Spill it, Morgan."

Ronnie turned to Aunt Millie, feeling trapped between two hard places. "Why are you doing this to me?" she whispered, even though Grady could hear her.

"Because you're in trouble and you need him. Trust me on this," Aunt Millie whispered back. She reached out and clasped Ronnie's hand. "Don't worry," she said, "my nephew doesn't bite pretty young things, especially when he stares at them as much as he does you."

Grady squinted from his aunt to Ronnie. "Why are you in trouble? Does this have to do with the FBI?"

Aunt Millie squeezed Ronnie's hand. "Tell him about the

diamonds, Veronica" she ordered, sounding bossy like Gramps.

"Diamonds?" Grady's eyebrows pulled together. "You mean the real gems this time, not that costume jewelry you were pawning off on my aunt?"

Ronnie's pride got snarly at his underlying accusation. "I wasn't pawning anything off on your aunt. She knew it was all fake from the start." Ronnie looked down at the ice cubes floating in her water. "What your aunt is referring to are the real things. I found a stash of them last month, and now it appears the owner wants them back."

Grady sat back, his jaw rigid as he looked from his aunt to Ronnie and back again. When he spoke, his voice had that authoritative tone to it that usually only came out when his badge was pinned in place. "Why don't you rewind and start at the beginning, Veronica. If you want my help, you're going to have to fill in the details—all of them."

"Okay, but for the record, I didn't want to bother you with this, Grady. I got Claire and me into this mess, and I'd planned to get us out without involving the law."

"Claire's in on it, too?"

"Well, she's the one who actually found the stash of diamonds, but I'm the one who kept them when the mule was hauled off to prison."

A range of emotions rippled across his face, none of them close to ending with a smile. "From the beginning," he iterated.

She obeyed, starting with the day she and Claire found the box of glass eyeballs and ending with her asking Aunt Millie for help with finding the camper. "Your aunt was supposed to meet me today and give me the details she learned about the camper, but instead here we sit and now you're involved, which makes this an even bigger mess."

"His job is to help clean up messes, not make them bigger," Aunt Millie added her two cents. "And before we go any further, I need to add another chapter to this story."

Ronnie turned to her. "So you did find out something about the camper."

"Yeah, and you'll be glad I made you come clean to Grady when I'm finished."

"You mean the camper we apprehended from the R.V. park?" Grady confirmed.

"That very one. Turns out that after Ronnie's mule was sent to prison, the state moved the camper to the auction yard with the other confiscated vehicles. A week later, it went up for sale and was purchased by a man named Pete Morshire, who hauled the camper back to his home in Pinetop. Last week, Pete's neighbor stopped by to see if Pete wanted to split the cost of a load of firewood. Only someone else had paid Pete a visit first, someone who had torn Pete's house and the new camper apart looking for something. When they didn't find what they were looking for, they tore Pete apart, too. According to the police report, it appears a chainsaw was used to do the worst of the damage."

Ronnie felt the blood drain from her face. "What?" she breathed more than spoke.

"There's a killer on the hunt, honey," Aunt Millie squeezed her hand again. "I'm scared clear down to my stockings that the trail now leads to your family's R.V. park."

"Oh, Jesus," Ronnie felt sucker punched, unable to catch her breath.

Aunt Millie frowned across at her nephew. "And after he finishes with the R.V. park, if Grady can't stop him, he'll follow the tracks to the end of the line—you and your sister."

* * *

Claire was nailing on a strip of molding while Chester and his can of beer supervised from one of Ruby's barstools when she heard the door in the General Store slam open.

Before she could do more than look over her shoulder in the direction of the curtain dividing the two rooms, her finger hovering over the trigger of the nail gun, Ronnie raced into the room. Her sister's cheeks had red blotches, her hands twisting together.

"We have a problem." She looked over at Chester, stole the beer from him, and chugged it down.

Claire was impressed, especially with her lack of gagging and burping. That was some bitter tasting shit. She turned back to the task at hand. "What's Kate done now?"

She hit the nail gun trigger twice. *Pop! Pop!*

"It's not Katie this time. It's me."

"I thought you said *we* have a problem." Claire moved further down the strip of molding.

"And you by association."

Pop! Pop!

"Well, whatever this problem is, it can take a number and get in line. Thanks to Chester, I have a toilet to fix out in the new restroom."

"It wasn't me," Chester said, lighting a cigar. "I told Carrera to fish the thing out, but the old bonehead thought flushing it would be better."

Claire pointed the nail gun at Chester. "Either way, you're going in there with me, or I'll nail both of your asses to the wall."

"Claire," Ronnie strode over and stole the nail gun from her. "This is serious."

Claire glared up at her sister. "Give me that nail gun back."

"No. Not until you listen to what we have to say."

"Who's we? You and Casper the Ghost?"

"Your sister and me," said a deep voice from behind the curtain. The voice registered in Claire's brain at the same time Sheriff Harrison joined them in the room, laying his cowboy hat on the bar.

"Claire," Chester said around his cigar, "Now might be a good time for you to tell me where you stashed my bird-watching binoculars in case you go to the hoosegow for a while and I need to keep a lookout."

"No. You're still grounded."

"What if I promise to bring you a special cake with a little gift inside while you're in the slammer?"

"Chester," Ronnie huffed at the old smartass. "This is serious."

"So is you stealing my beer." He leaned over and patted Sheriff Harrison on the arm. "I'd like to report a crime."

"Claire." Ronnie kneeled in front of her, her brown eyes and forehead lined with worry. "I'm talking life and death here."

What? Claire sighed, leaning back against the wall. "Criminy, Ronnie. What did you do now?" She glanced over her sister's shoulder at the Sheriff, who was checking out Ruby's collection of beer steins behind the bar. "And why is the Sheriff of Cholla County standing in our rec room?"

"It's about the diamonds."

Oh, hell. Ronnie had said that aloud, which meant the Sheriff was in on this. "What happened? And don't try to tell me Grady seduced the truth out of you, because that always sounds so lame when they use it in books and movies."

"You know the camper where you found the diamonds?"

"*We* found them," Claire corrected. She crossed her arms over her chest, wondering just how many details her sister had spilled to Grady. "Of course."

"It's been torn apart from top to bottom. Someone was looking for them. And the guy who recently bought the camper at the state auction was also left in pieces for the cops to find."

"In pieces?"

"Yeah, as in murdered with a chainsaw."

"Holy shit." Claire squeezed her forehead. "And now we're next in line."

"Yeah." Ronnie looked over at the Sheriff. "That's why Grady is here."

First those people over the border had been gunned down, then the mule had been stabbed twenty-three freaking times, and now the camper's new owner had been carved up with a chainsaw.

Claire stared across at the Sheriff, her gaze drifting down to the firearm he had holstered on his hip. "He's here to see the other eyeballs?"

"Yes." Ronnie sat down, leaning back against the wall next to Claire. "And to help us."

"I guess that's good." Claire frowned at her sister, "But will one lawman and his gun be enough?"

Chapter Twenty-One

Kate followed Butch inside Biddy's Gas and Carryout, Jackrabbit Junction's equivalent of a mini-mart. Thanks to the heavy flow of bikers on all makes and models, The Shaft was running low on buns, condiments, and eggs. Butch's usual supplier wasn't able to deliver until tomorrow morning, so tonight they were going to make do with whatever they could scrounge up between Biddy's and the General Store.

"I'll grab the buns and you load up on eggs," Butch told her, his gaze twinkling with mischief. His hand snaked toward her hind end.

She caught his wrist mid-reach and wagged her finger in his face. "That was slick, Valentine, but your eyes gave you away from the start. I'll get the buns. You're in charge of eggs."

Pulling free, he tweaked her chin. "Can't blame a guy for trying, Crazy Kate."

He headed toward the in-wall refrigerators filled with beer, soft drinks, and deli goods. Kate watched his buns as he went, enjoying the view along with the lighthearted banter they were sharing more often lately. It reminded her of life before the baby had come along.

She crossed her fingers this meant the future wasn't as bleak as it had seemed when she had gotten the pregnancy test results weeks ago. Butch wanted to be a father; she had no doubt about it. Next she needed to persuade him that he and she and baby made three, a happy start to a wonderful family life. At least things appeared "happy" in her recent daydreams.

Then again maybe the baby was making her delusional.

Kate's arms were loaded with hamburger futures, when the door chimed and Dory Hamilton walked in heading straight toward the chips section. She froze, clutching the buns, and watched Dory try to decide between several different flavors of chips.

"Kate," Butch's voice in her ear snapped her back to life. "While I enjoy it when you squeeze my buns most days, you might want to take it easy on these so we can serve them to customers."

She stepped back out of Dory's view, motioning with her chin for Butch to follow. "That's Dory Hamilton," she whispered, nudging her head toward the other aisle.

"I know," he whispered back, taking a bag of buns from her as it began to slip off her pile. "Why are we whispering?"

She peeked over the top of the row of laundry soap, bug spray, and other sundries. Dory had narrowed his choices down to a green bag of sour cream and onion potato chips and an orange bag of corn chips. "Because he's the caller."

"The caller of what?" Butch caught another slipping bag of buns as she shifted her load.

"Last week, he called the R.V. park and left a threatening message with Ronnie that freaked her out."

Butch pushed aside some boxes of matches and set the cartons of eggs he was holding on the shelf. "What threatening message?" He took another bag of buns from her, lightening her load even more.

"He said, 'He's coming for you,' and then hung up."

"How do you know it was Dory?"

Going up on her toes, she leaned into Butch and explained the whole shebang as fast as she could in his ear, including how Claire had confronted Dory the other day while Kate had snatched his phone, getting the prison's numbers from it.

"Damn, Kate," Butch leaned back, frowning down at her. "You've been busy—first stalking motel guests and now stealing phones."

"I didn't steal it." She glanced over, watching Dory dwell over which dip for his green bag of chips. "I merely borrowed it and then put it back the next day."

"*Borrowed.* Right."

Dory picked a dip and started toward the cash register.

"Shit." She shoved the rest of the buns at Butch. "Take

these. I have to confront him."

Butch pushed the buns back at her. "No, you don't."

"Yes, I do. I need to find out who put him up to calling the R.V. park." Buns still in hand, Kate started toward the register where Dory was handing the cashier some bills. "I'll be right back."

"Oh, no you won't, sweetheart." Butch grabbed her by the waist and spun her around.

"Butch, let me go." Dory was going to get away, damn it.

"Absolutely not." He pointed at the floor. "You stay right here and guard my buns. I'll take care of this." Then he was gone, following Dory outside.

Kate moved over to watch through Biddy's plate glass windows, shading her eyes from the setting sun. From her viewpoint next to a revolving rack of sunglasses, she saw Butch approach Dory, calling out to him, getting him to stop and look back.

She watched Dory as Butch spoke. His jowly face changed from friendly to surprised, his eyes widening. But the surprised look quickly turned defensive with a narrowed glare and a lot of tense gesturing.

At that point, Butch moved in closer, tapping the Tucson Electric Power patch on Dory's coat as he talked. Red, blotchy spots formed on Dory's cheeks before he replied. Butch crossed his arms over his chest, his stance determined as he spoke again.

Dory nodded and when his lips moved again, Butch took a step back. Based on his profile Kate guessed Butch was skeptical. About what though? She leaned closer to the window, as if it would help her hear through the glass better.

Butch's lips moved again, and Dory nodded. Then Dory turned and climbed into his pickup, spinning out of the carryout's drive.

The bell over the door chimed.

Butch strode down the aisle toward her, his lips curved down. When his dark blue gaze met hers, a storm brewed behind them.

Her pulse giddy-upped. "What happened?"

"Grab the buns please, Kate. We need to get out of here."

"Butch." She followed on his heels as he moved over to where they'd left the supplies. "What did he say?"

"I'll tell you on the way back to The Shaft."

They hauled everything to the counter and Butch tossed some bills down, offering the cashier a free drink on Thanksgiving if he stopped by again this year. Kate loaded the buns into several bags along with the eggs, and they left the mini-mart in silence.

The sun dipped below the horizon, the chill of night seeping in from the east. She could smell the smoke from The Shaft's grill in the cool air, reminding her she hadn't eaten anything since the madness rumbled into the parking lot right after they'd opened for lunch.

Halfway across Biddy's parking lot she couldn't stand it anymore. "Damn it, Valentine," she jogged up to him as they walked diagonally across U.S. 191. "What did Dory say?"

He slowed, his face lined when he glanced down at her. She couldn't tell for certain, but he looked sort of pissed off. "You're not going to believe it."

"Believe what?"

"Who's spurring Dory on."

"Who?" She grabbed him by the waist of his jeans, dragging anchor. "Come on, you're killing me here."

Stopping in his tracks, he turned. "Sophy."

She gasped. "You mean Sophy Wheeler?" As in the loony bitch who tried to shoot holes through Claire last spring?

"The one and only."

"I don't understand. Why would he call the Gila Flats complex when Sophy is in a prison east of Phoenix?"

"Because Sophy was moved to Gila Flats a month ago. She's been blackmailing Dory."

"Blackmailing with what?" What could a woman locked away behind bars have over the man?

"For one thing, he falsifies meter readings in exchange for favors. He's been sloppy about that for years, counting on nobody looking too closely at his records. Sophy could turn him in, get him investigated, and he'd lose his cushy job with that nice retirement the company offers."

"You sound like you knew about that before."

"I did. He had a deal with The Shaft's previous owner for free drinks whenever Dory came into the bar and made the mistake of assuming I'd continue with their arrangement after I took it over. That was how I got him to come clean at Biddy's. Sophy is the one who clued me in about keeping an eye on Dory years ago. I confronted him then, and he hasn't messed with my readings since. But apparently he's still making deals with others, and Sophy somehow has records that can prove it."

"Jeez. That woman is like a human scorpion. She keeps stinging and stinging."

"Blackmail isn't her only tactic when it comes to playing puppet master with Dory these days."

"What do you mean? What else does Sophy have on him?"

Butch grimaced. "Sex."

"What? Did he commit a sex crime?"

"No, he claims she's been having sex with Dory during his visits in exchange for 'favors.'"

She grimaced at the level that woman was willing to go to, but for what? A quick scare? A toothless threat? No, there must be a bigger purpose. "You mean favors like calling the R.V. park and leaving a threatening message?"

"Exactly." Butch began walking toward The Shaft again. "Come on, I need to get back and help with the orders."

She followed, feeling dazed. Sophy Wheeler. Holy moly. Claire was going to flip her lid when she found out. Maybe Kate should wait until the crowd had died down tonight to tell her the news. "So," she said to Butch's back, falling behind again. His legs were too freaking long, although she did like to trail her nails up them and watch him writhe under her touch. "What do we do now?"

"You don't do anything, Kate, except keep out of trouble and help me run the bar."

"I need to help my family. We have to figure out what Sophy is up to. If it has something to do with Ruby or Claire or both."

"I know." He waited for her to reach his side, lowering his voice. "That's why I'm going to take tomorrow off and go to Gila Flats. It's been a while since I've touched base with Sophy about her house."

Oh, yeah. Butch was still watching Sophy's place for her while she was in the pen. Kate had forgotten about that detail while trying to keep a toehold just this side of deranged, no thanks to the baby hormones.

"You think you can get her to talk?"

"I think I have a better shot at it than your sister or Mac. One way or the other, I'm going to find out what the hell she's up to before this goes any further."

"Why?"

He cocked his head to the side. "Why what?"

"Why are you helping us?"

His smile returned, his face softening under the glow of the red OPEN light in the window. Leaning down, he dropped a kiss on her lips, hovering just long enough to make her want more.

"Kate Morgan," he shifted the bags in his hand and ran a finger down her cheek. "Coming from a brainy, highly-educated teacher like yourself, that's a really dumb question." His gaze moved from her lips to her eyes.

"Butch," she started, blinking up at him. She wasn't sure what she wanted to say exactly, but she needed to let him know how much it made her heart feel all warm and fuzzy that he was helping her and her family, yet she didn't want to sound super-duper corny in the process and end up soaking his shirt in silly tears. Or something worse, like blubbering slobber.

He didn't give her the opportunity to finish. Pulling open The Shaft's door, he reached down and patted her on the butt. "Back to work, Baby Momma."

* * *

Thursday, November 15th

Mac checked his watch, squinting at the clock face under the bright afternoon sunshine. He looked down the street, keeping an eye out for a familiar Silverado pickup. No sign of it yet, only the wind kicking around the remains of a tumbleweed that had played chicken with a car a few minutes prior.

He leaned back against his tailgate, ready to get out of the city after a week of long hours and even longer nights at home alone. But this afternoon, instead of his normal routine of leaving work early and heading straight to his aunt's R.V. park and Claire, Jackrabbit Junction was coming to him in the form of Butch Carter.

They were going on a field trip, driving south to Gila Flats to pay a visit to the woman who'd tried to kill him and Claire. A trip that hadn't been on his radar until late last night when Claire had called and filled him in on the latest excitement, including Sophy Wheeler being the one behind Dory Hamilton's threatening phone call. Then Claire had put him on the phone with Butch. After hearing Butch's plan, Mac had offered to keep him company on the trip to the prison since the purpose behind Sophy's meddling likely had something to do with Ruby.

The sound of an engine coming closer made him look over. Butch's pickup rolled into the parking lot.

Mac climbed into Butch's passenger seat. "Your rig looks good. I can't even see any dents."

"Kate plays a mean game of demolition derby, but my buddy at Buck's is a pro." Butch pointed out the windshield. "There's no problem leaving your truck here?"

"No. We subcontract with these guys. They know I'll be back for it later." Mac secured his seatbelt. "How was the drive here?"

"Uneventful." Butch drove out of the lot and headed toward the Interstate. "It gave me some time to think about how to come at Sophy. She thinks I'm visiting to discuss buying the property her diner sits on."

"You want the property across the street from The Shaft?" At Butch's shrug, Mac said, "I wondered how you got her to agree to see you."

"I've been in contact with her off and on since she was sent away." Butch turned onto the entrance ramp, heading south on Interstate 19. "I agreed to keep an eye on her house and property for a year to give her time to decide whether to keep it or sell it."

"Is she paying you for house sitting?"

Butch shook his head. "She offered, but I turned her down."

"That was generous of you."

"When I first bought The Shaft, she helped me out, recommending certain local suppliers, hooking me up with my accountant, sending patrons my way. We worked as a team—she covered breakfast and lunch, I catered to the afternoon and evening crowd." Butch settled in the center lane and hit cruise control as the city buildings grew further and further apart, the desert landscape taking over.

"I don't know if you remember The Shaft back when I bought it, but it was a real dive."

Mac's history in that part of the state didn't go back that far. "You were in Jackrabbit Junction a while before my aunt married Joe and took over the R.V. park. By the time I came along, you were already in the thick of cleaning up the place."

"It took a chunk of capital to get the bar up to health code standards, and I wanted a little better than that. Sophy did what she could to smooth out the inspections and to keep the money flowing by sending customers my way. I owed her for her help, so when she asked me to keep an eye on her place, I told her I'd do it on one condition—she'd let me buy Joe's old El Camino."

Right, the El Camino. The souped-up, midnight blue mean machine that Sophy had been storing in the same shed where she'd tried to blow a hole through Claire with her shotgun. "I wondered how you ended up with Joe's baby."

"It's a sweet ride. I've drooled over it since moving to Jackrabbit Junction."

"That reminds me of Mabel." Harley's sexy Merc had caught Mac's eye from the first moment he had seen her out there in the moonlight.

Butch nodded. "That Mercury practically gives me a hard-on every time I see her. You think he'd ever consider selling it?"

"No." Mac adjusted the vent to blow on his face. The western sun blasting through the window was starting to cook him. "She's the love of his life. It shares the first place spot on the podium with my aunt. You should see the steam come out his ears every time Claire gets a scratch on her."

"Maybe if I got him a deal on fixing her scratches, he'd let me take her for a drive."

Mac looked over, wondering if Butch hadn't realized yet that he was now almost part of the Ford-Morgan family and all that entailed. "Since you're about to become the father of Harley's first great-grandchild, you may be able to land some time behind the wheel in exchange for something else."

"Like what?" Butch glanced his way, one eyebrow lifting. "A wedding band?"

Mac couldn't tell by his tone if that were a good or bad swap. "I don't know what. Harley is funny that way. He gave me advice on how to keep Claire from pulling a hit and run on me relationship-wise."

"What was his advice?"

Mac chuckled, remembering that warm spring day inside of Harley's stifling Winnebago. How he'd squirmed as Claire's grandfather demanded to know what Mac had planned for the future when it came to Claire. "He told me that if I wanted to keep her from leaving me when things got serious, I needed to storm the beach with my guns cocked and take no prisoners."

"No shit?"

"No shit. And when her tanks arrived, he said to call in for an air raid and level her defenses."

"What's that mean?" Butch asked.

"I wasn't sure at the time and I'm still not positive, but I've thought about it off and on for a few months. I think he meant to dig in and hold steady whenever things got rough between us, and if she tried to retreat, swing around and come at her from another front."

"You're making me want to watch more World War II footage on the History Channel." Butch hit his blinker and dodged into the left lane to pass an old VW bus. "You think that strategy would work on Kate?"

"I don't know. Kate's a different bird than Claire. She's not as flighty when it comes to commitment."

"I've never thought of Claire as flighty." He shifted back to the right, the Interstate now narrowed to two lanes. "Especially with how she's been digging in over at the R.V. park, putting so much work into repairing and cleaning up the place."

Claire's relationship with the R.V. park was different. That particular wooer would never slip in the middle of sex and tell her it loved her. It would never ask her to move to Tucson and leave her family behind. It would never risk asking her to marry it or unintentionally do something that might make her feel like her wings were being clipped.

Rubbing the back of his neck, Mac stared out his window at the passing fence line draped with tumbleweed garland. There was a lesson in there, damn it. Maybe he needed to start taking better notes.

"Claire enjoys working with her hands," Mac told him. "She takes after her grandfather that way, I guess. I don't know what Ruby would have done if Claire hadn't come along to help with the R.V. park. The hands-on labor of love needed there is right up Claire's alley."

"Your aunt certainly put a lot of her own elbow grease into that place before Claire showed up. I was impressed that she made it profitable again."

"Yeah, she was doing pretty well until Joe died and left her in a shitload of debt."

"Joe always was an asshole first and foremost," Butch said. "I don't know what Ruby ever saw in him. She was too nice for him."

"According to her, Joe could be quite charming, especially when he was throwing his money around. She believed that she loved him. I think in the end she realized that what she loved was the idea of escaping being a waitress in a small town in Oklahoma and running her own business somewhere far, far away."

They rode for several miles in silence. Mac watched as they passed Green Valley, remembering the fire in his aunt when she'd first moved to Arizona. Those flames had almost gone out when Claire and Harley had arrived and filled her with fuel and hope again.

"Your aunt once told me that the R.V. park was her wedding present from Joe." Butch changed lanes to pass a slow tractor-trailer. "I remember thinking at the time that Joe should have given her a pair of earrings instead, because fixing up that park was going to take as much blood, sweat, and tears as The Shaft when I got hold of it."

"You've done an incredible job turning it around."

"Thanks. It's doing much better than I'd planned."

"You don't sound thrilled about that."

"Don't get me wrong, I'm not complaining because business is good. I just didn't figure on it taking this much of my time. When I bought it, I was looking for a hobby project that would keep me busy while I tried to figure out what I wanted to do next. I never expected it to do this well, and I certainly don't want to continue spending so much time there. My heart isn't in it."

Mac wondered what that meant for the future of The Shaft. Would Butch sell it? Was he already trying to line up a buyer?

Rather than prod where it wasn't his business, he changed the subject. "I heard from Kate that you grabbed yourself several fine examples of Detroit steel at a classic car auction in Texas. What did you get?"

Butch filled the rest of the ride with tales of what he'd seen and bought at the auction, explaining his plans for each vehicle he'd acquired, inviting Mac to go with him sometime and see the auction in person. By the time they'd exited the Interstate and turned onto the road leading to the prison, Mac wanted to go over to Butch's place, roll up his sleeves, and rebuild something of his own.

The trip through the security gates at Gila Flats went smoothly. They parked in the prison lot along with a handful of other guests arriving in time for visiting hour.

Butch started to pull his keys from the ignition but then looked over at Mac. "I'll leave the keys here with you. I don't expect to be more than twenty minutes, thirty tops."

Mac nodded. "Why are you doing this, Butch?" He'd wondered that since they'd spoken on the phone last night. "This is Ruby and Claire's mess, not Kate's."

"I'm the only one who can get Sophy to talk. You and I both know that. She's not going to give you an inch, nor anyone else, especially your aunt and Claire."

That was true. "This is going to mess up things for you when it comes to Sophy. You have a decent history together, but after today you'll have gone to the dark side."

"She went to the dark side when she got herself mixed up

with Joe again and killed his cousin." Butch frowned over at the doors where people were entering the prison. "Whatever respect I had for her disappeared when she tried to take out you and Claire. I agreed to watch her place because I repay my debts, and that seemed harmless enough." He pushed open his door and stepped down onto the asphalt. His lips flat-lined when he turned back to Mac. "If she'd have just let sleeping dogs lie and kept to her own business in prison, I would have followed through for the year we agreed upon. But now she's back to harassing your aunt or Claire or both, and I can't abide that, especially with you guys being practically family now."

Family. Huh. So if Butch married Kate, that would make Ruby his step-grandmother-in-law and Mac his ... hell, that was too twisted to figure out. It'd be simpler if Claire would just say "I do" and make them brothers-in-law.

"I'll be here when you're done. Watch her tongue, it's forked and pointy."

"Better to face her tongue than the wrong end of her favorite shotgun." Butch closed his door and headed toward the prison's visitor entrance.

Mac cracked his window to let in some fresh air and leaned back in the seat. Everyone who had come to visit an inmate was now inside, and a silence fell over the parking lot.

He yawned. The long hours at work had been taking their toll on him, and he still needed to drive back to Jackrabbit Junction tonight after Butch dropped him off at his pickup. There was always the option of sleeping in his own bed and heading east tomorrow, but he wanted to wake up next to Claire.

Claire. Soft, curvy, warm to his touch.

He yawned again.

His thoughts turned to Butch's comment on how Claire was working so hard to fix up the R.V. park.

She'd told him to take the promotion, assuring him she wanted to join him in his travels, but he wasn't born yesterday. She was lying. Well, maybe lying was too strong, but she didn't really mean it, not in her heart.

Yet she was willing to sacrifice what she wanted for him.

Was he willing to make sacrifices for her? And how big?

Claire.

Her big brown eyes, sweet smelling hair, sexy skin, heated touches …

His thoughts switched to fleeting dreams, flying by too fast to catch and hold.

The sound of the pickup door opening made him jerk upright.

"Hey, sleeping beauty." Butch shut his door and started up the pickup.

Mac rubbed his hand over his eyes, shaking the sleep from his brain. He checked his watch. Butch had been gone for almost a half hour.

"How'd it go?" he asked. "Did she admit she put Dory up to making that phone call?"

"Yes, with a little coaxing. She also admitted a couple of other things." Lines crisscrossed Butch's forehead. "I'm not sure what to believe."

"What do you mean?" Mac frowned across the cab.

"For one thing, she said she had Dory send your aunt the letter about the Humdigger mine."

How in the hell had Sophy found out that Joe owned that mine? Had she known all along, or had she been using her spare time in prison to dig deeper into Joe's past?

"What else did she say?" Mac asked.

"You know that line Dory gave on the phone?"

"*He's coming for you?*" Mac repeated Dory's words.

Butch nodded. "Well according to Sophy, she wasn't talking about any hit man coming for Ronnie. Hell, she didn't even know Claire's sisters' names."

"That will ease Ronnie's mind."

"Grady's, too," Butch said. "I don't think the Sheriff has gotten a full night's rest since Ronnie came to town."

"She has a way of messing with your calm." Mac knew first hand after living with her for a month. "If Sophy wasn't talking about a hit man, who was she talking about?"

Butch shot Mac a quick frown. "I think prison life is getting to Sophy, scrambling her gray matter."

"Why's that?"

"Because she claims that the 'he' she was talking about in her message to Ruby was someone it can't possibly be."

"Who?"

"Joe Martino."

"What?!"

"Yeah, for some bizarre reason, Sophy doesn't believe the man is really dead."

* * *

If this insanity kept up, Butch was going to need to change the name of The Shaft.

Ronnie was thinking that "The Madhouse" was more appropriate these days, what with the place full night after night with rowdy customers. Currently, it was standing room only. Those who couldn't get a table were waiting with drinks in hand for one to become available. Slipping through the bodies was like wading through spawning salmon.

With Butch not home from Gila Flats yet this evening, Ronnie and Claire were both chipping in. Ronnie waited tables while Claire ran the bar so that Gary the bartender could help in the kitchen. If this didn't slow down soon, they were going to need another waitress or two and a hostess to keep things orderly.

Ronnie dropped onto a barstool exhausted, her chin resting on her palm. The Shaft buzzed and crackled with energy around her. On the jukebox, the late great Marty Robbins sang about his white sport coat and pink carnation, but the dance floor was too busy for anyone to swing and sway to the music. Ronnie tried to relax for a couple of minutes while Claire poured drinks for one of her tables.

A hand on her shoulder made her turn.

"My feet are killing me," Katie said, her face drooping with signs of exhaustion.

There was nowhere else to sit, so Ronnie started to rise to give her sister the stool.

"Sit still. Just let me lean against you for a moment." Katie's back pressed against hers. After a moment, she said, "Your FBI buddy is playing pool again tonight."

Good. It was nice to have him around, especially with what she'd learned about Pete, the camper owner. Sort of like having a Doberman Pincher chained up within reach. "Mississippi should help us wait tables," she told Katie. "After all, our taxpayer money helps pay his salary."

"I agree. The black apron will match his Johnny Cash outfit tonight."

Ronnie glanced over her shoulder at the pool table area. As if he had a tracking device on her eyeballs, Mississippi looked up and caught her glance. He gave her a two-finger come-hither wave. She gave him a one-finger hold-on reply, the nice finger this time. Claire was almost done filling her drink order.

As soon as Claire finished, Ronnie gave up her stool to Katie and parted the Flesh Sea. She dropped off the drinks, tucked her tray under her arm, and joined Mississippi at the pool table where he was wrapping up a game of Eight Ball.

"I need to talk to you for a moment."

"All I have is a moment, so let's get to it."

"Not here. We need privacy."

That couldn't be good. "How about Butch's office?"

He nodded. "You go first. I'll follow after a minute or two."

Dropping off her tray at the edge of the bar, she passed through the swinging doors and waited for him in the empty office.

Mississippi followed shortly, closing the door behind him.

"What's going on besides you dressing up like Johnny Cash tonight?" she asked.

Mississippi brushed some lint off his sleeve. "What can I say? I'm a big fan of the man in black."

"So was Ruby's dead husband."

"I noticed." He straightened the cuffs of his shirt and then hit her with a double-barreled frown. "I have bad news."

"I didn't figure the lottery commission sent you with a big check. Let's hear it."

"Your ex-husband rolled over on a big ticket player today. The FBI is paying the felon a visit *en masse* soon."

"Isn't that a good thing for the FBI?"

"Yes, but not for you."

"Let me guess, Lyle owed this felon something and now that he tattled on him, the guy will be wanting blood to spill."

"Exactly and since they can't easily get to Lyle, you're next in line."

She sighed. "Why can't they easily get to Lyle?"

"Part of the deal he made with the FBI was to be moved into a safe, low-security facility away from potentially violent inmates. He'll be tucked away with fellow informants."

"That no-good, yellow-bellied weasel." When Ronnie stopped grinding her molars, she said, "Someone needs to tell these blood thirsty assholes that I divorced Lyle. Hurting me will not even make him blink."

"You and I know that's true, but the people who hired him to do their dirty laundry don't know it. As far as they are concerned, sending Lyle pieces of you would be a fitting payback for him running his mouth."

"Fuck me," she whispered, feeling like she'd been tossed overboard into shark-infested waters. "What am I supposed to do now?"

"Well, I could see if you're eligible for the federal witness protection program, but I don't think you'll qualify since you're divorced from Lyle and no direct threats have been made on your life ... yet."

"Mississippi, I don't want to spend my life running from these bastards."

"I don't blame you, but as long as your ex-husband is breathing, you're at risk."

She nodded, wishing she could go back in time and say, "I don't" at the altar and then drive off into the sunset with the Bandit in his iconic black Firebird.

"What does this mean for you and me?" she asked.

He smirked. "If you're wondering if you have to give my high school letterman jacket back, you can keep it."

"Since when did they install a humor chip in you FBI robots?"

"They didn't. I've gone rogue."

"Thank the FBI makers for that."

He sobered. "As far as I know, nothing has changed with my assignment. I'm still supposed to keep an eye on you and see what kind of flies you draw."

"Flies? How about something nicer sounding, like bees."

"So you're honey then?"

"Yes, that's much better than the usual substance that draws flies."

"Fine, Ms. Honey. I advise you to keep your head low and your eyes peeled."

She nodded, opening the door for him to leave.

Pausing on his way out, he added, "And let me know if you see anyone who looks suspicious or catch wind of anything threatening."

"Define threatening."

He grinned. "Someone pointing a firearm at your head."

Or someone coming at her with a chainsaw? "You FBI folks are so helpful."

"We serve to rankle and rile." Mississippi left her standing in Butch's office.

She was so screwed. If she ever got the chance to wrap her hands around Lyle's neck, she might end up in prison herself for squeezing the life out of the rat-faced, selfish, philandering prick.

Hells bells!

What were Claire and Gramps going to think about this? They wanted her to stay, but the longer she graced their doorstep, the more danger she brought to their world.

And what about Katie? Pregnant, crazy, and more vulnerable by the day Katie. If anything happened to her or the baby because of Lyle's big mouth, Ronnie wouldn't be able to live with herself.

Then there was Grady. He was going to be positively thrilled to hear that more trouble might be coming to his county thanks to her. Any chance of a future with him was shriveling up before her very eyes. Who wanted a woman who was a homing beacon for goons and hit men?

She blew out a breath of frustration. The way things were looking it would be easier to fit a coyote through the eye of a needle than make it through this calamity in one piece.

Chapter Twenty-Two

Friday, November 16th

Claire sat at Ruby's bar, inspecting her and Chester's finished product—the rec room.

"What do you think?" she asked.

"The floor is too fancy," Chester answered from the stool next to her. "And the walls are too green."

"There's only one green wall." Ocotillo green, according to the paint swatch, which looked great with the bamboo flooring. The other three walls were a neutral sand color. "Besides, I wasn't asking you, big mouth," she backhanded his shoulder. She looked over at Mac, who was standing in the kitchen doorway sipping a mug of coffee while checking out their work. "I was asking Ruby's nephew."

Mac's focus shifted to her. "What? I've been demoted to being 'Ruby's nephew' now?" The corners of his hazel eyes creased, his smile teasing. "Yet to hear you this morning, I was the sexiest, most amazing man alive."

What did he mean "hear" her? She'd tried to be quiet about her appreciation for his rousing demonstration on how much he'd missed her this last week, but he knew her buttons and was really good at pushing them.

"Get in line, Sweet Buns," Chester said snickering. "You're still wet behind the ears when it comes to knowing how to romance a girl."

"Guess I'll have to keep practicing." Mac leaned against the wall. "You up for it, Slugger?"

"It's more important that you're up for it," Chester beat her to the punchline. "I hear you got offered some big promotion."

Claire looked away. While she'd kept her thoughts on Mac's

promotion positive when sharing the news with Chester, she didn't trust the old man not to speak his mind with Mac like he had with her. The last thing Mac needed to hear was how her leaving this place was trouble in the making for the two of them.

"Yep." Mac took another drink of coffee. "The rec room looks great. Ruby's going to be thrilled." His optimism was a relief. "I'm surprised you two didn't find anything stashed away in the walls or floor when you tore the room apart."

"Damn, we forgot to check under the floor boards," Claire told Chester. "I knew we were skipping something important."

"Screw Joe and his hidden treasures, girlie. They bring you nothing but more fretting and headaches."

He had a point. She stood up and stretched. "I need to clean up the last of our paint mess out back and get things ready for Ruby and Gramps to come home."

Home. She realized she'd used that word too late, noticing the frown Mac gave her.

"You want some help?" he asked.

She shook her head. "Did you bring the claim paperwork for Humdigger mine with you?"

"Yeah, it's down in the basement office. Why?"

"I'd like to look it over when I'm done." When his frown deepened, she explained, "I'm a curious cat, you know that."

"Which life are you on again, kitty?" Chester asked.

"The one where I take you out with me when I go."

"Can I make a last request before that time comes?" At her nod, he said, "Make sure you include a couple of strippers, too. If I'm going to be underground, I want to be *under* some pretty girls while I'm down there."

"You don't get to pick and choose the party guests. This isn't ancient Egypt and you're not King Tutan-Chester." She grabbed her gloves and headed for the back door. "I'll find you when I'm finished outside, Mac."

Two hours later, the sun had hit its high point for the day and was on its way back down the western side. Claire washed her hands in the kitchen sink and then made herself a sandwich. Grabbing a Coke from the fridge, she went in search of Mac.

She found him down in the basement office.

"Hey, Slugger," he said, glancing up at her from where he sat at Joe's desk, papers spread out across the top of it. He leaned back, running his hand up and down the back of her thigh as she stood next to him. "You want help moving the furniture back in the rec room?"

"Yes, but not now." She pointed her sandwich at the papers. "What's all this? The Humdigger claim documents?"

"Some of it. The rest is some work I brought along."

"What work? Stuff for your new position?"

"Sort of."

She bent over the claim information, scanning through the copies. The text looked like it was typewritten rather than printed from a computer. It listed specifics like area on a quad map by township, section, and range. The various owners of the stake before Joe were listed; the name of the mine had not changed since it had first been claimed. Her gaze drifted to the bottom, screeching to a stop on Joe's signature.

She swallowed the bite of ham and Swiss she'd been chewing. "That's not right," she said, tapping on the signature.

"What do you mean it's not right?"

"That's not Joe's writing.'

"Since when are you an expert on Joe's penmanship?"

"Since I went through all sorts of signed documents while I was sitting in that very chair." She leaned over Mac and opened the file drawer on the lower right, pulling out a couple of folders. After fingering past the second one, she found some hospital paperwork with his signature. "See, compare this one from Cholla County General to the Humdigger mine claim."

Mac set the hospital paper next to the claim and leaned down, his gaze playing ping-pong between the two. "It's similar, but I can see why you say it's different."

"Why would there be two different signatures?"

"Two slightly different signatures," he corrected.

"Quit splitting hairs. Do you think Sophy is onto something here?"

"No, I think Sophy is plum nuts. There could be several explanations for this difference." He grabbed her by the waist and pulled her down onto his lap.

She shifted so she could look at him, careful not to bump his shoulder or ribs. "Oh, yeah? Give me three."

"Maybe he was in a rush on one of them and got sloppy." He plucked her sandwich from her hand and took a bite.

"Okay, that's one." She reached for the sandwich, but he held it out of reach, swallowing.

"Or he could have injured his hand and had to sign with the other one." He tapped his cheek for a kiss.

He had another good point there. "Two." She leaned over to pay up and he turned at the last second, planting a kiss on her mouth.

Handing the sandwich back, he added, "Or maybe Ruby forged the hospital paperwork for him because of his stroke."

"Yeah, but this signature on the hospital papers matches all of the others I've seen throughout his files. The one you have on that old claim is not just sloppy different. Look at the different style he's using for the J and the O at the end." She took a bite, chewing as she stared down at the papers.

"Haven't we had this argument before?"

Yes, actually, they had. "And I won that argument, too."

"You're premature on the final ruling here today, Slugger."

"I'm telling you this is different." She stuffed the last of the sandwich in her mouth.

"If this is different, what does that mean in your brain?"

She finished her bite before answering. "Maybe this is what has Sophy thinking Joe is still alive. She would probably know his signature after years of marriage. Maybe she saw the Humdigger claim papers online or somewhere else and she knows something else we don't about Joe that made her come to the conclusion that he's still alive … somehow." Although how Joe could be alive without Ruby knowing it made Claire scratch her head.

"What else could Sophy know?"

Mac's question was rhetorical, but she answered anyway. "I don't know, but that woman is no backwoods idiot. Something has her gnashing her teeth again." Having been on the receiving end of Sophy's wicked bite before, Claire wanted to stay well out of the bitch's leash range in case Sophy lunged again.

Mac looked at her, his brow scrunched. Then he shrugged.

"One thing I do know is I need to go back in that mine."

"You mean WE need to go back in that mine."

He slid his hand up inside the back of the "Dolly Parton for President" jersey she'd found in Ruby's closet, the calluses on his fingertips lightly scratching over her skin. "Fine, we'll go together, but you need to let me lead while we're in there."

"I always enjoy it when you lead," she flirted, wrapping her arms around his neck, leaning against him. "When do you want to go?"

"The sooner the better."

She nuzzled his neck, breathing in the scent of his skin. He always smelled like the sundrenched desert. If she got homesick while they traveled for his job, she could carry one of his shirts around with her and sniff it off and on all day like a sad puppy.

"How about we go now?" she asked.

"No." His fingers strummed her ribs. "Not in the light of day."

"Ahh, covert and secretive. I like this new darker side of you." She moved her lips up close to his ear and whispered, "It's hot."

He chuckled. "You would, ya jailbird."

Pushing back upright, she stared down at him in all seriousness. "How about we go late tonight after things slow down at The Shaft?"

"That'll work. I can pack up some of my gear and pick you up."

"Should I mention anything to Butch?"

"I hate to bother him after he drove all of the way to the prison to help out, but we'll need him to pave the way with old Dick Webber so we don't end up full of bullet holes. Maybe he can call Webber and let him know we'll be passing through."

"Good idea. I'll mention it to him when I head over there in a bit." She looked back at Joe's signature on the claim paperwork, wondering what booby-traps there'd be in store for them tonight. "Are you bringing your gas detector?"

"Yeah, along with Ruby's shotgun."

She grimaced at him. "You think that's necessary, huh?"

He caught her hand, lacing his fingers through hers. "If

you're going to be there with me, I'm not taking any chances."

* * *

Something was out there in the darkness.

Something that had Mac's neck hairs standing at attention.

He peered into the night, but without the full moon to bathe the world in silver light, he was stuck using his ears instead of his eyes. Breath held, he listened for a few more seconds, hearing nothing besides the normal sounds of the desert—whistling wind, rattling greasewood and sage, the occasional yip of a coyote. He sniffed, smelling nothing in the cold fresh air. Adjusting his pack, he shifted the shotgun to his right hand as a precaution.

"Okay. Let's go," he whispered to Claire, who'd waited in silence after he'd shushed her for the second time in the last ten minutes since they'd left his pickup.

"You should let me lead," Claire whispered back, stepping around him, starting up the animal trail they'd used to descend from the mine the last time they had been there.

He caught her by the elbow, pulling her up short. "No way, Slugger."

"Then give me your pack. You don't need to have it yanking on your shoulder as you climb."

He appreciated her thoughtfulness, but there was no way she was going first. "My shoulder is fine."

"What about your ribs? Your pack is going to bump into them all of the way up."

His ribs were still a little sore, but she didn't need to know that. "I'm good. I'll probably have to take it slower than usual on the climb, but I'll still beat you to the top, no contest." He chuckled at her growl.

"Keep it up, big talker," she poked him in the gut, making him grunt in between his snickers, "and I'll bruise another one of your ribs."

Mac took a couple of steps up the trail and then froze.

There it was again, a creaking sound, coming from further back down the trail. Without a word, he grabbed Claire and tucked her behind him, shining his light around below, lighting up the mesquite, greasewood, and desert willows.

Something small and furry dashed under a bush when his light hit it. That would explain the sound of bushes rattling but not the creaking sound he kept hearing.

His flashlight beam glinted off something metal at the same time a crusty voice shouted, "Hold it right there, trespassers."

"Shit," Claire whispered, yanking him back a step.

"Unless you want to spend the night picking shotgun pellets out of yer hide," the voice below called out, twigs snapping as their visitor stepped out into the open, "you'd better get those hands in the air and tell me who you are."

Claire huddled deeper into his back, practically crawling up inside of his flannel jacket.

A bright light shined in Mac's eyes. Squinting, he raised his hands slowly, keeping his fingers clear of the shotgun trigger so their visitor didn't decide to shoot in self-defense. "My name is Mac Garner."

"Garner, huh? What's yer business here?"

"My aunt, Ruby Martino, owns the mine up this hill."

He heard a grunt from the other end of the flashlight. "Who's that hiding behind you?"

"Claire Morgan," he said.

"Morgan, you say? Let me see her face." The beam of light moved to Claire, who'd popped her head around his shoulder. "Are you one of them Morgan sisters I heard one of the Sheriff's deputies complaining about last week?"

"Probably," Claire admitted.

"Step out into the light, girl."

Claire did, but Mac held tightly to her forearm, ready to tuck her behind him again if things went sour. She shielded her eyes from the beam of light when it moved from Mac to her.

"I know you," the voice said.

"You do?" Claire shot Mac a worried frown.

"You were at my house a couple days back."

"I was?"

"Sure enough. You were giving that half-wit Dory Hamilton trouble about some phone call."

"That was *your* house?"

"Yep." The flashlight beam lowered. The creaking sound came closer, along with footfalls on the gravel. An old man wearing a dusty, sweat-stained cowboy hat and a long white beard stepped into Mac's beam of light, squinting up at them. "The name's Webber. Dick Webber." He rested the Remington 12-gauge pump-action shotgun Butch had warned Mac about on his shoulder, barrels aimed at the stars. "You two must be the folks Butch called me about earlier tonight."

"That's us," Claire said, staying close to Mac's side.

Mac would've dragged Butch along with them for this very reason, but the poor guy practically had been asleep on his feet when Mac had arrived to pick up Claire. Apparently the bartender had called in sick, so Butch had bounced back and forth between the bar and the grill all night.

Old Mr. Webber waved them toward him. "Come on down here. I need to give you a bit of advice and don't feel like hollerin' for the world to hear."

Mac gripped her hand. "If this goes bad, get behind me," he said under his breath and led her back down the trail.

Webber waited for them at the bottom, leaning on his metal four-footed cane. That explained the creaking sound.

When they came to a stop in front of him, Webber tipped his hat back. "I'm gonna help you out because you're a Morgan sister." The shadows exaggerated his grin, making him look as crazy as the rumors claimed. "Anyone who gives the law a run for its money is golden in my book."

"You'd love my younger sister, Kate, then."

"Why's that?"

"She's the craziest of us three girls."

"I don't know about that," Mac muttered, thinking of the precarious situations Claire had gotten into since he'd met her.

Claire elbowed him, wrinkling her nose at him.

"Like how crazy?" Webber asked.

"Like sneaking into the Sheriff's office and locking a deputy in jail without him knowing who did it crazy."

"You think it's wise to tell him that?" Mac asked.

"You won't tell anyone, will you?"

"My lips are sealed." Webber snickered, pulling out a tin of chewing tobacco and smacking it against his thigh. "You know, I'm liking you girls more and more. Is your younger sister as pretty as you?"

"Prettier," Claire said.

"I disagree." Mac put his arm around Claire, pulling her close. Old man Webber may seem friendly, but it would be foolish to trust him completely with that Remington in his hand. Mac kissed Claire's temple, breathing "Careful, Slugger," against her skin.

She nodded once.

"This yer man?" Webber asked Claire, pointing his four-footed cane at Mac.

"Yes."

"You married?"

"Not yet," Mac said.

"Why not?"

"She's a tad skittish."

Webber looked Claire up and down, pursing his lips. "Not taking to being saddled yet, huh?"

"Just the sight of a saddle makes her start bucking." He winced at Claire's pinch.

Webber shook his head. "That's too bad."

"Why's that?" Claire asked.

"I like you. I could use a feisty wife, especially one with a little marbled meat rounding out her frame."

"Claire does have some fine marbled meat," Mac said, trying not to laugh. "But she's downright allergic to wedding rings."

This time she poked him in the kidney, hard enough to make him grunt.

"What about yer sister," Webber asked. "The crazy one?"

"Kate? She's pregnant with Butch's baby."

"No shit?" He shifted the Remington to his other shoulder. "Good. That boy needs a woman to fill that big ol' palace of his with babies." Webber snorted and then spit on the ground beside him. "What about the other sister?"

"You don't want Ronnie," Mac said.

"Why not?"

After living with her, Mac's list was long, but he went for what would probably be the most off-putting for Webber. "She's involved with the Sheriff."

"Grady Harrison?"

"That's the one."

"Well, I'll be a pile of javelina turds. After the way that ex-wife of Grady's left him tied up and twistin' in the wind, I didn't figure he'd ever want to get involved with another woman." Webber opened his tobacco tin and stuffed a pinch under his lip. "Your sister must be mighty distractin' to have caught that boy's attention."

"That's one way of putting it," Mac said.

Webber sighed. "Well, then I'll just have to keep looking for a wife. But if you get tired of this one," he directed the light at Mac's chest, "come on by the house. You know where I live."

"I'll write your name on my dance card," Claire told him.

"Now, back to this mine business. If you two are thinkin' of going up to that mine," he pointed his flashlight up the hillside, "you're taking the wrong path."

"What do you mean?" Mac asked.

"There's another way in."

"Where?"

"Around the side a ways. But you need to be careful."

"Is the climb steeper?" Claire asked.

"No, but the trail is used every now and then."

"By what?"

"Goddamned coyotes. They've been using this mine off and on over the years."

Hell. Mac had heard of problems closer to the border further south but not up in this area until now.

"Coyotes?" Claire asked. "Are they using the mine for their den? I thought most of them were afraid of humans."

"Not that kind of coyote."

"He's talking about the drug and people smuggling kind of coyotes who come across the Mexico border," Mac said.

"Ohhhh." Claire peered up at the mine. "Those nasty sons of bitches."

"Exactly. Come on, follow me back to your rig and I'll show

you the other way up." Webber turned and creaked off into the shadows.

"Should we go?" Claire whispered to Mac.

"Might as well." He took her hand. "Although there is the chance that he may try to shoot me and drag you off to be his wife."

"I might just let him, too," her tone was ringed with laughter, "after the way you ran your mouth about my allergy to matrimony."

"In that case, maybe I should offer to trade you. That Remington of his is an antique, but it's still in great shape."

She grabbed his shirt and hauled him closer. "Just try it, MacDonald Garner, and you'll *feel* the error in your ways when I go Tasmanian devil on your ass."

"I think you've already done that and then some."

Patting his cheek, she said, "Face it, there's no easy way of getting rid of me. I'm dug in like an Alabama tick."

"Yeah, but you're a sexy Alabama tick with a tool belt, so I guess I'll have to make do. Come on, he's waiting."

They caught up to Webber, who was moving more slowly with a cane. According to the crusty old timer, he'd taken a fall recently and had a hitch in his giddy-up ever since. When they got to Mac's pickup, Webber's beat-up old 1967 Chevy truck was parked behind them, blocking any retreat.

A half hour later, with Webber leading the way in his truck, they'd backtracked a couple of miles and turned down what looked like more of a four-wheel trail than a road. Part of the time, they used a dry wash for a road, which was smoother than the washboard up above on the hard and bumpy flats. Finally the old guy came to a stop and waved them forward.

Mac idled alongside his Chevy while Claire rolled down her window.

"You can park over there behind that grove of mesquite. If you walk north about a hundred yards or so, you'll see a square-ish boulder as tall as an outhouse. Take a left at the boulder and you'll find yourself on an animal trail like the one you were planning to follow back yonder. Follow the trail until you cross a runoff, then take another right for about fifty yards and you'll come to a vertical wall. Slide along it to the north for a short bit and you'll come to an unmarked tunnel that leads into the mine. But be careful. Like I said, the coyotes use it."

"How do you know?" Claire asked. "Have you run into them?"

"Not face-to-face, but I've seen a flashlight beam bouncing around inside the entrance several times over the years."

"Why don't you turn them in to the Sheriff?" Mac asked.

"They don't bother me, so I don't bother them. Besides, in my experience, law dogs are like bedbugs. Once they get inside yer walls, nothing short of Hell's fire will get them to leave." He patted his door. "I'll be headin' on home now. Need to rest my bum leg."

"Thank you for helping us, Mr. Webber," Claire said.

"Any chance I can help a pretty girl, I take it." He pointed at her. "Remember, if you get tired of fooling around with this boy, I have a fancy new mixer at home and a double-wide jetted tub."

Mac covered his mouth, blocking his laughter.

"Wow, tempting, but I'm sort of hooked on this guy."

"Oh, yeah? What's he got that I don't?"

She glanced over at Mac. The dash lights making her eyes sparkle. "The patience to put up with my mother."

Webber groaned. "I forgot about mother-in-laws. They're deal breakers."

"Mine's a real doozy, too."

Doozy? Mac could think of a few more accurate adjectives.

"Well, good luck to you both." Webber rolled up his window and rumbled off, his taillights bouncing into the distance.

"You know," Mac said, parking behind the grove of mesquite, "old Mr. Webber has a valid point about mother-in-laws being deal breakers."

"You were the one running your mouth about rings, dear hobbit. Now that the Eye of Mordor is locked onto you, don't think you can escape her deadly wraiths and orcs that easily."

"Well, at least there are no flying monkeys."

"Says who?" She faked an evil cackle as she climbed out of the pickup.

They gathered his gear and flashlights and headed out again, following Dick's instructions as well as they could remember up the hillside. When they reached the entrance, Mac hesitated, sniffing the air.

"What do you smell?" she asked.

"Nothing." And that was a good thing. He got his gas detector out anyway and checked the air. All clear. "Ready to go inside?"

"Try to stop me."

Mac led the way, one hand holding his flashlight, the other with a firm grip on Ruby's shotgun, Claire tiptoeing along behind him. They wound deeper into the mine, keeping an eye out for booby-traps as they trekked but encountering nothing more than vermin droppings and animal tracks. If any drug runners had been in this place, they'd either covered their footprints well or had floated in and out.

Several turns later, they came to a short passage on the left that led into a large cavern about as big as Mac's living and dining room put together.

"Holy shit," Claire whispered, following him into the cavern. She shined her flashlight along the high-ceilinged room. "Is somebody living here?"

"I don't think so, but it looks like they might be using it to camp out now and then." Dick Webber was right, somebody came up here periodically. He walked over and shined the flashlight on the two cots leaning against the wall. Army supply store specials from the looks of it, he thought, along with the containers of rations packed away in an alcove carved out of the wall between them.

"Look," Claire whispered. "There are three drifts leading off from this." The tunnels spoked from the main room, each filled with shadows.

Mac scanned the room with his own light, feeling more and more like they'd walked into a trap. "We need to get out of here."

"Why?" Claire walked over to a pile of rocks littered with rusted old cans and other garbage remnants. She started nudging each piece with her toe, making small clinking sounds. "You think someone else is in here?"

"I don't know. Probably not." He took a couple of steps into one of the drifts, the darkness swallowing his beam about thirty feet ahead. The other two were the same, leading off into the blackness. He'd brought rope, spray paint, and other precautions, but his internal alarms were tripping left and right. "But something just feels wrong."

He looked over at Claire, who was squatting down, picking up a rusted old can that looked like it had been opened with a knife. She shook it lightly. A rattling sound echoed around the room.

"What are you doing?" He joined her. "Why are you going through the garbage?"

"I don't know. It seems like hidden treasures are often tucked away almost in plain sight, at least in Joe Martino's world."

Something clattered from the dark depths of one of the drifts.

Mac stood, aiming his beam down each tunnel in turn. He waited, clutching Ruby's shotgun tightly—watching, seeing nothing.

After several seconds of silence, Claire turned the rusty can upside down, emptying it into her palm.

Mac saw something shiny fall into her palm. "What is it?"

"A key." She held it up. The shiny piece of metal reflected his flashlight beam.

Shouldn't it be as rusty as the can?

The clattering of stones falling onto the floor came from the drifts again, this time closer. He guessed the middle drift as the source.

His chest tightened, his pulse throbbed in his ears. "Someone is in here with us," he whispered.

Standing, Claire said quietly, "I don't think I want to find out who it is."

"Or how many there are," he added. He raised the shotgun, aiming it at the center drift.

Claire pocketed the key and grabbed his shirt, pulling him back toward the main spur. "Let's get out of here."

"You lead the way."

All of the way out, Mac kept checking behind them,

expecting to see a snarling pack of coyote drug runners pointing machine guns at them. The sight of the star-littered sky was a relief.

They made their way back down the hill in silence. It wasn't until he was behind the wheel of his pickup that his chest loosened.

"What do we do now?" Claire asked as he reversed onto the weather-beaten trail.

He shifted into drive and hit the gas. "We go home, lock the doors, and crawl under the covers." At least that was his plan after nearly having a heart attack twice tonight—first down in the desert when old Mr. Webber was sneaking among the mesquite and willows, and then up in the mine.

"And then what?"

"That depends."

"On what?"

He grinned. "Whether you're naked or not, of course."

She looked over at him. "I'm serious."

"You think I'm not?" When she squeezed his thigh hard, he laughed and tried to pull away. "Okay, okay. Next, I think we need to come up with a plan on how to sneak Sheriff Harrison up to that mine without letting Dick Webber know."

Her grip on his thigh loosened. "Right. The law."

He covered her hand with his. "Then we get you naked."

Chapter Twenty-Three

Saturday, November 17th

Kate woke up screaming, her left calf knotted in a muscle contraction. After frantically massaging the charley horse away, she flopped back on the bed. The bedside clock showed that it wasn't quite six, which explained why it was still dark outside the window.

Her focus darted around the bedroom of her grandfather's R.V., from the dark wood paneling to the vintage pleated orange curtains. The world on the other side of the window was silent, the birds not even warming up for their morning recital yet.

Something wasn't right. Unease lurked in her, spurring her senses into high alert, but she couldn't figure out the source. Was it something to do with Butch? Ronnie? Claire? Or maybe the baby?

At the sound of footfalls on the gravel outside the Winnebago she scrambled out of bed, grabbing the baseball bat Claire had insisted she keep next to the bed. She tiptoed out into the living area, her breath fast and tight in her chest.

A knock on the door nearly made her pee her pants.

She didn't move, didn't answer. Who would come knocking this early in the morning? Her pulse thumped in her ears like a flat tire.

Her visitor knocked again, harder. "Kathryn?" a low, muffled voice spoke.

Manny!

She tiptoed over, turned on the porch light, and opened the door a couple of inches. She kept the bat still clutched in her hand in case someone was holding him at gunpoint.

Manny stood there alone, wrapped in her mother's hot pink

satin dressing gown which barely reached his knobby knees, looking up at her with wrinkled salt-n-pepper eyebrows. "Are you okay?"

After peering into the darkness behind him and seeing no sign of goons or mobsters or big burly guys with the nickname Polar Bear, she opened the door wide and waved Manny inside.

He took a seat at the table while she got two cups of water heating in the microwave. "I heard you scream, *mi querida*. Did you have a bad dream?"

She dropped into the booth seat opposite him, yawning. "My leg cramped in my sleep. Where's Mom?"

"Sleeping off last night's cognac *fiesta*." Leaning back, he crossed his arms over his chest. The lacy cuffed sleeves inched up his hairy black forearms. "What are you doing, Kathryn?"

She looked over at the microwave, then back at him. "Making tea?" she asked back.

"What are you doing sleeping in this camper all alone?"

"Ronnie got first dibs on the spare room at Ruby's."

She had an idea what Manny was really asking but wanted to avoid thinking about that right now, let alone discuss it with her mother's lover. Never mind that he'd known her since she was in diapers.

He reached across the table and took her hands in his. "Do you like the boy?"

Her cheeks warmed and she lowered her gaze, suddenly feeling shy. She thought about trying to redirect the conversation to her mother's drinking problem, but the affection warming Manny's brown eyes made hers rim with tears before she could stop them.

"Dang it, Manny. Stop being so nice to me." She pulled her hands free, moving over to the counter to grab a napkin. She dabbed her eyes. "These pregnancy hormones are turning me into a big crybaby."

"I don't think you are happy, Kathryn. That's why you cry so easily these days. The hormones are just making it harder to hide your feelings behind your pretty face."

Manny had pinned the tail on *el burro*. She didn't want to sleep alone in this damned R.V. anymore. But the bed she wanted to crawl into each night had someone in it and words needed to be said before he'd invite her back into it. Words that her tongue was too chicken shit to say yet, too afraid that after he'd listened to these words, he'd still say, "No thanks." Butch had rejected her before. She had no doubt he could do it again.

She looked back toward the bedroom, swiping away another rush of tears. "I'm afraid."

"What's to fear?"

"Butch wants the baby but not me."

Manny chuckled, coming over to lean against the counter next to her. "*Mi amor*, if that is true, then it is his loss. You are a bloom in the desert."

She sniffed. "You're only saying that because you're sleeping with my mother."

"Being married to *tu madre* has nothing to do with how much I care for you three girls." His satin draped arm rested on her shoulders. "And now you're going to make me an *abuelo*." He squeezed her in a side-hug.

Kate's brain screeched to a smoky stop. She leaned slightly away and frowned up at him. "What did you say?"

"I'm going to be a grandfather." When she continued to stare up at him without moving, his smile slipped a little in the corners. "Well, a *step*-grandfather. I meant no disrespect to your father."

She waved his words away. "Not that part, the stuff before that."

"I care for you girls?"

She shook her head. "The part about being married."

"*Sí*. What about it?"

She stepped back, her mouth falling open. "What the … When did …" she looked down at his left hand. "There's no ring there."

"We're getting it resized."

"You married my mother?!!"

"*Sí*. In Vegas."

"What!!!" Kate sank all ten fingers into her hair, tugging it back from her face. "When? How did I miss it?"

"You were in South Dakota with your sister."

"Does Claire know?"

He nodded.

"Ronnie and Gramps?"

He nodded again.

"How come nobody told me?"

"Maybe they thought you knew."

He'd married her mother. "Why?" She shook her head, flabbergasted. "Why did you go and marry her, Manny? You were enjoying the milk for free."

"I wanted more than free milk. I wanted *familia*."

"Family?" She laughed in disbelief. "Why would you want us as your family? We're as dysfunctional as they come."

"I disagree, especially when it comes to you three girls. You're adventurous and full of life."

That was literally true for Kate, with the baby growing inside of her. "We're messed up in the head and always landing ass deep in trouble. Haven't you seen how much we make Gramps bark and growl?"

Manny shrugged. "Eh, *es verdad*, but his eyes also shine when he talks about you three. Now mine will shine, too."

Kate scoffed. "I can't believe you willingly wanted all of this … this … insanity we call family life."

"It's exciting, Kathryn."

"But Mom's turned into a drunk."

"That will pass as soon as she's finished exorcising her demons."

Kate had been waiting for that exorcism to be complete for going on thirty-two years now.

"I've never had a stepdad before." She contemplated him as a father figure, thinking how absurd he looked in his beat up cowboy boots and her mother's pink robe. A feather boa would really make his outfit. She smiled. "What do you want me to call you?"

"What do you want to call me?"

She shrugged. "Manny."

"Manny it is." He tightened the satin belt. "Now what are we going to do about you living alone in this camper and all of those tears you keep leaking?"

"I don't know," she frowned, her angst returning.

"I do. You're going to tell that *muchacho* that you want to move back in with him and that he is going to make you his wife before that baby is born."

"Wife?" She grimaced. The idea of speaking that word in front of Butch incited a rash of terror up and down her limbs.

"Wife," Manny iterated, crossing his arms over his chest. "And if he isn't willing to put a ring on your finger, you tell him that your stepfather comes from a long line of Mexican gunfighters and isn't afraid to face off in the street at high noon."

"Oh, Manny." Her eyes filled again, damn it. "Thank you for marrying my mother." She stepped closer and wrapped him in a hug. "You smell like Mom's perfume."

He patted her back. "I think I will keep this robe for me. It's very soft."

Chuckling, she stepped back and straightened his collar. "Chester might find you sexy, especially in those boots."

He made a face. "Never mind." His gaze moved to the window. "Look, the birds are up. It's time for us to get dressed and go take on *el mundo*." He said that last bit like he was broadcasting a soccer game on Spanish television.

"Good idea." Kate headed for the bedroom, adding over her shoulder, "But first I need some ice cream for breakfast."

An hour later, Kate pulled her Volvo into the almost empty parking lot at the grocery store in Yuccaville. A tub of mint chocolate chip ice cream was in the forefront of her thoughts, along with what she planned to do to her sisters when they got their secret-keeping butts out of bed. She'd teach them a lesson for not telling her about their new stepfather.

With spots plentiful, she parked up front near the door. Purse in hand she climbed out of her car. The rumble of a muffler interrupted the squeaks and croaks from a pair of grackles fighting over half of a sandwich near a trash can, jousting with their beaks in between snatching at the bread.

The sight of the Polar Bear pulling into the lot made Kate gasp and duck down behind her car. She peeked through her window, watching as he parked his motorcycle in one of the marked handicapped spots right up front. He climbed off his bike and strolled inside the store, walking without any sign of a limp.

Kate popped up. "He parked illegally!" she told the grackles, who looked over at her, cocking their heads one way and then the other.

She planted her hands on her hips. As if plotting to terrorize and torture her sister wasn't enough, the son of a bitch had parked in a handicapped spot, and he was clearly walking just fine. "It's not as if the damned lot is full with nowhere else to leave your ridiculously shiny bike."

One of the grackles whistled at her. The other took advantage of the distraction she was creating and plucked up the remains of the sandwich. He flew off with the other bird chasing his tail feathers.

She walked over to the motorcycle, circling it. Where did he get the money for such a pricey machine? From torturing innocents for information? Killing for money? Her vision shifted through shades of pink and ended up at red.

That was it. She was done sneaking around worrying about what happened next in his game of hide-and-go-kidnap.

She glared over at the grocery store's front doors. "You're messing with the wrong family."

Stalking back to her Volvo, she snapped on her seat belt, jammed the keys in the ignition, and shifted into reverse. She backed up about fifty feet and hit the brakes. A final search of the lot found it clear of pedestrians.

All systems go. She shifted into drive.

With a war cry that would have made Gramps smile in pride, she hit the gas pedal. The speedometer was close to forty when she slammed on the brakes, the motorcycle front and center in her windshield. The brakes pulsed, but her car's momentum carried her forward. She winced in preparation for the *BOOM!* of the airbag going off in her face.

Her Volvo rammed into all of that pretty polished chrome with a clanging crash. Shiny parts and pieces flew everywhere catching rays of sunlight, sparkling in their final glory before smashing back to earth. The bike itself skidded sideways several feet and then keeled over and slid to a stop on the pavement. It lay like a dead horse in clear view of the store's front doors, its leather saddlebags ripped loose, the front tire spinning slowly.

Huh. The airbag hadn't gone off. Go figure.

"Whew!" Kate blew out a breath of relief. After weeks of watching the Polar Bear's comings and goings, lying awake at night worrying about his next move, fearing for her sister's future, she'd done something proactive to keep Ronnie safe.

At the sight of a handful of people rushing out of the store, she pushed open her car door. Stumbling out, she held her forehead and groaned good and loud for effect.

"Are you okay?" a man in an apron asked, coming to her aid.

"I think so."

"What happened?"

"I don't know. I started sneezing as soon as I turned into the lot and couldn't stop. You know how it is with the winds kicking up all kinds of dust and mold spores this time of year." When the bagger nodded in agreement, she faked two sneezes in rapid succession. "Anyway, I must have accidentally hit the gas instead of the brakes. I tried to stop, but—"

"What the fuck?!!!" a voice bellowed.

Kate looked across the hood of her car. The Polar Bear stood in front of the store, his eyes bugging as his sites locked onto his dead chrome horse.

"Uh-oh," she said to the bagger. "He looks perturbed."

"Maybe you should get back in your car, miss, and lock the doors."

The Polar Bear stumbled over to his crunched bike, his jaw opening and closing with no sound coming out. He grabbed the handlebars with one hand trying to haul it upright, but the bike slipped out of his hand and crashed to the ground again. The remaining mirror fell off and shattered on the pavement.

His eyes were black, menacing holes when they scanned the crowd, stopping at her. "Who did this?"

Kate expected him to start snorting and pawing at the ground at any moment. She crossed her arms over her chest, gearing up for battle. "I did."

"You hit my bike."

"It was an accident.'

"You hit my goddamned bike!" he roared.

She raised one eyebrow, slipping into teacher mode. "I heard you the first time, sir." She walked around her car, standing across his mangled motorcycle from him, feeling safe in the middle of a growing crowd of onlookers. "Where's your cane?"

"What?" His big face was beet red, the rims of his eyes almost the same color.

"Your cane. You were parked in a handicap spot. I'd expect you to have a cane or wheelchair, something that would make you impaired enough to need to park right up front."

His lip snarled. "I'm vision impaired."

"And yet you ride a motorcycle." She tapped her chin with her index finger. "My, that sure seems dangerous. And odd. Where do you keep your handicap sticker?" She looked over the bike. "I sure don't see one anywhere."

"What the hell does it matter where I parked? You hit my fucking bike!"

"Yes, but if you hadn't been parked illegally in a handicap spot, I wouldn't have hit it." That was the bona fide truth. Had he not been so blatant about disrespecting a parking spot set aside for those in need, she would happily have bought her ice cream and gone on her merry way, his bike and her car intact.

He clenched his fists, his eyes issuing death threats. "Lady, I hope you have insurance, because this here bike costs a lot of pretty pennies."

"I have lots of pretty copper pennies, but unfortunately no insurance."

He strode over to her car and slammed his fist down on her hood, making a huge dent in the middle of it.

"That wasn't very smart, especially with all of these witnesses." She spread her arms wide toward the murmuring crowd.

He shook his fist at her, the same one he'd used to dent her hood. "Listen, you ditzy blonde bimbo."

Her scoff interrupted his threat. "Come on. Ditzy blonde bimbo? Is that the best you can come up with, you slope-headed cretin? Somebody please give this guy a thesaurus."

He took a menacing step toward her.

Her heart panicked, throwing itself against her ribcage over and over. She should have brought Claire's bat along. A good lesson for future ice cream runs.

The sound of a siren coming their way made everyone turn toward the street. The screeching of tires followed as a Sheriff's Bronco careened into the lot and slid to a stop in front of the Polar Bear's bike, almost adding another dent.

Kate shielded her eyes, trying to see who was behind the wheel, but the morning sun ricocheted off the windshield.

Please let it be Grady. Please let it be Grady. Please let it be …

The door opened. Black boots came into view.

"Well, well, well. If it isn't the notorious Kate Morgan."

The Bronco door slammed shut.

Shit.

It wasn't Grady.

* * *

"The phone's ringing." Jessica said, joining Claire at the kitchen table.

"So answer it." Claire took a bite of pancake.

"I can't. My nails are wet."

"Criminy, do I have to do everything myself?" Claire stood up from the table, taking her can of soda with her into the rec room. She grabbed the receiver next to the bar. "Hello?" she spoke through a mouthful of pancake.

"Claire, it's Butch. I need you to come with me."

"What?" She swallowed the food in her mouth. "Where?"

"To Yuccaville."

It wasn't even nine o'clock yet. Did he need more supplies? Why her? Why not Kate or Ronnie? She took a sip of Coke to help wash the pancake down her throat. "Why?"

"I just got a phone call." Butch sighed. "Kate's in jail."

She gasped, spitting Coke on the bar and down the MoonPie T-shirt Mac had bought her last month. Damn it, what had Kate done now?

"I'll pick you up in ten minutes."

She grabbed a rag from behind the bar. "I'll be ready."

Manny stepped out of the kitchen, spatula in hand. "You

ready for some more pancakes?" he asked as she wiped off the bar.

She shook her head. "Put the pancakes on hold." She tossed the towel on the bar, not sure how to deliver the news she'd just received other than straight up. "Kate's in jail."

"No!"

"Yes."

"*Ay yi yi.*" He smacked his forehead. "This is my fault."

"How is Kate landing in jail your fault? You've been in the kitchen making breakfast for us all morning."

"I should not have told her to go take on the world."

Jessica poked her head out from around Manny, a piece of bacon sticking out of her mouth. "Kate's in jail again?" she practically yelled.

Claire shushed her. "Let's keep this to ourselves."

"How cool! Can I come with you to spring her?"

"Who's in the hoosegow now?" Chester asked, pushing aside the curtain leading to the General Store.

Shaking her head, Claire headed back to her bedroom to grab her shoes and purse. The shower was running next door. She debated on stepping into the bathroom and telling Mac what was going on but then decided against it. This was her problem not his. She'd fill him in when they got Kate home.

On her way back through the rec room, Manny handed her a wad of cash.

"What's this?"

"Bail money."

"You don't have to pay her bail." While she was in the bedroom, Claire had grabbed one of the credit cards Gramps had left behind for her to use in case of an emergency.

"I told you, this is my fault."

"Kate is nuts, Manny. Whatever reason she's in jail is undoubtedly due to another bout of temporary insanity not something you said."

He pushed it into her palm and closed her fingers over it. "Just take it."

A horn honked out front.

"That's Butch," Claire said, pocketing the cash. "Tell Mac I'll be back in a bit."

"Can I tell him Kate's in jail?" Jessica asked.

A screech of surprise came from the hallway leading back to the spare bedroom. "Katie's in jail?" Ronnie hollered.

"Way to keep it a secret, Jess!"

Ronnie joined them in the rec room wearing yoga pants and a long sleeve T-shirt, her cheeks red, her hair pulled back in a ponytail. She must have been exercising in her room again. On colder mornings, she shied away from heading outside to do her yoga. "What happened?"

"I don't know. I gotta go. Butch is waiting."

Ronnie grabbed Claire's flip-flops by the back door and snagged her purse from the barstool. "I'm coming with you."

She followed Claire down the General Store's porch steps. "You take the front seat. I don't want to stink out Butch after my workout."

"You stink him out on a daily basis, Ronnie," Claire said, reaching for the door. "What makes today so special?"

"Shut your lips, brat." Ronnie shoved her into the pickup.

Butch waited for them to click on their seatbelts before rolling out of the park. The Doobie Brothers were cranking good old *Black Water* out of the speakers, wanting to hear some funky Dixieland.

"Who called you?" Claire asked him, flipping down the sun visor. "Kate?"

"Grady did." He turned the radio down. "He said he got a call from his deputy that Kate was in the holding cell. She wouldn't come out to call anyone to come pick her up because she insists the deputy wrongfully arrested her."

"Oh, dear God." A groan came from the back seat.

"That's not all," Butch continued, glancing in the rearview mirror at Ronnie. "She refuses to leave the jail cell until the deputy says he's sorry."

"Jiminy Cricket," Claire grimaced out the window. "Her marbles have truly rolled away, scattering every which way into the desert."

"Did Grady mention what she did to land in jail in the first place?" Ronnie asked.

"He was on his way into the office when he called me. He had only a few details at that point regarding the charges against her." Butch turned toward Yuccaville. "All he knew for certain was the fact that she was in an accident."

"What?" Ronnie sat forward. "Is the baby okay?"

"Yes. From what he'd gleaned, Kate caused the accident."

"That sounds fishy."

"Not really," Claire said. "Just ask Butch about Kate's history as a demolition derby driver."

Butch chuckled but then sobered. "Grady asked if Kate had spoken to me about a man staying at The Rowdy Coyote Motel who she calls the *Polar Bear*."

"Oh, no." Ronnie gripped Claire's headrest. "She didn't."

Claire laughed in disbelief. "It sounds like she did."

"She definitely did," Butch told them. "According to his deputy, Kate claimed to have accidentally hit the Polar Bear's Harley Davidson during a sneezing fit. However, the deputy didn't believe her sneezing story."

"Is that why he took her to jail?"

"No, but Grady asked me if I'd realized she doesn't have insurance."

"Can you go to jail for driving without insurance?" Ronnie sounded worried.

"Not usually."

"Then why did Deputy Dipshit take her to jail?" Claire asked.

"According to what Grady was told, his deputy jailed her for assaulting an officer. But Grady was making his deputy wait to write up the paperwork until he'd had a chance to hear both sides of the story."

"What did Katie do?"

A grin rounded Butch's cheeks. "You're not going to believe this."

"What?"

"I told you Carter babies make women a little deranged, right?" He tried not to laugh and failed.

"I think someone needs to let Grady in on that fact," Ronnie said.

"What did Kate do to Deputy Dipshit now?"

"She threatened to pull the back of his underwear up over his head in front of a crowd of onlookers."

Claire burst out laughing.

"A wedgie?" Ronnie's tone jumped up several octaves. "Katie got arrested for threatening to give the deputy a wedgie?"

Butch nodded, laughing along with Claire.

"And what did the Sheriff have to say about that?" Claire asked when she could speak again.

"I think he was still too stunned to comment at the moment," Butch said. "Other than telling me to stop laughing because it wasn't funny."

"He's right, it's not funny. It's downright hilarious." Claire swallowed a bubble of laughter. "I'm sure it's not every day that a pregnant woman gets hauled in for threatening to give one of his deputies a super wedgie and then refuses to leave the jail cell because she wants an apology first."

"Actually," Ronnie said, "I wouldn't be surprised if his Aunt Millie has done that very thing, minus the pregnancy part of course."

"Wait until Manny and Chester get a load of this."

Ronnie grabbed Claire's shoulder. "You can't tell them."

"This is a small town, remember? They'll know the details by nightfall, especially since Chester is planning on heading over to pay Cherry a visit at the strip club."

"He's spending a lot of time at her joint, isn't he?" Ronnie let go of her shoulder, settling back in her seat. "You think it has to do with the naked women or the owner?"

"Probably both."

Claire's thoughts returned to Kate. Man, she wished she could have been in that parking lot to hear Kate tear into Deputy Dipshit. A hiccup of laughter made its way to the surface. Then several more. When they passed the Yuccaville city limits sign a few miles later, she was still wiping the tears from her eyes.

The streets were mostly empty in town. Another sleepy Saturday morning for work-weary miners, no doubt.

Butch parked in front of the Sheriff's office. Claire could see the Sheriff inside sitting at his desk, holding his head in his hands. It was a regular Norman Rockwell painting in the making:

Saturdays at the Sheriff's Office.

Straight face back in place, she climbed out of the pickup and followed Butch to the door. Ronnie brought up the rear, pausing to check her face in the passenger side mirror.

"You look fine," Claire told her, waiting at the door. "Let's go get *your* crazy sister."

"Morning, Sheriff." Butch led the way inside. "I'm here to transfer a prisoner."

The Sheriff looked up, his eyes bouncing from Butch to Claire and then Ronnie, where they seemed to get stuck.

"I am not going anywhere," Kate's voice echoed out from the holding cells in back. "Not until his deputy apologizes."

Claire looked over at Deputy Dipshit sitting at his desk, his face full of thunderclouds and downpours.

He pointed at Claire. "You and your sister need to be put away in a nut house. You're both royal pains in my ass."

"You hear that, Kate?" Claire called. "Your deputy friend says we're noble hemorrhoids."

"How is it, Sheriff," Kate yelled, "that your employee can insult me and my sister, but when we insult him back, he gets to throw us in jail?"

The Sheriff aimed a frown at Butch. "Carter, you need to go get that and remove her from this facility."

"I have rights, dang it," Kate continued. "Claire, bring me a reporter from the Yuccaville Yodeler."

"You will not," the Sheriff warned Claire, his tone keeping her feet locked in place. "Kate," he hollered back, "I asked you nicely to quiet down and you agreed, remember?"

"Yes, but you also promised you'd bring me ice cream, and I'm still sitting here without the taste of frozen milk in my mouth."

"She has low blood sugar in the morning," Ronnie defended Kate. "It makes her a little cranky."

The deputy snorted. "Cranky? She's a downright—"

"That's enough!" The Sheriff's gravelly voice lowered menacingly, taking control, demanding respect. "This is not Mayberry or a Marx Brothers' movie." He aimed a finger at Deputy Dipshit. "You went too far this morning."

"But she started it."

"And I'm ending it. As of today you're on temporary leave."

"What?" Deputy Dipshit pushed to his feet, his face turning blotchy with red splotches. "You can't do that to me. You know who my dad is."

"Yes, I know exactly who your father is. I'm sure when he gets word that you cuffed and hauled a pregnant woman to jail for arguing with you in front of a crowd of local citizens, he'll agree that you need a break." When Deputy Dipshit sputtered, the Sheriff raised his palm for silence. "Ernie, the stress of your state exams is getting to you. Now leave your badge and firearm on the desk and go home."

"Fine!" The deputy tore off his badge and slammed it down on his desk along with his firearm. "I'll go. But I'm not apologizing to that stupid psycho bitch."

Butch bristled visibly. "Is Ernie off duty now, Grady?"

The Sheriff nodded.

"Good." In two strides, Butch was in the deputy's face. "You watch your mouth, you spoiled brat." Claire's eyes widened at the hostility in Butch's tone. She'd never seen Butch tear into someone before. He was usually cool and calm, playing the peacemaker role. "I don't give a shit about your daddy being the mayor. If I catch you bullying Kate again, I'll fuck up your world so much that your daddy will ship you off to another state just to keep his job."

Deputy Dipshit retreated, using his desk as a barricade. "Are you going to let him talk to me like this, Sheriff?"

"Threatening to mess up someone's world is not a detainable offense." The Sheriff sighed, rubbing his forehead. "Go home, Ernie. Get some rest. Take some time to think through your actions over the last two weeks. When you're ready to talk, give me a call. We'll go to lunch."

The deputy snatched his jacket off the wall, trading glares with Butch the whole way out the door.

When the doors closed, the Sheriff leaned his elbows on his desk and looked down the corridor leading to the cells. "Kate," he called.

"What?"

"Ernie has left the building. You can come out now."

There was a clang of metal on metal, then footfalls on the concrete. Kate stepped out into the main office, dressed in her baby blue pajama pants and an oversized Dancing Winnebagos R.V. Park hooded sweatshirt. "Sorry about the mess, Grady." She included Ronnie and then Butch in her apologetic frown, ending with Claire. "I sort of have no patience when it comes to your deputy."

"Apparently the feeling is mutual. Tell me something, Kate," the Sheriff said, moving around to sit on the front corner of his desk. "Why did you hit that man's motorcycle?"

"Like I told your deputy, it was an accident."

"We both know that's not the case. Remember," he crossed his arms over his chest, "I've been at the scene of an accident with you before, Crash Morgan. I know all about your ability to twist the truth."

Kate's forehead turned pink. She looked back toward the jail cells, chewing on her lower lip. "Would you believe me if I told you that the guy who owns that bike is a dangerous criminal?"

"Yes."

Claire did a doubletake. He would? He did? "Why do you believe her?" she asked him.

"The motorcycle owner didn't want to press charges against your sister or pursue further investigation into the accident."

Butch rubbed his jaw. "Why not?"

"Unfortunately I wasn't there, so I'm not sure."

Kate collected her personal possessions from the tray on the Sheriff's desk. When she finished, she looked over at Butch. "As soon as Deputy Di ... *Ernie* showed up on the scene, the Polar Bear got antsy. He mumbled something about not thinking I'd meant any harm and that his bike wasn't worth enough to get his insurance company involved." She focused back on the Sheriff. "Both of those are outright lies."

"Didn't that strike the deputy as odd?" Ronnie asked her.

"He was too busy fighting with your sister," the Sheriff answered first. "That's why I gave him some time off. If he'd been focused, he should have found that more of a concern than Kate's false account."

Ronnie grunted in agreement. She walked over to the front plate glass window, frowning out at the world. Judging from her stiff spine, Claire had a suspicion Ronnie was hiding something more worrisome than what plans the motorcycle owner might be thinking up as revenge for his dead bike.

"That son of a bitch shouldn't have parked illegally in that handicap stall," Kate muttered.

Claire grinned. "Is that what set you off, Crazy Kate?"

"I'll have you know that there are people who are truly in need of those front row spots." Kate's chin lifted. "The rest of us play by the rules. What gives him the right to ignore them?"

"Where's Kate's car?" Butch asked, taking her hand and not letting go.

"In the tow yard out back."

"Are you done with it?"

The Sheriff nodded once. "Since no charges have been filed, there's no reason for us to hold it."

"I'll have someone come and get it, haul it out to my place. Send me the towing bill for getting it here." His focus turned to Kate. "How bad is it?"

"The front is a mess." She grimaced, leaning down to rub her calf muscle. "That big asshole dented the hood with his fist, too. But at least the air bags didn't deploy this time. That'll save me some money."

"Her keys are hanging on the wall." The Sheriff glanced over at the open lockbox with keys dangling inside.

"Are we free to go then, Grady?" Ronnie asked, still staring out the front window.

He looked over at Ronnie, his eyes narrowing. Claire had an idea he was picking up warning flares from Ronnie's body language, too. "Sure, but don't go far. I'll want to talk to you later."

That snagged Ronnie's attention. "Me or Katie?"

"Both of you. But first I have to get the paperwork on this morning's fiasco written up." His focus shifted to Kate. "Then I'll do some digging on this man you think is the hitman known as the Polar Bear."

"I'm telling you, he's the one."

"Well, if you're right, you sure made it easier to catch him now that you took his Harley out of commission." He exchanged a look with Ronnie that gave Claire the idea the two of them had already put their heads together about the hitman. "If this guy really is a notorious hitman, we have a bigger problem than a smashed up car and bike."

Ronnie held her clenched fingers up to her mouth. "What do you suggest we do, Grady?"

"Lay low and stay out of Yuccaville for a couple of days, especially you and Kate." His gaze shifted to Kate. "After the stunt you pulled this morning, he's probably fantasizing about wringing your neck."

"He can fantasize all he wants," Kate shot back. "Where does Ruby keep her guns, Claire?"

The Sheriff grimaced.

Claire snorted. "No way am I letting you touch Ruby's guns, spaz. Not with your instant rage button on the fritz. You'll shoot Chester or me and claim it was another so-called accident."

"Katie," Ronnie cut in, "you can't sleep alone in Gramps's Winnebago anymore."

"Maybe she should move in with Chester," Claire suggested, trying to keep a straight face. "All of that *chili con carne* he eats works as a chemical weapons force field."

"I have a bed," Butch said. "It's big, soft, and safely tucked away behind a top-rated alarm system."

"I'm not sleeping in your bed just because of *this*, Valentine," Kate said huskily, not meeting his gaze.

He raised his eyebrows at her. "Who said I was talking about *my* bed? I have two fully furnished spare rooms, remember?"

If mortification came as a paint, Kate would have been three coats thick in red. "I'm sorry, I was just … I thought …" She blew out a breath and shot Claire a help-me look. "Can we go now? I'm hungry."

Claire took pity on her and swooped in to the rescue. "Sure. Manny has pancakes waiting for me when I get home. Maybe I'll share one with you." She pulled open the door and held it wide for Kate.

"You mean Manny Carrera, our new stepfather?" Kate

accused more than asked, pausing on the threshold in front of Claire. "A fact that you and Ronnie forgot to share with me?"

"That was Ronnie's responsibility." Claire glared at her older sister, who was having a heated stare-off with the Sheriff.

Butch draped his arm around Kate's shoulders, leading her out into the sunlight. "Let's go, Baby Momma. As soon as you get some pancakes in your stomach, we have a bar to restock and open for another exhausting day."

Visibly shaking off the Sheriff's spell, Ronnie said, "Maybe we should postpone tonight. I have a feeling I'm going to need to help out at the bar."

What was supposed to happen tonight?

With a sigh, the Sheriff nodded. "I'll stop by around closing if I can."

With a nod, she rushed past Claire, who stared after her with a frown. What in the hell was going on with her?

Claire shook her head and smiled. "I'm sorry for all of this, Grady."

He waved off her apology. "Do me a favor, will you?"

"Sure."

"Keep a close eye on Veronica."

"Why?" What did the Sheriff know that she didn't?

"According to the FBI, thanks to her ex-husband she has some new targets on her back."

* * *

Late that evening, Claire slid her coat on, thinking about how good it would feel to crawl into bed next to Mac, who had gone home a couple of hours ago after almost falling asleep in his drink. This morning's adventure at the cop shop sponsored by Crazy Kate seemed like a month ago rather than mere hours.

The Shaft had kicked Claire's ass tonight, the crowd holding out until closing this time. Her ears still rang from the noise.

"I'm heading out," she told Ronnie, who was next to the front door finishing up the last of the mopping. "You sure you don't want me to wait for you and Kate?"

"Yeah." Ronnie glanced toward the swinging doors that led

back to Butch's office. "Butch offered to take Katie and me home when we're finished."

"She should quit being so silly and stay with Butch."

"I know that and you know that, but I get the feeling she's holding back for some reason. She can sleep with me tonight."

Claire shrugged. "Her loss. Butch smells better than you." She laughed and dodged when Ronnie threatened to hit her with the wet, looped-end mop head. "See you back at the R.V. park."

She stepped out into the cold night, zipping her coat up to her chin to keep out the freezing air. She sniffed, the smell of cooked burgers branded on her olfactory cells. Butch really needed more help, or a bigger place to hold everyone, or both.

She crossed the lot to where Ruby's old Ford was parked in the back at the edge of the shadows, pulling out the keys to unlock the door as she neared. Footfalls crunching in the gravel behind her didn't surprise her. "You change your mind?" she asked her sister.

The sound of a shotgun being cocked made the spit dry in her mouth. She knew what that sound meant all too well. After facing off with Sophy in that old shed, Claire had endured weeks of nightmares filled with it.

It wasn't her sister.

Claire froze, raising her hands in the air, the keys dangling from her fingers.

"I'm gonna need a ride into town," a familiar voice said.

Before Claire had a chance to turn around and assess how deep good old Shit Creek was at this particular crossing, something slammed into the back of her head, dropping her to her knees.

Chapter Twenty-Four

Mop in hand, Ronnie slowly backed out the front door of The Shaft, trying not to slosh the dirty mop water on her boots. She set the bucket down on the concrete walkway and paused at the crunching sound of someone walking across the gravel coming from the mostly empty parking lot.

Claire must not have left yet. She peered into the darkness toward where Claire had parked earlier. The sight of two figures at the edge of the parking lot's orange glow instead of one made her stand upright.

Was that Arlene? The hair sure looked like it, along with that lanky yet busty frame of hers. What was she doing here? She'd asked for the night off. And why was Claire on her hands and knees? What was Arlene doing with a …

Her breath caught.

Holy fuck! That's a shotgun!

As Ronnie watched, the older waitress kicked Claire in the side, knocking her onto the gravel.

"Get up," she heard Arlene say, the cold air of the desert night made a great sound conductor. "We're going to take a little drive, darlin'. I have a friend who wants to meet you. He has a couple of questions about those diamonds you've squirreled away."

A groan rolled across the gravel lot, followed by the sound of someone spitting.

Claire was hurt.

Adrenaline dug its spurs into Ronnie's hide. Crouching, she slipped off her boots. There was no way she could sneak across the gravel in boots.

Stones poked through her socks as she stepped off the concrete walkway and slid along the side of the building, still clutching the mop handle. She hid in the shadows under the awning as much as possible as she slinked closer to the action. At the corner of the building she waited, forming a plan of attack. The mop handle slipped from her sweaty palm, but she caught it before it clacked to the ground.

Not fifteen yards away, Arlene had opened the driver's side door. "Come on, Claire. According to Katie-doll, you're supposed to be the tough sister." She scoffed. "You don't look so tough now." She kicked Claire again, this time in the hip as she was trying to stand, knocking her into Ruby's truck with a solid thump.

Claire slid down the pickup, slumping onto her side in the gravel. Another groan filled the air, followed by a pain-laced "Fuck you."

Fury mixed with fear and rage adding a dose of nitro to the adrenaline coursing through Ronnie. Her muscles tightened, ready to spring into action.

She needed to do something, but Arlene was still holding that shotgun. *Shit!* If only she had Katie's cellphone to text Grady for help.

"Get in the pickup, Claire. No more fucking around."

"Make me," Claire mumbled.

The sight of Arlene pointing the shotgun at Claire's head snapped Ronnie out of her hesitation. Gravel chewed through her socks as she sprinted across the lot, hell bent on stopping that bitch from shooting her sister.

Arlene turned as she neared, the barrel of her shotgun lining up with Ronnie's chest.

But she was too slow and Ronnie was ready, mop handle raised. With a grunt, she swung the mop handle like Babe Ruth. Months of pent up rage and frustration from playing the part of prey fueled her muscles. The wood handle cracked against the gun barrel, knocking it aside. Ronnie used her momentum to propel her shoulder-first into Arlene's chest, slamming her back into the front quarter panel of the truck.

An "oof" flew from Arlene's lips, but the older woman recovered and shoved Ronnie back, sending her flailing. She lifted the shotgun, but Ronnie sprang again, bringing the mop handle up hard under the heavy barrel as Arlene pulled the trigger.

The *BOOM!* echoed across the empty parking lot into the desert. Ronnie's ears rang, muffling the world around her. There was no time to recoup because that damned shotgun barrel was swinging around, lining her up in its sights again. Tightening her grip on the handle, she made a sideswipe strike and smacked the back of Arlene's hand with a solid *thwack!*

Arlene cried out but held onto the gun.

Gasping for breath, Ronnie wiped the back of her mouth. Damn this battle-ax was tough. She had to get that shotgun away from Arlene and the mop wasn't going to cut it.

Before Arlene had fully recovered, Ronnie lunged, aiming at her hand again, connecting with the meat of her forearm with a solid *thwap*. Arlene recoiled in pain.

Ronnie dropped the mop and grabbed the gun barrel. Digging her heels into the gravel, she yanked back hard, stepping to the side of the barrel.

Arlene stumbled forward into Ronnie. Without boots for traction in the loose gravel, Ronnie lost ground. There was no way she could win this match in her stocking feet. While Arlene was still off balance, Ronnie wrapped one arm around the woman's neck and lifted both of her feet off the ground, letting her weight take them both down.

Gravity did its job a little too well. Ronnie's left hip took the brunt of the fall along with Arlene's knees. The shotgun bounced and slid out of their reach.

Pain shot down her leg and clear up to her shoulder, but she gritted her teeth and shoved sideways, rolling across the gravel with Arlene, wrestling to get on top of her.

The battle-ax refused to cry "Uncle." She struggled under Ronnie, scratching at her arms and eyes. Ronnie was too busy blocking claws and elbows to look for the shotgun. Arlene bucked her hips, knocking Ronnie off balance. She rolled over on top of Ronnie, sitting on her stomach, pinning her to the biting gravel. She wrapped her hands around Ronnie's neck, squeezing.

Ronnie slid her hands up and under Arlene's arms, using one of the tricks she'd learned in her self-defense classes to knock the older woman's grip loose. When her hands were between their faces, she shoved the heel of her palm upward, slamming it into Arlene's chin.

Something crunched.

Arlene reared back with a grunt, but her knees tightened on Ronnie's ribs, squeezing hard enough to make her cry out in pain.

"You're going to pay for that, you stupid whore," Arlene snarled, breathing hard. She reached behind her back.

Ronnie heard a click and realized Arlene had a switchblade. She bucked, but the older woman must have been a rodeo star in her past life.

"Hold still," Arlene ordered, "or I'll gut you."

Crack!

One second Arlene hovered over Ronnie with the knife in the air, the next she timbered face forward onto Ronnie's chest. The knife clattered onto the gravel next to them.

It took Ronnie a second to focus on Claire standing over them, the mop handle pulled back and ready for another swing.

"How tough do I look now, bitch?" Claire asked.

Ronnie lay her head back on the gravel, trying to catch her breath under Arlene's weight. "Now I see why Mac calls you *Slugger.*"

The gritty sound of footfalls running across the gravel toward them made Ronnie catch her breath. Claire stepped over Ronnie, blocking her with her body.

"Claire!" It was Butch, thank the stars. He held up his hands as he drew near. "Grady's on the way."

She lowered the mop handle, her whole body slumping. "I need to sit down." She limped over to Ruby's pickup, sliding back down onto the gravel to lean against the tire.

"Butch," Ronnie gasped. "Get Arlene off me." Her left hip hurt like a son of a gun, pissed off at her for using it as a landing pad and then pretending to be a bucking bronco.

Butch lifted Arlene off, rolling her onto her back. He checked for a pulse. "Still alive."

"Damn," Claire mumbled. "I'll use a bigger stick next time."

He scooped up Arlene's knife and closed it, shoving it in his back pocket. Then he held his hand out for Ronnie and helped her upright.

"Where are your boots?" he asked, leading her over next to Claire, whose head was tipped back, her eyes closed.

"I left them by the front door."

As Butch jogged over to grab them, she eased down next to her sister. When he returned with her boots in hand, he tried to pry Claire's fingers from the mop handle, but she wasn't letting go.

She opened one eye. "There may be more, Butch."

"I got your back." He held up Arlene's shotgun.

Claire let go of the mop.

"Where is Katie?" Ronnie asked him, tenderly touching the heel of her right foot. She must have come down hard on some sharp pieces of gravel. Walking was going to hurt for a day or two.

"She's calling in the cavalry."

"Good."

"Be right back," Butch said and walked over to Arlene, kneeling next to her.

Ronnie looked over at Claire. "You okay?"

"I'm pissed as hell."

"Why's that? Because you got beat up by an old lady?" she teased.

Claire chuckled and then groaned, holding her side. "No, I'm pissed because she picked on me instead of you about those stupid diamonds."

"Oh, poor baby. If it makes you feel better, she got a few good licks in on me, too."

"I'd feel better if I could kick her in the side once as payback. She got off easy."

"What are you talking about?" Ronnie pointed at Arlene's still form. "You knocked her out cold. Her head's going to hurt for days after she comes to."

Claire sniffed. "I should have shot her in the ass before Butch got out here and tried to stop me. Teach her for tangling with a Morgan."

Smiling, Ronnie leaned her head back on Claire's shoulder. "We make a good team."

"Yeah? You think we should take up mud wrestling over at Dirty Gerties? Maybe go pro? Chester could be our manager."

Butch came over still holding Arlene's shotgun and squatted in front of them. "You two going to live?"

"Probably not," Claire said.

"That's too bad."

"Ah, you'd miss us?" Ronnie asked.

She could see his grin clearly in the orange light. "Hell yes. It's damned hard to find help as cheap as you two."

Claire flipped him off, making him laugh outright.

"Butch?" Katie called from over by the door.

"They're both over here," Butch hollered back.

Katie ran to them, kneeling next to Claire. She tenderly tucked Claire's hair back. "When I heard that gunshot I thought you were dead." She wrapped her arms around Claire, hugging her tight, making her moan in pain.

"No such luck, crazy." Claire patted her little sister on the back. "You're still stuck with me." She grabbed Ronnie's hand and squeezed. "You, too, knucklehead."

Ronnie's eyes watered. "Takes one to know one, brat."

The blare of sirens cut through the air. Ronnie looked toward the road, waiting to see Grady's Bronco.

Fifteen minutes later, Arlene was still out. Claire had really rung her bell. One of Grady's deputies, whom Ronnie hadn't met before, had handcuffed the battle-ax and carried her over to the ambulance.

The Sheriff himself hadn't arrived on scene yet. According to Butch, who kept having quiet conversations off to the side with the two deputies who were there, Grady was dealing with another matter at the moment and had sent the two officers in his place.

Ronnie approached the deputy who'd taken her account of what had happened. She asked him what the so-called *matter* was that had the Sheriff tied up.

"It's police business," he told her.

Grady had trained his men well, it appeared. Anxiety pooled in her stomach. Grady would be here if he could. She hoped that whatever was keeping him away wasn't life threatening.

Claire still sat on the ground over by Ruby's truck. Mac was there with her, hovering nearby as one of the medics who'd arrived on the tails of the Sheriff's deputies checked her over. Ronnie had been there when they lifted the side of Claire's shirt to get a look at where she'd taken the kicks from Arlene's pointy toed boots. The good news was her ribs seemed to be bruised but not broken. The medic said she probably had a slight concussion and should go to the hospital to make sure.

The bad news was that Deborah had declared she was going to play Florence Nightingale and watch over Claire night and day. Ronnie told the medic she was fine when he came to check her over with Deborah in tow. She'd sooner run a marathon with her throbbing hip than have her mother play nursemaid with all of the wacky herbal concoctions and new-age ideas about psychic healing she had gotten from Mrs. Parker, their ex-flowerchild neighbor back in Rapid City.

Butch walked over, watching with Ronnie as Claire fought off Deborah's coddling. "I'm taking Katie inside," he said. "She's dead on her feet."

"Good idea. We're fine out here."

"You sure?"

Ronnie put on a brave smile when she met his searching gaze. "Sure enough for now."

He looked her over, measuring. "I guess so."

She must have passed his inspection. To her surprise he grabbed her and gave her a quick hug, then frowned down at her. "You did good, grasshopper. Way to save your sister from the evil villainess."

Ronnie shrugged. "All in a day's work."

Chuckling, he headed over to Katie, who was leaning against Manny, her eyelids drooping.

Truth be told, Ronnie thought, it was the other way around. Claire had saved her.

Before Ronnie had come to Jackrabbit Junction, she'd been a lonely, angry mess. Now she had her life back and more. Her gaze moved from Manny and Katie to Jessica standing next to Chester, who was puffing on a cigar as he watched Mac, who was helping Claire to her feet while Deborah fussed, pecking at him the whole time about being gentle with her daughter.

Yep. So much more.

"Ms. Morgan," Grady's deputy said.

"Yes?" She turned to find him right behind her

"I have a call for you." He handed her his cellphone.

She stared at it in surprise and then took it.

"Hello?"

"Veronica?" The sound of Grady's voice made her body hum with relief.

"Yes."

"Are you okay?"

"Yep." Pretty much so now that he'd called.

"Good. You'll never guess who I just put in my holding cell."

Ronnie looked around. Claire and Katie were both there with her this time. "Who?"

"The Polar Bear. Tell Crash Morgan that I owe her an apology along with that half-gallon of mint chocolate ice cream."

"You do?"

"Yep. She was right all along about this one."

* * *

Kate leaned back against Ruby's pickup, surveying the red and blue flash filled world in front of her. She still couldn't believe she'd been right about Arlene … well, right after she'd been initially wrong about her being a friend.

She was so relieved Claire hadn't been shot.

Kate had been wiping down the bar, enjoying the sound of silence after a whirlwind day, when she'd heard the blast go off outside. Butch had burst through the swinging doors, calling her name. When he saw her standing there with a bar rag in hand, he'd asked where her sisters were. Kate hadn't realized Ronnie had gone outside, too. She had thought her older sister was mopping in the bathroom.

Butch had killed the lights and looked out through the front window.

"Claire was parked toward the back," Kate whispered.

He moved to one of the side windows next to the door, peering between the blinds. "Oh, shit," he said just loud enough for Kate to hear.

"What's wrong?"

"Call 911," he told her, locking the front door. "I'm going out the back. Don't come out until I tell you it's okay." Racing back through the swinging doors, he left her standing there behind the bar with her heart hammering. She reached for the phone and started making calls, starting with 911 and then Mac and Manny.

"Kate?" Butch's voice pulled her back to the present.

She blinked, looking up at him. "Yeah?"

"Come to my office for a few minutes, will you?"

The intensity in his gaze gave her pause. "Why?" What was wrong now?

"Because you're dead on your feet. After the day you've had, you need to take it easy."

"I'm pregnant, Butch. Not dying." It was nice of him to be concerned, but her family was out here.

His jaw tightened. "I know that."

Manny nudged her shoulder. "Go rest for a minute, *chica*. I can take you home if you're feeling tired."

Truth be told, her body did feel worn out and achy, and the parking lot party seemed to be wrapping up. "Is Mac going with Claire to the hospital?" she asked Manny.

"*Sí*, with *tu madre*."

Kate winced. Poor Mac and Claire. Deborah was going to drive Claire to find another mop and start swinging.

"Okay," she turned to Butch. "I'll go get my purse."

He followed her through the back door of the bar without a word. Inside his office, he waited just over the threshold as she shouldered her purse.

Pausing in front of him, she gave him a polite smile. "What a day, huh? An accident, jail, and attempted murder."

"Life with you Morgan girls never gets boring." His words were light, but his dark blue gaze was heavy.

Kate felt the weight of it, suddenly unsure of what was going on. "Are you okay, Butch?"

He shook his head slowly.

"What's wrong?"

He jammed his hands in his pockets, pulling his shoulders inward. "Kate," he started and then hesitated.

"Butch, you're freaking me out a little. What's going on?"

His chest rose and fell a couple of times. "Stay with me," he whispered.

Her heart leapt up, tail wagging, but her brain ordered it to sit its ass back down. After all, they were unsure what he meant. They'd assumed too much once before in this very office and ended up the fools for it. "You mean stay here? Tonight? At the bar?"

"No." He licked his lips, glancing over at the couch and then back at her.

"Oh," she snorted. "You want to have sex." She'd heard near death experiences often incited lust, a way to celebrate still being alive.

"No, I don't mean sex." He grimaced. "Wait, that's not entirely true. Part of it involves sex." He licked his lips again, shuffling his feet. "What I meant was …"

She'd never seen Butch so uncomfortable. Usually she was the one who stuttered, hesitated, and bumbled during their conversations. She waited for him to finish, her defenses crouched and at the ready just in case, while the rest of her senses were one hundred percent tuned in to see where he was going with this.

"Stay with me, Kate." He tapped the left side of his chest. "In here."

Her heart throbbed loud and slow in her ears.

Was he saying what she thought he was saying? Common sense still held her in check, wary from her past screw-ups. She gave him a crooked smile and joked, "Are you saying you want me to play Jiminy Cricket and climb into your pocket?"

He didn't laugh. Pulling his hands from his jean pockets, he stepped closer and took her by the shoulders. "No. More."

Did he mean "more" as in more *more*, or did he mean more of something else? Her tires spun on that garbled mess for a moment, but she quickly yanked on the brake cable. She was too exhausted for guessing games tonight.

"Valentine." It was her turn to whisper. "What are you

saying?"

She hoped like hell his answer would put her out of her misery, because if this was his way of asking her to put in longer hours at the bar, she was going to stomp on his toe and sock him in the gut.

He slid his hands along her cheeks, his thumbs lifting her chin as he lowered his face toward hers. His mouth lined up with hers. She grasped his shirt, holding on for dear life. Her eyes fluttered closed, his scent waking a deep need.

"Please," she breathed, wanting him so bad she ached.

"Kate," he kissed one corner of her mouth, "stay with me tonight." He kissed the other corner. "And tomorrow." He brushed his lips over hers, so tender, stealing her breath. "And for all of the tomorrows after that."

Her eyes opened when the kisses stopped.

Butch stared down at her, holding back, waiting for her answer.

"I'm afraid." There, she'd come clean with the reason she'd pulled away from him since seeing those pink lines on the pregnancy test weeks ago.

His mouth curved upward. "What if I promise to be gentle with you the first time?"

She tried to smile, but her heart had too much riding on this moment. She gulped and then held the beating organ out there for him, come what may. "Valentine Carter, I'm in love with you. There's nothing I want more than to have your child. But I don't want to end up like my parents in twenty years, full of bitterness and hatred for each other."

His brow creased. "Why would we?"

"Because you feel trapped in a relationship that started because of a pregnancy."

"Our relationship didn't start with a pregnancy."

"Before this happened," she placed her hand on her stomach, "we were just having some fun."

He shook his head. "That's not true. Before this," he put his hand over hers, "I was already hooked on you, enjoying what was building between us." His hand slid upward, curving around the outside of her breast. "But now I'm plumb crazy about you. I don't want to ever let you go." He took her hand and laced his fingers through hers, then used their joined hands to reach around her lower back and pull her against him. His other hand cupped the back of her head. "Stay with me, Kate." His lips feathered over hers. "Stay with me and make the long nights and lonely days go away."

Well, when he put it that way. "Okay."

He pulled back slightly, his brow raised. "Okay? Really?"

At her nod, he kicked the door closed and turned her around, backing her into it. His mouth teased hers as his hands caressed, returning to their old playground favorites.

She heard the lock click behind her and moaned in agreement. She fumbled with the buttons of her shirt, wanting to feel skin on skin. He pushed her hands aside, taking care of the buttons in a flash. His palms brushed her bared stomach, tender yet possessive, before climbing higher.

"Your body," he said as his mouth skimmed across her shoulder. "It's changed already."

"I'm turning into a balloon animal."

"No." He lowered to his knees, his mouth trailing down between her breasts, which were spilling out over her old bra. "You're blossoming with *my* child." His lips feathered over her stomach, his hands spanning her hips. "It's incredibly hot."

She clutched his shoulders as his tongue circled her bellybutton. "You say that now," she sank her fingers into his blond hair, tipping his head back so she could look him in the eyes. "But in a few more months you'll think I look like I swallowed a basketball."

His gaze was a dark, inky pool of lust. "I'm in love with you, Kate. Whether you are with child or not, I'll be nuts for your body."

This had to be a dream. This kind of shit never happened in her waking life. Dream or not, she didn't want it to end, but her feet had a request after tonight's hectic shift serving gallons of beer. "Why don't you show me how nuts you are over on that couch?"

In a flash he was standing, scooping her up and carrying her to the couch. After he set her down he pulled his shirt off. He reached for his jeans and she shoved his hands away, unbuttoning them for him. It was her turn. She ran her palms over his briefs and skin as she slowly pushed his jeans toward the floor. He groaned as she taste-tested along the way, reacquainting her mouth with his salty skin.

When she finished teasing him, she lay back on the cushions, raising her arms over her head. "Your turn."

His hands flexed over her as if he weren't sure where to touch first. She stretched out like a cat, offering herself without reservation. He got over his dilemma quickly, starting in the middle. He kissed and caressed her flesh as he undressed her. She closed her eyes and sank into the pleasure of his touch.

Eventually he slid over her, his mouth seducing hers with a kiss that cranked her need into a frenzy. Then he slid between her legs. She arched, taking him in, her soul filled to the brim but her body craving release.

He took her to the edge and then eased back repeatedly, teasing her into a clawing, sweating, gasping mess. "Damn it, Valentine." She wrapped her legs around his. "If you don't stop teasing me, I'm going to hurt you."

He laughed under his breath. "You know I like your brand of pain."

Running her fingers down his back, she moved against him, holding him in her sights. What was happening finally reached her core. She was here with Butch and he wanted her, he loved her. No more nights curled in a ball for hours on end in Gramps's R.V. No more tears about facing the future on her own with a baby. No more aching to touch him but holding back. She stared up at him, her emotions spilling out on her face she had no doubt. "I'm a lucky girl," she whispered.

His expression grew serious, his gaze holding hers for several seconds. Then he lowered his mouth, tenderly kissing her as his body took hers with a fierce need. The combination made her cling to him as her body pulsed, her muscles contracting around him.

"Kate," he gasped, holding her still as his muscles locked for several seconds, a mixture of pain and pleasure on his face. Then he collapsed on her, the couch sinking under their weight.

She trailed her fingers down his damp back, her legs still wrapped around him. She didn't want to break the connection.

As their breathing returned to normal, he rolled sideways into the cushion, relieving her of his weight. His fingers trailed over her breasts, circling, cupping, his gaze mesmerized. "You're beautiful."

She chuckled. "We already had sex. You don't need to seduce me now."

"I mean it, Kate." His focus moved to her eyes. "I was afraid I'd never get to touch you again." His fingers trailed down to her stomach, his palm rubbing over where the bump would begin to show soon. "I'm not letting you go. Not even if it means sleeping in your grandfather's R.V. for as long as you want in order to keep you by my side."

"No way are we sleeping there. That bed is killing my back already and it will only get worse the bigger I get."

"You'll come home with me then?"

She nodded.

"For good?"

"On one condition."

His eyes narrowed slightly. "What?"

"You promise not to leave me there alone for weeks at a time when you travel."

"I'm not going to go anywhere for a while."

"What about the classic car auctions?"

"I have plenty of work to keep me busy for now after that auction in Texas. By the time I need to go again, you and the baby can come with me."

… and baby makes three. She smiled. "Okay."

"Okay what?"

"I'll go home with you."

He leaned down and kissed her, his hand still spanning her stomach.

When he lifted his head, she traced the lines on his face. "It's good you'll be home for the duration of my pregnancy, because I'm not sure who would spring me from jail next time if you're gone."

He frowned. "Kate, you need to be more careful."

"Come on, Butch. You know I'm not very good at being careful." She shifted, tugging him around so he was underneath her, flat on his back. She straddled his hips, teasing him with her body as she continued tracing her finger down his chest.

"You're not, huh?" He folded his arms behind his head, his smirk cocky yet content.

"Nope." She leaned forward, hovering over him eye to eye. "How do you think I ended up pregnant with your baby?"

He laughed. "I don't know, teacher. Maybe you should give me the lesson about the birds and the bees once more."

He didn't need to ask her twice.

Chapter Twenty-Five

Sunday, November 18th

Sunday morning eased in on a warm gentle breeze, rattling the yellowing leaves of the cottonwood trees down by Jackrabbit Creek. Ronnie took a deep breath, inhaling the fresh scent of the desert as she raised her arms toward the sun, exhaling as she folded her torso down and touched the yoga mat between her bare feet.

It was the perfect opportunity for some yoga sun salutations in the great outdoors, modified slightly after last night's injuries. Even more opportune since Deborah was maintaining her vigilant watch over Claire inside Ruby's walls.

She breathed in, raising her arms high again.

In addition, Gramps had called early this morning from somewhere in New Mexico. He and Ruby would arrive home later this afternoon. With them needing their bed back, Deborah had insisted on moving Claire and Mac into the spare room.

So Ronnie had packed her things back into her suitcases and headed out the door … landing at Gramps's Winnebago, her new home away from no-home. Her lack of an abode was yet another reason she'd love to beat Lyle with a sock filled with bars of soap. If he hadn't secretly mortgaged their house to the hilt and then lost it to the bank after skipping off to prison, she wouldn't be stuck in this leaf-in-the-wind position.

She breathed out and folded down to touch the mat again.

Although, it was her own fault as much as his. She shouldn't have had her head in the sand for all of those years. Oh well, lessons learned and all of that shit. Holding onto her rage only gave her heartburn. Unless she was willing to drive up to South Dakota, break into prison, and strangle the son of a bitch until she put him out of *her* misery, she needed to move on with her life and try to focus on the positives.

Take what happened with Katie and Butch last night. Somehow they'd managed to work through their differences, which meant Ronnie would get Gramps's queen-sized camper bed to herself. Bonus!

She inhaled, hands reaching for the sun, trying not to think about the loneliness factor. After all, she had Manny sleeping in the camper right next to her, and Chester right across the gravel drive. She exhaled and bent over to touch the mat again. Maybe she could start having nightly Euchre games, take up cigar smoking, drink beer instead of gin and tonics.

On the inhale up to the sun yet again, she tried to clear her thoughts of the world around her, relax her mind, block out the sound of someone walking past the front of the Winnebago on the gravel drive. Back down with her hands on the mat, she did her best to ignore the dull pain radiating out from her left hip where she'd taken the brunt of the fall last night while fighting with Arlene.

The kaleidoscope of blues, purples, blacks, and yellowish-green bruises coloring her left side from ribcage to upper thigh had made her grimace when she'd gotten dressed in front of the bedroom mirror. Sexy they were not. She'd have to make sure her mom didn't catch her in the midst of changing her shirt for the next week.

She walked her hands forward on the mat, shifting into the downward facing dog position to start loosening the back of her thighs and calf muscles. Pain pulled on her lower back as she pushed her butt higher into the air, making her wince when she was supposed to be zoning out.

It was taking longer to clear her thoughts today, which was no surprise after last night. She wondered if Arlene was hurting as bad as she was. Probably worse after Claire's attempt to bat her skull out of the infield with that mop handle.

Clear your mind, dammit.

Two more breaths and she'd …

"Keep that up, Veronica," Grady's voice surprised a gasp from her, "and somebody might get arrested for lewd conduct in public."

From her upside down viewpoint, she looked over to where he leaned against the back of Gramps's R.V. in his Sheriff's uniform, albeit a very rumpled and wrinkled version of it minus the shiny badge. His hat shaded his face, his sunglasses shielding his eyes from her.

"It's called yoga, Sheriff Hardass," she said, still holding the pose, "and I'm wearing all of my clothes."

He cocked his head sideways, making it obvious he was staring at her butt. "Who said I was talking about you?"

That made her smile. She walked her hands toward her feet and then stood up, unbending slowly. "I didn't hear you drive up." She pulled her T-shirt down over her stomach.

"I parked up at the General Store. Mac said I could find you here. It's a nice morning, so I decided to walk."

She shook out her yoga mat and then rolled it up. "Welcome to my new abode." She slipped on the flip-flops she'd borrowed from Claire and headed for the Winnebago "Come inside and I'll pour you something to wet your whistle."

"Coffee would be great." He followed her inside.

She tossed the mat on the floor next to the couch, slid out of the flip-flops, and walked over to the kitchenette to see what she could drum up in the coffee department.

"You're lucky. Katie hates instant coffee, so this rig is stocked with an actual coffee grinder and maker." She opened the bottom pantry cupboard door, not finding any beans, and then checked the top. Going up on her toes, she grabbed the little bag of coffee.

"Do you like it black or with—" She turned to find him staring at her backside again, his sunglasses and hat off now. She looked around at her butt. "Do I have something on my pants?"

"No." His gaze lifted to her chest. "I'm having trouble thinking clearly after being up all night, and your choice of clothing this morning isn't helping."

Finally his amber gaze met hers. His eyes looked tired, but heat still shimmered in their depths.

"Look, Sheriff, if my clothes are bothering you, I could always take them off."

That brought a grin to his face. "First coffee and then we'll work on your debriefing."

She grinned. "That line doesn't quite work unless I'm wearing briefs."

"De-pantying?"

"Well, that would require me to be wearing panties." She pulled the waistband of her yoga pants away from her hipbone and peeked down at her bare skin before letting it snap back. "Nope, none to be found in there."

He groaned and walked over to the table, obviously putting distance between them. "We need to talk about a few things, Veronica." He sat down on the edge of the table.

She had a feeling he was reminding himself of that more than informing her. "Okay. Give me a minute to get some coffee going and then we can talk." She'd rather skip the talking herself, since it probably had to do with the troubles she was bringing to his county, but she doubted much would dissuade him from speaking his piece.

When the coffee was brewing, she turned around and leaned back against the counter, giving him the space he apparently wanted. "Okay, Grady, let 'er rip."

He grimaced, rubbing his right eye. The poor guy was nearly asleep on his feet.

"I heard all about your fight with Arlene."

He must have talked to Butch. "It was more of a tussle."

His gaze drilled her. "You could've been shot."

"But I wasn't."

"You should've gone inside and immediately called 911. Let us handle situations involving firearms."

"And let Arlene kidnap my sister in the meantime? I think not. I made the right choice at the time."

"I disagree."

"Really? So if you'd been there watching your sister get the shit kicked out of her, you would have gone inside and called for backup first and worried about saving her life second?"

His jaw tightened.

"Yeah," she said, "that's what I thought."

"But I'm trained in hand-to-hand combat."

"So am I." After all of those self-defense classes, she knew enough to get herself out of trouble … most of the time, anyway.

He growled under his breath. "Christ, you're so damned obstinate."

"What does it matter how Claire and I took down Arlene? She's behind bars now and we're both still alive and kicking."

"It matters because you're my girlfriend, damn it. I don't want you to get hurt."

It was sweet that he cared, but … "Listen, if you want a girlfriend who runs for help or hides at the first sign of trouble, we should probably put an end to this thing we have going between us right now."

"Veronica," he started, but she wasn't done.

"Because you need to understand something, Grady. I'm done letting assholes fuck with me and my family."

He stood, his arms crossed, his legs wide in that I'm-the-Sheriff-in-this-town stance. "Are you done?"

With a shrug she said, "For the moment."

"Good."

"But I reserve the right to be stubborn again during this conversation if necessary."

He shook his head at her, his lips pinched tight.

"What else do you have to say to me, Sheriff?" she egged him on.

"Arlene's real name is 'Shirley Arlene Rancor.'" He said that name as if she should know it. When she continued to look at him without recognition, he added, "Her nickname is 'the Husky' in the criminal world."

Her jaw fell open. "You're kidding. Arlene was the Husky?" At his single nod, she covered her mouth. She'd taken on the Husky in hand-to-hand combat. Sure, she might have gotten her guts sliced and diced if it hadn't been for Claire, but still, "Holy fucknuts."

"Now you understand the reason I'm not thrilled that you rushed into the scene of the crime."

"Yeah, but I got her—I mean *we* got her," she corrected. "Maybe Claire and I should become professional bounty hunters."

"Bad idea."

"We could help the law."

"I highly doubt it."

She wrinkled her nose at him. "We helped you didn't we? Along with Katie."

"Kate made a lucky guess."

Ronnie shook her head. "Never underestimate a woman's intuition."

"You three are going to be the death of me. I should just hang up my badge now and join one of those monasteries over in the Himalayas."

"Come on, Grady," she said, pushing off the counter and strolling toward him. She took his elbow and tugged him over to the couch. "We're not so bad are we?"

"Don't ask me to answer that until I finish with the paperwork on last night's mess."

She shoved him down onto the middle of the couch and then sat next to him. She patted her lap.

One of his eyebrows rose. "You want me to sit on your lap? Are you Mrs. Claus now?"

"Not sit, smartass. Lie back," she tugged on his arm until he consented. "Now put your feet up and rest your head here." She patted her lap again.

He looked at her warily for a second and then did as she ordered. "Now what?" he asked, staring up at her. "Are you playing shrink?"

"No," she trailed her fingers through his black wavy hair. "I'm being your girlfriend."

"In that case," he lifted the hem of her shirt, peering up it.

She playfully pulled his hand away. "Behave, Sheriff Hardass. I'm trying to help you relax."

"Looking up your shirt is very relaxing."

"You can look up my shirt later."

"And down your pants, too?"

"Sure." She laid his hand on his chest and returned to massaging his head.

His eyes locked onto hers. "Why are you doing this, Veronica?"

"Because I want to show you how much I appreciate your concern for my safety."

"I don't want anything to happen to you."

"Really? Even though I sometimes drive you crazy?"

"It's more often than sometimes." He grunted when she tugged on the hair near his temple, and then settled more into her lap, closing his eyes, kicking his boots off.

She trailed the pads of her fingers down his face, using a relaxation method she'd learned about during a weekend at a renowned spa just outside of Deadwood. His whiskers tickled her fingertips. "Tell me about the Polar Bear."

"Not much to tell. After Crash's so-called accident, I made a phone call to the manager of The Rowdy Coyote Motel, asking him to help me out with the guy's identity. He came into the office and looked through some Wanted bulletins, pointing him out. So, I got a hold of your pal from the FBI—"

"You called Mississippi."

"Yes. I knew they were all fired up to nail this guy for several past crimes in various locations throughout the country."

"Then what?"

"The FBI requested our help as backup. We started with his room at The Rowdy Coyote. He wasn't there, but we found a breadcrumb—an address of an old empty building on the east side of town. It used to be a butcher shop back when I was a kid but had to close its doors when the grocery store came to town and took most of its business."

"He just left the address sitting out?"

"No. He'd written it on the motel notepad, and we were able to see the imprint enough to determine what he'd written."

"That trick really works, huh?"

"Sometimes, but only if they write hard enough."

"So what did you find at the old butcher shop? Was he waiting there?"

"No, but we found a chair, some duct tape, a blow torch, and a box of knives."

"Surgical knives?"

"No."

"Throwing knives like they use at a circus?"

His eyelids opened. "Now I see where your sisters get their wild imaginations."

"What? Maybe Arlene and the Polar Bear used to be performers in a circus. She threw knives and he was the Strong Man. But that didn't pay the bills, and they soon realized they could make more money as killers for hire."

His forehead wrinkled. "Really?"

"You never know."

"Well, we do now, and they weren't in a circus act together. Undoubtedly the plan was to kidnap Claire and take her to the old butcher shop and make her talk."

"About the diamonds?"

"Yes, about those."

"So, are Arlene and the Polar Bear the ones who killed those people in Mexico and the guy who bought the camper?"

"No."

"You sound pretty sure about that."

"I am. For one thing, that's not the Polar Bear or the Husky's usual style of execution. For another, the description given by the witness doesn't match either of them."

She blew out a breath. "Damn."

He reached up and ran his thumb along her jaw. "We'll get him, too. One killer at a time."

She caught his hand and kissed his palm. "There are going to be more coming," she told him, thinking about what Mississippi had told her about her ex rolling over for a better deal in the pen.

"I know."

"You know?"

"If you're talking about the possible side effects from your ex-husband playing tattle-tale on another one of his previous business partners, then yeah, I know. Mississippi warned me about it."

She frowned down at him. "Are you mad?"

"Why would I be mad?"

"Because I'm bringing more trouble to your county."

He turned on his side facing her and pushed up so he was looking her in the eyes. "Veronica, I'd like to wrap you in bubble wrap and lock you away in my bedroom to keep you safe, but I'm not mad. This isn't your fault. You're the victim here."

"I'm tired of being the victim. I'm not going to play that role any longer."

His dark eyebrows creased. "What does that mean?"

"I'm not sure yet. Probably something you won't like."

His lips flat-lined. "Undoubtedly."

"I'll let you know as soon as I figure it out so you can lecture me about why it's a bad idea."

"I'd appreciate that opportunity."

"Lie back down, Sheriff. I'm not done with my massage yet, and you're not done with your story."

"Okay, but while I'm up here, you should probably give me a kiss."

"Why should I do that?"

"Because you haven't yet."

"You didn't seem interested."

"That's not true. I wanted to slide my hands all over you, starting with those yoga pants, and then take you on that table over there. But I resisted, trying to be a gentleman."

"Your first mistake would've been taking me on that table. It's not even a little comfortable, especially without the seat cushions that turn it into a makeshift bed. Second, I'm not in the mood for a gentleman right now."

"What are you in the mood for?"

"You and your handcuffs."

His pupils dilated, his gaze dropping to her lips. "Are you really not wearing any panties?"

"Maybe I'll show you the answer to that question after you finish telling me about how you captured the Polar Bear."

He leaned forward and stole a kiss, taking his time with his thievery, and then settled back down on her lap. "We waited for him next door to the abandoned building. He pulled up in Arlene's car about the same time Claire and you were taking turns trying to 'restrain' her in Butch's parking lot."

"So you didn't know about Arlene until then?"

He shook his head. "She's a master of disguise, changing her appearance significantly for each job. The only picture I'd seen could have been any middle-aged woman. The feed was from a cheap security camera and so grainy and out of focus it didn't offer much help. I'd kept my eye on her, of course, since Kate found the scarf in the Polar Bear's room and Butch had me look into her, but many people prefer to live off the grid, especially here in Arizona. It wasn't until we saw the Polar Bear pull up in her car that we were certain they were linked."

"All of this time she was playing undercover killer, scoping out me and my family, biding her time." Her hand stilled on his face. "She must have found out about the stolen diamonds from our conversations at the bar."

His brow wrinkled as he stared up at her. "You and your sisters need to be more careful in the future."

"Yeah, but you have the diamonds now." She'd handed them off to Grady when he'd followed her home days ago to inform Claire about the camper guy's death.

"True, but you guys are still a pit stop on the road to finding them."

"So you think Arlene figured the diamonds were the result of Lyle's skimming from her boss and planned to take them back to fulfill her contract?"

"I don't think, I know." He yawned, his eyes drifting shut again, his forehead smoothing out. "She admitted that much when she came to. She also turned on the Polar Bear when the FBI offered her a deal."

"Wow, that's heartless."

"It turned out he's one of her ex-husbands."

"Oh, well, then that makes complete sense." She scraped her nails lightly over his scalp. "Anything else to tell me?"

"Yes. You're putting me to sleep."

"You need some rest." Although the coffee was about done judging by the sounds coming from the coffee maker, she said, "Just relax. Let me take care of you for once."

"Okay, but when I wake up, I'm going to take a closer look at those bruises on your left side."

She blinked in surprise. "Did you see those when you looked up my shirt?"

"No, when you were doing that stretch outside that nearly drove me to do a lewd act in public with you."

"You like that pose, huh?"

He yawned again, the lines around his eyes softening. "More than like." A hint of a grin played on his lips. "Have you ever done yoga while wearing handcuffs?"

She chuckled. "No."

His breathing slowed, deepening. Just when she thought he'd fallen asleep, he mumbled. "You wanna try it?"

Smiling, she tenderly rubbed his unshaven cheek. "Go to sleep, Grady, and I promise that after you wake up I'll show you a few yoga positions that will really light your fire."

He listened to her for once, falling into a sleep so deep that her shifting out from under him didn't disturb it.

Several hours later when he began to stir, she put down the book she'd been reading, shed her shirt, and showed him her kaleidoscope of bruises. When he'd finished kissing them better, she followed through on her end of their deal.

It turned out she was right about the yoga poses. He went down in flames not even a minute into her routine, burning white hot as he carried her back to the bedroom where he showed her a few back arching positions of his own.

* * *

The General Store's front porch beckoned along with the old codger relaxing out there after his long drive south. Claire sat down on the bench seat next to Gramps. Henry growled up at her from his favorite snoozing spot at her grandfather's feet. She stuck her tongue out at the spoiled beagle. "Long time no miss, ya little shit."

Gramps chuckled.

The sun was setting, coloring their view to the east in a myriad of dusty pinks, deep blues and pale purples. Cigar smoke laced the cool evening air. The land was nice and still, unlike the inside of Ruby's house now that Deborah had a new project—healing Claire.

"How's your head?" Gramps asked, puffing on his cigar.

"Sore but the headache is gone."

"Your ribs?"

"They complain with each breath but not so loudly now." Painkillers were wonder drugs.

He nodded. "Glad you're okay."

"We can thank Ronnie for that." She stared out at the horizon, watching the colors languish in the darkening sky. "Have you seen Mac?"

He shook his head.

"What about Chester?"

"Nope." He took another puff on his cigar, letting the smoke roll out. "You did a good job on the rec room. Spent a bit more than I would have liked, though."

"Sorry about that. I probably could've saved some money going to Tucson for supplies, but I wanted to keep things local, you know?" At his nod, she asked, "What about your wife? Did she approve?" Claire had been sleeping off her beating when Gramps and Ruby had arrived, so she'd missed their initial reaction to her changes.

He patted her leg. "Like I said, you did good."

Whew! She leaned back into the bench, relaxed now that she knew they didn't hate what she'd done to the rec room. "How was South Dakota?"

"Colder than a witch's tit, but it was nice to spend some time back home."

"Was it weird to have a new wife in your house?" He hadn't taken any women "home" since her grandmother had died, at least as far as she knew.

He grunted, whatever that meant. "I was thinking about selling the place on my way up there, but Ruby really likes it."

"I don't blame her." His house in Nemo sat in a beautiful valley in the Black Hills, with rocky outcrops overlooking the small ranch and a creek gurgling along the edge of it. "Wait until she sees it in summer when it's all lush and green."

He grunted again, taking another puff on his cigar. "Natalie sends her love."

She wondered how soon her cousin could arrange a trip back down here. Then Claire remembered she'd be gone with Mac and his new job most of the time and decided not to get her hopes up. "How's Nat doing?"

"She seemed distracted, half a bubble off plumb even. She kept frowning at blank walls, or laughing when nobody was around."

"Was she drinking at the time?"

He shook his head. "Speaking of drinking, Jessica told me your mom's been hitting the bottle too much."

Grimacing, Claire nodded. "Manny thinks she's going through a midlife crisis sort of deal."

"Well," he rolled the ashes of his cigar in the ashtray he'd carried out with him, "she's his problem now, not mine. That's what the jackass gets for robbing *my* cradle."

The sight of Mac's white pickup rolling over the bridge into the R.V. park followed by a dark green Jeep Wrangler—the four door kind—snagged Claire's focus. She waited as both vehicles came to a stop out in front of the General Store. Mac's pickup door opened and Chester stepped out.

"Evening, Babe Ruth." Chester said as he climbed the steps. "Good to see you up and ready for some more batting practice."

"What are you doing driving Mac's truck?" she asked.

"That's not my story to tell." He pulled open the screen door, waving at Gramps to follow him. "Haul ass, Ford."

"I'm finishing my cigar."

"Finish it inside. I need to talk to you about settling my bill for all the electrical work Claire made me do while you were gone. I'm not cheap labor. This is going to cost you at least a case of beer, maybe more."

Grumbling, Gramps stood up, taking his cigar and ash tray with him.

Claire watched the two of them disappear inside the store. What was going on? Gramps would normally have told Chester off and finished his cigar wherever he wanted.

The sound of the Jeep door slamming drew her gaze back to the twilight lit gravel drive in front of her.

Mac walked toward her, his long-sleeved white T-shirt seeming to glow in the growing shadows. "How you feeling, Slugger?" he asked as he climbed the porch steps.

"Confused."

"Confused and in pain?"

"Just plain confused. The pain is mostly dulled."

He sat down on the bench next to her, his arm snaking around her shoulders. He made a point of avoiding the lump on the back of her head where Arlene had clocked her. "Confused about what?"

"Why Chester was driving your pickup and you were driving that Jeep."

He reached into his back pocket and pulled out a black rectangular box, holding it out toward her.

"What's this?" Her heart thudded. It looked like a jewelry box. Too big for a ring but not a bracelet.

"I got you a present."

She frowned at him, wondering why he'd buy her jewelry. She wasn't the jewelry sort of girl and he knew it. Had he hit his head recently? Then another thought came to her. "Did Mom put you up to this while I was knocked out from the drugs?"

He grinned. "No. She doesn't know about it." He tapped the box. "Open it."

Warily, she pulled the lid open. Inside, lying on a bed of black velvet, was a key.

Huh? Was this some kind of metaphor? Like the key to his heart. "I don't understand."

"It's a key."

"I can see that, wiseacre." She wasn't that drugged up. Plucking the key out of the box, she held it up between them. "What do I need a key for?"

"To start your Jeep."

"I don't have a ..." she paused, looking out at the Jeep parked next to his pickup. "You mean *that* Jeep?"

"That's the one."

"I don't ... you mean you ..." she turned back to him. "Did I buy a Jeep while I was heavily sedated?"

"No, I bought you a Jeep while you were heavily sedated."

"Why would you do that when we're going to be traveling so much with your job?"

"We're not going to be traveling so much after all."

"I don't und … dammit, Mac, would you quit messing with me while I'm still flying high on pain meds and tell me what in the hell is going on."

He crossed one leg over the other, resting his ankle on his knee, looking like he didn't have a care in the world. "I didn't take the promotion."

"What?!"

"You heard me, Slugger."

"Why not?"

"Because I realized something. After all of the years I spent busting my ass to get that job, there was something I wanted more."

"A Jeep?"

"You."

"But you already have me."

"Taking that job meant possibly losing you."

"Says who?" Besides Chester, the bristle-topped oracle.

"Come on, Claire. I'm no fool. You said you were willing to travel with me, but we both know it wasn't your dream."

"But it was yours."

"I have other dreams, too. It turned out that particular one wasn't as tempting as it used to seem."

"But I don't want you to sacrifice your dream for me."

"That's enough 'buts' from you for tonight." He leaned over and kissed her temple. "I love you, Claire. Happy Jeep Day."

"Mac, take the job, please."

"We both know you would've been miserable leaving your family for weeks at a time."

"You're wrong. It turns out that I don't really like them that much."

He laughed. "Liar."

Staring out at the Jeep, she chewed on her lower lip. "I don't know how soon I can repay you for this." Cash wasn't exactly flooding into her pockets these days.

He grabbed her hand and placed it on his thigh. "There's no repayment necessary. I bought it for you as a gift."

"That's an expensive gift."

"You need a vehicle."

"Why? I can always borrow Ruby's truck or Gramps's car."

"Because you're going to be driving back and forth to Tucson to visit me more often."

"I am?"

"I hope so, anyway." He spread his hand over hers where it still rested on his thigh. "You see, instead of taking the promotion, I arranged to work four ten-hour shifts from now on and secured Fridays off. That way I can come here for three days each week instead of two." When she continued to frown at him, he squeezed her hand. "And I was thinking that if you have your own wheels, maybe you could spend a night or two with me in Tucson during the week now and then."

A compromise. She stared down at the key, her eyes watering at his thoughtfulness. "Damn you, MacDonald Garner," she whispered, blinking back tears. "Have I told you lately how much I love you?"

"Does that mean you'll keep my present?"

She leaned into him. "Come closer," she smiled up at him, hearts undoubtedly floating around her head. "Let me thank you properly."

Taking her face in his hands, he kissed her instead. "You're welcome, Slugger," he said, after making her feel even rummier on top of her slight drug haze.

"You didn't go up into the Humdigger mine without me while I was drugged up, did you?"

"Nope. Whatever—or whoever—is up there can wait until the Sheriff has time to check it out with us."

"Good." She looked out into the darkness that had fallen over the desert. "You think Sophy is right about Joe still being alive?"

"How could that be possible?"

"I don't know." She shivered at the idea of it, though.

"Sophy has some wires loose. She's searching for villains where there are only ghosts now."

Mac was right. Nobody in their right mind committed the crimes she had before they finally put her away. Greed had lured her to the cliff edge and then shoved her over into the abyss.

"You want to go for a ride in the Jeep?" Mac asked, sounding excited to show off the new toy he'd bought for her. "I'll drive."

"Yes! Please get me out of here before Mom finds me and makes me drink more of that special herbal tea of hers that tastes like moldy hay and smells like Henry's breath after he's licked his butt."

Chuckling, Mac helped her up and into the Jeep, showing her the bells and whistles as they drove toward Jackrabbit Junction. He pulled into The Shaft's parking lot and cut the engine.

"What do you think?" he asked.

"I think that you spent a lot of money on this present and I am forever in your debt."

"I told you it's a gift. There is no debt." When she started to balk, he interrupted, "Claire, it's no secret that I'm crazy about you. I want to take care of you, but you make it damned near impossible with your hardheadedness. Let me do this for you. Please."

"Okay."

He leaned over and kissed her, distracting her from her residual aches and pains.

When he sat back, she shook her finger at him. "But don't think for a minute, buddy boy, that this means I'm going to sleep with you just because you buy me expensive gifts."

His grin softened his face in the glow of the dashlights, making him look even more heartbreaking than usual. "Of course not, Miss Morgan. We'll keep that virginity of yours intact until marriage."

He stepped out and came around to help her down.

"Mac," she said as her feet hit the ground.

"Yeah?"

"I changed my mind."

"About what?" He shut the door and took her hand, leading her toward The Shaft.

"I'll sleep with you tonight."

"That's a good little sex kitten." He pulled open the front door, holding it for her.

"Because it's you or Nurse Mom in my bed, and you kick less and smell better." She laughed as he chased her inside.

"No drinking alcohol tonight, Slugger." He followed her to the bar. "Doctor's orders."

She had no desire to add beer to the heavy duty drugs she was taking, but joked, "Why are we here then?"

"You wanted to escape your mother, remember?"

"Oh yeah." She sat down on a barstool. Mac took the one next to her.

Butch was filling glasses with beer from the tap on the other side of the bar. "How are the new wheels?" he asked, setting a tray with four foaming mugs on the counter.

Claire looked at Mac. "He knows about the Jeep?"

"I bought it from a friend of his."

Of course. Butch knew just about everybody in town, and those he didn't, Grady undoubtedly did.

"I love it," she squeezed Mac's leg under the bar. "And there's plenty of room in the back for my brand new niece."

One of Butch's eyebrows raised. "You mean nephew."

"Oh no, it will be a niece. Another wild Morgan girl to make your life even more hair-raising."

Butch laughed. "There's not enough room in this town for

four of you."

"The Sheriff will need to build a bigger jail," Mac said before sipping on the mug of beer Butch slid his way.

She slapped his leg at the same time Kate dropped onto the barstool next to Claire.

"Damn, my feet are killing me."

Butch frowned. "Maybe you should take a break, go rest on the couch in my office for a bit. I can pour and deliver drinks."

"No way. Your couch gets me into trouble whenever I lie on it." She winked at his smoldering gaze. "It's partly to blame for my being knocked up with your kid."

Oh, Lord. Claire grimaced, thinking of the times she'd sat on those cushions. "Dang it. Did you two have to do it there? I liked that couch, too."

"You're one to talk," Kate said. "You and your tool-belt loverboy there have ruined Gramps's car for me."

Claire tapped her index finger on the bar. "But we've never had sex in there."

"Whatever." Kate turned Claire's chin her way, staring into her eyes. "How are you feeling today? Should you be out of bed already?"

Claire pulled back. "I'm fine. What's with this mothering thing you're doing lately?" Kate had come into the spare room several times this morning checking on her, threatening to call the doctor if she didn't follow his orders to a T. "Are you practicing mommy-hood or something?"

Kate shrugged, sitting back. "Maybe I'm nest building."

"One wanna-be-nurse in this family is plenty." Her mother needed to return to her glass of cognac as far as Claire was concerned. "I prefer Crazy Kate to mommy dearest."

"Fine but don't cry the next time you end up in jail with me, then."

"No more jail," Butch said, setting down the glass of water Mac had requested for Claire. "Both of you need to try harder to stay out of it."

"Who's going to jail?" Ronnie asked, setting an empty tray on the bar. "Two pitchers of pale ale for table seven," she told Butch.

"Kate's threatening to drag me to jail with her again," Claire told her. "You think the Sheriff will give me a couple of get-out-of-jail-free cards?"

"Maybe he could start a loyalty card promotion," Kate said. "You know, a punch card. After the tenth punch you get something special."

Ronnie's smile seemed extra wide suddenly. "I'll have to ask him when I see him later tonight." She tittered and then giggled.

What the hell? Ronnie wasn't one to giggle, let alone titter. Claire narrowed her eyes. "Have you seen the Sheriff lately?" she asked Ronnie.

Her sister's cheeks darkened. "Uh, yeah. He sort of stopped by Gramps's Winnebago earlier to fill me in on Arlene and the Polar Bear."

"So that's why you tittered."

"I don't know what you're talking about."

Claire looked at Kate. "Good news! Ronnie had sex with the Sheriff again. With luck, she'll marry the poor guy and our jail cell blues will be no more."

"Nobody is getting married," Ronnie said, sobering.

Claire heard a tinge of bitterness in her sister's tone. She searched Ronnie's face, seeing traces of sadness and something else dark there. Instead of poking at the sore spot, she changed the subject. "What did he say about Arlene and the Polar Bear?"

Ronnie filled Claire, Kate, and Mac in, with Butch joining them at the end.

Kate raised both hands in a cheer, hitting Claire with a wide, gloating smile. "I told you that guy was trouble from the start, but you thought I was nuts."

"You are nuts."

"Yeah, but I was right this time."

Claire rolled her eyes. "Mac, call Mt. Rushmore and have them hire another sculptor. I have a feeling we're going to need a big-ass monument to memorialize this moment in order to shut Kate up."

He chuckled until Kate reached around Claire and pinched him on the back.

"So," Claire said, "it sounds like the Sheriff doesn't think our troubles are over yet."

"Far from it." That dark ripple passed over Ronnie's face again. "But he's confident Arlene and the Polar Bear won't be bugging us again. The FBI has been looking for them for a while, and now that they have them with fresh evidence of attempted kidnapping and possibly worse on their hands, they'll both go away until they are too old to do more than whack you with a cane."

"Grady's aunt and her Geritol gang have done that plenty enough to Claire and me," Kate groused.

"Oh, that reminds me of something else I meant to tell you," Ronnie said, but then hesitated.

Claire crossed her arms over her chest. "Now what have you done?"

"Well, I sort of invited Grady's aunt to Thanksgiving dinner."

"You did what?" Kate asked, her forehead turning bright red. "After she threatened my life in the library bathroom?"

"She was just playing around," Ronnie said, her laugh fake. "Besides, Grady will be there to keep her under control."

"Ronnie!" Claire glared at her. "You invited the Sheriff of Cholla County to break bread with us? You know all of the shit we have hidden in Ruby's house. What if he says he's going to go to the bathroom and sneaks a peek in the basement office?"

"I'll keep an eye on him. Besides—"

"What else do you have hidden?" Mac asked, interrupting Ronnie, giving Claire his squinty-eyed Eastwood glare.

"I don't know. Lots of stuff," Claire whispered out of the side of her mouth. "Don't get me wrong," she told Ronnie, "I think the Sheriff can be a nice guy when he's not threatening me with jail time, but he's the last person we need sniffing around Joe's old stomping grounds."

Butch set a glass of water in front of Kate, indicating for her to drink up. "You're not having Thanksgiving at Ruby's place."

"We're not?" Kate asked, lifting her glass.

"No," he leaned his elbows on the bar. "We're having it here, right, Ronnie?"

She nodded. "We'll be in neutral territory, so you don't need to worry about Grady finding out our family secrets." When Kate started to object about the Sheriff's aunt, Ronnie cut her off. "I told you, Grady will be there to keep Aunt Millie in line." She picked up the tray with the pitcher of beer Butch had poured. "I can guarantee you two piss-pots that it's going to be an uneventful dinner with the worst crime being a dry turkey if Mom's in charge of cooking again this year."

Claire would believe that when the day came and went without a snag. She watched Ronnie carry the drinks over near the pool tables, her gut telling her something was wrong with this picture. Her sister was acting like things were fine and dandy, but there was something she wasn't telling them. Claire wasn't sure if it had to do with Grady or something else. Or *someone* else. Someone who was shadowing Ronnie's world. She'd have to ask her later when they were alone and these damned meds weren't scrambling her brain.

"Was it just me," Butch said, coming around the bar to grab the other tray he'd loaded up with four glasses of beer, "or did Ronnie's prediction sound more ominous than heartening?"

"What are you doing?" Kate asked, reaching for the tray.

Butch knocked her hand away. "Switching places with you." He leaned down and kissed her hard and fast on the lips. "Scoot on behind the bar and get to pouring."

"But I get better tips out on the floor," Kate said. "Especially in this T-shirt."

"I noticed that." Butch ogled the cotton stretching across her chest for a second before grinning up at her. "Did I tell you I've decided to institute a new dress code for my female wait staff— matching burlap sack shirts and pants?"

"Burlap itches," Kate said.

"I'll scratch wherever you itch, Baby Momma." He gave her a wink and headed off to deliver the drinks.

"Men are so bossy," Kate said, smacking Mac on the shoulder as she passed by him.

He shot Claire a frown. "What did I do?"

"Grew testicles while you were in the womb."

"Your sisters have issues."

"I know." She slid off her stool, turning him to face her and then looping her arms around his neck. "You'll get used to living with them." She smiled. "They're like herpes that way."

His arms wrapped around her hips, gently pulling her between his legs. "You ready to go home?"

"Sure, if you promise to nail the bedroom door closed so Mom can't come in and rub any more of her herbal creams on me when I'm sleeping." The last one had made her dream she was a cow eating grass in a cow pie littered paddock.

His eyes were level with hers, so were his lips. "I'll grab some two-by-fours and nails on our way to bed." He kissed her. "And your tool belt." His eyes sparkled.

"You're going to have to wear it then, because I'm injured, remember?"

"We'll improvise." He stood, leading her toward the door. "I may not be as crafty as you, but I've been told I'm pretty good with my hands."

She laughed, following him out into the night. "You're very good with your hands, but let's not discount your talent with your other parts."

"Oh, yeah?" He opened the passenger side of her new Jeep, helping her up and in. "What other parts are those?"

She waited for him to come around and join her inside the cab. "Well, your tongue is damned amazing."

Shifting into gear he pulled out of the lot. "What else?"

"Your lips are pretty nice."

"Just 'pretty nice,' huh?" He glanced across at her. "I'll have to work on improving their rating."

"You can certainly try."

Later that night, after they'd managed to escape the rest of the household, Claire lay next to him on the sheets, sweat-covered, her body still humming from his touch. She smiled at the ceiling like a lovesick fool. "I changed my mind, Mac."

"About what?" he asked, his breath tickling her earlobe.

"Your lips."

"Yeah?"

"Yeah. They're freaking incredible."

She felt his chuckle in his chest, which was pressed against her arm. "That's more like it."

She lay there in silence for a bit, listening to the sounds of the old house settling down for another cold desert night.

"Mac." She wrapped his arm around her bare stomach. "Thank you for the Jeep."

"You're welcome." He nuzzled the hair at the base of her neck. "You have to promise me something though, Slugger."

"Anything."

"You won't use it to go out to Humdigger mine and sniff around when I'm gone—or any of Ruby's other mines for that matter."

"Uh, sure, okay." She turned her head and kissed him, enjoying his lips some more.

"Claire," he said when she let him come up for air.

"What?"

"Were your fingers crossed behind your back when you made that promise?"

She uncrossed her fingers. "Maybe just a little."

"Claire," he warned.

Laughing huskily, she pulled his mouth back to hers. It was a good thing he hadn't asked about her toes.

The End … for now

* To read some "bloopers" from *The Rowdy Coyote Rumble*, check out the following hidden page on my website.
(Note: To open the Bloopers page, type the password: Rowdy)
http://www.anncharles.com/?page_id=3032

Connect with Me Online

Ann Charles Website: http://www.anncharles.com

Sign up to receive my newsletter:
http://www.anncharles.com/?page_id=196

Facebook (Personal Page):
http://www.facebook.com/ann.charles.author

Facebook (Author Page):
http://www.facebook.com/pages/Ann-
Charles/37302789804?ref=share

Twitter (as Ann W. Charles): http://twitter.com/AnnWCharles

Instagram (as Ann_Charles):
https://www.instagram.com/ann_charles/

About the Author

Ann Charles is an award-winning, USA Today Bestselling author who writes romantic mysteries that are splashed with humor and whatever else she feels like throwing into the mix. When she is not dabbling in fiction, arm-wrestling with her children, attempting to seduce her husband, or arguing with her sassy cats, she is daydreaming of lounging poolside at a fancy resort with a blended margarita in one hand and a great book in the other.

Ann's Fun Random Arizona Facts

SOURCE: arizonaexperience.org/land/az-habitats

Arizona's biotic communities represent all but one (tropical forest) of the world's biomes (BIOME: a large naturally occurring community of flora and fauna occupying a major habitat, e.g., forest or tundra).

High plateau, low desert, rugged mountains, hidden canyons, and riparian ecosystems sustain a unique and complex web of life. From northeast to southwest, the subdued topography and shimmering rocks of the Colorado Plateau give way to the ruggedly folded and faulted mountains of Arizona's Transition Zone, which in turn yields to the mountain ranges, sky islands, and intervening valleys of the Basin and Range Province. Each area has unique vegetation and wildlife that has adapted to thrive in that specific habitat.

SOURCE: topockazschool.com/Arizona Fun Facts.pdf

Arizona has 3,928 mountain peaks and summits—more mountains than any one of the other Mountain States (Colorado, Idaho, Montana, Nevada, New Mexico, Utah, and Wyoming). Of these peaks, 26 are more than 10,000 feet in elevation.

All of New England, plus the state of Pennsylvania, would fit inside Arizona.

There are more wilderness areas in Arizona than in the entire Midwest. Arizona alone has 90 wilderness areas, while the Midwest has 50.

Arizona has the largest contiguous stand of ponderosa pines in the world stretching from near Flagstaff along the Mogollon Rim to the White Mountains region.

SOURCE: legendsofamerica.com/az-facts2.html

In Arizona, it is against the law for donkeys to sleep in bathtubs.

In Arizona, it is unlawful to refuse a person a glass of water.

No one is permitted to ride their horse up the stairs of the county court house in Prescott, Arizona.

The age of a saguaro cactus is determined by its height. A saguaro cactus will take between 50 and 100 years to grow an arm.

The sun shines in southern Arizona 85% of the time, which is considerably more sunshine than Florida or Hawaii.

It is illegal to hunt camels in the state of Arizona.

Arizona became the 48th state on February 14, 1912, the last of the contiguous states to be admitted into the Union.